# *One Tempting Proposal*

T0033936

**Also by Christy Carlyle**

*One Scandalous Kiss*
*One Tempting Proposal*

**Coming Soon**
*One Dangerous Desire*

# One Tempting Proposal

## AN ACCIDENTAL HEIRS NOVEL

# CHRISTY CARLYLE

**AVON**IMPULSE

*An Imprint of HarperCollinsPublishers*

Excerpt from *One Scandalous Kiss* copyright © 2015 by Christy Carlyle.

Excerpt from *Montana Hearts: Her Weekend Wrangler* copyright © 2015 by Darlene Panzera.

Excerpt from *I Need a Hero* copyright © 2015 by Codi Gary.

Excerpt from *Blue Blooded* copyright © 2015 by Shelly Bell.

Excerpt from *Best Worst Mistake* copyright © 2015 by Lia Riley.

EPub Edition NOVEMBER 2015 ISBN: 9780062428011
Print Edition ISBN: 9780062428035

23 24 25 26 27  LBC  8 7 6 5 4

## ABOUT THE AUTHOR

**SARAH REMY** writes fiction to keep real life from getting out of hand. She lives in Spokane, Washington, where she shows horses, works at a local elementary school, and rehabs her old house. Follow her on Twitter at @sarahremywrites.

www.sarahremy.com
www.harpervoyagerbooks.com

Discover great authors, exclusive offers, and more at hc.com.

*For John, your love and support*
*encourages and humble me.*

## Acknowledgments

This heroine would never have had her happy ending without the guidance and wisdom of my fabulous editor, Elle Keck. Thank you!

*One Tempting Proposal*

## Chapter One

*London, April, 1891*

KITTY ADDERLY STRAIGHTENED her back and planted her feet flat and firm against two enormous pink cabbage roses decorating the Osgood's drawing room rug. She resisted fidgeting with the ribbon along the skirt of her gown and tried summoning a pleasant expression, though the tremor in her cheek probably meant she'd only managed to transfer a restless quiver to the corner of her mouth.

The gilded timepiece over the mantel had to be broken. Despite the hour it seemed she'd spent perched on the edge of the settee, the clock's hands insisted only fifteen minutes had passed. Even the vase of sunny daffodils and white narcissus on a table at her elbow failed to inspire any cheer.

Time did tend to move slowly in the Osgood's drawing room, especially when Cynthia, this week's hostess of their regular ladies' gathering, appeared determined to turn afternoon tea into a tedious skirmish. She'd already insulted one lady's hairstyle, dismissed another's taste in music, and implied that a third was such an awful dancer that she should consider avoiding the upcoming ball altogether. All of that in a quarter of an hour. She was efficient, if nothing else.

"We're looking forward to your mother's ball, Kitty. Wait until you see my gown. My dressmaker is a true artist, and there's never been a mauve like mine, I assure you." Cynth's boast had more to do with claiming a position among Kitty's circle of friends than with fashion or balls. The leader of their group always chose the color of her gown first.

Any other day, Kitty would put the younger woman in her place, but social ranking, announcing the color of her dress, and being the one to offer the cleverest set down seemed less important with every passing season.

"Shouldn't Kitty be the first to choose her gown's color? Her mother *is* hosting the ball." Bess Berwick occupied the other half of the couch and spoke low enough that the rest of the ladies at the tea party might not hear her retort.

She was Cynthia's younger cousin and the newest addition to their group, with a figure as round as her cheeks and a soothing softness in her tone. Kitty assessed Miss Berwick and wondered what it would be like to be soft, to allow herself to be meek and gentle. Would it smooth over her sharp edges? Compared to Bess's curves, Kitty was all angles. She'd been taught to be steely on the inside too. After a childhood of sickness, her father demanded that she grow up strong.

"What do you know of picking colors, Bess? You've chosen a bland white dress for the ball, which no one will even notice."

Neither the petulance nor the dismissal in Cynthia's tone surprised Kitty. Cynth had a terrible talent for preying on the weak, and from the day Bess joined their circle, she'd become the main target of her older cousin's snipes.

Yet Miss Berwick refused to play the game. She offered no set downs, flung no insults, and made it a habit to speak as little as possible. Perhaps she simply waited for her moment, watching and learning from the rest of them.

Kitty knew the power of waiting. She'd waited four seasons while all of her friends rushed into romances and engagements.

If the girl refused to spar, Kitty would join the fray. "I don't mind you choosing your gown's shade first, Cynth. Mauve will suit you. Your complexion always benefits from a bit of color."

Except now, of course, when a rosy stain rushed up their hostess's cheeks.

"Thank you," Bess whispered as she lifted her teacup, casting Kitty the quickest of glances.

The girl had much to learn. None of them thanked each other in such circumstances. Bess's gratitude was a faux pas. Acknowledging a barb or praising a retort opened the door to honesty, and truth was their nemesis. Truth would force each woman to admit the game they played at social gatherings, exposing their false smiles, backbiting whispers, and the art of cutting others to the quick with a few words.

"What color *have* you chosen for the ball, Kitty?" Cynthia bit out.

Now was her moment. Kitty could upset all of Cynth's plans. If she chose a rose or pink or any color that might clash with Cynth's mauve, the young woman would have to relent and chose another gown for the ball. Her father's title and wealth gave Kitty status in their little group, and her popularity among their circle still exceeded Cynthia's, despite the younger woman's attempts to dethrone her.

Yet Kitty couldn't rally a cool smirk as she held Cynth's dark gaze.

These battles were ridiculous. Frivolous. Petty. Worst of all, they seemed to form the confines of her life. Explorers were out climbing mountains while great thinkers innovated technological marvels. One American lady journalist had even managed to travel around the world in seventy-two days. Other women, like the members at the Women's Union meetings Kitty sporadically attended, focused their energies on advancing the cause of women's voting rights or charitable endeavors.

Now her main task for the day would be deciding whether to smash the plans of one of her dearest and most false friends. Was this her mountain? Were these trifling battles all she had to look forward to during another social season?

The airy, flimsy silliness of it all brought no laughter, only a dizzying queasiness that intensified when she thought of doing this again, and again, for the next several months. The next several years. The rest of her life.

"Not to worry, Cynth. My gown is cream," Kitty offered, infusing her voice with a reassuring tone she didn't often employ in this company.

Cynth frowned and pursed her mouth as if she'd accidentally taken a sip of something sour. "Cream? Isn't that just a muddier version of white?"

"My modiste calls the shade ecru and assures me it is all the rage in Paris."

Mention of Paris never failed to do the trick, and several ladies nodded approvingly while Cynth sniffed and turned her attention to pouring more tea.

With the gown nonsense settled, Kitty considered raising a more interesting topic. Something that mattered. Any subject that might turn their thoughts to the world beyond the walls of fashionable drawing rooms and ballrooms.

One of the ladies began describing the dress she'd wear to the dance. Then the others began a round-robin, each lady enthusing over the cut and details of her ball gown, while the rest joined in with comments of approval or challenge.

Kitty released the breath she'd been holding on a long sigh, but dizziness blurred the room's walls whenever she tried to inhale deeply and met the restraint of her corset. She tried again, fighting the confines of laces and stays. If only her emotions were as easily bound as her waist and breasts.

*Poise. Decorum.* She was the Marquess of Clayborne's eldest daughter. She'd be his heir if the laws that decreed only men worthy of inheriting were ever overturned. Crumbling in public was not allowed. Her father's admonitions were always with her, imparted in youth and repeated so often they'd become tattooed in her mind. *Never display weakness. Never cry or lose oneself in sentiment. Never let them best you.*

Today the energy required to appear flawless—to move with elegance, to smile at the right moment, to fight these silly drawing room battles while being witty and charming and never, ever boring—had all been sapped by a fearsome row with her father.

His shouts still echoed in her ears. Angry words spewed past a sneer that twisted his features until she'd barely recognized him.

She'd been a fool not to anticipate his outburst.

Four years of rejected suitors had worn down the modicum of patience he possessed, and he'd never had much where Kitty was concerned. He insisted this season she must relent and accept an offer.

This season she must give up the freedom of being unmarried and place herself under a man's control. Or, more accurately, another man's control. Exchanging her father's disapproval and admonishments for a husband's sounded as appealing as spending a lifetime of afternoons sparring with Cynthia Osgood.

He'd called her a disappointment, a cruel daughter, an unnatural woman for her lack of enthusiasm for marriage and children and a settled future.

She swallowed and sat up tall. Not even her father could overturn the poise she'd worked years to perfect, and she couldn't let her circle of friends glimpse any sign of weakness. The sweet-natured few like Bess might offer comfort, but others would love to see her falter and rush to claim her place in their social circle, or attempt to push her out of the group entirely.

"Are you looking forward to the season, Kitty?" Bess took a bite of scone while waiting for Kitty's answer.

"There can't be much to look forward to when it's your sixth season." Cynthia had a talent for infusing every sentence with a sting.

"It's actually my fifth season, Cynth. And I look forward to it as I did all the others." Which was to say, not much at all.

Dancing could be invigorating, and she enjoyed attending social events to hear the latest gossip and speculate about who would be shackled to whom by the season's end. But as to the main purpose of the season for every unmarried young woman—the game of being gazed upon and measured for the role of some fop's wife—that prospect held no appeal. Independence called to Kitty more and more every year as she steeled herself for dozens of visits by overeager and utterly unappealing gentlemen.

"Well, perhaps your fifth season will finally bring you some success." Cynthia spoke with all the pomposity of a woman who'd "succeeded" in her second season. She'd captured a priggish earl who spent too much time twisting his mustache or patting his ample waistline and far too little time saying anything intelligent or interesting. Their engagement had lasted nearly a year and soon she'd have to commit to the man who held more appeal in prospect than he likely would in reality. Knowing Cynth, she judged him steerable and already plotted ways to manipulate the poor besotted fool for her own gain. Thirty thousand pounds per annum and a title could make almost any man tolerable. She'd become Lady Molstrey, and that's what mattered most.

"I can only dream of catching a gentleman as charming as yours." Kitty couldn't quite manage a grin, as Cynth always did when delivering one of her barely veiled set downs.

Miss Berwick choked on her scone, and a few other ladies tittered behind their teacups. Lord Molstrey wasn't anyone's notion of charming.

Cynthia narrowed her eyes. "Yes, well, I doubt you ever will when you chase away every man who offers you a bit of attention."

Kitty held Cynthia's gaze as sparks of challenge and disdain electrified the air between them and the other ladies chattered among themselves.

She longed to tell Cynth and the rest of them the truth. A loathing for marriage and the prospect of motherhood had less to do with her reticence to accept a proposal than the men who'd proposed. None of them moved her. None of them inspired trust or desire. None of them gave her any reason to hope that a life spent with them would be any different than living in the glare of her father's judgments.

Men had been disappointing her since her first season, and she'd been disappointing them in return. Snubbing gentlemen had practically become a skill. She'd turned away countless suitors and refused several offers of marriage.

"Of course, there's always Lord Ponsonby," Cynthia purred before reaching for a neatly trimmed triangle of sandwich.

Gasps echoed in the high-ceilinged room and Bess pressed a hand to her mouth to stifle hers.

Lord Molstrey might be a bit of a farce, but Kitty knew precisely what the rest of them thought of Lord Ponsonby. He'd rout Molstrey in a game of wits any day, but the man was old. Half their fathers were younger than Ponsonby, and yet the earl retained enough energy to haunt the London season, his eagerness to find a young bride swamping the air around him like a miasma. He'd served with Kitty's father in the army, and she had long been his favored candidate to serve as broodmare. He'd all but bribed her father for the honor, but Kitty refused him. Several times. But he was as persistent as a weed, springing up at this ball or that social event when she least expected him.

"Unlike some young women"—Kitty scanned her gaze from face to face before turning to stare at Cynthia

Osgood—"I am not eager to marry. Why should I give up my freedom and choices to a man?"

She thought of her sisters, both of whom longed for marriage and motherhood. Why was she different? She'd always imagined having a child one day, but it was impossible to envision being a wife, especially if she found herself married to a man like her father—impossible to please and determined to mold her to his liking.

"There are some worthy gentleman, surely." Miss Lissman, who was usually content to let her older sister do the speaking at their gatherings, frowned at her declaration, as if she didn't quite believe it either. "Our cousin married last summer and seems quite blissfully happy," she added as further evidence of her dubious pronouncement.

"But her husband is a bit of a saint, you must admit. How many of us will snare one of those?" The elder Lissman sister spoke matter-of-factly, but the younger seemed to take the words as chastisement and said nothing more.

"A saint sounds terribly daunting. I think I'd prefer a sinner." Bess's soft voice sometimes went unnoticed during a particularly lively discussion, but in the quiet of the room, her words fell like a solemn decree. Cynthia wore a disapproving scowl but the rest of them lifted hands to cover grins or outright smiles. Kitty raised her teacup in a symbolic toast. The girl had the right of it.

After striving to live up to her father's expectations and forever falling short, the notion of a spending the rest of her life with a saintly man turned her stomach. If she did capitulate to the pressure to marry, it would be to a flawed man. Or, at the very least, one who could love her beyond her own flaws.

She heard laughter echoing in the silence and realized it was her own. What a notion. A man who would love a woman for her flaws. Each woman in the room had been taught to eradicate their flaws, or at least give the appearance they had. Her own mother bought tonics to cover blemishes, salves to soften skin, unctions to make one's hair glossy, and powder to whiten her teeth. And those only redressed physical flaws. What of the rest? Was there a miracle cure to improve one's inner flaws, to turn unkind thoughts sunny, to fill the empty spaces in a heart and light up dark corners of doubt? If she could bottle that tonic and sell it, she'd never need any man's income to sustain her.

As their weekly teatime drew to a close, Bess moved to occupy the empty spot on the settee next to Kitty.

"Are you all right, Kitty? You seem a bit unsettled."

"I'm well, Bess. Thank you."

The girl's query wasn't an accusation or a warning that her weakness would be used against her. Bess Berwick didn't seem to possess that sort of malice.

"You're too sweet."

And she was. Sweet and naive and kind without expecting anything in return. She feared for anyone so gentle. In this company it was better to be hard, to wear one's armor, as well as perfecting one's noncommittal grin. If Bess ever challenged someone like Cynthia, she'd be cut down before she ever saw the scythe.

"I don't disagree with your notion of independence."

Even when espousing women's independence, Bess spoke softly. "But what of love?" She waited a beat and turned to watch Cynthia leave the room to see the Lissman sisters off.

When Bess turned back, her delicate features tensed as she whispered, "What of passion?"

Yes, what of passion? Kitty had been waiting to feel it for four seasons. There'd been moments of excitement— the thrill of catching a handsome man's gaze, the zing of physical attraction when a gentleman took her in his arms before a waltz, and even the heady pleasure of conversing with a clever man interested in topics beyond sports and gentlemanly wagers.

Every spark of intrigue fizzled, and not a single burst of initial enchantment ever grew into a flame. If a man's attention toward her didn't quickly wane, her interest in him did. In Kitty's experience, most men's appeal lasted the length of one ball or perhaps a single other afternoon social call. If a gentleman didn't drone on endlessly about himself, he took to telling Kitty what *she* must do. *You must see the new play at Drury Lane. You must go riding with me in Hyde Park tomorrow. You must come see my horse run the Derby.*

Few asked her opinions or considered her preferences. Just like her father.

When she found herself unable to wrap four years of disappointment into a few words, Bess nudged her arm.

The girl's eyes were huge and danced with mischief as she spoke in a low voice meant for secrets and intrigue. "If you have no plans to marry, will you take a lover?"

Apparently Miss Berwick could be as fanciful as she was kind.

Passion. A lover. Kitty couldn't imagine either when she anticipated a season of struggling with her father to make her own choices.

## Chapter Two

*Cambridgeshire, May, 1891*

SLASHING THE AIR with a sword was doing nothing to improve Sebastian Fennick's mood. As he thrust, the needle-thin foil bending and arching through the air and sending tingling reverberations along his hand, he glared across at his opponent, though he doubted she could see any better than he could from behind the tight mesh of her fencing mask.

His sister parried before offering a spot-on riposte of her own, her foil bowing in a perfect semicircle as she struck him.

"Are you making any sort of effort at all?"

Seb bit back the reply burning the tip of his tongue. Fencing was the least of his concerns. In the last month he'd learned of the death of a cousin he'd barely known and inherited the responsibility for one dukedom, three thousand acres of land, hundreds of tenants, twenty-eight staff members, one London residence, and a country house with so many rooms, he was still counting. He could find no competitive pleasure in wielding a lightweight foil when his mind brimmed with repairs, meetings, investments, and invitations to social events that spanned the rest of the calendar year.

And all of it was nothing to the bit of paper in his waistcoat pocket, separated by two layers of fabric from the scar on his chest, dual reminders of what a fool he'd been, how one woman's lies nearly ended his life.

He wouldn't open her letter. Instead, he'd take pleasure in burning the damn thing.

*Never again.* Never would he allow himself to be manipulated as he had been in the past. He had to put the past from his mind altogether.

Fencing wasn't doing the trick. Give him a proper sword and let him dash it against a tree trunk. Better yet, give him a dragon to slay. That might do quite nicely, but this dance of lunges and feints only made his irritation bubble over.

Yet his sister didn't deserve his ire, and he'd no wish to stifle her enthusiasm for the newest of her myriad interests.

"I fear fencing and I do not suit, Pippa." As she returned to *en garde* position, preparing for another strike, Seb hastened to add, "Nor shall we ever."

Pippa sagged in disappointment when he reached up to remove his fencing mask. "I'd hoped you might find it invigorating. A pleasant challenge."

In truth, his mathematical mind found the precision of the sport appealing, and the physical exertion was refreshing. But when he'd inherited the dukedom of Wrexford, Seb left his mathematics career at Cambridge behind. And weren't there a dozen tasks he should be attending to rather than waving a flexible bit of steel about at his sister?

"Invigorating, yes. Challenging, absolutely. Pleasant? No."

When he began removing his gloves and unbuttoning the fencing jacket Pippa insisted he purchase, she raised a hand to stop him.

"Wait. We must do this properly." She approached and offered him her hand as if they were merely fellow sportsmen rather than siblings. "Politeness is an essential element of fencing."

Seb cleared his throat, infused his baritone with gravitas, and shook his younger sister's hand. "Well done, Miss Fennick."

She'd tucked her fencing mask under her sword arm and met his gaze with eyes the same unique shade as their father's. Along with her dark hair and whiskey brown eyes, Pippa had inherited their patriarch's love for mathematics and sporting activity of every kind.

"Fine effort, Your Grace." And father's compassion too, apparently.

Pippa smiled at him, her disappointment well-hidden

or forgotten, and Seb returned the expression. Then her words, the sound of his honorific at the end, settled in his mind. *Your Grace*. It still sounded odd to his ears.

Seb and his sister had been raised for academic pursuits, children of a mathematician father and a mother with as many accomplishments as her daughter now boasted. Formality, titles, rules—none of it came naturally. The title of Duke of Wrexford had passed to him, but it still rankled and itched, as ill-fitting as the imprisoning fencing mask he'd been relieved to remove.

As they exited the corner of the second ballroom Pippa had set out as her fencing strip, she turned one of her inquisitive glances on him.

"Perhaps you'd prefer boxing, like Grandfather." Their grandfather had been as well known for his love of pugilism as his architectural designs, and had reputedly been one of Gentleman Jackson's best pupils.

Taller and broader than many of his classmates, Seb had engaged in his own share of scuffles in youth, and he'd been tempted to settle a few gentlemanly disagreements with his fists, but he never enjoyed fighting with his body as much as sparring with his intellect. Reason. Logic. Those were the weapons a man should bring to a dispute.

"Unless you're like Oliver and can't abide the sight of blood."

It seemed his sister still sparred. Standing on the threshold of Sebastian's study, Oliver Treadwell lifted his hands, settled them on his hips, and heaved a frustrated sigh.

"I did consider medical school, Pip. I can bear the sight of blood better than most." Ollie's eyes widened as he scanned the two of them. "What in heaven's name is that awful getup you two are wearing?"

Seb didn't know if it was his lack of enthusiasm for fencing or Ollie's jibe about their costumes that set her off, but the shock of seeing Pippa lift her foil, breaking a key point of protocol she'd been quite insistent upon— "Never lift a sword when your opponent is unmasked"— blunted the amusement of watching Ollie rear back like a frightened pony.

"Fencing costumes," she explained through clenched teeth. "I tried instructing Sebastian, though he says the sport doesn't suit him." She hadn't actually touched Ollie with the tip of her foil and quickly lowered it to her side, but the movement failed to ease the tension between them.

Turning back to Seb, she forced an even expression. "I'll go up and change for luncheon." She offered Ollie a curt nod as she passed him, her wide fencing skirt fluttering around her ankles. At the door, she grasped the frame and turned back. "And don't call me Pip. No one calls me that anymore."

"Goodness. When did she begin loathing me?" Ollie watched the doorway where Pippa exited as if she might reappear to answer his query. "Women are terribly inscrutable, aren't they?"

Seb thought the entire matter disturbingly clear, but he suspected Pippa would deny her infatuation with Oliver as heatedly as Ollie would argue against the claim. They'd been friends since childhood, and Ollie had been an unofficial member of the Fennick family from the day he'd lost his parents at twelve years old. Seb wasn't certain when Pippa began viewing Ollie less as a brotherly friend and more as a man worthy of her admiration.

As much as he loved him, Seb secretly prayed his sister's interest in the young buck would wane. Treadwell had never been the steadiest of fellows, particularly when it came to matters of the heart, and Seb would never allow anyone to hurt Pippa.

"Welcome to Roxbury." He practiced the words as he spoke them, hoping the oddness of playing host in another man's home would eventually diminish.

"Thank you. It is grand, is it not? Had you ever visited before?"

"Once, as a young child. I expected it to be less imposing when I saw it again as a man." It hadn't been. Not a whit. Upon arriving thirty days prior, he'd stood on the threshold a moment with his mouth agape before taking a step inside.

Seb caught Ollie staring at the ceiling, an extraordinary web of plastered fan-vaulting meant to echo the design in the nave of an abbey the late duke had visited in Bath. Every aspect of Roxbury had been designed with care, and yet to match the whims of each successive duke and duchess. Somehow its hodgepodge of architectural styles blended into a harmonious and impressive whole.

"You mentioned an urgent matter. Trouble in London?" A few years older than his friend, Seb worried about Ollie with the same ever-present paternal concern he felt for his sister.

After trying his hand at philosophy, chemistry, and medicine, Ollie had decided to pursue law and currently studied at the Inner Temple with high hopes of being called to the bar and becoming a barrister within the year.

"No, all is well, but those words don't begin to describe my bliss."

Bowing his head, Sebastian closed his eyes a moment and drew in a long breath, expanding his chest as far as the confines of his fencing jacket would allow. It had to be a woman. Another woman. Seb had never known a man as eager to be enamored. Unfortunately, the mysteries of love couldn't be bound within the elegance of a mathematical equation. If they could, Ollie's equation would be a simple one. Woman plus beauty equals infatuation. If Ollie's interest in this woman or that ever bloomed into constancy, Seb could rally a bit happiness for his friend.

*Constancy.* An image of black hair came to mind with a piercing pain above his brow. How could he advocate that Ollie learn constancy when his own stubborn heart brought him nothing but misery?

"Tell me about her."

Ollie's face lit with pleasure. "She's an angel."

The last had been "a goddess" and Seb mentally calculated where each designation might rank in the heavenly hierarchy.

"With golden hair and sapphire eyes . . ." Ollie's loves

were always described in the same terms one might use when speaking of a precious relic Mr. Petrie had dug up in Egypt, each of them carved in alabaster, gilded, and bejeweled.

"Slow down, Ollie. Let's start with her name."

"Hattie. Harriet, though she says she dislikes Harriet. I think it's lovely. Isn't it a beautiful name, really?"

Too preoccupied with unbuttoning himself from his fencing gear, Sebastian didn't bother offering a response. Ollie rarely had any trouble rambling on without acknowledgment.

"She's the daughter of a marquess. Clayborne. Perhaps you know him."

Seb arched both brows and Ollie smiled. "Yes, I know. You've only been a duke for the space of a month. Don't they introduce you to all of the other aristocrats straight away, then?"

A chuckle rumbled up in Seb's chest, and for a moment the burdens that had piled up since the last duke's passing slipped away. He laughed with Ollie as they had when they were simpler men, younger, less distracted with love or responsibilities. Seb felt lighter, and he held a smile so long his cheeks began to ache before the laughter ebbed and he addressed the serious matter of Oliver's pursuit of a marquess's daughter.

"I think the better question is whether you've met Harriet's father. What are your intentions toward this young woman?"

Ollie ducked his chin and deflated into a chair. "Goodness, Bash, you sound a bit like *you're* Hattie's father."

Only Ollie called him Bash, claiming he'd earned it for defending him in a fight with a particularly truculent classmate. The nickname reminded him of all their shared battles as children, but if Ollie thought its use would soften him or make him retreat, he was wrong. Ollie needed someone to challenge him, to curb his tendency to rush in without considering the consequences. If he lost interest in this young woman as he had with all the others, a breach-of-promise suit brought by a marquess could ruin Ollie's burgeoning legal career.

"I intend to marry her."

"May I ask how long you've been acquainted with the young lady?" Mercy, he did sound like a father. As the eldest, he'd always led the way, and with the loss of their parents, Seb had taken on a parental role with his sister too. Pippa might wish to marry one day, and it was his duty to ensure any prospective groom wasn't a complete and utter reprobate.

"Not all of us fall in love with our childhood friend." The barb had no doubt been meant to bring Seb's past heartbreak to mind, but Seb thought of Pippa. Thankfully, she hadn't heard Ollie's declaration.

"Indeed. I would merely advise you to take more time and court Lord Clayborne's daughter properly. Her father will expect no less."

Even with a properly drawn-out courtship, a marquess would be unlikely to allow his daughter to marry a man who'd yet to become a barrister and may not succeed once he had.

"I must offer for her now. Soon. She's coming out this

season, and I couldn't bear for another man to snatch her up."

"You make her sound like a filly at market."

"Will you come to London and meet her? I know you'll approve of the match once you've met her."

Seb had already given into the necessity of spending the season in London at Wrexford House. Pippa had no interest in anything in London aside from the Reading Room at the British Museum, but their aristocratic aunt, Lady Stamford, insisted he give his sister a proper coming out. She'd also reminded him that a new duke should meet and be met by others in their slice of society.

"You hardly need my approval, Ollie."

"I need more than that."

If he meant money, Seb could help. Cousin Geoffrey and his steward maintained the estate well over the years, investing wisely and spending with restraint. Sebastian had met with the estate's steward once since arriving at Roxbury and emphasized his desire to match his predecessor's good fiscal sense.

"We should discuss a settlement of some kind."

Waving away Seb's words, Ollie stood and strode to the window, looking out on one of Roxbury's gardens, perfectly manicured and daubed with color by the first blooms of spring.

Oliver Treadwell had never been a hard man to read. Seb knew him to be intelligent, but he used none of his cleverness for artifice. A changeable man, Ollie blew hot and cold with his passions, but he expressed himself honestly. Now Seb sensed something more. Another emotion undercut the giddiness he'd expressed about his most recent heart's desire.

His friend seemed to fall into contemplation of the scenery and Sebastian stood to approach, curious about what had drawn Ollie's attention. The sound of Ollie's voice stopped him short, the timbre strangely plaintive, almost childlike.

"She says her father won't allow her to marry until her older sister does. Some strange rule he's devised to make Harriet miserable."

It sounded like an unreasonable expectation to Sebastian. At two and twenty, Pippa found contentment in pursuing her studies and political causes. She'd indicated no desire to take any man's name. Never mind the way she looked at Oliver. If they had a younger sister, the girl might have a long wait to wed if some ridiculous rule required Pippa to do so first. Then again, not all women were as reticent to marry as Pippa.

"Does this elder sister have any prospects?"

Ollie's whole body jolted at Seb's question and he turned on him, smile wide, blue eyes glittering.

"She has more suitors than she can manage, but she's not easily snared. I assure you she's just as beautiful as Hattie, with golden hair . . ."

"Yes, yes. Eyes of emerald or sapphire or amethyst."

Oliver tugged on his ear, a frown marring his enthusiastic expression. "Well, she is lovely. Truly. You should meet her."

A sickening heaviness sank in his gut at the realization of Oliver's real purpose for their *urgent meeting*.

"You're very determined to convince me, Oliver."

Ollie sighed wearily, a long gusty exhale, before sinking down into a chair again. "You only call me Oliver when you're cross. Won't you hear me out?"

Sebastian had a habit of counting. Assigning numbers to the objects and incidents in his life gave him a satisfying sense of order and control. Not quite as much satisfaction as conquering a maddening equation, but enough to make the incidents he couldn't control—like the small matter of inheriting a title and a home large enough to house a hundred—more bearable.

He wished he'd counted how many times he'd heard those same words—"Won't you hear me out?"—from Ollie. Whatever the number, it would certainly be high enough to warn him off listening to the man's mad schemes again.

"All right, Ollie. Have it out then."

"Do you never consider finding yourself a wife?"

"No."

"You must."

"Must I? Why? I have quite enough to occupy me."

Ollie took on a pensive air and squinted his left eye. "The estate seems to be in good order, and you've given up your post at the university. Pippa has her own pursuits." He glanced again at the high ceiling over their heads. "Won't you be lonely in these grand, empty rooms, Bash?"

Sentiment? That was how Ollie meant to convince him? Seb had put away sentimentality ten years before, dividing off that part of himself so that he could move forward with the rest of his life. If its power still held any sway, he would have opened the letter in his waistcoat pocket the day it arrived.

"I will manage, Ollie."

And how would a woman solve anything? In Seb's experience, women either wreaked havoc on a man's life, or filled it with noise and color and clever quips, like his mother and sister. Either option would allay loneliness, but he did not suffer from that affliction. Sentimental men were lonely. Not him. Even if he did live in a house with ceilings so tall his voice echoed when he chattered to himself.

He narrowed his eyes at Ollie, and his friend sat up in his chair, squared his shoulders, and tipped his chin to stare at Seb directly.

"She's the eldest daughter of a marquess, Bash, and much more aware of the rules of etiquette among the wealthy and titled than you are."

"Then we won't have much in common."

Ollie groaned. "She would be a fine partner, a formidable ally in this new life you've taken on."

"No."

Denial came easily, and he denounced Ollie's mad implication that the two of them should marry sisters from the same family. But reason, that damnable voice in his head that sounded like his father, contradicted him.

At two and thirty, he'd reached an age for matrimony, and with inherited property and a title came the duty to produce an heir. No one wanted Roxbury and the Wrexford dukedom to pass to another distant cousin. If he had any doubts about his need for a wife, he was surrounded by women who'd happily remind him. His aunt, Lady Stamford, had sent a letter he'd found waiting for him the day he'd arrived at Roxbury suggesting that marriage was as much his duty as managing the estate. Pippa also dropped hints now and then that having a sister-in-law would be very nice indeed.

Ollie had yet to multiply the bride-taking encouragement, but he was making a fine effort at rectifying the oversight.

"Acquiring a dukedom is a vast undertaking." Ollie stretched out his arms wide to emphasize the vastness of it all. "Why not have a lovely woman by your side in such an endeavor?"

"I didn't acquire it, Oliver. It passed to me." He loathed his habit of stating the obvious.

A lovely woman by his side. The notion brought a pang, equal parts stifled desire and memory-soaked dread. He'd imagined it once, making plans and envisioning the life he'd create with the woman he loved. But that was all sentiment and it had been smashed, its pieces left in the past. Now practicality dictated his choices. He spared emotion only for his family, for Pippa and Ollie.

Ollie watched him like a convicted man awaiting his sentence.

His friend's practical argument held some appeal. A marquess's daughter *would* know how to navigate the social whirl, and Seb liked the notion of not devoting all of his own energy to tackling that challenge. He might even find a moment to spare for mathematics, rather than having to forfeit his life's work entirely to take on the duties of a dukedom.

And it would give Ollie a chance at happiness. Perhaps this younger daughter of Lord Clayborne's would be the woman to inspire constancy in Ollie, and Seb might assist his friend to achieve the family and stability he'd lost in childhood.

Seb spoke on an exhaled sigh. "I suppose I do need a wife." And there he went stating the obvious again.

Oliver turned into a ten-year-old boy before his eyes, as giddy as a pup. If the man had a tail, he'd be wagging it furiously. He jumped up and reached out to clasp Seb on the shoulder.

"Just meet Lady Katherine, Seb. See if you suit. That's all I ask." It wasn't quite all he asked, but Seb had learned the futility of quibbling with a giddy Oliver.

A marquess's daughter? Lady Katherine sounded like just the sort of woman a duke should seek to marry. Seb could contemplate marriage as a practical matter, but nothing more.

Would he ever feel more?

He hadn't allowed himself an ounce of interest in a woman in ten years, not in a lush feminine figure, nor in a pair of fine eyes, not even in the heady mix of a woman's unique scent under the notes of some floral essence.

"I think you'll enjoy London during the season." Ollie couldn't manage sincerity when uttering the declaration. His mouth quivered and he blinked one eye as if he'd just caught an irritating bit of dust.

Seb doubted he'd enjoy London during the crush of

the social season. As a Cambridge man raised in a modest home in the university's shadow, he'd enjoyed occasional jaunts to London but had always been content to return to his studies. As he opened his mouth to say as much to Ollie, Pippa strode into the room and drew their attention to the doorway.

She'd changed into one of the day dresses their aunt insisted she choose for the upcoming season, though Pippa signaled her disdain for the flouncy yellow creation by swiping down the ruffles that kept popping up on her chest and around her shoulders.

"Luncheon is laid in the morning room. Are you joining us, Oliver?"

Ollie stared wide-eyed at Pippa a moment and then turned to Seb.

"We're almost finished here," Seb assured her. "Ollie and I will join you momentarily."

She nodded but offered the still speechless Ollie a sharp glance before departing.

After a moment, Ollie found his voice. "I've never seen her so . . ."

"Irritated?"

"Feminine."

Seb took a turn glaring at Ollie. The man had just been thrilled at the prospect of a match with Lady Harriet. He had no business noticing Pippa's femininity, especially after failing to do so for over a dozen years.

"She chose a few new dresses." Seb cleared his throat to draw Ollie's attention.

"It's odd," Ollie said, his face still pinched in confusion. "I've known Pippa most of my life and never truly thought of her as a woman."

His friend's words put Seb's mind at ease, but he suspected Pippa wouldn't find them nearly as heartening.

"Ollie, let's return to the matter at hand."

"Yes, of course." Ollie rubbed his hands together and grinned, the matter of Pippa quickly forgotten. "Will you come to the Clayborne ball and meet Lady Katherine?"

"I will." Meeting the woman seemed a simple prospect. Practical. Reasonable. A perfectly logical decision in the circumstances.

"If you're still planning on presenting Pippa this season, by all means, bring her along too," Ollie added. "Why leave her to ramble this house alone?"

Pippa preferred to spend her days at Cambridge where she'd been studying mathematics for much of the previous year. Yet Seb felt the pull of his aunt's assertion. His sister should have a London season, or at least spend some time among London society. He wished to open as many doors for Pippa as he could. Give her choices and options. If his title meant his sister might be more comfortably settled in life, all the better.

"She's not convinced of the appeal of a London season." Seb worried neither of them was equipped for it either. Gowns and finely tailored clothing aside, they didn't possess the aristocratic polish others would expect of a duke and his sister.

Ever undaunted, Ollie grinned. "Then you must convince her."

Seb lifted his gaze to the ceiling, following the tracery,

lines in perfect symmetry, equidistant and equal in length, forming a perfect whole. The geometric beauty of the design melted a bit of the tension in his shoulders. Still, he doubted the propriety of allowing his sister to attend a ball when she'd not yet formally come out. And, most importantly, he feared Pippa was unprepared for the sort of attention she would encounter in London.

Pippa unprepared? She'd fence him into a corner for even entertaining the notion.

"Very well. We'll both attend, but I make no promises regarding Lady Katherine."

He'd accept the invitation in order to give Pippa her first glimpse of a proper London ball, meet this marquess's daughter, and do what he could to assist Ollie's cause. But marrying Lady Katherine was another matter entirely. He'd only ever intended to marry one woman and that had gone so spectacularly pear-shaped, he wasn't certain he could bring himself to propose ever again.

## Chapter Three

"You'll defend Oliver, won't you, Kitty? Papa can be a bit ferocious."

*A bit?* Kitty Adderly's middle sister, Hattie, the diplomat of the family, had a tendency to smooth over others' flaws, especially their father's. Heaven knew the Adderlys needed a peacemaker. Conversations often turned to rows and petty scrambles for a bit of high ground, even if it meant putting everyone else out of sorts. Left to their own devices, Kitty thought she and her sisters could carry on very amicably, but their parents often forced them to take sides.

No one could doubt that of the three sisters, Hattie most deserved a happy ending. Hattie knew how to embrace joy with open arms, whereas Violet was their resident worrier, far too concerned with being precise and fussing over what might or might not come to be, and every tragic possibility in between. Too much like Mama.

Kitty preferred not to dwell on her own foibles, though she knew them with intimate certainty. It was agony to admit the truth—that she'd inherited her father's nature, his tendency to overestimate his own worth and see others as somehow less clever and therefore less worthy. Worst of all, it was a terrible bore. It made everyone she met far too easy to maneuver and mold. It was the single thing Kitty might change about herself, if she was pressed to change anything at all.

Only her sisters gentled her. With Hattie and Violet, there was never a need for pettiness and foolish games. Their influence even melted a bit of her anger toward their father.

"If you love Mr. Treadwell, I'm certain I will too. You know Papa barely speaks to me these days, but I shall do all I can."

Since the first moment the nurse had placed Hattie in her five-year-old arms, a plump squalling bundle with a tuft of blond hair and soft pink skin, Kitty hadn't been able to deny her sister anything. If Hattie truly wished to marry the man, how could she douse her joy?

Hattie had never been one for childish infatuations, so Kitty believed her enthusiasm for the young man sprang from genuine emotion, however short their acquaintance.

But there was still Papa to manage. He wouldn't approve of Hattie's barrister-to-be easily, and he'd taken to the ridiculous notion that his first daughter must marry before his second or third. He'd only mentioned the idea in the past weeks, and Hattie covered the hurt of his declaration by teasingly claiming it was a harebrained scheme the gentlemen at his club helped him devise to give them a new cause for a wager.

But Kitty knew the truth of it. She and Father had been engaged in a grand chess match for as long as she could remember. He would move to best her, she would attempt some bit of strategy to impress him, and he would invariably choose exactly that moment to call checkmate.

Father had been the one to teach her to play chess when she was a child. During one memorable lesson, he'd lectured her on ways to limit an opponent's options, to hem them in, forcing the direction of their next move.

This new insistence that she marry first was meant to do just that. To cobble her, take away her options, and perhaps punish her for her continued refusal of Lord Ponsonby. Mama might allow her to be discerning and terribly choosy when it came to accepting a proposal, but her father couldn't seem to forgive her rejection of a man he considered a friend and political ally.

"I've had a note from dearest Oliver this morning. He will be at the ball tonight, of course, but he tells me he's bringing friends, the Duke of Wrexford and his sister."

"He's friends with a duke? You should have mentioned that to Papa first. Nothing impresses Desmond Adderly like money and good blood."

Hattie nodded eagerly, the pinned curls around her ears coming loose in her fervency. "A quite handsome duke from all I've heard. And rich. He's only just inherited a beautiful estate in Cambridgeshire. Roxbury Hall, I believe it's called."

Kitty had been flipping pages in a lady's magazine as their maid, Elsie, arranged her hair and Hattie's. When Elsie reached up to sort out Hattie's loosened curls, the meaning of her sister's ramblings finally dawned on Kitty.

"Hattie . . . I do hope you don't mean to match me with Oliver's duke."

"I'm not Papa. I wouldn't presume to match you, but I thought Wrexford might intrigue you. Beyond his friendship with Oliver, the man's a new duke."

Wouldn't their father love such a match? She might finally, for once in her three and twenty years, actually please him. It was a prospect she'd given up long ago. What he most wanted from her, she could never give him. She couldn't change her sex. She could never be the Clayborne son and heir he'd hoped for.

Mama would be over the moon too. What a coup to marry off her first daughter to a duke. It might even cover the embarrassment of admitting Oliver, the not-quite-a barrister, into the family. And it could sweep away all of Kitty's sins—the incident she'd instigated with Lord Grimsby, and her refusal to marry a man three times her age.

But what might it cost her? A duke, higher ranking than her father, might outrank him in imperiousness too. If her every action was watched and appraised now, how might she be scrutinized as Duchess of Wrexford?

Hattie, clever girl, said nothing more, but watched Kitty from the corner of her clear blue eyes. She waited, allowing Kitty to sift her worries and the benefits of such a match, which were impossible to deny.

Kitty laughed, a lower naughtier tone that she reserved for moments alone with her sisters.

"I look forward to meeting him." She lifted a finger when she saw Hattie beaming. "Only that. I promise you nothing. He's a new duke. Anyone would be curious."

SEBASTIAN TRIED TO ignore the whispers and stares as a footman announced him and Pippa at the Clayborne ball. They were a fresh spectacle, something new for London society to chew on. He expected others to be curious, though his sister seemed to bristle at the inquisitive glances.

"Will we be able to overcome our shyness and talk to these people?" she asked as her gaze darted from the shimmering chandeliers to livered footmen to a cluster of ladies whose jewels glittered in the gaslight.

"I wasn't aware we suffered from shyness."

His sister attended classes in which she was often the sole female in the room. She gave speeches at the half-dozen ladies' groups she'd joined. Pippa had as much mettle as most men he knew.

Seb preferred to listen and observe before speaking, and he strove to choose his words carefully. Still, their parents had taught him and Pippa the power of words, encouraging them to form educated opinions and speak their minds. Neither of them could truly be called bashful.

Pippa seemed to disagree. Looking up at him, she tipped her head, assessing him. "You rarely speak to those with whom you're not acquainted, and I'm dreadful at making new friends."

"I call that discerning. Not shy."

He was relieved to see the hint of a smile and feel Pippa loosening her grip on his arm. Despite her reticence about attending the ball, she'd prepared carefully, choosing one of her new gowns, and one afternoon the previous week he'd even caught her dancing in her sitting room.

This ball was a much more formal affair than the winter country dance he'd attended previously, but for the most part the whisperers seemed benign. He spied nods of approval and even a few genuine smiles of welcome among the gathered guests.

Lady Clayborne greeted them warmly and Lady Harriet, the object of Oliver's affections, truly was a bejeweled goddess. Alabaster fairly described the lady's skin, and her hair shimmered as bright and enticing as any golden relic.

Her sister, Lady Katherine, the woman whose noble qualities Ollie had been extolling for the entire train ride down from Roxbury to London, was absent from the introductions. Perhaps she'd caught a whiff of the grand scheme to match them and found a way to avoid the ball, as Sebastian half wished he'd done.

Not only did he doubt his suitably to marry any woman but, in general, he loathed scheming of any kind. He refused to be manipulated like a marionette on a string. He'd danced to one woman's tune a decade ago. *Never again.*

When he stopped moving and began woolgathering, Pippa unlatched herself from his arm to go off in search of lemonade with Lady Harriet. Seb watched his sister be swept away, and took a strategic position next to a potted palm, letting his eyes range over the assembled guests. Who was who? Why had Lord Clayborne selected these particular guests? He feared there'd be no space in his mind for mathematics at all once he'd filled it with lords and ladies and all of polite society's rules of etiquette.

Ollie had arrived before them and approached Sebastian.

"Apparently there was some snafu with Lady Katherine's gown. You know how ladies are about their gowns. Hattie says she'll be down direct . . ." Oliver had been glancing around the room as he whispered and stopped short at the sight of a tall statuesque blond woman in a gown of buttercream satin. "Wait. There she is. Shall I make the introduction?"

Lady Katherine was a stunning woman—gilded hair, emerald eyes, all the precious adjectives one could devise—with delicate features almost too perfectly arranged. Her hair was lighter than her sister's and glittered as if spun through with threads of gold, and her skin glowed as if she'd painted herself with diamond dust. The lady drew attention and she knew it. She moved with purpose, a measured glide, meting out a smile here, a grin there, as she floated across the ballroom. A group of giggling young women seemed to be her target, and Seb watched as she sailed toward them as sure as an arrow shot from a master archer's bow.

"Let me watch awhile."

Ollie cast him an amused expression before striding off toward his young lady.

The group of three young women welcomed Lady Katherine with smiles and kisses and, from the appreciative way they all glanced down at the intricate beading of her gown, praise for her dressmaker's creation. The eldest Adderly daughter accepted their accolades with a grin and several nods before the quartet drew closer to each other, flicked their wrists, and began whispering behind the painted silk of their fans.

Seb noticed their attentions turn outward and their gazes alight on an individual just long enough to laugh and whisper at their expense before moving on to the next object of ridicule. Most people seemed oblivious to their attentions. The musicians had begun to play and couples were beginning to pair off and ready themselves for the first dance.

He scanned the room for Pippa and found her conversing with a pretty chestnut-haired young woman against the far wall. The two interacted as if they were old friends, smiling and laughing as they chatted, completely caught up in whatever topic they'd lit upon.

Oliver had secured the first dance with Lady Harriet, and even Lord Clayborne seemed pleased, the firm set of his mouth softening a bit at the sight of a couple so clearly enamored with each other.

Those who weren't dancing turned their attention to those who were, couples moving with grace and precision in a series of complex steps that reminded Seb just how unprepared he was for a ball.

The eagerness in Pippa's expression drew a deep sigh from low in his chest. Her tapping toes and moving feet, a mimicking echo of the ladies on the dance floor, signaled her desire to dance, yet she'd never had a chance to learn the intricate steps. Seb couldn't abide the notion of Lady Katherine and her group tittering at Pippa behind their fans if she took to the dance floor and faltered.

The young woman at Pippa's side reached for her arm and whispered close to her ear before both young ladies turned their attention to a lanky bronze-haired buck striding the length of the ballroom as if *he* was master of Clayborne House. The gent carried himself with too much confidence, managing to make his black suit and stark white tie, a variation of which all the male guests wore, look better suited to him than anyone else in the room.

Seb rolled his shoulders, pressing against the restraint of his own evening attire. The tailor had stitched the jacket so close, it fit like a second skin. Even if he'd been so inclined, the garment would never yield enough for him to swagger like the gadabout drawing all the ladies' attention.

He was just the sort Seb imagined Pippa putting in his place, and his chest deflated on a relieved exhale when she dismissed the man with a single glance. Her companion, on the other hand, bit her lip as a poppy-red flush crept up her cheeks. The lady darted her gaze toward the musicians, the dancers, back to Pippa, all in an obvious effort not to gape at the young man, but after every momentary glance away, she'd turn back, drinking him in, naked admiration writ in every aspect of her face.

As the man approached them, Seb found himself hopeful for Pippa's new acquaintance. A young woman so infatuated with a man surely merited a bit of his attention. But as the gent drew near, and the ladies' eyes widened, he didn't turn a single glance their way before sauntering toward Lady Katherine and her gang of gossips.

After bowing and smiling—an irritatingly drawn-out show of white above his square jaw—he took one of the young lady's hands and led her toward the dance floor. Lady Katherine seemed to pout, her bow-shaped mouth bowing out further, while two of her friends turned toward Pippa and her disappointed companion and began snickering. One even had the gall to point. And this time their derision was felt in full measure. Pippa's new friend turned away, lower lip quivering, and his sister turned her back too, drawing close to the distraught young woman, no doubt consoling her as best she could.

Fisting his hands, Seb fought the heartburn sear of anger. It didn't match the provocation and he recognized it for what it was. An echo from the past, a vein of ire buried deep and meant for another woman who smiled one moment and mistreated others the next.

Whatever his ballroom failings, he couldn't stand by and watch. Tension twisted a vice between his shoulder blades and he was gritting his teeth so forcefully, he feared those around him would soon hear the crunch.

He strode forward to ask Pippa's companion to dance, if only to distract the young woman. With any luck, his lack of skill as a dance partner wouldn't cause her more embarrassment.

Ollie stopped him midstride.

"Who is that man, Ollie?" Seb narrowed his gaze at the young man dancing past with one of Lady Katherine's cohorts in his arms.

"Wellesley. Robert Wellesley, a family friend of the Adderlys. Why?"

"He seems to leave disappointed women in his wake. Excuse me."

Continuing toward Pippa, Seb saw rebellion break out among Lady Katherine and her ladies, and he suspected the tall smirking peacock was the cause. He watched as Wellesley returned his dance partner to the quartet and the four women slowly drew apart from each other, their faces twisted in frowns of anger and irritation. Surprisingly, most of the wrath seemed to be directed at their leader.

Seb drew close enough to hear their exchange.

A dark-haired young lady asked, "Who is she and why did you invite her?"

"Yes, and how dare she look so forlorn that Wellesley won't dance with her?"

"Her name is Annabel Benson, and she's not the only lady disappointed to find Mr. Wellesley's name missing from her dance card." Lady Katherine addressed the group, an eyebrow arched knowingly.

"And who's the tall forbidding girl in that awful blue dress?"

Turning as one, they gazed across at where his sister stood clad in the new blue gown he'd watched her smooth down a dozen times to alleviate her nervousness during their carriage ride to the ball.

Seb knew little of women's gowns, but Pippa's seemed every bit as elaborate and fashionable as those the other ladies wore. He considered declaring as much to Lady Katherine and her cronies, but Pippa would never forgive him for making a fuss about her clothes or drawing attention to her at all. As it was, she'd spent every moment since they'd arrived clinging to the ballroom's wall.

Lady Katherine and her friends were forced to move as breathless couples stepped off the dance floor.

Seb could no longer hear the women's exchanges but their expressions indicated continued discord. After another moment of listening to whatever condemnations her companions offered, Lady Katherine withdrew from the group and strode away.

She moved with the same lithe elegance with which she'd entered the room, and if not for the patch of pink marring her cheek, none could have guessed at her distress.

He gave into impulse and followed her, skirting the edge of the ballroom's perimeter, his heels clicking on marble as he entered a darkened hall. When he glimpsed the train of her gown slip through a doorway, he stretched his long legs into a deeper stride to catch up before she locked herself away.

Pausing at the threshold of the door she'd left ajar, Seb sucked in a deep breath, expanding the confines of his evening jacket to ease tension in his neck and shoulders. He waited, closing his eyes and drawing in another long inhale, striving to tamp down his irritation. Turning back would be the prudent path. He didn't need a guide to aristocratic behavior to tell him a duke shouldn't chase women into empty rooms to chastise their rude behavior.

Yet there was the rub. Who would ever tell a marquess's daughter and her coterie of lady critics to treat others respectfully? Even his sister, who'd done nothing but keep to the ballroom's edges, had found herself in their crosshairs.

One more shallow breath and he took a step toward the threshold. Vanilla. He tasted its sweetness on his tongue. Her scent. The simple flavor didn't suit Lady Katherine, and yet as he peered through the doorway at the expanse of her pale shoulders and the corn silk strand of hair that snaked down her back, somehow escaped from her perfect coiffure, he could easily imagine the skin at her nape tasting of vanilla.

Despite the seemingly endless stretch of years since he'd touched a woman, he knew that swath of skin on her neck would be smooth, warm to the touch. A tender spot, vulnerable. Few men would ever be allowed to caress her there.

He flexed his fingers as he stepped past the threshold,

moving quietly, still doubting with every step whether he should confront her at all.

She stood before the unlit fireplace, shoulders curved in, hands gathered in front of her, and he noticed too late that her body trembled and she emitted an unmistakable whimper.

When she whirled on him, Seb reared back at the sight of a glistening tear caught in the fan of lashes beneath her eye.

*Good God.* Tearful women were his Achilles' heel. Pippa's rare tears reduced him to mush.

He cleared his throat and bounced on his heels. "Lady Katherine, I—"

"We haven't been introduced. Don't you know you shouldn't speak to a lady until you've been introduced?" She turned back toward the fireplace and peered at him over her shoulder a moment before executing an elegant swivel that drew the skirt of her dress around in a flash of sparkling beads bobbing on a river of satin. There were no tears now, not a single vestige of distress, just a snappish bite in her tone.

"I'm not terribly fond of rules." Seb knew the basics of etiquette, but he was much more interested in the laws of mathematics. Surely here on the cusp of the next century, the silly list of *dos* and *do nots* could be discarded now and then.

"I'll introduce myself now," he offered, stepping toward her as he spoke.

"No." She lifted a hand to halt his progress. "I know who you are. You're the Duke of Wrexford, and you've been a nobleman for less than a month." She jutted her chin and threw the words at him as an accusation, a reminder that he was a novice in this world of balls and etiquette, regardless of the accident of inheritance that had given him a dukedom.

Her haughty tone kindled the irritation he'd felt in the ballroom back into a hot spark. "Yes, and you've been a noble lady all your life, yet you laugh at your guests for sport."

She crumbled for a fraction of a second, a slight frown marring her brow, and then lifted her chin even higher. If the lady raised her head any farther, she'd tip over.

Her discomfort did not please him. Winning the point brought no victorious thrill.

"You're right, my lady. I do lack social graces." Seb took another step and far too much pleasure in the way her eyes widened a fraction as she straightened her back, holding her ground.

"Not to mention finesse." She lowered her chin, though her back remained ramrod straight.

"Perhaps you could teach me." He'd meant to infuse his tone with sarcasm, but the words came out low, catching in his throat. More petition than scold.

"Surely you didn't follow me into this room to learn etiquette." Despite her stiff posture, her tone softened to a lower pitch. A disarmingly warm, almost jovial sound that made Seb duck his head and work to steady his breathing. Her vanilla scent enveloped him now, its potency multiplied by the warmth of her body.

"Tell me. Why did I follow you?" He still wasn't

sure of the answer himself, and her certainty stoked his irritation. Yet the instant he asked the question, she seemed less sure—of herself, of him, and of whatever had brought them to this moment, alone together in a dimly lit room.

"To charm me?" Her question made him grin. She was a beautiful woman, but when she faltered and let her perfect façade slip, she was enticing. What had Ollie called her? *Difficult to snare*. This woman *was* a snare.

When he didn't reply, she frowned, and the temporary flaw in her too perfectly arranged face made her more beautiful, more human, a woman whose hair he could imagine mussing in passion, whose clothes he could envision disheveling in a desperate race to uncover more of her radiant skin.

Lifting her hands to her hips, she demanded, "Go on, then, Wrexford. Charm me."

Despite the hint of a smile curving her mouth, the tone of command in her voice sank into his gut like a lead spike. He'd been free from a woman's dictates for ten years. All the denial and solitude had been nothing to knowing his choices were his own. Yet her challenge pushed him the final long stride toward her. The confidence she exuded, her vibrancy, compelled him near her, but even her potent allure did not blot out the memory of her pettiness in the ballroom.

He'd followed her into this room to chasten her. Hadn't he?

"Do men often try to charm you?" He was close enough to feel her breath against his chin, to see the lighter flecks of burnished gold in her eyes, to spot the tawny beauty mark at the right edge of her upper lip.

"Yes." She released the word instantly, a hiss of heat against his skin.

He swallowed down an ache in his throat, but the soreness traveled, burning in his chest, tightening his body.

"Do they touch you?" He reached out, gripping her arm lightly above her elbow.

"Only if I let them."

He'd gone beyond simply breaking the rules of etiquette now. Beyond logic and reason. Her skin was warm and smooth, and touching her was a mistake. But it was heady one, as if he was a green boy touching a woman for the first time, a reckless man taking the first step on a grand adventure.

She felt it too. Her eyes went limpid, brighter, the black center growing larger and the lower crescent of green glowing like absinthe lit by candlelight.

Her lips parted and he lowered his head.

When he moved, she jolted, fluttering her lashes and then glaring up at him, her marble perfection slid neatly back in place.

The chill in her gaze tempered his arousal, but he couldn't stop touching her.

"I did not follow you into this room to charm you."

"No?"

He shook his head. "I came to tell you . . ." What? That she was the most contradictory woman he'd ever met? Beautiful enough to snare any man, and yet thorny the moment he approached. Despite her distasteful behavior in the ballroom, she'd done what no woman had in ten years—driven him to take action, made him ache after a decade of denial.

"No one in that ballroom wishes to be the object of your ridicule, Lady Katherine."

"Perhaps some of them deserve it." She trailed her gaze down his body and back up again in one sweeping glance, leaving no doubt she thought him one of the deserving sort.

"Not from their hostess."

"My mother is this evening's hostess."

"Ah, so she invites them, and you snicker at them behind their backs?"

She narrowed her eyes and drew in a breath so deep her pale shoulders lifted.

"No lady wishes to be chastised by a stranger in her own home." After tugging her arm from his grasp, she took two quick steps, backing away from him.

Her reprimand found its mark and Seb clenched his fists, ignoring the tingling sensation in the fingers of his left hand, the warmth from her body captured against the flesh of his palm. Speaking of strangers, what the hell was he doing verbally sparring with a woman he barely knew while leaving his sister on her own in a ballroom full of people she didn't know?

He'd been a fool to follow her, a madman to touch her. And he wished to regret every moment near her more than he did.

"Forgive me, Lady Katherine." Seb wasn't certain

whether he needed forgiveness, or she did, for being so damned confounding, for making him ache. He nodded, ducking his head without quite bowing—that seemed a bit much—and turned to return to the ballroom and find Pippa.

"Wait, Your Grace, if you please."

## Chapter Four

HE WOULD LEAVE. The duke was already two steps away from the threshold, and there was a firm, decided solidity in the line of his back. The man seemed quite finished with her and their strange encounter. Then he shocked Kitty by halting midstride and spearing her with a glance over the wide span of his shoulder.

Those eyes of his were a nuisance.

"Perhaps we can dispense with a bit of formality, Your Grace." She paired the words with one of the simpering smiles she'd perfected over the years. It wouldn't do to make an enemy of the man. "Please, call me Kitty."

Many called her by the diminutive. There was no true intimacy in what she offered, but he wouldn't know that. Gifting the concession drew people in and tended to soften them toward her.

He turned fully and snapped his head up, his inscrutable gaze tangling with hers. His eyes widened, but irritation still furrowed lines between his brows.

"Kitty?"

Ignoring his incredulous tone, Kitty lifted a hand to her elbow and pulled her white evening glove snug on her right arm. She brushed a fingertip across the spot where he'd touched her. Held her. As if he had any right to do so.

"That's what my friends call me. So you must do so too." She pasted on a grin and turned her chin down at the precise angle to allow her eyes to tilt up at him flirtatiously.

He'd succumb like all the others, and *she* would choose what he called her and when he touched her, *if* she ever allowed him to touch her again.

Then he stalked toward her, and her sense of control faltered. A tremor skittered across her skin, but she refused to retreat. She stood firm, only reaching up to twine her long strand of pearls through her fingers, twisting the gems tight to cover her pulse where it flickered wildly at the base of her throat.

He tipped his head and studied her in a slow agonizing perusal. "No, I think not."

"No?" With him standing close, his rich verdant scent scrambling her wits, she wasn't certain what he refused.

Her name. He was denying the invitation to call her Kitty. No, that wasn't the way of it. Men didn't refuse her. She refused them.

He closed the distance in one long stride. Warm man and the aromas of oak moss and bay assaulted her senses.

Shock arced through her body. Shock that he affected her, and that she craved any man's body so near.

"Is that truly what others call you? It can't be your name. There's nothing kittenish about you."

She gasped, to breathe him in, to catch her breath, and when he moved his arm, she had the mad notion he might reach up and trace her lips with his fingertip, and then claim her mouth with his, letting her taste his woodsy cologne directly from his skin.

His gaze locked on her eyes.

"You're not a kitten. You prowled that ballroom as sure-footed as any woman I've ever seen. And while you manage to appear disinterested in everyone and everything, I'd wager nothing escapes your notice."

He lifted a hand as if to touch her but hesitated.

She held her breath, drawn taut and tense.

"You're much more cat than kitten." He grinned, the lines between his brows softening, and a glint of satisfaction lighting his gaze. "Yes. Kat suits you far better than Kitty."

What a foolish thing to say. It was the height of audacity for him to suggest any name for her.

He lifted his hand again, and she knew he would touch her. She wanted him to, if only to have the satisfaction of pushing him away. But he didn't touch her. He licked his lips and reached up to straighten his necktie and smooth down his waistcoat. Stepping back, he nodded and then began to retreat, glancing at her only once more.

"Good evening, Lady Kat—" His tongue seemed

stalled on her name. Or perhaps he was merely insisting on his new name for her. *Kat* was all he managed before swiveling on his heel and striding away.

Kitty gripped the cool marble of the mantel a moment after he stalked away and willed her legs to stop trembling. In the space of ten minutes, the Duke of Wrexford had smashed her composure to bits, and she closed her eyes, struggling to fit the puzzle pieces back together. She grappled for any thought beyond the cloud of frustration and irritation he'd left in his wake. They were familiar emotions, especially after any encounter with her father, but her brief clash with Wrexford left her swaying off-balance.

The man had taken her utterly by surprise, and the predictability of men was something she'd come to rely on. Those like Father were driven by power and money. Status and reputation mattered most. Young rogues like Rob Wellesley were lured by a pretty face and women who filled their idle hours with frivolity. And a man who followed a woman into a room without a chaperone was intent on seduction or, at the very least, flirtation.

But Wrexford wasn't interested in flirting so much as giving her a set down, and she'd been completely unprepared. The duke wasn't at all what she'd expected. Hattie had described him as a university don, and Kitty envisioned a stodgy, studious man more keen on equations than titles. No one had warned her he'd be so impressive, with a broad chest and shoulders filling out his evening jacket in ways most men never managed, nor that all the masculine angles of his face aligned in a beautiful whole that stole her breath when she stared too long.

Kitty returned to the ballroom on wobbly legs and cursed the Duke of Wrexford—for his arrogance, that knowing grin on his far too sensual mouth, and the scent of something fresh that still tickled her nose, as if he'd brought a bit of the Cambridgeshire countryside with him to London.

She craved privacy and something to drink, but escaping to the room Mama had set aside for refreshments was out of the question. A long absence from the ballroom would start tongues wagging, and she'd already had her moment of escape. How could she have known it would be spoiled by the one man at the ball who found fault with her?

It didn't help that he seemed faultless himself. Aside from his rudeness in teasing her about her name, and the apparent pride he took in throwing etiquette aside as if it had gone out of fashion. Knowing he'd only come into his title recently, and that he'd never planned to be a duke, she'd anticipated a less polished man. But Sebastian, Duke of Wrexford, was tall and elegant, with a square jaw, sharp cheekbones, cool blue eyes, and a mouth that . . . Heaven help her, she'd wanted him to kiss her with that perfectly sculpted mouth, even when he was tilting it at her in derision.

"There you are. I've been looking for you everywhere." Hattie paused between her words, attempting to catch her breath, and her cheeks glowed as if she'd just run across the length of a field. Kitty guessed she and Mr. Treadwell had danced every set since the ball began.

"It's this silly dress. I thought Elsie's stitches had pulled loose again."

Hattie didn't even pretend to believe her hastily fabricated excuse. "I saw Miss Osgood and the others, though I couldn't hear what they said. They upset you."

Everyone knew Hattie was the sweetest Adderly. The fact that she was sharp-eyed and perceptive tended to be overlooked.

"Cynth goaded me about Lord Ponsonby. They'll tire of teasing me about him eventually."

"Cynthia Osgood will never tire of tormenting others. She's been perfecting the skill since we were children."

Wrexford's words about making sport of her guests echoed in Kitty's mind. Was she truly as snide and unkind as Cynthia Osgood?

Gazing across the ballroom, past couples sailing around the dance floor in the first waltz of the evening, she spied Annabel Benson, an acquaintance and now fellow Woman's Union member she'd met at a country house party before year's end. Young and good-natured, eager for new friendships, she'd reminded Kitty of Hattie. Extending an invitation to her mother's ball had seemed a simple kindness, but she certainly hadn't treated the young woman as a friend tonight. She'd taken the easy way, avoiding another skirmish with Cynthia Osgood, when the others snickered at Annabel after Wellesley snubbed her. But it hadn't prevented a row with Cynth, who'd turned on Kitty, just as she had at their ladies' tea.

"She's unkind. I cannot fathom why she's such a popular young woman." Hattie rarely condemned anyone, and Kitty's skin itched at the realization her sister's dismissal of Cynth could as easily be applied to her own behavior. "She's certainly caught Mr. Wellesley's eye."

"Any pretty thing catches Rob's notice." Kitty knew him to be an incorrigible flirt.

The Adderlys and Wellesleys had been connected for years, and Rob Wellesley had attended the same house party where Kitty befriended Miss Benson. Apparently the two had been acquainted since childhood, but Rob was as blind as he was handsome, and Annabel's infatuation, which was obvious to everyone who saw the two of them together in the same room, remained a mystery to him.

"Well, he should have a care for how he treats your new friend."

The admonition was meant for Wellesley, but Kitty hadn't treated the girl any better.

"I should speak with Annabel and make sure all's well."

It wasn't because of what Wrexford said. If she bucked Papa's commandments, she certainly wouldn't change her behavior because of a stranger's admonition.

"And you've picked just the right moment. The duke has joined them. That young woman with Annabel is his sister, Lady Philippa."

Annabel stood side by side with the tall brunette in a blue gown and the broad-shouldered duke. He stood with his back to the ballroom and the notion of approaching him under the bright light of the gaslight chandeliers set bees buzzing inside her belly.

Hattie didn't hesitate another moment before urging Kitty to follow her around the edge of the ballroom and join the trio.

As soon as they approached, he turned to look at her and Kitty's skin burned. Her cheek, her neck, everywhere his gaze touched.

She kept her eyes fixed on Annabel. "Annabel, might I have a word with you, my dear?" Kitty needed to apologize, but to do so under the duke's unnerving watchfulness was unthinkable.

Hattie cleared her throat with feminine delicacy and nudged Kitty's arm.

"Your Grace, may I introduce my sister, Lady Katherine?"

Ah, yes, she'd forgotten the niceties, and the fact that no one knew they'd already made their own awkward introductions privately.

"Pleasure to meet you, Lady Katherine." Wrexford hadn't completely forgotten the niceties, it seemed. He bowed as well as any nobleman born to his title, but Kitty didn't offer him her hand for the pretense of kissing it. If their tangle in the sitting room taught her anything, it was that the Duke of Wrexford loathed pretense.

"Everyone calls her Kitty," Hattie offered.

His brow winged up. "Do they?"

Kitty closed her eyes a moment before glaring at her sister. Hattie looked confused, but then merrily carried on with the introductions.

The duke caught the exchange, and that alluring grin crept over the curve of his mouth.

"Your Grace, may I introduce your sister to mine? Kitty, this is Lady Philippa, His Grace's sister."

The young woman lifted her chin and squared her shoulders, but her mouth curled into a displeased pucker, as if she'd taken a bite of something sour.

Wrexford looked down at his sister with one arched eyebrow, though if he intended to correct her, the grin still lingering on his mouth—why could she focus on nothing but the man's mouth?—ruined the effect.

"My goodness, it's the first time I've heard someone call me that. It sounds shockingly formal. I hope I can live up to it." Lady Philippa cast a wide, wary gaze up at her brother, and he nodded, offering her a look brimming with such love and encouragement that Kitty found herself, for the first time in her life, wishing she had an older brother.

"Everyone calls me Pippa. I don't think I'll ever get used to being called Lady Philippa."

Her comment revealed more than a hint of disdain for her honorific. Cynthia Osgood and the other young ladies would no doubt disparage the girl for her lack of delicacy. Titles were more valuable than currency to men like Kitty's father, and she suspected all the ladies in her circle had been instructed in deportment as she had. Those lessons included admonitions not to be too delighted, or disgusted, with anything, never to appear overly enthusiastic, and to absolutely refrain from bald truth. The refreshing charm of Pippa's honesty and her lack of feigned exuberance made for a delightful change from the usual ballroom inanity.

"Would you care to join us in our search for a bit of fresh air, Lady Philippa?"

Pippa nodded and Kitty turned to the lead the two young women away, relieved for the opportunity to offer Annabel an apology, and even more eager to remove herself from Wrexford's scrutiny.

She glanced back to offer him a nod and take her leave, but before she could dip her head, he cut in.

"Actually, I was just attempting to entreat Miss Benson to dance with me. She insists she is disinclined to dance this evening."

That slate gaze of his held her again, though less demanding than in the sitting room. In fact, she imagined a flash of the heat she'd glimpsed when he touched her. Before he'd scolded her and left her trembling like a fool.

"Would you to join me for the next waltz, Lady Katherine?"

Kitty swallowed hard. Then once more. She struggled to make her tongue obey. *No.* She couldn't dance with him. That would require touching him, that he touch her. She'd already allowed him that liberty once, and he'd dashed off as if the experience horrified him.

When she took too long to answer, Kitty sensed the weight of their gazes on her, especially Hattie's, who no doubt expected her to be amenable to Mr. Treadwell's aristocratic friend.

"Yes, I will dance with you, Your Grace."

*Move, go, walk away.* Her glued-to-the-floor feet were

the least of her problems. Every individual in the circle around Kitty broke into a grin. Even the duke who'd been so eager to castigate her in the sitting room wore a pleased smirk that tilted precariously toward smug.

She usually made a man work a bit harder to secure a dance with her, and the little group seemed terribly pleased with her acquiescence. As if she'd finally transformed from an obstinate mare into a tame show filly, as compliant and biddable as every daughter of a marquess ought to be.

But it was only one dance. She hadn't agreed to marry the man. No matter how much his gaze unsettled her, her determination not to take the bridle her father had been attempting to impose all her life hadn't wavered. Not even when Wrexford touched her. One dance with the man meant nothing. He was a wealthy duke, practically the brother of the man Hattie wished to marry. Dancing with him would be impossible to avoid. Why not dispense with it now and settle any awkwardness between them? Perhaps it would ease the buzzing in her belly.

SEB'S GRIN WIDENED as Kitty rushed away, Miss Benson and Pippa falling in behind her in a symphony of swishing satin and taffeta silk. But the mirth ebbed and his face stiffened until he was certain he was grimacing rather than indicating an ounce of the pleasure he felt at the notion of having Lady Katherine in his arms.

*What have I done?*

He'd given into impulse again, as if he'd abandoned

ten years of staid studious behavior the minute he crossed the threshold of the Marquess of Clayborne's front door. Waltzing was nothing he excelled at. He'd danced one waltz in life, and done it very ill. Lord Moreland's daughter had been incredibly patient as he'd whirled the girl around her father's ballroom. She'd stifled her winces of pain with the fortitude of a soldier. But no one had missed how the poor thing had hobbled away afterward.

"Well done, Your Grace. My sister is very particular about who she admits onto her dance card." Lady Harriet stared at him as if he'd just trounced a dragon. Or a tigress.

"Yes, well . . ." Seb glanced down at his feet, a chance to glare them into submission and avoid Lady Harriet's overeager gaze.

"What's this I hear? Seb, are you to stand up with Lady Katherine? Well done, indeed." Ollie added his exuberance as he approached and then turned his attention to Lady Harriet. "Shall we join this set, sweet?"

Now it was the young lady's turn to avert her gaze. She blushed, the peach stain setting her skin aglow, and nodded before taking Ollie's arm and allowing him to lead her back into the fray of dancing couples.

Which left Seb alone to contemplate his foolishness.

Lady Katherine had stared at him with such indifference after their encounter in the sitting room. As if none of what passed between them had affected her beautiful practiced composure. As if her eyes hadn't widened and her pulse hadn't thudded as his had the moment he'd touched her skin. But however much he wanted to know if Katherine Adderly was soft and pliant in his arms, or as sharp and flinty as her green glare, making a fool of both of them wouldn't help Ollie's plan to woo her sister.

He longed for a bit of Pippa's resourcefulness. As a child she'd had an agile mind, but now, as a young woman, she was absolutely fearsome in her pursuit of skills and knowledge. Pippa assured him one could learn anything by reading a book on the subject and then practicing to the point of proficiency.

Why hadn't he at least perused a damned book on dancing?

Ollie and Lady Harriet swooped past him. The man's eyes were alight with a contented bliss the likes of which Seb had never seen, and certainly never experienced himself.

He stretched up, straightening his back, reaching out to align each cuff. He could do this. For Ollie. For old Wrexford and the title he'd left to Seb, one he was still learning to accept as his own. And for Pippa, who deserved a brother who was, if not brilliant at dancing, at least better than a complete ballroom dunderhead.

Now to wait for the next waltz and ignore the tingle at the center of his palms. One of his palms would soon be pressed against hers, his other nestled in the curve of her waist. Would she be warm in his arms? He vowed then and there not to lick his lips when he tasted vanilla in the air around her, and heaven forbid he duck his head to draw in the aroma mingled with the unique scent of her skin.

He flicked his gaze left and right to ensure none

glimpsed whatever ridiculous expression settled on his face while he indulged in lascivious meanderings—and about the worst-behaved woman at the ball. Lady Katherine engaged in just the sort of petty gossip and trouble-making he loathed.

But he'd glimpsed something else beyond her formidable exterior. When he'd found her in that empty room, she'd been crying, and he had no doubt the malicious sneers of her friends had been the cause. Why had they turned on her? Perhaps those who engaged in idle talk about others were most likely to become the victim of it themselves.

"Don't let her lead."

Seb had been so consumed with thoughts of Lady Katherine that he hadn't noticed her sister and Ollie return to his side.

"Beg your pardon?"

"Kitty," Lady Harriet continued in a conspiratorial tone. "Papa says from the moment of her first formal dance, my sister has always tried to lead. You shouldn't let her."

*Wonderful.* Not only did he need to worry about not treading on the lady's feet, but he would have to wrestle the reins from her too.

## Chapter Five

LONDON HAD BEEN flirting with spring for weeks, with warm sunny days followed by rain and cool breezes. The day of the ball brought an onslaught of showers that had her mother fretting about muddy floors and drenched guests, but Kitty welcomed the embrace of dense moist air as she stepped onto the balcony. She needed it to chase away the overheated flush she'd been unable to shake since her encounter with the Duke of Wrexford. Resting her hands on the balustrade at the balcony's edge, she drew in long drams of fresh air.

The longer she contemplated it, the more certain she became. She couldn't dance with the man. Feigned illness or a broken heel would suffice as an excuse. Why should she endure another moment of his self-righteous disdain? He was in *her* home. And he was a novice at the games involved in a London season. He could look as elegant as he liked in his well-tailored evening suit and flash that irritatingly lovely grin, but she didn't miss the little tells of distress—the pinch of his mouth, the occasional narrowing of his eyes and clenching of his fists—as he stood along the edge of the ballroom. He looked lost, completely out of his depth. For a man used to dusty lecture halls at Cambridge, the heat and noise and constant movement of a ballroom must seem quite an overwhelming muddle. And whom did he know? Beyond his sister and Mr. Treadwell, was there a single face he recognized among the guests?

Even if she hadn't perceived his discomfort, the fact that he'd asked her to dance proved his ineptitude. The man didn't have the sense to know his host's eldest daughter wasn't on offer like all the other eager misses. Was she unaware she'd turned down six offers of marriage and refused thrice as many suitors? Perhaps he'd yet to hear her referred to as Cruel Kitty or Coy Kitty or, as one blunt nobleman had put it, "not at all worth the effort."

That comment had cut her, a stunningly sudden and sharp pain, and brought her as close to fainting as she'd ever come in her life. She hated the baron who'd said it for that most of all, that he'd found a weak spot, the chink in her armor of polite smiles and practiced poise.

"Are you well, Lady Katherine?"

At Lady Philippa Fennick's resonant voice, Kitty drew in a bracing lungful of cool air, straightened her shoulders, and turned to face the two young women who'd followed her out of doors.

"I brought Miss Benson out to ask her the very same question."

Annabel stiffened and began shaking her head before replying. "Me? Yes, of course. I'm fine. Why do you ask, Lady Katherine?"

So it was to be ice between them now, the frosting over of any of the easiness they'd achieved beyond polite civility. Men did wreak such havoc on female friendships, and they weren't even vying for the same one. But Annabel's cool tone wasn't wholly undeserved. Kitty should have shielded the girl from Cynth and the others, or at least seen to it that Robert Wellesley asked Annabel to dance.

Annabel had never been anything but kind, if a bit too naive about men and the wide world around her.

"If you mean Mr. Wellesley . . ." The girl tried to say more, but his name seemed to tangle her in knots and she twisted her gloved hands and turned away to compose herself.

"Balls and soirees, particularly the first of the season, seem to bring out the worst in all of us." In herself especially, but Kitty bit back the admission. After all, Cynthia Osgood had been the one to laugh and point at Annabel. Kitty suspected it was half inspired by Cynth's wish that *she'd* been the one Wellesley had asked for the first dance. The man was handsome enough to turn friend against friend, but Kitty couldn't comprehend why the ladies bickered over him. Rob was almost too pretty, and he was overly fond of his own witticisms. No woman would ever impress him as much as he amused himself. His too obvious charms had never unsettled Kitty half as much as a few minutes spent in the Duke of Wrexford's company.

"Why should balls make people cross and unkind?

I imagined them as nothing but music and merriment and the stuff of happy memories." Lady Pippa's achingly sincere tone caused a pinch of jealousy in Kitty. Could any young woman truly possess so much youthful innocence? The duke's sister had to be nearly her own age, yet she seemed so fresh and unbruised by life's disappointments. Love must have been showered on her as a child, and what a blissful family the Fennicks must have been to produce such an optimistic young woman.

Kitty couldn't imagine familial bliss. Not anymore. She'd tried as a child, with her cutout paper doll family, smiles carefully drawn on their faces, but years of family rows and resentments, and her failure to obtain an iota of the approval and love she'd sought from her father, had taught her differently.

Stepping toward Lady Philippa, Kitty studied the young woman's high cheekbones, waves of glossy dark hair, and stunning amber eyes. She was a beauty, and a singular one. With a bit more guile and understanding of how to play the game, the duke's sister could best them all.

Tapping her bottom lip a moment, Kitty considered how many of the young woman's illusions to shatter.

"Some see it less as a ballroom and more as a battleground."

It was the only battleground on which she held the balance of power against her father. After four seasons, dozens of suitors, and all her rejected marriage proposals, her final *yes* to a man of whom he would approve was the only weapon remaining in her arsenal, and she wouldn't deploy it carelessly. That withheld *yes* was her single portion of independence. After twenty-three years, she'd learned to manage her father's attempts to exert control. But how might a husband stifle and control her? Why give another man the power to dictate her actions and choices?

The duke's sister narrowed her gaze, lowering her sable eyelashes as if Kitty had just read the opening lines of the worst sort of penny dreadful, and she considered every word of it dubious at best.

"If we could all step into the basket of an aeronaut's balloon and ascend high above that room . . ." Kitty stepped toward the French doors that led back into the ballroom, staring through the windows until the living palette of rich-hued gowns and men dressed in evening black and white blurred in her field of vision. "We'd see men and women moving with as much strategy as any battle commander has ever employed."

Lady Philippa had drawn to Miss Benson's side by the time Kitty turned her attention back to them. The two were shivering, but she couldn't be certain if a glimpse of harsh reality or the increasingly bitter wind was the cause. She didn't wish to frighten the young women, merely to equip them. Ladies like Cynthia Osgood would relish the opportunity to take advantage of Lady Philippa's naiveté and Miss Benson's infatuation.

"Women's futures depend on their success in that room. Men's happiness rest on the choices they make. Is it any wonder we all take it far too seriously?"

The young women stared at her, lips parted, as if they

might offer a retort. Perhaps they were wondering why they'd decided to accompany Kitty onto a balcony so that she could drain all of the enjoyment from their evening. The music filtering out from the ballroom had reached a lull, a brief respite before the musicians would play the next waltz. The duke would come looking for his sister, or perhaps for Kitty herself to claim his dance. And Wellesley might search out Annabel. The man couldn't see that the girl was besotted with him, but he was hawkishly protective of her in a brotherly way.

"Though I admit to having doubts before, I now appreciate the appeal of a grand ball, and I intend to enjoy every minute of this one," Lady Philippa announced. Her lip quivered and Kitty feared she'd have to explain to the most daunting man she'd ever met why she'd caused his sister to cry, but then the young woman pursed her lips, turned, and stomped toward the doors, wrenching one open before calling to Miss Benson.

"Are you coming, Annabel?"

Annabel nodded at Lady Philippa before turning back to Kitty. "You should come too, Kitty. It's freezing out here." Kitty heard a hint of Annabel's usual warmth in her tone. It was the opening she needed to swallow her pride.

"Forgive me, Annabel."

They were the wrong words to say. A tear welled up, glittering in the moonlight, and Annabel blinked her eyes a moment to set it on its path down her wind-rouged cheek. "Of course I do. Thank you for an invitation to the ball."

The words were still too polite for Kitty's taste.

"It's not your fault he doesn't notice me, Kitty. You can't make Rob see me, or force him to dance with me."

As Kitty watched Annabel follow Lady Philippa back into the ballroom, a scented swell of warm air rushed through the doors to surround her, to lure her back into the fray.

It truly had turned bitterly cold, and Kitty wrapped her arms around herself as she considered Annabel's plight.

Kitty acknowledged that she might not possess the power to make a man recognize a woman's love for him, but this was her father's home and her mother's meticulously planned ball. Surely, she did have the ability to force one silly man to dance with one terribly smitten girl.

THERE WAS NO hope for it. He'd have beg off. It'd been bad enough treading on the Moreland girl's feet. He couldn't hobble a marquess's daughter at the first grand ball of the season, especially when Oliver was determined to marry the woman's sister.

And judging by what he'd seen of the Marquess of Clayborne, Seb didn't envy Ollie the task of convincing the nobleman of anything. Every time Seb thought he caught a bit of pleasure in the marquess's expression, the man's face turned hard in the next instant and he glared at his guests as if wishing them all anywhere but in his ballroom.

Seb was beginning to wish he were anywhere else too. The musicians had struck up again, and couples paired off and took their places in the center of the ballroom for the second waltz. Oliver and Hattie were among the dancers, standing much too close to one another, cocooned in the bliss of young love and oblivious to anything as unromantic as propriety or those rules of etiquette of which Lady Katherine seemed so fond.

Then he saw Pippa and Miss Benson enter the ballroom. Their mouths had gone pale and they chafed their hands and upper arms as if to ward off a chill. Worse, they were unaccompanied. Had they truly followed their host's daughter onto the balcony only to leave her out in the cold on her own? And why was he so concerned with the woman's whereabouts? The next time he saw her, he'd have to manage a waltz without trouncing on her toes.

Seb made his way toward his sister, wending past Lady Katherine's group of friends, ignoring stares and trying not to bristle at the sense of being stripped bare as they assessed him. He turned his head to meet the gaze of the boldest among them who'd moved to position herself in his path, a dark-haired beauty with eyes as cold and devoid of warmth as chips of onyx.

"Your Grace." The young woman dipped her head and made a slight bending motion, an uninspired version of a curtsy.

They hadn't been introduced, but Seb couldn't bring himself to be as rude as she'd been to Miss Benson. He nodded to acknowledge her and continue on his way just as Katherine Adderly stepped into the ballroom, halting him midstride. Half expecting her to approach and claim the waltz he'd offered, he shivered with a trickle of anticipation at the prospect. But she didn't spare him a single glance before making her way toward the young buck. Wellesley, Ollie had called him.

Seb almost felt sorry for the peacock. Eyes flashing with determination, stride quick and forceful, Lady Katherine looked like Athena marching into battle. And Wellesley defended himself as well as he was able in the middle of a ballroom, crossing his arms over his chest and taking two steps back when she reached his side.

They were too far away for Seb to hear their discussion but from the vigor of the man's nods and the way she kept wagging her finger at him, Seb guessed the lady would get her way, whatever she was after. He suspected she usually did.

The Wellesley gent tipped back the glass of whatever he'd been drinking, handed the vessel to an unsuspecting chap nearby, sketched a half-hearted bow in Lady Katherine's direction, and set off on the mission she'd given him. His stride nearly matched hers for determination as he beelined toward Pippa and Miss Benson. Both young women looked as shocked as Mr. Wellesley had been when Lady Katherine approached him, if a good deal less frightened. Miss Benson blinked several times before allowing the young man to take her hand and lead her to the edge of the ballroom floor to wait for the next set.

"Do you think it's a trick?"

Seb heard Pippa's voice before he saw her emerge through a group of ladies and gentlemen gathered near his edge of the ballroom. Rather than move around them, she'd reached out an arm to force her own path, whispering excuses and ignoring their irritated glares and tuts of disapproval as she passed.

"Careful, Pippa." She stumbled as she drew near, and Seb reached out a hand to steady her.

"If she's engineered this to humiliate Annabel, you can't possibly dance with her." She was upset and a bit disheveled, strands of hair breaking free every which way. She scooped several behind her ear. "And despite Ollie's hopes, you mustn't dream of marrying her."

Pippa couldn't know it—she'd been young and occupied with lessons in the nursery—but Seb had heard the same words once before. Not the bit about Annabel Benson, of course, but the plea that he not allow the notion of marrying Miss Alecia Lloyd to enter his mind. His father's face had been sad when he'd said it, his tone fearful, much more pleading than stern. Their father had never managed stern. And Seb hadn't required the admonition. He'd already begun to see beyond her façade and unravel a few of her lies.

"Ollie mentioned his hopes to you?" Seb asked, unaware the chill between his sister and friend had thawed.

"He can't contain himself. He speaks of nothing but Lady Harriet and how fine a match his sister would make for you."

The moment she mentioned her, Seb caught sight of the woman Pippa insisted he not marry. Though the strains of the next waltz filled the room, Lady Katherine seemed completely uninterested in taking him up on his offer of a dance. She stood near the edge of the waltzing couples, fully occupied with trailing her gaze after Annabel Benson, who moved around the ballroom in the arms of Mr. Wellesley. A grin softened Lady Katherine's face, tipping her mouth unevenly.

She was a fetching woman. For a moment he let himself imagine they'd danced together, that he'd taken her in his arms and guided her around the ballroom. That he'd pressed his hand to her waist, felt the skirts of her gown slipping between his legs, and tasted her vanilla scent in the air between them. He should have touched her again when he'd had the chance.

*No.* No to the unexpected rush of desire she ignited in him. No to the notion of giving in to the impulse that made his fingers itch to touch her. No to letting passion addle his brain and weaken his reason as it had once before. *Never again.*

He could admire a stunning woman attempting to redeem her actions, but nothing more.

"I believe she's trying to make amends." Seb indicated Lady Katherine with the dip of his head and his sister turned to watch her too. He expected her to perceive the pleasure Lady Katherine took from matchmaking a couple in need of a nudge, but Pippa seemed thoroughly unimpressed. She crossed her arms and glanced at him obliquely.

"I still don't like her. She's not at all what she seems."

He waited for more, an explanation, but Pippa continued to bounce wary glances from Lady Katherine to Miss Benson and back again.

"She reminds me of that white rose at Roxbury," she finally added.

Dozens of white roses bloomed at Roxbury, but Pippa was as fond of specificity as he was. They only differed in kind. Pippa's literary mind saw symbolism and analogies in her experiences, while Seb saw the world in numbers and the beauty of fixed equations.

"What rose?"

"The first day we arrived. Don't you recall when I bent to smell that extraordinary white rose and a bee flew out and nearly stung me?"

He didn't recall the incident, but he knew the rose and the bee weren't the point. "And is Miss Adderly the bee or the rose?"

She sighed, emphasizing her frustration with an unmistakable eye roll.

"She's both! She's the rose that hides the bee. She looks lovely and lures you in. She makes you wish to draw close, like I wished to smell the sweet scent of that rose, but watch out . . ." She pointed a finger at him, wagging it much as Lady Katherine had at Mr. Wellesley. "She's as likely to smell sweet as to sting you."

Pippa turned back toward the dance floor, wrapping her arms around herself.

"Are you still cold?" It might not be done at proper London balls, but he'd damned well offer his sister his coat if she needed it.

A jerky shake of her head was her only reply. He watched her from the corner of his eye as she bit her lip and her frown deepened. Seeing her upset stoked an anxious unease that made him itch to do something, anything, to fix it.

"I take it something unpleasant occurred on the balcony. I'm happy to hear it if you wish to tell me."

Pippa dipped her head and stared overlong at the toes of her new shoes, their embroidered tops peeking out under the hem of her gown. A few curling strands of her hair slid down, sheltering her eyes, and Seb clenched his fists, fearing she'd look up at him with a tear-filled gaze.

But when she finally swiveled to face him, jaw clenched, eyes glittering, there was nothing of sorrow or defeat in her eyes. She looked angry and every bit as fearsome as Katherine Adderly had when she'd stomped up to Mr. Wellesley.

"She doesn't even like balls. They're like battlefields, she said, and I couldn't help thinking of all of us charging at each other with sabers and bayonets while rifles and cannon fire burst out over the music."

Seb glanced out over the ballroom. The measured movement of the dancers and clamor of music, laughter, and conversation suddenly seemed tame compared to what Pippa envisioned. And yet despite the beauty of the gowns and jewels and the lavish decorations, Seb saw the furtive gazes of debutantes assessing prospective suitors and heard the unsettled chuckles of eligible young men commiserating with each other about being sized up like thoroughbreds before a race. He'd never been to war, never seen a battlefield, but he suspected

Lady Katherine's comparison was more apt than his sister allowed.

"I'm not sure I'll ever be able to enjoy a ball again, and I've never even had my first dance."

Pippa was as resilient as she was hopeful, and she had years of seeing the world as a very fine place ahead of her before experience's bruises and disappointments might temper her perspective. He prayed she'd never know heartache, even while acknowledging his inability to prevent it.

"You'll dance at many balls, Pippa. And I suspect you'll enjoy every one of them."

It was wrong of Lady Katherine to burst his sister's illusions. Time and tribulations would see to that soon enough.

"Promise?"

It was a question she'd asked of him as a child, securing promises as often as she'd ask for a sweet. She was old enough to know that promises weren't simple to come by and, sometimes, even harder to keep. But she still asked him. And he still promised.

"I do."

That finally brought a smile to her face, and a bit of the tension in his chest eased.

"And will you promise me something else?"

He crooked an eyebrow. Promises weren't as plentiful as sweets anymore. They'd both seen promises broken.

"I'll consider it. What is it?"

She glanced around, as if to ensure none of the half-dozen people standing within arm's length might hear and whispered, "As a marquess's daughter, I know she's just the sort of lady you should be considering, but please have a care. Lady Katherine is not . . . what she seems. Remember the rose and bee."

His sister cast him a long look, brow furrowed in concern. There was no need for her to mention his past foolishness, that he'd been taken in by just such a woman once before.

*Never again.*

## Chapter Six

"I cannot imagine anyone less appropriate for her." Desmond Adderly, Marquess of Clayborne, had a tendency to voice his very definitive opinions in extreme terms. On Lord Clayborne's scale, you were the worst or the best, the most or the least. There was little room for gray.

Kitty reached up, smoothing the patch of skin between her eyebrows, and inhaled deeply, gathering strength before replying to her father's declaration. He pounced on any sign of weakness. Leveraged any vulnerability. Becoming overwrought or allowing him to see the effect of his words was equivalent to losing the battle. And she needed to win this one. For Hattie's sake.

Though he'd tolerated Oliver Treadwell's presence at the first ball of the season, the marquess had done little but complain about the young man since.

"Hattie is in love with Oliver Treadwell. Whatever his

shortcomings, we cannot change her mind. Hattie has always been led by her heart. Did you think it would be any different when she chose a man to marry?"

Her father bent his head and shook it in denial. Anyone watching might conclude he simply disagreed with her assertion, but Kitty knew her father's mannerisms better than her own. He was disgusted, disappointed. With her. And she was familiar with that most of all.

Panic welled up, an irrepressible need to please him warring with her determination not to be tamed. She swallowed to keep herself from blurting out defensively, stifling the desire to appease him.

"Will you never learn, girl? There is no aspect of our constitution, no organ of our body more susceptible to deception and more likely to deceive its bearer. Never trust the heart. It is weak and fragile. Trust what you know—about yourself, and especially about others. Use that knowledge to your advantage."

Kitty realized she was moving her lips, silently mouthing the words he had repeated so many times before. He'd been a soldier during the Crimean War, but if the boasts of his army cronies were to be believed, he'd been a bit more. It was no stretch to imagine Lord Clayborne had been a brilliant tactician, a skilled collector of information and coordinator of men and arms, and a master spy, if the rumors that he'd always refused to confirm were true.

Relegating himself to the marital machinations of his daughters must have been a very great letdown. Kitty sometimes wondered how he could bear it, and if he secretly wished for another war to fill his life with excitement, to make him feel truly useful. She understood the desire to be of use. It was why she'd joined the Women's Union and attempted to organize charitable initiatives among her circle of friends.

"She loves him." Kitty feared he would interrupt her and hurried on to stave him off. "And he does seem to be an ambitious young man."

"Ambitious for her dowry."

"The Duke of Wrexford considers him a brother. Will the duke not wish to see his brother well settled? Mr. Treadwell is to be a barrister. He may yet make a splash with his legal career."

When she'd finally said it all and allowed herself to take a breath, she lifted her gaze to her father's face, only to encounter a virtual expressive wall of displeasure. His mouth was fixed in that disgusted moue he often wore, and his two graying brows dipped and drew together, meeting in the center of his forehead.

"No splashes, thank you very much. I would simply like the man to have the ability to care for your sister as she deserves."

Kitty edged forward in her seat. Might he truly accept Hattie's young man without a full pitched battle? If Wrexford saw fit to settle a reasonable sum on the young man, they could live very comfortably with the addition of Hattie's dowry. A tight clamp of tension released in the center of her chest, and she realized how anxious she'd been. It had been weeks since she and her father had spoken privately, face-to-face, and she'd expected awkwardness. She'd half expected him to order her out of his study before she'd even managed to put in a good word for Mr. Treadwell, as she'd promised Hattie she would.

"So your only objection relates to means? If the gentleman can provide for—"

"Let us not parse it until supper. If the man can give her a fine home and take over her dressmaker, milliner, and jeweler's bills, I shall consider giving him my blessing."

He would imply it was all about money and lady's finery, though the truth was the Adderly sisters had as hefty a bill with the book vendors as the designers. Her father never gave in gracefully. He growled and grumbled and made sure he got in a final blow when he finally surrendered.

Relief and gratitude had Kitty on her feet. If he were a different kind of father and she was a better sort of daughter, she would move toward him with arms outstretched. But her father loathed hugs and kisses and any kind of physical display of warmth or affection. He hadn't touched her in years. She recalled only one embrace he'd given her as a child. She'd been ailing with a fever, and Papa had come into her sickroom to watch over her while the nurse stepped out for fresh water and linens. He'd encouraged her to test her strength, to get out of bed after three days of resting. *Stand on your own two feet, child.*

She'd been eager to please him and scrambled out from under the covers. The cool floorboards under her bare feet, dizziness that set the room spinning, the fearful trembling she couldn't stifle however hard she tried—it all rushed back as if she was still a desperate little girl. Failing at her first step, she'd reached out to stop her fall, and he'd been there. His impossibly strong arms surrounded her, gathering her near, and he'd squeezed her tight a moment before lifting her back into bed. Covering the top of her head with this hand, he'd patted her gently before turning away. Though he'd said nothing more to her, he shouted at the nurse as he departed. *See that my child gets well.*

"Thank you, Papa."

Excitement bubbled up. She had to tell Hattie, couldn't wait to see her sister's face when she heard that the biggest hurdle to her match with Mr. Treadwell had been managed. Their father's approval was contingent only on the duke's support of the match, and Kitty had no doubt he'd give it.

"I must go and find Hattie."

"Not so swiftly, Katherine. That's not the end of the matter."

All of the anticipation of a moment before dipped in her belly and Kitty held stiff and still, waiting for the rest. She wasn't going to like it. The smirk on her father's face told her as much.

"Sit."

Reaching up to swipe away a strand of hair tickling at her ear, Kitty shook her head. "No, Papa. I'll stand."

He loathed minor skirmishes. He found them a waste of precious time and energy. So he'd let her stand, but his stare was cold, his jaw tight.

"You've always been obstinate."

"Yes, Papa." She'd learned from his own supremely stubborn example. One might think a woman as agreeable as their mother would make for at least one docile daughter, but Desmond Adderly had been cursed with three young women under his roof who'd inherited a portion of *his* intractable nature. Kitty most of all.

"While I'm willing to consider Hattie's barrister, that comes later. First, there's the matter of your marriage."

She'd told herself he wouldn't insist on the ridiculous and only just instituted rule that she marry first, but of course he would.

"Yes, well, I'm afraid there's no one I wish to marry."

"My patience for your wishes and preferences has run thin. Your mother and I will decide, if you cannot."

He moved and the very air in the room shifted as he stood to ring the bellpull. It was too late for afternoon tea unless he was thirsty and didn't mind being casual about his tea taking, but Papa was never casual about when he took his tea.

Then she heard her mother's footsteps, measured and precise, and the softest of knocks at the door before she entered and seated herself on the settee. Once her mother had settled her gown and Papa had taken his place beside her, Lady Clayborne flicked her wrist toward the chair next to her, indicating her eldest daughter should sit.

Kitty clenched her jaw, debating whether to press the issue and insist on standing. While she took satisfaction in holding fast to her own choices where Papa was concerned, her relationship with her mother was sometimes chilly, but rarely a tug of war. Kitty simply didn't understand her mother. Her obsequiousness and overly agreeable nature were the opposite of Kitty's strong will. Yet Mama, through her softness and meek ways, still managed to wield a uniquely powerful sway over her husband. To Kitty, that was the greatest mystery of all.

"Come sit by me, my dear."

Kitty relented and took the seat next to her mother, but she couldn't relax against the fabric and sat forward, perching just on the edge.

"You say there is no one you wish to marry, but I am done with heeding your wishes, Katherine." Her father's tone was matter-of-fact, emotionless, as if he was discussing a business investment or the results of the horse races at Epsom. "Long past done."

Mother lifted a hand and placed it gently on her husband's arm. "Marriage and the selection of a husband are among the most important decisions a woman will make in her life. I understand your wish to take care with your choice, my dear."

Mama's voice was like a soft stroke of fingers on harp strings after the bark of Papa's tone, but he cut in at the very instant her mother stopped speaking. "If you cannot decide, you must trust our judgment to guide you along."

A squeeze, like the constriction of a too-tight collar, pressed at Kitty's neck and throat. She couldn't breathe, couldn't move, couldn't think except for one word.

"No." She wouldn't be forced into anything. Her father might remind her of what a frightened eager-to-please little girl she'd been, but she was no longer a child. And she wasn't going to pinch her nose and take her medicine just because Mama added a bit of treacle to the mix.

Kitty hadn't noticed the clammy dampness of her mother's hand the first time she'd touched her, but she felt it now. "Now hear us out, my dear."

Papa's gruff voiced intruded over her mother's soothing tone. "You mentioned Wrexford. Secure a proposal from him."

"No." She'd feared it and more than half expected it, but hearing the words and seeing the flinty resolve in her father's eyes made her want to bolt. Marriage wasn't a fate she expected to escape. Not forever. She simply wanted it on her terms. In her time. And with a man of her own choosing.

And the Duke of Wrexford was the last man she could imagine being shackled to for the rest of her days. He unsettled her. A few moments in his presence had tipped everything inside her on end. And they'd begun on a footing of disappointment and derision. She'd had her fill of that as Desmond Adderly's daughter. Binding herself to a man as critical and overbearing as her father was unthinkable.

"He's inherited well and seems clever enough to maintain it or even improve on the late duke's investments. And he'll need a wife to get an heir on. No one will wish to see the dukedom pass to another Oxford don."

"Cambridge." Kitty knew that much about the man at least, and she suspected the duke would take the distinction quite seriously.

"He's very handsome," her mother chimed in, as if Kitty hadn't corrected her father at all.

Her father turned a momentary glare on his wife, as if a man's countenance was of little importance, and yet the Duke of Wrexford's face was the one thing Kitty could like about the man unreservedly. It was perhaps the finest face she'd ever seen, perfectly proportioned and yet not too Rob Wellesley beautiful. The Duke of Wrexford's face was graced with lines of age and laughter, and he wore them well. Yes, he was handsome. Unforgivably so. And well-proportioned—tall and broad-shouldered with wide masculine hands.

And why shouldn't a man's beauty be as important in the marriage game as a woman's? She'd been urged from childhood to brush her hair to make it shiny, stand up tall to straighten her back, and later to pinch her cheeks and bite her lips to make them pink. She'd been taught how to walk to emphasize her bustle and bosom, how to dip her gaze and practice her grins. She'd been praised for her appearance more often than any other skill or accomplishment she'd acquired through practice and effort.

Whatever admiration she'd seen in the Duke of Wrexford's gaze when he'd studied her had surely been about her outer beauty. The man made his disgust for her behavior all too clear.

At the sound of her mother tapping her toes and clearing her throat, Kitty's woolgathering smashed to shards and she recalled the dire matter at hand. If she wouldn't go willingly into a match, her parents would force the matter.

And they possessed powerful leverage. A match with the duke wouldn't just see her settled. It would ensure Hattie's happiness. Her father could hardly refuse to admit his own son-in-law's closest friend into the family.

"Why didn't you dance with the Duke of Wrexford at the ball, my dear? I understand he did ask you."

"How do you know that?"

But of course she'd know. The ball had been her mother's event and while there'd been too many guests to track everyone's movement, the behavior of a freshly titled duke would have been worth watching. In her own way, Kitty's mother was every bit as adept as gathering information as her father.

"I was concerned with Miss Benson. I wanted to make sure Mr. Wellesley danced with her. The duke and I . . . missed our chance."

It wouldn't do to acknowledge that she'd planned to avoid dancing with him even if he'd sought her out again, or that their first encounter had included a chastisement for her bad behavior. Her parents could imagine a match with Wrexford all they liked, but it wouldn't change the duke's opinion of her, or the fact he'd thought her in need of a scolding from the first moment he laid eyes on her. They'd commenced an acquaintance on abysmal terms and nothing indicated that furthering their connection would improve it.

"Nonsense." Clearly her father didn't agree. "You'll soon have another chance to claim your waltz with the duke. We've been invited to Lady Stamford's ball Friday next."

"How can you be certain he'll be at the Stamford ball?"

"Didn't you know, my dear? The Countess of Stamford is his aunt."

His aunt? With a noblewoman in the family, the man couldn't be as much a novice at gentlemanly behavior as she'd accused him of being. And despite conceding his lack of social graces when they were alone in the sitting room, he'd played the gentleman well enough in the ballroom.

Blast the man for being a conundrum. Men invariably proved simple to suss out, and yet this mathematician-turned-duke posed a mystery.

Kitty had never been able to resist a mystery.

## Chapter Seven

IT WASN'T SATISFYING enough to rip the letter to shreds. Seb crumpled the fragments, clenching his fist until his knuckles strained against his skin, and strode over to throw them on the grate. But the remaining embers flickered with a waning heat, not enough to turn the pieces of the second unopened letter to cinders. A few flecks began to smolder and hiss, but he wanted to see them burn, to watch the flames and hear the satisfying crackle as he seared her from his life for good.

Alecia Lloyd's beauty and cleverness had enthralled him, and he'd been full of enough youthful arrogance to believe he alone had caught her interest. Those first few months had been bliss, and then learning he was one of three gentlemen she was playing for a fool, and uncovering each of her lies, had been a hellish descent that stripped him of ideals and naiveté.

Memories of her ebony hair streaming out as he'd followed her through the woods didn't haunt him anymore, but he could still feel the weight of the bulldog revolver he'd carried in his overcoat pocket. He'd been so determined to protect her.

"I've been sent to fetch you in to dinner. You're joining us, aren't you?" Pippa strode into his study as she questioned him.

"Yes, of course." Seb gripped the fire poker and stirred up the coals, kindling a few flames to consume the shredded paper. That was what he needed. A tumbler tripped inside of him, unlocking a few bars of tension constricting his chest.

"May I speak to you before we go in?" The catch in her voice had him curious, as did the object she clasped in her hands as if she wished to conceal it. "Does he really mean to marry her? From what he's said, he barely knows Miss Adderly. Ollie is a romantic. We all know that. And he's had his fair share of sweethearts, but he's never been set on marrying any of them."

Ollie's infatuation with Lady Harriet had become a favorite topic of conversation at Wrexford House, and Pippa's recent reserve toward Ollie had warmed enough for her to at least *appear* happy for him. Until the night of the ball. Whatever had passed between his sister and the contradictory Lady Katherine on the balcony, it soured Pippa on the notion of Ollie marrying into the Adderly family.

"Have you taken against Lady Harriet because you don't like her sister?" Bearing grudges was one of his flaws, but it wasn't in Pippa's nature to remain angry with

anyone. She was usually the first to tamp down her pride
and make amends, as Seb thought she'd done with Ollie.
Now her irritation with his friend flared again.

"No, but Ollie's suggestion that you marry Lady Katherine is absurd. He cannot dictate your future. None of
us have the right to ask you for such a sacrifice." Face
flushed with color, she spoke through clenched teeth as
she twisted and crumpled the paper in her hands. "Don't
forfeit your happiness for his."

He'd been a selfish bastard in the past, especially
where Alecia was concerned. He found it curious that
Pippa even believed him capable of such a sacrifice.

"Besides, you're the family dictator. Not Ollie." The
amusement in her eyes softened the accusation, and it
wasn't one he could deny.

"Ollie's mistaken, Pippa."

In this instance, Seb doubted sacrifice would be necessary. He'd speak to Clayborne on Ollie's behalf and
offer a settlement to allow the couple to start their life
together, but Pippa was right. He couldn't marry Katherine Adderly to suit Oliver's plans. The woman hadn't even
claimed the waltz he'd offered and snubbed him for the
remainder of the ball. He doubted she'd welcome a social
call from him, let alone an offer of marriage.

"I won't be marrying Lady Katherine."

He expected his reassurance to bring his sister a
measure of satisfaction, but Pippa twisted her mouth
and stared at her lap. "I'm not saying you should remain
alone. Perhaps you *should* be considering marriage."

The thought of it held as little appeal now as it had when Ollie suggested it back at Roxbury.

"You're being as inscrutable as Ollie says all women are."

She thrust the crumpled bit of paper at him. "I'll never be as confounding as this woman."

It was another letter from Alecia. Her slanted scrawl was unmistakable, and the sight of it sickened him, ruining all the pleasure he'd taken in burning the second letter to dust.

After a long pause he reached for the letter, but his sister drew it back. "Why is she writing to you? She brought you nothing but misery. I fear she'll only stir up trouble."

Given half a chance, she most certainly would. It was the money, of course. After their ugly parting, Alecia hadn't contacted him in ten years. But now, with his title and newfound wealth, she seemed quite determined to worm her way into his life once again. It had always been about money with Alecia. She'd never understood how he could be content to follow his father into an academic professor and plan a future based on a modest salary. In the end, she'd proven her love had nothing to do with sentiment and everything to do with practicality. She'd rejected him for Lord Naughton, the richest of her many suitors, a pompous earl as blind to her schemes as Seb had been.

"Let me worry about Lady Naughton."

Pippa chewed the edge of her thumbnail a moment before leaning toward him. "I'd rather see you married to Kitty Adderly than attached to that woman again."

"And there you go changing your tune again. I do wish you'd make up your mind." Were his choices limited to those two? One woman who loathed him and another who hadn't bothered to chance letting him tread on her feet. *Clever woman. Beautiful woman. Distracting woman.* She'd invaded his thoughts far too often since the Clayborne ball. Whatever his initial disgust at her actions, he'd also witnessed her attempt to redeem them. That peek at her vulnerability when he'd caught her in the sitting room vied with his opinion of the haughty beauty she became the moment others might see. Whatever the lady's contradictions, she was an undeniably bright spot of luminous skin and cream satin lighting up the corners of his mind.

"None of us ever liked her." Pippa jumped at the sound of Ollie's voice as he joined them.

"Do come in, Oliver."

Ollie ignored the sarcasm in Seb's tone and positioned himself in front of the fireplace, arms crossed. "Pippa told me about the letter. No idea what you ever saw in Miss Lloyd, but I know you've better sense than to let the woman into your life again."

He'd kept the worst of it from his family. None of them knew she'd lied about being with child and stoked jealousy in Seb until he'd been prepared to rip the child's purported sire to pieces. He prayed they'd never know how depraved he'd become, how easily she'd twisted him.

"I've no intention of communicating with Lady Naughton or reading her letters."

Seb considered saying more, offering further reassurance. It wouldn't require exaggeration. There was nothing he desired less than an entanglement with Alecia. But Pippa settled back in her chair with a satisfied sigh, and Ollie nodded sharply as if a promise had been made, and it was sufficient to put him at ease.

Then in the next moment, he looked anything but tranquil as he thrust a hand into the wave of overlong hair dipping perilously close to his eyebrows. After massaging the back of his neck, he stuffed both hands in his pockets and bowed his head as if utterly forlorn.

"Enough fidgeting, Ollie. Tell us what's the matter." Pippa had never appreciated Ollie's flair for melodrama.

"I have a fresh dilemma." Ollie drew out the suspense, waiting for a long theatrical pause before satisfying their curiosity.

Seb restrained the impulse to indulge in a Pippa-style roll of his eyes.

"Clayborne has refused my request to call on him. Twice. How can I ask for Harriet's hand in marriage if the man won't speak to me?"

Seb opened his hand and lifted it toward Pippa. She stared a moment at the crumpled letter before laying it in his palm.

He didn't indulge in destroying this one slowly, cursing his stupidity under his breath as he had with the first and second. This one he simply crushed in his fist before tossing the walnut-sized mass onto the fire. A tiny spark responded to the fragment of kindling and a flame licked out to consume it.

With one matter behind him, he could tackle the other.

"The Marquess of Clayborne has requested I meet with him tomorrow morning."

"He did?"

"Why didn't you say so?"

Seb lifted his hands. "We can discuss it at dinner, but rest assured I will do all I can." He hadn't yet divulged details of his plan for a settlement with Ollie, but he'd make his intentions clear to Clayborne.

He stood and Ollie reached out to shake his hand. "Thank you, Bash."

A swell of contentment warmed Seb's chest. It would be a heady kind of relief to see Ollie settled. His friend's life had been directionless and unfixed for too long.

Ollie linked arms with Pippa to lead her into the dining room, but she stopped him and turned back to Seb. "I'm still not sure I understand why Lord Clayborne wishes to see you."

Seb frowned. "I suspect he wishes to discuss the prospect of Ollie marrying his daughter. He can't be unaware they're enamored after how they carried on at the ball." He shot a stern glance at Ollie, who smiled brightly enough to deflect any censure.

Pippa twisted her lips in a thoughtful moue. "I think it's far more likely he wishes to speak to *you* about marrying his daughter."

SEB PACED THE floor of Lord Clayborne's drawing room. He'd misjudged the walk and arrived early, and nothing about the starkest four walls he'd ever seen in his life put his mind at ease. The Fennicks were given to covering their walls, every bare inch, not just with wallpaper but with art and sketches, even framing some of Grandfather's blueprints for majestic country houses and civic buildings. When Pippa turned out a fine watercolor, it had taken pride of place next to prized oil paintings by their late mother's artistic circle of friends.

The Marquess of Clayborne and his wife clearly didn't share his parents' lackadaisical notions regarding decor. Pristine whitewashed furniture seemed to frown on the pale pink of the walls and upholstery. Seb tolerated it for all of five minutes before tugging the bellpull.

When a maid popped through the door, he gave into the desire to escape the cold room.

"I'm a bit early for my meeting with Lord Clayborne. Is Lady Katherine at home?"

Like steel striking flint, speaking her name set off sparks of anticipation that disturbed him as much as the memory of their first clash. He reminded himself to approach softly this time and try to refrain from upbraiding the woman.

The maid seemed as dubious about leading him to Lady Katherine as he was about the wisdom of seeing her again. She chewed on her lip and scrunched her eyes, assessing him, before relenting.

"I believe she's in the conservatory, Your Grace. Right this way."

The room was far at the back of the Belgrave Square town house where Seb imagined the kitchens or laundry might be. But the maid took a sharp turn and led him into a room filled with light filtered through panels of frosted glass and dominated by enormous palms and ferns. The plants clogged the space, towering above his head, some branches seeming to strain against the limit of the glass ceiling. Scent assailed him and then lured him—the damp loam of earth, the fresh sweet scent of greenery and flowers, so many that it was impossible to sort out a single note in the cacophony of aromas.

And back in the corner amid a collection of glazed pots, shovels, and trowels, Lady Katherine stood at a bench crowded with seed packets and small seedlings in tiny clay pots. She wore a plain brown dress and her hair wasn't pinned but pulled back, a waterfall of gold waves caught in the knot of a simple blue ribbon. She scrubbed her bare hands together, as if dusting away dirt, but then turned to two small pots and carefully pressed her forefinger into one and then the other, burrowing pockets into the soil. Reaching for a packet, she carefully poured a couple of pea-sized seeds into her palm and rolled them about a minute as if studying the facets of precious gems before carefully dropping them into the holes she'd made.

Humming as she worked, she turned to one bud that had just begun to reveal the coral shade of its yet hidden flower. She touched the bud, then stroked its dark leaf, cooing encouraging words under her breath.

Though he stood out of her view, a few long strides would bring her close. He had no wish to disturb her, and yet here among her thriving plants she was as alluring as the lush blooms. Seb's body tensed as he resisted the wave of desire threatening to wash away his inhibitions and make him do something foolish. Like call out or reach for her. Clenching his fists, he held his ground, but each of her movements fascinated him, every subtle expression of pleasure he could read in her profile drew him.

She bowed her head to make notations in a journal, and he noticed a patch of dirt on her cheek that he itched to wipe away. He blamed the impulse on a sense of chivalry, insisting to himself that it had nothing to do with satisfying a desire to touch her again. He'd almost convinced himself to do it when she made it worse by tapping the end of her pen on her lower lip and leaving a dusting of soil there too.

Touching her mouth would be a definite mistake, never mind chivalry.

A clock chimed the top of the hour somewhere in the house, and Seb struggled to care that he'd be late for his meeting with her father if he continued staring at her. He preferred to stay and watch her work, but she'd likely loathe being observed.

He began to retreat, stepping carefully so as not to disturb her, but his boot heel scuffed against a tile. Her hummed tune cut off on a dissonant squeak, and he looked back to find her scowling.

"Who allowed *you* in here?"

It was no use blaming a maid for doing her job, but Seb couldn't resist revisiting their first encounter.

"Is that the proper etiquette for greeting a visitor? I'll make a note of it."

"Most visitors wait to be invited before pushing in."

Seb tried not to smirk. He even considered being contrite, but her green fire glare brought out a terrible streak of defiance.

"Am I not welcome?"

"You weren't invited." She swiped her hands down her hips, apparently trying to settle her gown or remove the dirt from her hands, but it only drew his attention to how the dress hugged her slim figure.

He forced his gaze away from her body and studied the fronds of an enormous spiky plant arching over his head. "Does anyone receive an invitation to join you back here?"

"No." In a less strident tone, she added, "I come here to be alone."

He felt the utter fool. He understood the desire for solitude. When he was wrangling with a vexing mathematical concept, he'd sometimes wander on solitary walks around the Cambridgeshire countryside for miles.

"I've intruded."

"You surprised me." Her tone had softened, but she still watched him warily. "Why are you here, Your Grace? Have you come to chastise me again?"

Seb ignored her sarcasm and focused on the more interesting question.

"You enjoy horticulture?"

She seemed unwilling to let go of her ire, lifting dirty hands to her hips, and then crossing her arms to hide dirt-stained fingers from his view.

"Yes, I love plants." The tentative catch in her voice when she finally answered made Seb swallow hard. It was a moment of honesty, vulnerability, and he wanted more.

Then her eyes went wide a moment before she tightened her crossed arms. "But I prefer to work in the conservatory alone. Annie shouldn't have brought you out here. If you'll excuse me."

She stepped toward him as if to move past, but the space was cluttered with ceiling-tall potted ferns on one side and wrought iron shelves overflowing with plants on the other. His shoulders spanned the space and she'd have to press in close, nearer than they would have stood if they'd danced the waltz, to get around him.

"I must go and change, Your Grace."

He didn't wish her to go. Or to change. With tendrils of hair framing her face, eyes brightened by the light filtering through the conservatory windows, and a smudge of dirt on her cheek, she was the most appealing woman he'd ever seen. He knew he should move, allow her to go on her way, but his body fought him. He wanted to draw closer, not move away. He took a step toward her and caught her scent. Not vanilla this time, something brighter, citrus with a sweet tang.

"What is that scent?"

"Which one?" She glanced at the red flowers beside her and then up at the hanging blooms above her. He thought they might be wisteria.

"Yours."

She reached up and placed a hand at the base of her throat. Her breathing quickened as he watched her, and his breath sped too.

He should have retreated when he'd had the chance.

When she turned, he feared he'd gone too far and she meant it as a dismissal, but then she reached up and plucked a leaf from an unassuming plant with spiky leaves.

After crushing the leaf in her palm, she lifted her hand toward him, and the sharp pungent fragrance made his nose itch. It was an overwhelming version of the scent she wore.

*"Aloysia citrodora.* Lemon verbena."

"It's powerful." *And smells much sweeter on your skin.*

She grinned. "It is. It must be diluted before use as a fragrance, but there's such a pure clean zest in the raw leaves. Don't you think?"

"Speaking of clean, there's just a bit of . . ."

He reached out to touch her but hesitated. His skin against hers would be the start of it, and one touch wouldn't be enough. He already wanted more—to hear about her plants, read that journal she'd bent over so intently, and taste the skin he was about to caress.

"Will you always find fault with me?" In the space of his doubt, she reached up to scrub at her own face.

But she missed the spot and Seb pressed his fingers to her cheek, wiping gently at the smudge, his fingers brushing against hers as the heat of her skin warmed his fingers and wound its way, somehow, all the way to his chest.

"It's not a fault. Just a spot of dirt."

It disturbed him how it easy it was, how right it felt to touch this woman, when he'd held back from touching anyone for so long.

"Did you get it all?"

He swiped his thumb across her cheek. "Here, yes, but there's more."

She spluttered and waved one hand. "Well, go on and get the rest."

The last mark was on the edge of her plump lower lip. He lifted his other hand and dabbed with one finger until all he could see was a lush crescent of skin as deep a coral as the bud she'd encouraged to blossom.

She didn't flinch away from his touch or turn her eyes down coquettishly. Lady Katherine used their proximity to appraise him, her eyes sharply assessing as she studied his face, roving over every aspect of his countenance but never quite meeting his gaze.

He'd done his good deed and wiped her face clean, but he still wanted to touch her. He cupped her cheek in one hand and rested the fingers of the other at the edge of her jaw.

Her voice was low and breathy when she asked him, "Have you got it all?"

When he dipped his head to nod, he drew closer to her mouth. And that was the greatest mistake of all. With barely a flex of his hands, he could tip her closer, taste the skin that was far softer than he'd imagined. But then there'd be no turning back. Hadn't he vowed to himself not to be drawn by a pretty face again? Not to lose himself in desire?

Lowering his hands, Seb slid one down her arm and felt her body tremble beneath his touch.

"Another time, will you tell me about all of these?"

He glanced around her conservatory.

She moved out of his grasp and glowered a moment, as if she took his question as a jest, a belittling of her interest and passion. But when he continued to stare at her expectantly, she seemed to lower her shield.

"Why do you want to know about my plants?"

He opened his mouth to tell her that he was curious by nature. The most difficult aspect of university had been narrowing his studies to just one or two topics. But the truth was more dangerous, impossible to admit. He wanted to learn more about *her*. Lady Katherine who called herself Kitty, when there was nothing frivolous or kittenish about her. Lady Katherine who laughed at her friends, and in the next moment scolded a man to set her insult aright.

Mysteries had always intrigued him, and he'd never met a woman who left so many questions unanswered in his mind. But he couldn't tell her that.

A woman cleared her throat behind Seb. "Beg pardon, my lady. His lordship says he will see the Duke of Wrexford now."

Seb stiffened and Lady Katherine sprang away from him at the maid's intrusion.

"You're here to see my father?" She seemed intrigued by the prospect.

"Yes, regarding a settlement for Mr. Treadwell and Lady Harriet."

She sighed with obvious relief. "My sister will be pleased to hear that."

"I haven't convinced the marquess of anything yet. But I will. Leave your father to me."

Seb turned to follow the maid. He'd come to assist Ollie and time spent in this perfumed room touching Lady Katherine wouldn't accomplish that goal.

"Your Grace?"

Turning his head, he caught her wiping again at the spot where the smudge had been. The spot where he'd touched her cheek.

"Yes, my lady?"

"Another time, I'll tell you whatever you wish to know. About the plants."

Plants were well and good, but *she* truly sparked his curiosity. He wanted to learn whatever he wished to know about *her*.

The desire was so fierce it terrified him. Desire and attraction—all of it led to loss of control. Losing one's heart, falling madly, trusting utterly—none of it held any appeal. But she did, and far too much for him to find peace of mind anywhere near her.

## Chapter Eight

"WHAT HAPPENED BETWEEN you and the duke?"

Kitty ignored Hattie's question and pushed the dirty cotton gown from her hips before pressing a cool damp cloth to her blazing face. The duke had flustered her, setting her nerves jangling until she'd agonized over trembling so fiercely her teeth might begin to rattle. And he'd touched her. Not as a possession or a prize, but tenderly, as if he couldn't stop himself. The way she stroked an orchid or passionflower blossom, awestruck by its beauty, fascinated by its shape and texture and color.

She turned in her seat and faced her sister. "He told me that he plans to provide a settlement for Mr. Treadwell. That should help bring Papa around."

It wasn't what Hattie had asked, but her sister squealed with delight, bouncing up and down like an excited child, and Kitty knew it was truly what she'd wished to know.

Kitty preferred not to explain her odd encounter with

the Duke of Wrexford. She suspected it would be as impossible to sort out as their first.

At least she'd kept a clear head this time, and she counted that a victory. Even when he drew near, even when he put his hands on her, even when he'd caused her to tremble, she'd had enough sense to study him. She'd search his eyes and facial movements for any emotion that might belie his words. After scrutinizing and assessing, she found him . . . extraordinary, at least in her experience of men. Wrexford's eyes matched his words. If anything, he seemed to hold the full extent of his emotions at bay and express only a fraction of the genuine interest and pleasure he felt. Try as she might, Kitty couldn't catch him using any expression to deceive, charm, or prevaricate.

"And did he come to speak of marrying you too?"

Their mother's lady's maid stood behind Kitty arranging her hair and tugged her back into place when she tried to turn and glare at her sister.

"Don't speak nonsense, Hattie."

"Why is it nonsense? The housemaid said he asked to see you. And in your hidden haven."

It was her haven, but it certainly wasn't hidden. Even the Duke of Wrexford knew where to find it now.

"Annie would do well to gossip less. She shouldn't have brought him to the conservatory."

"He clearly unsettles you." Hattie's voice held the singsong quality they'd perfected in nearly two decades of sisterly taunting. Kitty knew she spoke partly in jest, but there was a disturbing seriousness in her sister's voice.

Marriage to the duke didn't bear discussion. She'd met the man twice and all of their minutes in each other's company wouldn't see the sand in an hourglass turn.

"Very well. He unsettles me. Is that a fitting basis for marriage?" Kitty struggled to infuse her shaky voice with Hattie's teasing tone.

"At least he makes you feel something."

Her sister hadn't meant to be cruel. Hattie was never cruel, but her words pricked like rose thorns, scratching just deep enough to string.

"You think me unfeeling."

"I think you guard your heart. And I've never seen a man pierce through your defenses—unsettle you, as you say—as easily as the Duke of Wrexford."

Kitty sat still, allowing the maid to finish with her hair. She was grateful when Hattie turned away and began searching the wardrobe for a suitable day dress, finally emerging with a pale pink confection, far more frilly and frivolous than Kitty felt.

"This one?"

"That will do."

Anything would be an improvement over the plain muslin gown she wore when working in the conservatory. Goodness, she must have looked like a street urchin when he'd found her, begrimed and disheveled, with dirt under her fingernails and wisps of hair clinging to the perspiration on her cheeks and forehead. Adderlys never got dirty. Or if they did, they certainly didn't let anyone see.

No one ever ventured down to the conservatory when

she was working with her plants. Father considered the room to be much like the kitchen, a place of messes he'd rather ignore as long as delicious food and pleasing flower arrangements occasionally emerged from the chaos.

And Mother considered her interest in botany an unnatural pursuit for a young woman. Drawing flowers was well and good, even pressing them between the pages of a book until every bit of moisture and life had been snuffed out. But a lady who grew them from seed like a farmer, studied them, and enjoyed sinking her fingers into rich dark soil—Mother declared such pleasures wholly unacceptable. But Kitty had never relented, never caught Violet's interest in sewing and embroidery, never matched Hattie's skill in music. And why was her passion inappropriate? No one seemed to find it the least bit disturbing that Violet's hobbies revolved around stabbing things with needles, or that Hattie's favorite songs to sing outside their parents' hearing were bawdy dance hall tunes she'd learned from the housemaid whose sweetheart performed at a music hall near Leicester Square.

Now, after years of being censured for her interest in horticulture, the Duke of Wrexford wished to hear more about her plants.

The man was a puzzle, faulting her one day and finding her seemingly fascinating the next. If it was artifice, she couldn't detect a single flaw in his façade. Nor could she believe him so accomplished at feigning interest and tolerating those he disdained. Even Father's mask slipped now and again. Surely a man like Wrexford, who'd spent years pondering lofty academic topics, would have little reason to waste time honing skills in deception.

Hattie helped Kitty into the clean day dress. Turning to inspect herself in the long mirror, she almost stumbled. How simple it was to transform with a bit of polish and a fine dress. This is how she'd been taught to present herself to the world. Clothes in the height of fashion, tailored to fit. Clean skin and every hair in place. Jewels glittering at her ears and neck as proof of Clayborne wealth. A spotless woman, without taint or flaw.

She almost preferred herself as Wrexford had found her, engaged in a task she cared about, dirty and imperfect, but more herself than the woman who stared back at her now in the looking glass.

But that woman wasn't acceptable—not to her mother, not to their friends, and most especially not to her father. Kitty found it easier to give them what they wanted, even if it made for a life of pretense. She was skilled at pretense, after all.

"You look lovely." Hattie came around in front of her and straightened the bow at the edge of Kitty's bodice. Her thin fingers fumbled with the ribbon, and Kitty noticed her sister was quivering.

"What if the duke's money isn't enough to sway Papa?" Hattie dipped her gaze, a tear caught in her lash. "I hate that my marriage is dependent on yours. I have no wish to see you forced into a connection you do not desire."

The rest went unspoken, suspended between them. Hattie's mouth was still ajar, her breath seemingly trapped in her throat and waiting to escape.

Kitty knew what she'd say. Whatever they wished, their father's stubbornness and Hattie's desire to marry meant their fates *were* linked.

"But if you don't marry, I can't marry." Hattie didn't need to add that it wasn't simply marriage that Kitty would be keeping from her. For Hattie, marriage to Mr. Treadwell equated with happiness, contentment, the kind of future Kitty wanted for both of her sisters but rarely imagined for herself.

Unlike Hattie, she'd yet to meet a man she couldn't do without.

"That is Papa's decree, yes." In a lifetime of being Desmond Adderly's daughter, Kitty had come to expect arbitrary rules and high expectations. They'd all squirmed under his control at one time or another. But insisting on piano lessons when she didn't have an ear for music was a world away from choosing a man for her to wed and taking the most important decision she'd ever make out of her grasp.

"Let me speak to Papa again. No doubt the duke's support of Mr. Treadwell has reassured him." She laid a hand on Hattie's arm. Her sister's tremors were like the fluttering a bird's wings against her palm.

"Perhaps if you simply told him you'd consider the Duke of Wrexford. Would that satisfy him?"

More pretense. But feigning interest in a suitable young man to stem the pressure from her parents was practically a habit for Kitty. Some of them she had truly attempted to like. Others she merely tolerated because it pleased her mother or had been insisted upon by her father. But taking tea with a man, or entertaining his chaperoned visits wouldn't go far enough this time. Their father would see through it immediately.

Only marriage would satisfy him. And before that a very public engagement with the thrill of telling family and friends, the announcement in the newspapers, and the satisfaction of knowing they would be adding a duke to the family.

She glanced once more at her reflection in the looking glass. Pretense and polish. That she could give them. The pretense of an engagement. What if she gave her father what he wanted? Gave her mother the pride of declaring two engagements?

Rushing to the bedroom window, she looked down and saw no Wrexford carriage sitting in front of their town house. Had he already departed or sent his driver on an errand while he spoke with her father?

"Kitty?"

"Stay here, Hattie. I must catch Wrexford if I can."

Lifting her skirts, Kitty rushed down the stairs and saw Annie emerging from the entry hall.

"Is he gone?"

"He's just stepped out, my lady."

Moving past the maid, Kitty marched toward the front door.

"Did he travel by carriage?"

"By foot, my lady."

She pulled open the door, perched on the threshold, and scanned the pavement for Wrexford's tall figure.

"My lady, your jacket." Annie held her coat and Kitty

slipped her arms in and allowed the maid to begin buttoning her up when she spotted him. His long-legged stride would have him around the corner and out of sight if she didn't hurry.

"That'll do, Annie." Ignoring the gloves and hat the maid offered, Kitty sprinted down the pavement.

Attempted to sprint. Layers of petticoats and her overly flouncy skirt made speed impossible, but she pressed forward, her legs wrestling against the fabric as if she was treading waist-high water.

"Wrexford!"

Pram-pushing nannies and top-hatted gentlemen scowled at her as she passed. Haste was improper enough. Shouting and flapping one's arms could get her categorized as a hellion.

It took a final push against her leaden skirts and the jostling of a slow-moving nanny to get close enough to speak to him in an inoffensive volume.

"Your Grace, wait, please."

If she was a hellion, he was a rogue. Like her, he wore no hat. In a sea of black chimney pot-covered heads, his hair shone in rich shades of chestnut, with wheaten strands catching the morning light as he moved. The daylight performed magic with his eyes. She'd identified them as blue during that first encounter in the empty sitting room, but not the extraordinary shade she noticed now—the vibrant blue of a gentian flower.

He turned to look back at her. "Ah, Lady Katherine. I thought it was you. Somehow even your pleas come out sounding like commands."

"And yet you turned back."

"I've been told my curious nature will be my ruin." One of his wry grins accompanied the admission, and Kitty hated the way the sight of it stirred the silly fluttering in her belly.

"I promise not to ruin you. I simply need to speak with you."

He pursed his mouth and studied her a moment as if considering whether to refuse her.

"I was just going to take a turn in the park. Join me."

She swallowed down a tumbling sense of dread and nodded agreement. If he rejected the scheme she intended to propose, there could be no more public a setting for their falling out than Hyde Park.

She hoped to convince all of fashionable London that she planned to marry the man. Being caught in a quarrel with him wouldn't do.

"Was it a fruitful meeting with my father?"

He glanced at her, a quick brush of his gaze across her face.

"He's pleased at how determined I am to see Oliver and your sister comfortably settled."

"But?" She didn't miss the hesitation in his voice.

"Your father was more interested in talking about your marriage."

They'd just reached the edge of the park's green and he turned his body to guide her off the path and into a patch of shade under the pink-frilled branches of a cherry blossom tree.

He left her, pacing a few steps away, unbuttoning his

jacket and flicking the edges back to plant a hand on each hip. Then he stalked back toward her, head down, shoulders braced, a fearsome frown tightening his angular jar and drawing down his brows.

"To *me*, Lady Katherine. He wished to speak about your marriage to me. Our marriage. Yours and mine. Would you care to explain?"

Kitty winced as if he'd thrown his words at her rather than merely speaking forcefully enough to make her ears ring.

She'd feared this. Her father might be a great strategist, but he'd always lacked patience. And now he'd riled the man she very much hoped to cajole.

When she didn't find her words quickly enough, he turned away again. Pacing in a square, as if marking off a measurement. He grumbled as he stalked around his invisible path, and she thought he might be counting.

Forcing her mouth into a charming smile, Kitty dipped her head a fraction, and prepared to approach, but Wrexford turned and glowered, his blue eyes drained of all their vibrancy, his arms locked across his chest.

Mentally scouring her mind for the best strategy to quell his irritation, the most convincing words, the unassailable arguments to present to him, she came away with a shocking truth. None of her cunning would work on him.

For how little she knew of him, nothing about the man was as clear as his lack of artifice.

If she hoped to engage him in a scheme to lie to everyone, she'd have to tell him the unvarnished truth. Lay it out plain, unadorned with any gilding, unsweetened, and to such an honest man, perhaps unpalatable.

"Let's tell them we plan to marry."

His brows shot up, and his grimace faltered. Then his whole body went momentarily slack before he took a breath and stalked toward her.

"Pardon?"

"You wish to see Hattie and Mr. Treadwell married, as I do, but Father insists on my marriage first." Kitty sucked in a breath. "He will arrange a match for me if I do not accept a proposal this season, so why not allow him to believe we'll marry?"

"Allow him to believe? You mean lie? You want me to join you in a scheme to deceive your father?"

"And the rest of them. Our friends and social circles. Your family and mine. My sisters couldn't keep a secret to save their lives. I don't know about yours."

He looked up at the tree above their heads as if making a detailed study of the canopy of white and pink blooms.

Along the expanse of his throat, muscles rippled and moved, as if he was swallowing down each word that came to mind. Stifling angry words, she suspected. When he finally lowered his gaze and met hers, hope fluttered up on fragile wings in her chest. She read no denial in his eyes. He studied her face as she'd studied his in the conservatory, tracing each feature.

He shook his head. "I can't do it. I won't lie to my family or take part in your scheme. Fennicks aren't the scheming sort."

If he was obliquely saying the Adderlys *were* the scheming sort, she couldn't deny it.

Of course he wouldn't agree to a false engagement. She should have known. Only a fool would ask a plain-speaking man to lie.

The fragile wings shattered and hope crashed down, a sickening wreckage at the bottom of her stomach.

Kitty staggered forward, forcing him to back away, and started toward Clayborne House. The stony Hyde Park path caught at her feet like piles of sand and her damnable skirts made every step an effort. She couldn't manage a graceful glide or even a poised gait. If she made it back home without collapsing under the weight of her own failure, she'd count it a victory.

What would she tell Hattie? What could she say to convince her father to relent and allow her sister to marry the man she loved?

There were few enough happy marriages in the world. Why put a stop to a match with so much potential to achieve it?

"Lady Katherine—"

She stopped midstep, nearly toppling into the gentleman in front of her, and whirled on the duke.

"I do wish you'd call me Kitty." If nothing else, why could he not abide that simple request? It was her turn to be indignant and she bested his earlier glare as he approached.

He had his hands behind his back, and his head lowered, as if he could compress his breadth and height and seem less formidable. If he'd bothered wearing a hat, it would be in his hands.

"Let me consider the matter. I'll give you my answer at Lady Stamford's ball."

"And claim your waltz?"

The lines around his eyes softened. "You do owe me one."

"And you'll call me Kitty?"

He stretched up to his full height and crossed his arms again, not with the tension of anger, but as if pondering a weighty question. He tilted his head and thrust out his lower lip.

"What about Kat? I prefer it to Lady Katherine. May I call you Kat?"

When she clashed with her father, a pressure often built in her chest, burning up into her throat until she recognized it as a scream, desperate to escape. A cry of frustration, anger, powerlessness.

A tickle danced in her throat now, and she did long to cry out. In frustration, yes, but another emotion was there too. One that made no sense at all.

Anticipation.

She wouldn't give the Duke of Wrexford the right to rename her. Not when he'd conceded her nothing.

"No. You must call me Kitty, like everyone else. No one calls me Kat."

After the temerity of attempting to give her a new name, the man had the audacity to look bemused by her refusal. His amusement was of the brazen sort, causing his eyes to glitter and his distracting mouth to tip, emphasizing the perfect sculpted squareness of his jaw. Amusement seemed a natural state for the duke, effortless, in noticeable contrast to the way he seemed to restrain his reactions in the conservatory.

What if he didn't hold back?

That flutter tickled up Kitty's throat again and spread along her neck before she swallowed against it. She wanted to see him unrestrained, pouring out all the banked emotion reflected in his gaze.

"I shall look forward to our waltz and your answer at Lady Stamford's ball. Good day, Your Grace."

## Chapter Nine

SEB COUNTED AS he scanned the ballroom, letting the numbers settle his nerves and bring order to the chaos in his mind. He judged the room smaller than the Adderly's, though Lady Stamford's ballroom glowed brighter, with eight gaslight chandeliers, sixteen gas wall sconces, four arranged an equal distance apart on each wall, and two elaborate candelabrum blazing with long fresh candles. The room didn't allow for hiding at the edges or the anonymity of blending in with the crush. It was a room to be seen in, an elegant fishbowl where you could look your fill and be gazed upon in return.

He'd never longed for a shadowy corner more in his life. If he could find Lady Katherine, discharge his debt of dancing a waltz with her, and give his final refusal to lie to both of their families, he'd steal away early.

"I always knew white tie would suit you." Seb's aunt, Augusta, Countess of Stamford, swept toward him, trailing a rippling train of ruffled lavender silk in her wake.

Seb and his sister had only visited their father's brother, Uncle Edward, the Earl of Stamford, and his wife Augusta a few times as children, but there was no mistaking Lady Stamford. On each visit to their uncle's grand home in Wiltshire, her wit and irreverence made a lasting impression. Beautiful, intelligent, and wellborn, she was the most poised woman Seb had ever met.

At least until he'd seen Katherine Adderly glide across her father's ballroom.

"Does it? Then it must look better on the outside than it feels from the inside."

"You have your father's dry sense of humor, I see. A trait he and his brother shared. Have you any idea how many years it took to realize when Ned was teasing me?"

"Mother said the same of our father." Seb knew his mother and aunt had carried on a long-standing correspondence. Despite how rarely the families visited, the two women had formed a bond of friendship around their shared interest in women's suffrage, art, and literature.

"I do miss Rosamund." A mournful quality in her tone made Seb's throat burn.

Their father's death had been sudden, a heart attack when he'd still seemed vibrant and full of life. But their mother's death two years later had come after months of a debilitating ailment the doctors struggled to explain. One physician diagnosed acute ennui, and Pippa still insisted their mother died of a broken heart. It had broken all of their hearts to watch their brilliant and talented mother waste away.

"We all do."

"Of course you do, my dear. I'm glad to see you looking so well. Rosamund and Reginald would be proud of how you've taken on your cousin's title."

"Do you think so?" Seb doubted they'd be proud. His parents valued achievement, not titles bestowed because of an accident of birth or the lack of an heir on the correct branch of the family tree. Helping others through charitable good works or improving oneself through study—those were the achievements his parents valued above all others. If there was any benefit to his title, it would be the opportunity to help others. He felt the weight of his tenants' expectations, and he would make the needed improvements to the estate. But first he had to address Ollie's expectations and see the young man settled. His parents, who'd all but adopted Ollie after he'd lost his own parents, would wish it as much as Seb did.

"I know it, my boy. Enjoy yourself at the ball, Sebastian. There are several young ladies quite eager to make your acquaintance." She leaned in close and her rosewater scent reminded him of his mother. "Though I hear you owe Lady Katherine Adderly the first waltz."

A waltz and an answer.

He was ready for the waltz after studying the dance and its triple meter time signature and box-stepping pattern. Six steps repeated time and again. How difficult could it be? As to the answer he'd give Lady Katherine, the lady wouldn't be pleased. He should never have wavered. It was out of the question. Unthinkable. He'd never allow himself to be a woman's pawn again. And yet . . . it unsettled him how much he dreaded disappointing her. Or perhaps it was the notion of disappointing Ollie's plans that rankled most.

"Gossip seems to travel at breakneck speed in London."

"Isn't it wonderful?" Lady Stamford reached up to pat his cheek, a maternal gesture that warmed him. "And look, there's Lady Kitty. Such a lovely creature. I suspect you could win her if you set your prodigious mind to it, Sebastian."

Unfortunately, Kat provoked in him every emotion he'd prefer to stifle, and she clouded his mind. Nothing he knew of math or science would help him decipher the woman.

"You'd better move quickly and claim your waltz before Lord Ponsonby monopolizes her dance card."

Seb followed the direction of his aunt's gaze, and a rogue surge of pleasure swept through him. Kat glittered near the ballroom's entrance, the glow of her luminous skin set off by a deep sapphire gown, but he couldn't see nearly enough of her. Several men gathered around and one broad gray-haired hulk of a man stood far too close, leaning in, clearly eager to capture her attention.

"Who is Ponsonby?" Overbearing, irritating, and rude would be Seb's quick measure of the man, at least from across the room.

Even after flipping through *Burke's Peerage* and

numbing his mind with row upon row of names and titles and lists of lineages, Seb had no real grasp—nor a care—for who was who among the aristocrats crowding fashionable events of the season.

His aunt flicked her fan a few times as if contemplating how best to answer.

"Ponsonby is an earl, well connected, both politically and financially, and has a fine estate in Surrey. His age is the only barrier. He's Lady Clayborne's second favorite."

"Second favorite what?" She made him sound like a pet.

"Potential suitor for her eldest daughter."

Searing heat, like hot oil in his veins, replaced the ticking pulse of irritation he'd felt all evening. He recognized the sting of jealousy and fought the urge to walk away—from the unrelenting brightness of the room, from the sight of Lady Katherine being fawned over by a ridiculous suitor, and from his irrational desire to be the only man in the room to capture her attention.

He wasn't needed here. The woman appeared overwhelmed with suitors. Apparently, the Ponsonby sod wasn't even the favorite of her many admirers.

"Who's the first favorite?"

His aunt tittered and snapped her fan shut. "Silly boy. You, of course."

Seb needed a drink, something with a smoky burn to wash down the bitter flavor in his mouth. Favorite suitor? He'd competed for a woman's attention once in his life and been shot for his efforts. Alecia had played men for fools, and Seb suspected she'd ranked their worth too—

favorite, least favorite, not so appealing after all. Surely they'd all believed they were the woman's only love.

If he ever courted another woman, it wouldn't be like the last time. There'd be no room for games, no feigning and lies.

But his resolve not to play the game of suitors and false seduction didn't stop him from loathing how Lord Ponsonby hovered over Lady Katherine, the way the man found any excuse to touch her, repeatedly reaching out to pat her arm or hand. And Kat allowed it, simpering at the man as if she relished every moment in his company.

*At least the first damned waltz is mine.*

Lady Stamford patted his arm before leaving him alone at the edge of the ballroom. As she strode away, he caught Kat's gaze. She turned toward him and began to approach without even a word to Lord Ponsonby. Seb was far too satisfied by the sight.

With each step she took in his direction, he felt a bit of the fire of envy cool in his veins.

"Your Grace, the waltz comes next. I hope you haven't forgotten me."

"How could I? I've been looking forward to our dance." Now, with her near, he could admit to himself that it was the only aspect of the evening he'd anticipated. He'd happily never stuff himself into an evening suit again, but he'd looked forward to dancing with Kat, and touching her again.

Seb drew near her, as close as Ponsonby had stood, and her sweet floral essence made his breath catch and stumble.

"A new scent."

Her eyes widened and she blinked as if she found the candles and gaslight as difficult to bear as he did.

"You've yet to teach me about any of your flowers, so I can't identify it. Which is it tonight?" He needed to know. Seb wasn't certain why it mattered, but it did.

"I-it's not just one. I asked my perfumer to mix essence of gardenia and . . ." She narrowed her gaze, assessing him. "Do you really want to know what scent I'm wearing?"

"I do."

"Gardenia and essence of violet leaf, with a hint of jasmine."

He could see her in the conservatory tending to each of her plants, and he wished they were alone in that humid green space, rather than exposed and observed here in his aunt's ballroom.

"Is this one of them?" A white flower with a bit of glossy dark leaf clung artfully to a knot of pinned waves gathered near her nape.

He couldn't resist reaching up to touch the flower's petal. She jolted at the movement, rearing back, and his finger grazed her cheek. He didn't regret it a bit, especially when his touch sparked a ruddy heat in her cheeks.

A few dancers from the previous set left the ballroom for air or refreshment, and Seb led Kat to a spot near the center of the floor.

She seemed to struggle to meet his gaze when he reached for her, settling one hand at the delicious curve of her waist and clasping her gloved hand in his other.

He'd seen images of couples dancing the waltz in the books he'd studied, but none of the etchings and drawings conveyed a tenth of the pleasure of holding a perfumed woman so near. The edge of her bodice brushed his lapels, her blue velvet skirts tangled against his legs, and even before the music began, he knew his hands would hold her scent long after he stopped touching her.

"Have you danced the waltz many times, Your Grace?"

"Only once before."

"Truly?"

"We never spent much time dancing at university."

*One and two, three. Four and five, six.* Seb counted silently as he led Kat through the dance, but when the gaslight caught the gilded freckles in her eyes and she licked her lips before glancing up at him, he forgot to count. He forgot the box pattern and numbers around it, forgot everything beyond the enjoyment of holding her in his arms. He memorized the dip of her waist, the warmth of her skin through the fabric of her gown, and the intense pleasure of moving his body in rhythm with hers.

If this was dancing, whatever he'd done before had been something else entirely.

"You dance well for a man who claims this is his second waltz."

"It *is* my second waltz."

"Yes, of course. Fennicks never lie."

"I believe I said we don't scheme, but we do value honesty too."

"So you won't do it?" The hopelessness in her tone

made his chest ache, as if he'd gathered the pleasure of dancing with her there, and it was all draining away.

"No, Kat. I won't deceive our families, not even for Ollie's sake."

All her softness turned to tension as her body went rigid in his arms. Then it was over. The musicians played the final notes of the waltz and dancers stopped to clap a moment before gentlemen led their partners from the dance floor. Seb released Kat reluctantly, though she seemed eager to be away from him.

"My name is Kitty," she said brusquely before dipping her head once. "Thank you for the waltz, Your Grace."

Seb reached for her, but she'd already turned her back on him and hurried toward her sister, who stood with Ollie on the other side of the ballroom. Seb knew Ollie would be attending the ball, but he'd yet to speak to him. Despite Kat's obvious lack of interest in continuing their conversation, Seb approached the group. Before he could reach them, Ollie broke away and urged Seb out of the ballroom toward the refreshment room.

One glance and it was clear that his friend was over-wrought.

"You spoke to Lord Clayborne?"

"Good evening to you too, Oliver."

"Seb, will the man give his consent or won't he?"

Tipping back a glass of champagne did little to settle the thickness in Seb's throat. He'd already disappointed Kat, and nothing he had to say would please Ollie.

"He seemed gratified by my mention of a settlement."

"Then he'll consent?"

"You know he wishes to see his eldest daughter married first."

Ollie's wide-eyed expectant stare swept away the last bits of contentment he'd felt while holding Kat in his arms, and Seb sensed the return of the same gnawing irritation which had hounded him at the start of the evening.

"I won't marry the woman to suit her father, her sister, or you. The Claybornes want me for a title, without a care for their daughter's preference. I'm barely acquainted with Lady Katherine—"

"You seemed quite snug when you waltzed with her."

"She's a beautiful woman. Dancing with her is no burden. But I suspect there's a bit more to marriage than a few turns around a ballroom."

Ollie bristled at his answer, spun on his heel, and stalked from the room.

Seb followed his friend and found him pacing, marching in a tight rectangle back and forth across the polished floor. When Ollie's temper flared, it usually burned out quickly, and Seb couldn't blame him for his frustration. Clayborne's dictate about his daughters seemed to be making everyone miserable.

Seb waited. If he was patient, Ollie's pacing might wear him out enough to speak with more logic than emotion.

Finally Ollie turned, fists clenched, body tense. "We've waited long enough. If Clayborne won't give his consent tonight, Hattie and I plan to elope."

Grasping Ollie's lapels, Seb drew him close. "Are you mad? You'll bring scandal to Lady Harriet, to her entire family, not to mention the damage to your own reputation."

When Ollie's eyes flashed with fear, Seb released fistfuls of his friend's jacket, smoothing down the garment with the swipe of his hands.

"Do you truly wish to begin your career under a cloud?"

Ollie returned to his rigid stance and tipped his square jaw up. "I wish to marry Hattie. That's all that matters."

The boy served as a mirror. Seb looked into the face of the love-sopped fool he'd once been. He might have said the same words. If he hadn't, he'd certainly believed his love for Alecia and his desire to marry her were all that mattered. He clung to that truth with more fervency and fire than he believed in mathematics or a single God in heaven, more than he loved his family or even himself. The woman had nearly led him to his death, and there was a time when he would have walked into it willingly, just to please her.

"Trust me. It's not all that matters."

But Ollie was already shaking his head, his ears as clogged, his mind as set, and his devotion as tenacious as Seb's had once been.

"Let me to speak once more to Clayborne before you do anything rash. Agreed?"

Ollie wouldn't look at him. He glared at the wall to his left, jaw clenched, but he dipped his head once in agreement.

Seb took a deep breath and swiveled on his heel. Clayborne would give his consent. He had to. But he doubted he'd convince the man alone. Perhaps he'd listen to his firstborn. Lady Katherine wouldn't wish for the couple's elopement any more than Seb did. She'd understand the damage a scandal might do.

Striding back to the ballroom to find Kat, he'd just passed the refreshment room door when a woman called to him.

"Your Grace?"

The faint voice emanated from inside the room, and Seb stepped back toward the threshold. His legs turned leaden and stiff, shock fixing his body in place.

Alecia stood just beyond the half-open door, black hair and pale eyes glistening in the wash of light from the ballroom. *No.* He shook his head in denial as Ollie had done moments before. *No.* If he refused her letters, he sure as hell wouldn't allow himself to be ambushed at a bloody ball.

She wore the same look of entreaty he'd seen a hundred times before—an innocence that hid cunning, a helplessness that covered her competence.

"I must speak with you, Sebastian." She hissed over the S's in his name as she always had and a sickening shiver slid down his back.

"We have nothing to say to each other, Lady Naughton."

Lord Naughton stood near the back of the room, chortling with another gentleman, seemingly oblivious to his wife. She moved toward Seb as if she meant to follow him.

He held up a hand to stop her. "No, Alecia. It's over. Long over."

He wanted nothing from her, and he'd give her nothing of himself. She was a ghost, a reminder of his past, and finally, after years of pain and grief, he wanted to live in the here and now.

Stalking into the ballroom, he scanned the crowd for Kat. Ponsonby stood near, as if imparting some secret that required him to whisper.

Seb needed to speak to her, and he wanted her alone. That desire propelled him across the ballroom in a direct line, pressing between couples, pushing dancers out of the way.

Kat's eyes widened as he approached, but she didn't resist when he reached out to grasp her hand and tug her along beside him. She called a parting "Excuse me, my lord" back to Lord Ponsonby, all sweet civility, and then whispered to Seb in a far chillier tone.

"When most gentlemen wish for a second dance, they ask."

"We're not going to dance."

He led her onto the balcony, down its stairs, and into his aunt's garden. Forward movement and heat seeping into his muscles eased his tangled thoughts, and Kat's hand in his, clasped as tightly as he held onto her, was an unexpected balm.

By the time they reached the far edge of the garden,

both of them were breathless, their exhalations puffing out to cloud the night air.

"I take it you have something you wish to say to me, Your Grace."

He still hadn't released her. She was warm and smelled heavenly, and the grip of her hand grounded him. Here and now. That's what mattered. Not the past. The past was a broken place of mistakes and regret.

The April evening had turned chilly and Seb finally let her go to remove his evening jacket and settle it over her bare shoulders.

She pulled the lapels together across her chest.

"Is it to be a long discussion, then?"

Seb reached up to lift the coat's collar to cover more of her exposed skin, but he found himself touching her instead, stroking the soft warm column of her neck and then resting his hand at the base of her throat, savoring the feel of her speeding pulse against his palm. His heartbeat echoed in his ears, as wild and rapid as Kat's, and the longer he touched her, the more the sounds merged, until he could almost believe their hearts had begun to beat as one.

He shook his head. That sort of romantic drivel led only to misery.

But he couldn't bring himself to stop touching her. And he couldn't deny he wanted more. Leaning down, desperate to know if her flavor was as sweet as her scent, he pressed his mouth to her forehead.

"Your Grace?" she whispered, the heat of her breath searing the skin above his necktie.

He pulled back and lifted his hands from her, remembering who he was, who she was. He was a master at guarding his heart and avoiding intimate moments. She was the woman who'd thrown over multiple suitors during each of her seasons.

"We must speak to your father."

Even in the semidarkness, he could see her green eyes grow large. "You've changed your mind?"

Excitement hitched her voice up two octaves, and Seb wished he'd changed his mind, that he wouldn't have to disappoint her, or her sister and Ollie. If he hadn't wasted all his reckless choices in youth, he might allow himself a bit of freedom now. But controlling his emotions, regimenting his behavior, clinging to logic and order—that had seen him through the darkest days of his life. Control had been his salvation, and he was loathe to let it go.

"No. But Ollie tells me that he and Lady Harriet—"

"Plan to elope."

"You knew?"

"She just told me when you walked off with Mr. Treadwell, and I fear they're quite determined."

He jumped when she touched his arm, her exploring fingers jolting his senses, until each press, each stroke along his collar and then up to the edge of his jaw, made him ache for more. She caressed his cheek as he'd touched hers in the conservatory before sliding her hand down to his shoulder, gripping him as if to brace herself.

"Won't you reconsider my suggestion, Your Grace?"

When she lifted onto her toes and swayed toward him, a flash of reason told him to push her away, to guard against her feminine assault. But the thought had all the power of a wisp of smoke and dissolved just as quickly when he reached to steady her and found how well she fit in the crook of his arms.

He'd been a fool to drag her onto the balcony and touch her like a man without an ounce of self-control.

"If you're going to let me hold you this close, you should call me Sebastian."

"If we're to be engaged, you should call me Kitty."

He hadn't agreed to the engagement and still loathed the notion of a scheme. And yet . . . he couldn't deny the practicality of it. It would forestall Ollie's ridiculous plan to elope, satisfy the Claybornes and allow the couple to marry, and, best of all, it would keep all the young misses eager to make his acquaintance—as his aunt had so disturbingly put it—at bay.

"I'm afraid you'll always be Kat to me. Never Kitty."

"Very well. Is that your only condition?"

His skin burned feverish. He loathed lies. Hated pretense. And yet he loathed nothing about holding Kat in his arms. With her velvet-clad curves pressed against him and her thighs brushing his own, he found himself tempted to agree to her subterfuge. Almost.

"I have two more."

"Go on."

"We end it as soon as we're able." If holding her melted his resolve this thoroughly, what sort of wreck would he be after weeks in her company? "You can jilt me if you like. However you wish to do it. And we tell my sister the truth of what we're doing and why. Pippa's far too clever not to see through a falsehood."

"Agreed, Your Grace."

He caught the flash of white as she smiled and moonlight glinted off the curve of her cheeks. Pleasing her stirred an echo of pleasure in him, and it disturbed him how much he wanted to see her smile again, wanted to bring her pleasure, and not just for a moment.

Lifting a hand to caress her cheek, Seb drew Kat in close, dipped his head, and took her mouth in a quick mingling of chilled flesh and warm breath.

One delectable touch of her lips was electric and terrifying. In their too brief kiss, he tasted bliss, and all the havoc a woman could wreak on a man's heart. But the delectable buzz of sensation didn't bow him or buckle his knees. It simply made him yearn for more.

"Didn't we agree you'd call me Sebastian?"

Hearing his name on Kat's lips seemed as essential as aiding Ollie and sussing out each of her unique scents. It wasn't logical. Reason played no part in it, but he needed to hear her say his name.

"Sebastian?"

Seb gripped Kat tighter in his arms. It wasn't her lilting whisper he heard.

Alecia stood at the bottom of the balcony stairs calling out into the darkness. It was unlikely she could make them out at the far end of the garden, but she must have seen him dragging Kat onto the balcony.

"Who is it?" Kat peeked around his shoulder.

"It's Lady Naughton. She's—"

"I know who she is." She had a terrible habit of finishing his sentences.

"Do you?" Could she truly know his history with the woman? The thought of it sickened him, and then another notion teased at his mind. What if the two women had connived this very moment to shame him or force him into a more elaborate scheme?

Kat tugged his lapel. "Of course. I know who everyone is."

Momentarily relieved, Seb released a pent-up breath as Kat continued. "She's an earl's wife, though she comes into London society rarely. I wonder why your aunt invited her this evening."

Seb wondered the same, though finding a way to avoid Alecia and get Kat safely inside seemed a more urgent concern.

"More interestingly, why is she calling for you?"

"I've no idea, nor any wish to inquire," he whispered while tucking them further into the shadow of a towering shrub. Alecia could keep her letters, her secrets, and her lies.

Kat pulled away. "We shouldn't be hiding. She can be the first to hear our good news."

Before Seb could stop her, Kat stepped out and proceeded up the moonlit path as she called to Alecia.

"Lady Naughton, good evening. I take it you're looking for Wrexford. He's here, but I do hope you'll keep our secret. We haven't yet spoken to my father, but His Grace has just asked me to be his wife."

## Chapter Ten

SHE LOVED HIM. Or at the very least Lady Naughton knew the duke beyond a polite acquaintance. It wasn't just the way her dark brows arched high and her body stiffened at Kitty's pronouncement. Something in the way she bit her lip to stop it trembling and wrung her hands before turning toward the ballroom implied more.

Kitty peered back at the man still lingering in the shadows, the man she'd just declared to be her fiancé, the man who'd just stolen her breath with his kiss. He did not look pleased, and she didn't need discernment to know the blaze in his gunmetal eyes had nothing to do with desire.

He'd agreed to a feigned engagement and she could not allow him a moment to change his mind. Why not begin spreading the news immediately? With any luck, Lady Naughton wouldn't be able to keep it to herself and rumor would ignite the ballroom like a spark amid dry kindling.

"At least now you cannot renege on our agreement."

Wrexford stepped onto the path and glanced at the spot where Lady Naughton had stood. A muscle ticked at the edge of his square clean-shaven jaw.

"I had no intention of doing so." He enunciated each word, sharpening every consonant, his deep voice cool and precise.

All the warmth between them had fled, but Kitty couldn't regret it. She needed her wits about her, and the man's nearness turned her thoughts thick and sluggish.

Now was the time to plan their next steps. Father might not be pleased to hear of Wrexford's proposal after the fact, but he'd certainly welcome the man into the family. Convincing him to allow Hattie and Mr. Treadwell to marry first would take a bit of maneuvering, but Kitty already pondered several ways to accomplish the feat. She had the story of her romance with the duke to shape too. Among the lessons she'd learned from observing her father's political maneuvering was that gossip, in order to be truly effective, must be carefully managed.

"You'll need to trust me, Kat."

Sebastian reached for her, but she sidestepped out of his grasp.

"Do liars often trust each other, Your Grace?"

She'd been unable to avoid his embrace during the waltz, and she'd used their nearness here in the darkness for persuasion. But that was quite enough touching for one night. The man's hands had a terrible unsettling power over her. He didn't brush or lightly graze her skin. He stroked her, caressed her, as if he wished to give her pleasure rather than take his own. He almost made her want to believe the fib they were going to tell everyone— that he admired her, that he wanted her for his own.

To prove their false romance, she'd let him hold her hand or lock arms with him during a stroll in the park. But those moments would be of her choosing. She would dictate the when and where.

Tonight she'd been remiss and allowed him too much liberty.

Striking out too quickly for her to retreat, he clasped her hand.

"I'm not a liar by nature, my lady. This ruse is for Ollie's benefit, and your sister's." Loosening his hold, he snaked his hand up higher, stroking her arm, cupping her elbow in his palm and drawing her in close.

"But yes, liars that we are, we'll have to trust each other. Can you not see that you risk your reputation with this scheme?"

She didn't expect his concern. They each sought their own benefit, if not for themselves than for those they loved. He couldn't imagine her an innocent miss. She *had* suggested the arrangement, after all.

After watching her father work his machinations and Mama's subtle steering for as long as she could remember, getting others to join her games or nudging them in the right direction was as much a skill as tending to plants in the conservatory. No one looked out for her well-being or considered her wishes. If she'd abided by her father's demands, she would have been married off during her first season.

"Let me worry about my reputation." The poor man seemed to have no notion that a favorable match, even a feigned one, could only improve her image as an unmarried lady determined to remain stubbornly on the shelf.

"Very well. Shall we go in?"

He didn't even wish to touch her anymore. After releasing her arm, he straightened his tie and jerked his jacket lapels into perfect symmetry, as if their interlude had ruffled him and he wanted to put himself back in order.

Kitty thought he might leave her standing in the cold night air and go on his own to face whatever gossip might have begun to spread among Lady Stamford's guests. But he was too much of a gentleman for that. Lifting a hand toward the balcony, he gestured for her to precede him back into the ballroom.

"Have you been acquainted with her long?" The mystery of his connection with Lady Naughton hovered at the back Kitty's mind like a persistent bee, and it buzzed more fiercely the longer she attempted to ignore it.

"Who?" But he knew exactly who she meant. His gaze, which had followed her since their waltz, suddenly locked on the towering rhododendron to his right.

"You don't wish to tell me." Which only served to stoke her curiosity. Had they been friends? Lovers? For a man with a reputation for being an academic unconcerned with titles and society, he seemed to possess a plethora of noble connections.

"Were you lovers?"

Turning to face her, he took a step closer, too near to avoid noticing his scent and the way his breath warmed her skin wherever it gusted.

"What are we to be to each other, Kat?"

"I don't—" A simple question and yet the moment she began to answer, rational thought scattered like colored tiles tumbling in a kaleidoscope. If all went well, they'd be bound by family ties for the rest of their lives. But he didn't speak of some far-off future. His eyes had gone wider, his tone taut and tense. He spoke of immediacy. This handful of days when they'd feign romance and love, and Kitty knew nothing of either. She'd spent all her life avoiding both.

"Friends? Or merely players in a temporary scheme?" He dipped his head and then lifted it. "Your hesitation tells me we're the latter. So let's keep our secrets to ourselves."

The duke stepped back and glanced again at the spot where Lady Naughton had stood watching them. He reached around her as if he meant to embrace her, but she realized he merely intended to herd her back toward the balcony.

"We should return to the ball, and I must speak to your father, preferably before the gossips do."

"He'll be in the cardroom and won't appreciate being disturbed. Best to speak to him tomorrow." Her father rarely danced anymore, but he took his card games seriously. He never lost, though he was more interested in the leverage he could wield over the men he bested rather than any winnings he might receive.

Kat let the duke lead her to the balcony stairs, turning at the top to stop him so that she could slip off his evening coat. His jaw ticked again when he took it from her hands and settled it on his shoulders.

She could still smell his clean masculine scent on her skin and imagined his jacket now smelled like her gardenia-jasmine perfume. The notion that they'd imprinted their scents on one another shook her nearly as effectively as his touch.

Glancing at her, eyes hooded and expression inscrutable, Sebastian started toward the balcony door.

"She's one of your secrets, then?" The words came before she could stop them. He was to be her fiancé for the next few weeks. Their names would be linked in every scandal rag and dance on the tongue of every whisperer in the city. Didn't she deserve to know of an entanglement that might complicate their plan?

He didn't turn or acknowledge her question, but he froze in place, his back stiff, hands fisted.

Kat waited several beats and then started past him. He could stand out in the cold all night if he wished it. Without the warmth of his coat, her skin had turned to gooseflesh. But he caught her, lifting his arm to hold her back, not touching her, thank goodness, but indicating she should stop.

"If you truly wish to know my secrets, then I want to know yours. Every mistake, every regret, all the secret parts of your history you'd prefer to keep from judgment and scrutiny."

He held his breath, waiting for her answer.

She inhaled sharply, a sound of fear. He didn't want that. But nor did he wish to lay his soul bare for the woman. Her changing scent confused him as much as the many sides of her character. She was one moment the simpering debutante, the next a dedicated horticulturist, and now a master schemer. She was a tantalizingly snarled riddle of a woman, but sorting out her secrets would mean revealing his own. And that didn't interest him at all.

"Not so appealing, is it, Kat?"

Refusing to look at him, she stared straight ahead, shoulders back, chin up high, all the lines of her face limned by the moonglow. He almost wished he was willing to let her see inside, to let her learn of all his failings and fears, just so that he could glimpse the woman beyond her flawless façade.

Her refusal to answer brought as much relief as disappointment.

"No, I don't think so either, my lady. Let's see this plan through to its end. We'll see Oliver and Harriet married and put the rest behind us. No more questions about my past, and I won't ask any about yours."

She glanced down at his arm where he held it up, not quite touching her chest. "Very well, Your Grace." Looping her arm under his, she grasped it lightly as a lady might take a gentleman's arm during a promenade in the park.

Seb let himself breathe again, deeply, drawing in long drams of frosty air. The garden was overflowing with shrubs and blooming flowers, but he could only detect Kat's scent on the breeze.

"You should dance with me again," she commanded.

"I didn't step on your toes too much during our waltz?" Whether it was the chill in the air or her arm clasped in his, he felt lighter than he had all evening. The notion of reentering the ballroom and facing Alecia held no appeal, but the prospect of dancing with Kat again lured him. He fought his tendency to analyze, to worry over what a danger she might prove to be to his peace of mind. He would allow himself to enjoy a dance with her and avoid sifting the black thoughts Alecia stirred.

"People should see us dancing together again. At least once more, perhaps twice. Even if your Lady Naughton says nothing, we'll set tongues wagging about our budding romance." Kat's tone had gone flat, her voice low and bereft of its usual lilt. Focus, determination—she would be all about the game now. He'd set the rules and would have to abide by them.

He loosened his hold on her arm, touching her now as lightly as she held onto him.

"Ready?"

"Of course."

The noise and heat of the room attacked his senses and he blinked against the brightness until his eyes adjusted. He expected stares, whispers, perhaps even words of congratulations, but the glances of dancers skimmed over him, past Kat, and onto the others in the room. They seemed to be attracting no more attention than any other couple. Only one man kept his gaze fixed in their direction—the one his aunt had identified as Lord Ponsonby.

Seb scanned the room for the one woman he hoped never to see again. Several dark-haired ladies moved in the steps of a lively dance and a few gathered on the ballroom's edges, but none possessed frost blue eyes. He didn't see Lord Naughton's towering frame among the crowd either, though it was most likely he could be found wherever they were serving drink. Or perhaps in the cardroom with Lord Clayborne.

"I haven't had a chance to speak to our hostess yet this evening. I'll return before the next dance." Kat unlatched her arm from his and strode away, leaving him as exposed and out of place as the moment he'd entered the ballroom.

Securing an uncrowded corner, he darted his gaze from one feminine face to another. They were all strangers. None of them were Alecia, and that brought a rush of relief. The shock of seeing her had chilled his blood, like one of those doomed characters from the ghost stories Pippa loved to read. Most shocking of all, he hadn't burned with the loathing he'd expected. She was smaller than he remembered, almost fragile, somehow diminished. Not the temptress and ruiner of men he'd once known her to be. But he'd still wanted nothing more than to get away from her. Whatever time had done to alter her, there'd never be a place for her in his life again.

Years ago, she'd been so persuasive. If she'd turned her energies to something other than attaining a title and a rich husband, she might have been a leader, a reformer, a woman who inspired others to action. She'd certainly inspired him to act, leading him to a clearing in the woods on the far side of the River Cam to confront the man who'd purportedly ruined her. Poor Charles Page had been told an equal and opposite lie, expecting to save her from Seb's clutches. Seeing them together, the man hadn't bothered with questions before taking aim at Seb and firing his pistol. Luckily, he'd been a very bad shot.

One glimpse of Alecia brought it all back, and in that moment, Kat had seemed the antidote. A moment alone with her, a private moment away from the light and heat and noise was all he'd wanted. And then she'd touched him. Or he'd touched her. He couldn't recall the order of it. But their bodies connected as they had during the waltz. For a moment in the garden, she'd been his alone. No lords or eligible gentlemen could leer or lean on her.

Just one bloody fool who let a few whiffs of her gardenia scent scramble his senses and melt his resolve.

How had a moment in the shrubbery turned a lie into a solution? Why had he agreed to feign a betrothal with the woman when he'd never been able to pull off a real engagement with any success at all?

A few weeks of courting her only to allow her to jilt him. That sounded like a prescription for pure misery.

At least he had practice at it.

*What the hell have I done?*

He'd begun the evening determined to refuse Kat, manage a single waltz without bruising her toes, and return to Wrexford House. He had plenty to do and none of it involved dancing or strutting around a ballroom.

Only halfway through decoding the estate's ledger books when they departed for London, he'd insisted on bringing them along. The daunting pile of correspondence that seemed to breed on his desk at Roxbury had somehow followed him to London, and an unfinished paper he was due to present to the London Mathematical Society awaited a final polish.

"She's a beauty."

The barking volume of the man's voice disturbed Seb nearly as much as turning to find Lord Ponsonby looming by his side. For a bulky man, he approached with surprising stealth.

Seb crossed his arms, ignored the man's question, and cast Ponsonby a wary glance. His tone as he spoke of Kat's beauty, and the creeping way he trailed his gaze over her as she moved across the ballroom raised Seb's hackles, and he resisted a moment before shaking the man's offered hand.

"Wrexford, is it? Ponsonby, though I suspect your aunt has already told you my name. She offered to make an introduction, but she's no doubt orchestrating a match between some chit and her swain or overseeing a naval treaty or some such. Busy woman."

"She is indeed." Although Kat had gone in search of his aunt, he could now see no sign of either lady in the ballroom.

"I acquired a Rembrandt last week, Wrexford."

Seb was familiar with the Dutch master. His mother had been fond of art and made sure her children had a passing knowledge of art history. How the man's acquisition related to their stunted conversation, Seb hadn't a clue.

"Well done." Seb offered the accolade lightly as he reached up to straighten his waistcoat, preparing to take his leave of the rambling Ponsonby and go off in search of Kat.

"The seller refused my first three offers, but I wasn't daunted. Once I've fixed on my prize, I'm not a man to be easily dissuaded."

Seb focused on the wall sconce in his line of vision, gaslit, and with four crystals dripping from its gilded base. He worked to steady his breathing as he watched Ollie and Lady Harriet moving past him in the ballroom. She wore the same flower as Kat had in her hair. Ten waxy white petals framed by two glossy leaves. He flexed his fingers, but held the rest of his body still, resisting the urge to turn and tell the one pompous fool at his elbow just what to do with all his bluster.

The older man cocked his hip and leaned on the silver-handled cane under his right hand. He'd been watching the ballroom as he spoke, never quite meeting Seb's eye. Now he swiveled enough to gaze up at him.

"She is not on offer, Ponsonby." Seb turned to face the nobleman as he said it, enunciating every word so there could be no doubt as to his meaning.

"Nonsense, Wrexford. She's only refused me three times, and her resistance now will only make my eventual victory sweeter. Indeed, her refusals make her the only woman in this ballroom worth having." The man's hard gaze didn't match his jesting tone.

*She's mine.* A possessive impulse rushed Seb like the burn of single malt Scotch, a delicious fizz in his veins. Never mind that it was false. Never mind that it was temporary. Kat wouldn't be marrying this irritating nobleman, and that was a victory worth savoring.

"Perhaps you should take the lady at her word and accept her refusal."

Not that accepting a woman's word always made for a happy ending. Alecia had taught him that lesson well. Yet Seb wasn't foolish enough to expect dishonesty from all women any more than he expected honesty from all men.

"Ha! You've much to learn, Wrexford. Lady Katherine refuses all her suitors. That's her game." Ponsonby's barking chortle was as annoying as his booming voice.

The notion that Kat liked to play games with men and their emotions set the muscle in Seb's jaw ticking. Perhaps it was true. Was he not a player in her latest scheme?

Seb and Ponsonby glared at each other a moment, taking the other's measure, and then the elderly viscount snapped his head, sniffing the air and searching the ballroom as if he sensed Kat's approach.

She glided toward them and offered the nobleman a slight grin, but the corners of her mouth fell when she met Seb's gaze.

"Lord Ponsonby, has Wrexford not told you our news?"

The man's forehead furrowed and he stacked his hands on the head of his cane, leaning toward Seb with a menacing glint in his eye. "He has not, my lady."

She'd been unstoppable in her determination to blurt

the news to Alecia, and yet now Kat stood watching him, slim arms crossed.

An echo of that liquor-heat rush of victory welled up again, especially when she attempted to glare at him and only one eye truly narrowed, as if she was winking at him instead. Then his eyes locked on the beauty mark, the one at the corner of her mouth.

Kat pursed her mouth, drawing his gaze to her lips.

Lips he'd tasted, and wanted to kiss again.

A clicking sound set his teeth on edge and he turned to find the cause, only to realize it was her foot, slapping the parquet floor and flicking the edge of her dress.

"We're to be married." She blurted the words as unenthusiastically as he'd ever heard any news imparted.

Ponsonby's jowls began to quiver. "Impossible. I spoke to your father just this evening at the club. He said nothing."

Seb cut in. "I have yet to speak to Lady Katherine's father, but I am confident of his consent." At his only meeting with her father, Lord Clayborne had all but demanded Seb propose to Kat. Surely the marquess would be pleased to hear the news.

Ponsonby hung his head a moment and his shoulders sagged with defeat, but then he pushed against his cane and straightened. "Who gave you a title? You cannot even ask for a woman's hand properly. What kind of a gentleman are you?"

Kat moved as if to intervene, but Seb stepped forward to stand between her and Ponsonby.

"I am the gentleman she didn't refuse."

Kat stepped back, away from Ponsonby's gaze, but she clasped her hands in front of her, as if locking herself off from conversation or contact. Ponsonby nearly toppled forward to get a glimpse of her before sketching an awkward half bow and stomping toward the refreshment room.

Seb wasn't certain whether he pitied Ponsonby more for believing he'd ever had a chance to marry Kat, or himself for being the fool who'd be stuck by her side for weeks before being snubbed just as decidedly.

## *Chapter Eleven*

WAITING IN CLAYBORNE's sterile drawing room to ask the man for Kat's hand in marriage was far worse than pacing the halls had been as a first-year Cambridge student before a test. Seb rapped his knuckles against the arm of the chair and then began counting the polished studs at the edge of upholstery. He'd stolen a few moments in the morning to work on his paper for the Mathematical Society, and read a bit of Boole's *The Laws of Thought,* but anticipation, a sort of Ollie-like giddiness, had plagued his efforts to indulge in algebraic logic or any sort of useful thinking at all. Even now his pulse jumped in his throat and he couldn't keep his fingers from tapping the arm of the chair. He tried for a Fibonacci sequence— might as well have some order even if he couldn't achieve it in his mind—but lost count and had to start again.

It was ridiculous. Their whole engagement would be a ruse. *Nothing to be so damned pleased about, man.*

The only numbers that truly mattered now were the days until he could put the scheme behind him. A month, perhaps two? After Ollie's wedding, there'd be no reason to remain in London. A broken engagement with a marquess's daughter wouldn't earn him many invitations to balls and dinner parties. He would close up Wrexford House early and return to Roxbury. The grand estate still didn't feel like home, but he'd accepted it as his future, and his responsibility.

"Grab her! Get Persephone before Wiggins does."

Kat's voice rang out, high-pitched and panicked, and Seb shot up from his chair. Moments later, a blond girl bounded into the room, head down, arms pumping, and stopped just short of barreling into him.

She appeared to be about nine or ten, and her honey blond hair and green eyes reminded him so much of Kat that he deduced the girl was her younger sister, who he'd yet to meet.

As he studied her, the child planted a hand on each hip and speared him with a withering glare.

"Are you Persephone?" If he'd been told the name of Kat's youngest sister, he couldn't recall it.

"No, I'm Violet, and you're in my way, sir." As she spoke, her eyes darted around the drawing room floor. "Have you seen her?"

"Seen who?" The room had been empty from the moment the maid ushered him in and asked him to wait for Lord Clayborne.

The girl huffed out a sigh and rolled her eyes. "Persephone, of course. Haven't you been paying attention?"

When he didn't immediately answer, the child stepped around him and crouched down to look under a table. "Aha."

Her satisfied exclamation, like Sherlock Holmes finding the mystery-solving clue, intrigued him.

"You've found her?"

The girl pointed to the legs of an end table and Seb squinted at the polished wood before finally glimpsing the tip of a fluffy gray tail flicking against the rear left leg. Stepping back, he could make out the whole ball—all gray fluff except for two lime green eyes.

"Persephone's a cat." Stating the obvious didn't impress the girl, and she twisted her mouth at Seb as if he still had it all wrong.

"She's my kitten, but she's also a Greek princess who lives under the world." She frowned a moment. "Not my kitten, of course. She's English, not Greek. And she's not a princess."

Then the child who'd treated him with such gruff indifference began cooing lovingly at the ball of gray fluff. "Are you, Persie? Are you a princess?"

"Where is she?" Kat rushed into the room and skidded to a halt at the sight of her sister crawling under the table to retrieve the kitten. Then she noticed him.

"Wrexford. You're early."

"Sebastian." He reminded her to use his given name.

"Violet, come and bring that little mischief-maker."

"She won't come out." Violet straightened and looked down at her kitten with the same irritated glare she'd given Seb.

Kat crouched slowly, clearly trying for stealth, to retrieve the kitten.

"So you're the man Kitty's going to marry?"

In that moment, with her chin tilted high and one eyebrow arched, Violet reminded him more of Lord Clayborne than Kat.

"She did say she would." Seb watched Kat as he said it. Her long skirts had pooled around her as she knelt down and reached out to retrieve the recalcitrant kitten.

"Then she will. My sister always does what she says she will. That's why she couldn't accept any of the others." Violet leaned toward him and whispered, "And because they were all odious."

Kat drew back and stood with a gray ball of fur tucked in her arms. The kitten blinked up at each of them accusingly.

"I should introduce the two of you properly."

"Your Grace, may I present my sister, Lady Violet?" Violet stepped in front of him at Kat's pronouncement and bowed a graceful little curtsy.

"Violet, the Duke of Wrexford . . ." Seb straightened his back and bent to offer the girl a chivalrous bow. "He's not at all odious, as far as I can tell."

"Such high praise, Lady Katherine." Seb cast his feigned betrothed a wry grin.

"Let's hope you don't prove me wrong."

Before he could offer another retort, Kat turned to her sister. "I've made a place for your kitten in the conservatory. Shall we take her?"

The girl nodded and gazed up at Seb expectantly.

Apparently, it was her way of inviting him to come along.

"Don't worry, Persie. We'll hide you so that Wiggins will never find you."

"Who's Wiggins?" In for a penny, in for a pound. If he was to be a part of this cat-hiding mission, he might as well have all the facts.

"Our butler," Kat called back over her shoulder.

"He said he'd eat Persie," Violet insisted.

"That sounds rather extreme." He'd teased Pippa mercilessly when they were children, but he could easily imagine how well even a jest about eating one of her pets would have been received.

Kat turned back and lifted a hand to pat Violet's arm. "He was teasing you, sweet. You know Wiggins isn't fond of pets."

Slowing her pace as they approached the conservatory, Kat looked back and forth to make sure none of the housemaids or other staff saw them enter. Once inside, she led Seb to a corner near the edge of the glass wall that extended into the town house's outdoor garden. The morning sun had already warmed the spot, and as soon as she began to lean forward, Persephone jumped down and onto a plush pillow arranged near a dish of water.

Violet hunched beside her kitten and began stroking its fur into order while rambling through a series of questions. How did Persie like her new home? Was she frightened of Wiggins too? Would she like a treat before supper? Unless her languid blinks were a kind of cat Morse code, the kitten seemed disinclined to answer.

Kat drew close and whispered. "I don't think he'd do the kitten any real harm, but she'll be safe in here. The conservatory makes him sneeze and other staff rarely come in here."

"That puts my mind at ease." Seb grinned but didn't look at Kat. Both of them focused on Violet as she fussed over her kitten. "You've allowed me into your conservatory twice and claim I'm not odious. One might almost think you're growing fond of me."

He hoped his light tone might ease the tension between them, but Kat remained stiff and quiet at his side.

Then finally, without turning to look at him, she said, "Don't get ahead of yourself, Wrexford."

Seb turned to study her profile, but Kat ignored him and continued to stare ahead, watching her sister.

"Your father is expecting me. May we have a word after I meet with him?"

"I'll wait for you in the drawing room." Though she spoke agreement, the sharpness in her tone sounded like resistance to Seb's ears.

He leaned toward her and lowered his voice to a whisper. "You do still want to carry through with this?"

His question earned him a glance before she turned back toward Violet. "Yes, of course."

"Pleasure to meet you, Miss Violet."

The child lifted a finger to her lips. "Not so loud, Your Grace. Persie's almost asleep."

Seb took a deep breath, steeling himself for his performance with Lord Clayborne. He'd yet to tell his sister or Ollie about their plan. He hadn't lied to anyone yet. Kat had taken the initiative of telling Alecia and Ponsonby and he'd stood by mutely, lying by omission. But now he'd face the marquess alone, and he was the kind of man Seb suspected could spot a liar from across a room.

As he exited the conservatory, he frowned at the sound of lighter footsteps trailing his own. He turned and Kat reached out to grasp his upper arm.

"When you meet with my father, please don't mention the kitten. My sisters and I have learned that, in some cases, the less my father knows, the better."

He glanced over her shoulder. Violet had found a book and held it up for perusal with one hand while resting the other on the gray fluffball's steadily rising and falling back.

"Let's distract him with planning a wedding instead."

It was their one objective. The good that could come of all their subterfuge, and the reminder of it finally seemed to chip through the chill between them. Kat almost grinned. Seb hadn't realized how much he craved some sign of pleasure or camaraderie from her. He sighed, letting a bit of his anxiety about meeting Clayborne ebb.

As he gazed at her, Seb recalled the first time he'd found her in this green space. That studious, unfashionably dressed woman fascinated him, and he didn't like how much he looked forward to getting a few more glimpses of her over the coming weeks.

"I'll be waiting in the drawing room." Her practical tone drew him back to the matter at hand. "We have much to do."

"Do we?"

"Yes, of course. We both want this over with quickly. In a short time, we must carry on a courtship, prevent our own wedding, and plan Hattie and Oliver's."

Kat turned to retreat to her conservatory, but then she paused and gazed back at him over her shoulder. It was just what he needed to bolster him for the meeting with the marquess.

"Good luck, Sebastian."

"MARRY HER? MARRY Katherine?"

Seb loathed the way her father said her name with a hard emphasis on the three syllables and an incredulous tone, as if he doubted any man could desire her.

"Yes, my lord."

He'd said it twice, as clearly as he could. The direct approach seemed best. No use prevaricating or dragging it out.

The man was as confounding as his daughter. He'd all but insisted on a match with Kat the first time Seb met with him, and now he stared as if he thought requesting her hand meant Seb was bound for Bedlam.

The marquess seemed more interested in studying Seb than in giving due consideration to the request to marry his daughter. At first he'd glared from across the expanse of his desk, then stood and circled Seb's chair like a predator sniffing its prey, and now he'd positioned himself before the fireplace, a hand on each hip, starring at the back of Seb's head.

Not only could Seb feel the man's gaze boring into

him, but thanks to an ornate mirror on the wall before him, he could watch Clayborne assessing him.

"Why?"

"Pardon?" Seb turned in his chair, but the furnishing was too narrow and damnably uncomfortable. He stood, stretching his muscles, and faced Clayborne.

"The season breeds matches and hasty ones at that, I'll allow, but you've known my daughter for the sum of three days."

"It's a short acquaintance admittedly, but Lady Katherine . . . makes an indelible impression." It wasn't a lie. From the moment Seb laid eyes on her, she'd been a tenacious presence in the back of his mind.

"And your friend wishes to marry her sister."

Seb tried to grin or lift his mouth in the semblance of amusement, but his cheek spasmed instead. "A fortuitous coincidence, isn't it?"

"I shall consider Treadwell now, of course."

Seb inhaled and it was easier than it had been a moment before. Anxiety lifted, like a fever leaving his body, and his pulse danced as it had the first time he'd spoken to Kat. It was worth it. The torment of growing close to a woman only to break with her publicly in a few short weeks. The guilt of lying to those he loved. For this moment and the prospect of seeing Ollie happily wed, it was all worth it.

Clayborne cleared his throat. "Don't count your winnings until the race is finished."

Seb swallowed down joy as he nodded his head.

"Betrothals are well and good, Wrexford, but none

of it matters until the ceremony. If Mr. Treadwell meets muster, perhaps we should consider a double wedding."

"Yes, perhaps." He and Kat had decided nothing further than this moment. Beyond the plan to end the ruse in as few days as they could, Seb had no real notion how they'd pull it off. Clayborne intended to see Kat married. How could they dissuade him? He'd feared the marquess might slap Ollie with a breach-of-promise suit, but now he could foresee a legal battle in his own future.

"Cigar?"

Seb never smoked. "No, thank you, my lord."

"Well, sit at least."

Rather than returning to his desk chair, Clayborne seated himself in front of his study's unlit fireplace before flicking a hand toward the opposite chair, indicating Seb should sit. Like his daughter, the man moved with precision, as if sparing energy for comfort or giving into slouching was against his philosophy of life.

"You have my blessing, of course. But tell me how you convinced her."

"Convinced her?"

"To accept your proposal."

His lips were dry. His mouth was a desert. And his mind was momentarily as uninhabited as the Sahara.

"She's refused six others." Clayborne held still, watching Seb closely for a reaction.

Seb liked that she'd refused other suitors. Irrationally, pointlessly adored the fact.

Ponsonby would be among the six. And the others? He imagined men fumbling to impress her, to win her affection. His was no true victory, but whether ego or conceit, some part of him that refused to parse truth from fiction thrilled at the notion of being the only one who could rightfully call himself her betrothed. At least for a few weeks.

For a few weeks he would get to spend time with her, touch her, learn more about the woman, and then part from her. He was a fool to anticipate it at all.

"Kat . . . Katherine is a fascinating woman. It doesn't surprise me she's had six other suitors."

Clayborne's fingers twitched, jerking into motion, and then the movement spread to his face, until the staid controlled man actually broke into a grin around the stub of his cigar.

"Six proposals, Wrexford. There have been three times as many suitors. You're the nineteenth." He blew rings of smoke into the air to punctuate the revelation.

Seb coughed, less from the smoke of Clayborne's cigar than the unpalatable image of eighteen men crowding the Adderly drawing room bearing flowers and baubles to tempt Kat. He wondered if anyone ever thought to bring her a living flower or a seed? Perhaps some of the plants she tended in her conservatory represented failed suitors.

The nineteenth suitor and seventh proposal. At least they were special numbers, each an indivisible prime.

"Can you understand my curiosity now, Wrexford? You've pulled off quite a coup." Clayborne reached over to tap his cigar against a crystal dish on the table between them. "At least tell me what drew you to my daughter.

Most are distracted by her beauty and only realize too late that she lacks the soft, mild manner men desire in a woman."

Seb had touched her, held her. Kat's skin was achingly soft. He slid his thumb across the fingers of his right hand, remembering the silken curve of her cheek.

And mild? Weather could be mild. Bland soup was mild. A tamed horse might be mild. Who wanted a woman to be mild?

"Speak, man. Was it her meekness?" The marquess's tone turned derisive as his mouth contorted in a sneer. "Or was it her lack of opinions? No, no. It must be her willingness to be led rather than grasping the crown and scepter for herself."

Seb stared at Clayborne, studying him in the same cool manner the nobleman had raked Seb with his gaze. Is this what she endured? Did he mock Kat to her face or only to the men who asked to spend their lives loving and protecting her? Never mind that his own intentions were false.

No father had the right to belittle his daughter, simply because she knew her own mind. And no man in his right mind desired a silly, simpering wife.

Not that Kat would be his wife. Or that he was truly reconciled to having a wife. All of that changed nothing about Kat's cleverness or her appealing confidence. None of which her father seemed capable of appreciating.

"Quite the opposite. I look forward to hearing all of Lady Katherine's opinions."

"And do you look forward to engaging in skirmishes with her over every choice you make?"

"She is headstrong." Seb was quite content in the knowledge that there was no equation in which the addition of a women's confidence subtracted any of a man's. He'd spent his whole life surrounded by outspoken women.

"She is challenging." The marquess worked over the final word as if it was a bit of tough meat and hard to chew.

"I do enjoy a challenge."

Clayborne reached up to stroke his beard. "Then you've chosen well."

It should have been the end of it. The words were, Seb suspected, as much of a blessing as he was likely to get from the man. But none of it settled well with him. The marquess had changed his manner since their first meeting, and Seb feared his acting skills hadn't convinced him. More than convincing the man, Seb wanted to tell Clayborne he'd wronged his daughter. If his own father had held such outdated views about women, what would have become of Pippa when she decided she wanted to study mathematics alongside mostly male classmates at Cambridge? What of his mother, who had begun writing letters to her member of parliament at the age of eighteen, asking the man to consider the suffrage for women?

He'd encountered Clayborne's sort before, and he suspected many such men were fathers of intelligent, headstrong women. The notion that Kat endured discouragement from her father made Seb respect her more.

And respecting her more, when he was already battling an attraction that distracted and disturbed him, did not bode well for the day when their false engagement came crashing to an end.

## Chapter Twelve

KITTY PACED THE drawing room. Too much time had passed. Her father wouldn't deny a duke who wanted his daughter's hand in marriage, and he certainly wouldn't refuse the one man she'd been all but instructed to wed. But he could make the conversation miserable. He could interrogate and scrutinize until a man—or a daughter—wished to crawl out of their own skin just to get away.

What would utter shock look like on Desmond Adderly's face? Papa was used to reading every situation so well that virtually nothing came as a surprise. He was an undefeated chess master who could predict his opponents' next three moves.

But he'd be well and truly stunned when he heard she'd finally accepted a suitor's proposal. And that might be the sticking point. He wouldn't expect her to accept Wrexford. Perhaps he'd given up hope that she would accept any man. She'd once declared her intention to live out her days alone. Old maid, spinster, whatever they wished to call her, it had seemed a more appealing future than being viewed as a man's possession, his property. Any fate of her choosing held more appeal than marriage to a man she could not bear.

At the sound of her father's study door opening and closing, she peeked around the drawing room doorway. Sebastian exited in one piece but sighed deeply before turning and striding toward her.

Kitty closed the door behind him, slipping the lock with a decided snick.

"Is it prudent to close the door?"

"I'm afraid most of our housemaids are terrible gossips, and I've already mentioned my sisters' inability to keep a confidence."

He may have been thinking more of propriety than privacy, but Kat imagined Mama would allow her a moment alone in an overstaffed town house with the man she planned to marry. Privacy would be essential in order to plan their strategy and maintain their secret long enough to allow Oliver and Harriet to exchange vows.

She settled on the end of the settee and indicated the adjacent chair. He lowered himself into it but looked as uncomfortable as if she'd asked him to perch on a cushion of needles.

"It went well?"

He nodded sharply. "The best part is that it's over."

"You make it sound like you've had a tooth pulled."

Pursing his lips as if his jaw actually did hurt, he said, "I would have preferred that, I think."

She wouldn't make excuses for her father. He'd laugh at the notion of any woman defending him. Perhaps Papa didn't think her worthy of a duke's attentions. Perhaps he found it difficult to believe she'd finally given up her *yes*. Perhaps he refused to believe any man could love her for the very qualities he'd spent years trying to chastise out of her character.

Would any man ever love her that way? This false engagement might be as close and she'd come, and it was all artifice.

Kitty shook her head. Practical matters were far preferable to ruminating over romantic nonsense. Lifting a small journal from her skirt pocket, she slipped a finger into the spot she'd marked with a piece of ribbon and smoothed open the pages on her lap.

"Hattie's agreed to a simple ceremony, which should save a good deal of time. We needn't plan for anything elaborate. Mama will protest, of course." She reached up to tap her finger against her bottom lip.

"Hattie's happiness trumps a lavish display. Surely your mother will come around."

Kitty had never met such a practical man. His direct and decisive manner put her father's prevaricating ways to shame. Sebastian seemed unflappable, with a sanguine confidence that everything must fall into place. In Kitty's experience, it was better to prepare for the worst and be pleasantly surprised by good fortune.

Somehow he managed to make none of his rosy perspective feel like false assurance. Indeed, Sebastian seemed unable to speak anything but the unvarnished truth. No ambiguity. No polishing his sentences to make them more appealing. No couching his meaning in similes or metaphors.

"You don't know my mother." She glanced down at the list resting on her thighs. "The first obstacle is location. Many churches can't be scheduled on such short notice. There's Sunderly, our home in Suffolk, but Mama and Papa don't like to return to the country before the season's end."

"What about Roxbury?"

"That *would* impress my mother."

She'd heard of the estate, had even seen an etching of it in a book on English country houses. By all accounts, the structure had been built on a grand scale and situated on one of the most breathtaking pieces of land in Cambridgeshire. Not at all the house for a plain-speaking mathematician. Hattie would find the notion of a country house wedding romantic.

"Then it's settled."

The ease with which he made the gracious offer took Kitty by surprise, especially considering his initial resistance to the scheme.

He finally eased back into the chair he occupied, though he still sat with his feet planted firmly on the ground and a hand on each arm of the chair, a bit like a monarch perched on his throne. Pleased with himself, that's what he looked, and Kat allowed him a moment of satisfaction before moving onto the next item on her list.

"You'll need to . . ." The words stuck in her mouth like toffee. She'd convinced the duke to go along with her plan, but dictating his actions seemed a good deal more daunting. "You'll have to court me. And as publicly as possible."

She prepared herself for resistance. He'd said she risked her reputation, but he would have to risk his too. More so, since he would be the jilted suitor when all was said and done. The more publicly they conducted their engagement, the more public the judgment when it crashed. Yet it would be the only way to convince her father and their circle of friends.

Instead of anger, Sebastian seemed amused. He leaned forward, resting his arms on his thighs and clasping his hands in front of him. She was grateful for his clasped hands, having promised herself to insist on less touching.

"Then you'll have to help me, Kat. Tell me how you like to be wooed."

"I'll play my part, I assure you." He didn't like that, whether it was the reminder of the falseness of their connection or the flippant tone in her voice, his brow creased and he leaned back in his chair, moving away from her.

"Shall we get started?"

"Now?" He looked as miserable as when he'd left her father's study.

"Mmm. I thought we'd start with a ride in Hyde Park." The park where she'd first suggested their engagement seemed a fitting spot for their first outing as a betrothed couple.

"A carriage ride? Why not a walk?" he suggested.

The paths would be crowded with riders at this time

of day. The duke had to be aware of the tradition of a morning ride through Hyde Park.

"I prefer a horseback ride. You can borrow Harriet's horse, unless you prefer to return with your own." She stood, not giving him time to protest. "I'll go and change. Perhaps you can peruse my list while you wait." She handed him her little leather journal, keeper of her many lists.

"You have a list?" From his frown, it seemed he wasn't looking forward to any of it.

"We've only just begun, Sebastian. There's much more to come."

"YOU'RE STARING AT my hat." At first she assumed the duke couldn't take his eyes off of her, that he was as enthralled as he'd seemed at his aunt's ball. But every time she glanced over, his gaze was locked on her head.

"I'm not the only one." He turned to take in the groom and others assisting in the Clayborne mews. "I do believe everyone is looking at your hat."

"Nonsense." Kitty looked around to make sure he was, in fact, teasing. "It's the latest fashion."

He lifted both brows before glancing again at her feathers.

She stiffened her spine and lifted her chin in defiance as he studied her. The feathers were rather long, and perhaps a bit too numerous, but their excess would make her stand out among the crowd. So what if she had to tilt her head a bit to the right to balance the weight? The milliner's creation made her feel tall and regal. And no one could deny the iridescent lime, tan, and turquoise shades of the peacock feathers looked fetching with the dark green velvet of the hat.

Kitty loved her new hat. Absolutely adored it.

"Is it comfortable?"

"No, but it's beautiful."

If comfort were the criteria for fashion's value, she'd happily burn her bustle and divest herself of every corset in her closet. None of them were anywhere near as pretty as her new hat.

He grunted and smirked at the same time. "Hmm . . . the color suits you."

"Quite the concession." Kitty grabbed Majesty's reins and allowed a groom to boost her up. The horse dipped its head for a scratch and she reached out to brush her fingers through its mane.

When Junia, Harriet's horse, scraped a hoof against the path, the duke sidestepped away from the animal's side.

"You don't like horses." The realization stunned her. She'd never met a gentleman who didn't take his horse-flesh seriously.

"I have little experience of horses. Most I've known spent their time drawing a carriage."

"But you have ridden before?"

He opened his mouth and stood staring at the animals a moment, but no explanation came.

"Sebastian?"

"Once before."

She couldn't help staring. She consciously locked her lips so her mouth wouldn't stand agape. One horseback ride. One waltz. The man seemed to like his experiences in the singular.

"It didn't go well?"

Glancing down at his upper arm, he twisted his mouth. "The horse bit me."

"Why did you let him bite you?"

"I don't recall giving my consent," he said, throwing his shoulders back and puffing out his chest slightly. "He nudged my arm. I thought he was being friendly."

She couldn't quite imagine how his brawny arm ended up in a horse's mouth. She stared, wondering if a scar still marked the spot.

He bristled. "I was a child. No one told me a horse who nudges you is considering whether to take a bite."

She chuckled under her breath, then put a finger to her mouth to stay the laughter. "I suspect horses are like people. Some are more apt to bite than others."

Casting a wary gaze over Harriet's horse, he asked. "And this one?"

"Junia's never bitten anyone. Though it might be difficult, I'm sure she can resist having a bite of you."

"Very reassuring."

He tilted his head to catch the horse's eye, and then lifted a hand to grasp near the saddle's pommel. Sunlight glinted off his polished boot when he slipped it into the stirrup iron, and Kitty couldn't manage to avert her gaze from the firm muscled line of his thigh as he flexed to lift himself into the saddle.

Junia flicked her head and took a single step forward, nearly pulling him off his standing leg. Releasing his grip on the saddle and untangling his foot, Sebastian hopped back, crossed his arms, and offered Kitty an endearingly peeved frown.

"She's rejected me."

"Nonsense. She's testing you." Nodding her head at him encouragingly, Kitty added, "Don't be so indulgent at the start. Take the reins firmly in hand when you mount."

He turned his head slowly and gazed up at her, his mouth tipped in a beguiling grin. Voice low and seductive, he assured, "I shall certainly keep that in mind."

She caught her breath as the sunlight caressed the arch of his high cheekbones and the faint stubble at the edge of his jaw.

His words felt like a stroke down her back, a hot breathy whisper at the base of her neck. Kitty shivered.

When he approached Junia again, Kitty gripped her reins so tightly her own horse neighed and tipped her head in protest.

"Grasp a bit of her mane rather than the pommel."

He nodded and swung himself into the saddle. For a man who'd only ridden once before, he sat a horse well and controlled the reins masterfully. He was more insistent than Harriet, and the mare responded as if she appreciated a rider who knew how to take the lead.

As they trotted toward Hyde Park, she reflected how the duke had been the same when he waltzed with her. Other gentlemen stared at her too long and lost their footing, and some were so abysmal at ballroom conversation that she forced the lead from them in protest. But the Duke of Wrexford had been unexpectedly sure-footed, and she'd been as supple in his arms as that silly horse. Letting him guide her, trusting him to lead.

They'd ridden for only a brief time and were just approaching the banks of the Serpentine. A breeze kicked up and swept the lake's surface into a dancing bed of diamonds, rippling waves sparkling in the sunlight. They drew near a tree and the wind funneled around them, lifting tufts of the duke's bronze hair.

The duke turned to her, his expression grim. "How long must we do this?"

"You're not enjoying it." She didn't need to be as discerning as her father to recognize his dissatisfaction.

He flexed his fists around the reins and tried for an expression more pleasured than pained.

They might not look like London's most besotted couple, but their outing hadn't gone unnoticed. Kitty looked around them and noticed a young woman she'd met during her first season. The lady looked on from horseback and whispered to her companion, the Earl of Chessick.

Craning her neck, she noted other glances. They weren't quite making a scene, but perhaps they were making an impression that would set a few tongues wagging. If others remembered them at all, they'd probably recall her unique hat. She'd count that a victory, whatever Sebastian thought of her fashion sense.

A strand of loose hair caught at her neck, tugging a few pins free. Before she could fix it back in place, a breeze kicked up and snatched the hat off her head, sending it dancing like a whirling dervish above her head.

"My hat!" As it flitted on the air behind her, Kitty reached back, arms wheeling to grab it. Majesty startled at the awkward movement and pranced forward, shaking Kitty off-balance. Frantically grabbing for purchase, she rolled her hips and slid out of the sidesaddle, legs akimbo, and finally ended up bent across the horse, her backside pointing in Sebastian's direction.

All she could do was watch as her hat sailed past, landing on the banks of the Serpentine. It bobbed in the shallows, plumes standing tall like an extraordinary ship's topsail.

She heard Sebastian's cough behind her, and then felt his hands at her waist as he settled her safely back in the saddle.

"What are you doing?"

He handed her Junia's reins along with Majesty's. "I'm saving you from further embarrassment and fetching your hat. You do want it, don't you?"

Just then the wind caught the feathers and heaved the hat along, a forlorn little boat skipping on the water's surface.

"It's gone in too far now," she said, trying to keep the whine from her voice. "You'll ruin your boots."

"At least it got me off the horse."

He removed his overcoat and handed it to Kitty.

Rolling up his shirt cuffs as he marched toward the shore, he stopped when the toe of his boot dipped into the water's edge.

Kitty swallowed hard. Where had a mathematician acquired such muscular thighs? And why was she staring at the man's thighs at all?

He turned back to her. "I hope they're watching. Whoever we're supposed to be convincing."

Yes, of course. Being seen as a couple was why they were here in the first place, not for her to study the firm planes and sinewy swells of his body. Why *was* the man so muscled? The mystery of it gave her an excuse to stare longer.

No doubt he was one of those sporting gentlemen, preoccupied with running across fields or thwacking balls with bats. Men who talked of nothing but sports put her to sleep.

"You're quite fond of sports, aren't you?"

He'd just waded in, the water rushing up the length of his boots, then higher, pasting his black trousers to those thighs she shouldn't be so interested in.

"Is that what you wish to discuss now? While I'm . . ." He waved his hand ahead of him in the general direction of her doomed scrap of millinery. One determined peacock feather still poked its head above the water.

"I'm curious."

He inhaled deeply, lifting his inexplicably contoured chest, and peered back at her over his shoulder.

"I was on the rowing crew at Cambridge and have a

passing interest in other sports. I can swim, if that's what you're worried about."

Rowing? That explained the width of his arms and the strength in his legs. Perhaps some sports weren't so bad after all.

When she said nothing more, he continued treading water, releasing a hiss as a wave crested his thighs, swelling up over his shapely backside, and higher still until the sky blue shade of his waistcoat turned an inky dark indigo.

"I told you it was deep."

"Very helpful. Thank you," he called back drily.

The force of his movements pushed a surge of water ahead of him, which set the hat weaving along at a faster clip. With one long arm extended, he reached out to snatch the frippery from the lake. It looked like a pathetic bird that had crashed to a watery end, its feathers sodden and limp.

Sebastian hoisted the little hat with a victorious pump in the air as if he'd just pulled Excalibur from its stone.

Kitty lifted a fist to her mouth to stifle laughter, but she heard a giggle and echoes of throaty female delight erupting behind her. A throng of women had gathered at the lake's edge to watch Sebastian walk out of the water with his treasure. One lifted up a kerchief as if she considered throwing it out for him to retrieve, but most simply stood agog, watching water sluice down his long muscular legs, his painted-on trousers leaving little to the imagination. Water had seeped up his waistcoat and soaked the white shirt beneath, fabric clinging lovingly to each hard muscle as he moved. He was a gentlemanly Poseidon emerging from the Serpentine depths, and few seemed willing to miss a moment of the display.

When he finally stepped out of the water, a dainty applause broke out and then grew. A few gentlemen had drawn near and added their approval. Sebastian sketched a deep bow, waving her hat as if he'd just doffed a feathered cap at his gaggle of admirers.

He glanced down at her now ruined piece of headgear and frowned.

"It might be all right once it dries out."

"No, it's ruined."

"I'm sorry, Kat." She'd never seen more sincerity in a man's eyes than when he handed her the bit of drenched fabric.

"Help me down." He frowned at that and a twitch started at the edge of his jaw when he reached for her. She expected him to offer a hand to lean on, but he grasped her waist instead and took all her weight as he lifted her off Majesty and settled her on the ground, careful not to allow her body to brush against his wet clothing.

"We've attracted a good deal of attention." She opened her mouth to instruct him to bow over her hand or whisper in her ear, to take some action to seal their romance in the memory of their sizable audience.

The duke needed no direction.

He released her waist and reached for her hand, but he wasn't content to place a chaste kiss on the back of her glove. Turning her hand palm up, he snaked his fingers up to her wrist, peeling back the edge of her leather riding gloves and finding the bare patch of skin below her jacket cuff. He rubbed her flesh with his thumb, drawing all the sensation in her body to that single spot. Then he bent at the waist to kiss her there on the inch of territory he'd staked for himself.

It wasn't a simple kiss. His tongue darted out to wet the spot, then his hot breath teased against the dampness before she felt the firm warm press of his lips.

Her thighs quivered as if the ground below her feet had begun trembling and might not hold her up.

When he stood and looked down at her, eyes searching for her reaction, she bit her lip to stifle the moan pressing at the back of her throat.

He hadn't released her hand, but for once she was grateful for his touch. The strong wall of his body steadied her, reassured her. Then she glared up at him. His far too tempting touch was the reason she needed steadying in the first place.

Tugging her hand from his, she took a step to put distance between them.

"I think we've made an impression." He skimmed his gaze over a few ladies clinging tenaciously to the patch of grass near the water's edge, eager to catch his attention, or wishing she'd fall in, no doubt.

They'd made an impression all right. She could easily imagine some gossip rag scribbler preparing the next broadsheet in which her hat debacle featured prominently. But that wasn't the impression that still made rational thought a challenge and her skin tingle where he'd kissed her. The shape of his mouth seared into the sensitive skin of her wrist—that was the impression that kept her thoughts stumbling.

"Can we walk the horses back?"

"I suppose you've earned that."

As they walked and the horses clip-clopped behind them, ladies turned to watch their progress. Or, rather, his progress. He still hadn't replaced his jacket, and she noted how their eyes wandered to all the places she'd perused so brazenly.

Kat clenched her teeth.

"Are you embarrassed to be seen with a soaking wet man?" For a gentleman who made his own emotions so apparent, he had a shockingly poor ability to read others.

Sighing deeply, she turned, determined to give him a bit of his own unvarnished truth. But she couldn't admit that the sight of him with his clothes pasted to his body set her own humming in the most irritating manner. Or that something else kindled below the surface.

However much she enjoyed her moments with him, they were all for show. They could be as entertaining as the best theatrical, but it would all be just as fictional.

But whatever she thought to say was drowned out by the sound of a throaty female voice calling his name.

"Sebastian!" Pippa rushed toward them, lifting her skirts high enough to indicate she wasn't overly concerned about anyone seeing her practical black boots or the flash of white stocking above. "Did you fall in?" The last question bubbled out of her mouth, punctuated by bursts of laughter.

His sister reached out to touch his waistcoat. "This

will be ruined. You really do enjoy making your valet miserable, don't you?"

She smiled up at him and then finally seemed to notice Kitty at his side.

"Oh, hello, Lady Katherine. Did you fish him out of the Serpentine or were you the one who pushed him in? I wouldn't blame you if you did. He can be a bit overbearing."

Kitty considered conveying the embarrassing tale of her doomed hat, which would explain Sebastian's sodden physique, but Pippa steamed ahead like a train.

"When you didn't come back to the library for me, I decided to take a walk. What serendipity to find you." She turned again to Kitty. "And you, Lady Katherine."

Kitty grinned at the young woman. She was grateful for Pippa's exuberance. Better to focus on his sister's amusement at Sebastian's wet disheveled clothing than for Kitty to let her gaze drift to all those places where the fabric still molded to his body.

But as soon as Kitty acknowledged Sebastian's sister, Pippa fell silent and began examining both of them as if trying to solve a mystery. "So . . . what did happen?"

Pippa's tone turned suspicious, and her gaze locked on Kitty, as if her presence was more of a conundrum than the question of why Sebastian stood dripping water onto the grass. She looked shocked to see them in each other's company, and certainly seemed to have no notion that Kitty and Sebastian had entered into a scheme to tell everyone they intended to marry.

He'd insisted on telling Pippa the truth of their plan,

yet it appeared that he hadn't bothered telling his sister anything at all.

"You haven't told her."

He swallowed and jerkily shook his head.

His perceptive sister missed none of it. "Told me what?"

The duke looked as if he'd happily dive back in the Serpentine headfirst if it meant he could escape dual feminine interrogation.

"Sebastian, tell me what?"

He shifted his gaze from his sister's face to Kat's, then back again.

"Why don't we discuss it over dinner? Lady Katherine, would you join us? And Lord and Lady Clayborne, if they're free on such short notice."

Kat wouldn't ruin the moment for him. If he wished to tell his sister in private, she owed him that after his chivalrous attempts to save her hat. For a man who'd resisted her idea, he was committed now and it reassured her that they'd see Ollie and Hattie wed, hopefully by month's end.

"I look forward to it, Your Grace."

## Chapter Thirteen

"DID YOU BUMP your head when you fell in the river?"

"No. And you're being purposely inaccurate, Pippa. I didn't fall in. I waded in."

"To preserve her headwear?"

"She was fond of the thing." Seb still wasn't sure why.

Pippa held still after he said it. She'd been pacing as she railed at him but stopped, suspended midstride as if he'd given something away. Was it so difficult to believe he remembered how to be chivalrous? He'd had a long dry spell, admittedly. So long his romantic notions were buried under dust, but he hadn't completely forgotten how to be a gentleman.

She glared at him long and hard and then resumed her march across the carpet, turning with all the stiff precision of a soldier and then treading past the spot where he leaned against the edge of his desk.

"You can't do this. She'll make a laughingstock of you when this is all said and done."

"After today's performance, I suspect I already am."

"Nonsense. I'm sure you looked terribly heroic while saving a wealthy lady's overpriced hat."

Seb didn't bother to remind his sister that they were wealthy now too, and she could afford to buy as many ridiculous hats as she liked. It would be a futile argument. Give Pippa a hundred pounds and she'd probably spend it trying to assist those in need, only leaving a bit aside for a new tennis racket or fencing épée. She'd never given two minutes consideration to fashion, and he couldn't recall the last time he'd seen her wear anything beyond a practical straw hat to fend off the sun.

"I could care less about being a hero. We're doing this for Ollie and Harriet."

On this journey across the carpet she stopped near the window and crossed her arms, staring out through the fine gauze drapes at their quiet corner of Mayfair.

"Why does he insist on marrying her?"

Now it was his turn to keep still, to fight the urge to respond to the pained break in her voice and go to her. But even as a child Pippa refused coddling and comfort. She might shed a tear or two over a skinned knee or sulk about the loss of a game, but she'd push their mother away when she attempted a reassuring embrace, or turn from Father when he'd offer one of his truisms about loss and perseverance.

"He says he loves her." Seb uttered the words quickly, wishing for any way to mitigate his sister's pain.

"Ah, love." Pippa's shoulders lifted as she uttered an awful choked sound, a bitter semblance of laughter. "We should all believe in love, shouldn't we? Because that impulse covers all sins. Love is always true."

Beyond her infatuation with Ollie, as far as Seb knew, Pippa had never been in love. There'd been plenty of young men who indicated interest in her, but she'd either ignored their overtures or missed them entirely. Her interest in Ollie had become clear the previous year, if overlong gazes and sensitivity to their usual sibling-like banter was any indication. But she ignored Ollie as often as she spoke to him, and he seemed as oblivious to her feelings as she was to those of her besotted classmates at Cambridge.

Seb couldn't imagine where she'd developed such bitterness toward love and romance. A thought chilled him. He only knew one person more jaded about love, and he glimpsed a bit of the pathetic man's face in the mirror over the mantel. Had his own bitterness somehow infected Pippa? He thought he'd hid it well, buried his pain and carried on so that none of them truly imagined what had transpired between him and Alecia.

He didn't want bitterness and a lonely life for Pippa. Such a clever, accomplished young woman deserved to find happiness and never know the pain of betrayal and lost love.

"Pippa—"

"Do you intend to tell everyone you *love* Kitty Adderly?"

Horrible? Kat was a challenge, as her father had been quick to remind him, and her behavior at that first ball had been appalling, but there was a good deal more. Intelligence, determination, and a loyalty to her sister he couldn't help but admire.

"Until Oliver is married, yes."

"So you'll lie about love, and yet you think Oliver, who possesses as much constancy as feral cat, means it when he says he loves this marquess's daughter?"

She turned just as he began to approach her and held up her hands. "Can we stop for now, Seb?"

He hated the pain in her eyes, the white pallor of her skin. She looked like a haunted version of his lively sister, and he couldn't comfort her. Even if she allowed such emotional displays, he had no idea what he'd say. He believed in the power of love as little as she did, at least for himself. If Ollie thought he'd found his portion of happiness, it wasn't his place to question the young man's devotion to Kat's sister. But for himself, the prospect of giving his heart seemed laughable.

Seb wasn't certain there was anything left in him worth giving.

"They will be here in an hour, Pippa."

"Is Kitty coming? And Lady Harriet?"

"Ollie invited her."

"Very well." She wore the same expression he'd seen as a child when he'd bested her at a game of chess. Reticent concession, but something less than full-on defeat. If she loved Ollie and his determination to marry another woman broke her heart, she'd never let him, or anyone, see that agony. Seb thought back to the years after Alecia's betrayal and wondered if he'd managed to wear a poker face as well as Pippa.

"What if he changes his mind about her? If you tell these lies and woo a woman you don't even like, and Ollie fixes his admiration on another young lady, as he is wont to do? What then?"

Seb had no ready answer. But his lack of a response didn't bother him nearly as much as the presumption that he did not like Kat. Dislike wasn't there when he thought of her. In fact, the emotions she sparked in him were deeper, thornier, far beyond anything as simple as like or dislike. And that disturbed him most of all.

"You're certain she'll keep the secret until all is said and done?"

Kat whispered as Sebastian stood near her at the edge of his drawing room. Lord and Lady Clayborne engaged in conversation with Ollie while Harriet beamed at his side. Clayborne finally agreed to meet with Ollie in the afternoon, and no one could see the glowing smiles the young couple had been wearing since their arrival at Wrexford House and doubt the result of that meeting.

"Pippa can be trusted."

"How did she take the news?"

Seb tried not to watch the drawing room door for his sister's entrance. She'd left him standing in the middle of his study, midsentence, as he fumbled over explaining his complicated feelings for Kat. He wasn't certain Pippa would join them for dinner at all.

"She's unwell this evening."

Kat turned to face him. "You asked me to trust you once. Why not tell me the truth?"

He took a deep breath to explain, though revealing Pippa's affection for Ollie wasn't an option. Not only would it complicate everyone's plans, but his sister's feelings were her own.

"We didn't start well, your sister and I. Perhaps I frightened her."

Frightened? Pippa? As a child she'd only begged for a retelling of the most gruesome of fairy tales and now collected volumes of Sheridan Le Fanu and Wilkie Collins's ghost stories for her nighttime reading.

"Don't look at me like that, Sebastian. I meant no harm. I merely—"

The drawing room door swung open and Lady Harriet and her mother stood, perhaps thinking it was the butler calling them into the dining room. But it was Pippa. She wore a pasted-on smile, and Seb's neck itched at the thought of what she might be feeling, the dilemma he could not fix for her.

Before he could lead her over, Kat approached his sister and whispered some sentiment amusing enough to make her smile, or at least feign it convincingly. Kat took Pippa's arm and drew her to a corner of the room. Seeing the two clever women together with heads bent did nothing to settle his nerves.

A few minutes later, Pippa approached. "She's good

at this." Though Lady Harriet had smiled at Pippa as she crossed the room and indicated a seat next to her, his sister offered Kat's sister a pleasant smile and planted herself at his side instead.

"Who's good at what?" Seb was busy watching Ollie's interaction with Lord Clayborne. The older man gave little away, and he hoped Ollie didn't overwhelm the girl's parents with his exuberance.

"Lady Katherine is good at convincing people to like her. What if Lady Harriet is as false as her sister?"

"As you pointed out in my study, I am lying as well. We're not enjoying this." For the most part, it had been miserable. He hated lying, and the interrogation with Clayborne had been brutal. But he glanced up at Kat as he spoke, and he admitted, at least to himself, that it hadn't all been misery. "And as for Harriet, I know her as little as you do. But I do know Oliver. He's never shown this sort of devotion to any woman."

"Then I shall be happy for him." Seb suspected Pippa had no idea the words came out through clenched teeth. He leaned an inch closer but didn't reach for her. She blew out a breath, and then inhaled deeply. Peeking at her out of the corner of his eye, he saw a tear glistening on her cheek.

He considered offering his handkerchief, but the danger of drawing attention to her distress wasn't worth the gesture. She'd swiped away the evidence of her heartache before he'd finished the thought.

When the butler called them into the dining room a

few moments later, she bolted from his side. Kat maneuvered across the room and reached for his arm.

"Thank you for coming this evening." Trite words, though he meant them sincerely. Wrexford House took a bit less getting used to than Roxbury, but they'd yet to entertain any guests, and his parents had taught them that guests enliven any home.

"Of course." She lifted her shoulders and her turquoise dress rustled. "We'll be family when all is said and done. Might as well know what we're up against now."

He and Pippa and Kat made quite a trio. Each as cynical about love and happy futures as the other in their own way.

"I think I'm on the road toward making amends with your sister. I've invited her to go hat shopping with me, if that suits you."

"The feathered one couldn't be salvaged?" He wasn't sad to hear the news.

"Yours was a valiant effort. But no."

Dipping his shoulders, he tried for a slightly mournful expression. Whatever he thought of the monstrosity, Kat had adored the thing.

"Stop it," she whispered as she tightened her grip on his arm.

"What?"

"You really are a terrible liar. Are you trying for sorrow over my hat's demise?"

"I'm trying for polite." He really had done his best to save the bit of feathered velvet.

"Well, stop it. I assure you the next one will have feathers too."

"I have no doubt." He imagined she'd go for something grander and with bigger feathers just to see his reaction.

The Wrexford House staff knew how to impress dinner guests. The table glowed with spring flower arrangements positioned amid sparkling crystal stemware, a glinting silver service, and gilt-edged porcelain plates bearing an extraordinary Moorish pattern of crimson, gold, and cerulean blue. The butler informed Seb they'd been specially commissioned by the late duke after a visit to Spain.

Beyond the table itself, however, the seating arrangement posed the potential for disaster. For some reason, Ollie's card placed him with Harriet by his side and directly across from Pippa. She wouldn't meet his gaze but held her head up high as if she meant to endure the evening, no matter what transpired.

Seb took his place at the head of the table, with Kat to his right. Her father had been placed at the other end of the table. Seb hadn't requested that the man be seated farther away from him than any other guest, but he wasn't displeased with the turn of events.

They'd barely begun sipping their soup when Ollie sprang up from his chair, wineglass held high.

"I must say thank you, Lord Clayborne, for considering my request to marry your daughter. I know the value of family, having lost my own. I will be forever grateful to the Fennicks for taking me in, but I am so looking forward to gaining a new family, and a beautiful bride. Let us all raise a toast to Harriet."

Perhaps the boy would be a fine barrister after all. Seb couldn't deny he had a way with words. And judging by the ladies around the table dabbing kerchiefs to their eyes, a way of provoking emotions too.

After they'd all lifted their glasses and swallowed a drink for Harriet, Kat whispered between spoonfuls of bouillabaisse.

"How are you going to top that?"

"Must I?"

His answer came in the form a dull pain pulsing up his shin where she tapped him with her pointy-toed shoe.

Seb stood, dropped his napkin on the edge of his soup bowl, and nearly knocked over his water glass. It got him everyone's attention and he lifted his wineglass in the air at the precise moment his mouth went dry. He took a sip of wine and raised his glass again.

"I echo Oliver's sentiments, and I . . ." *Am a complete and utter fraud.*

Kat cleared her throat, a surprisingly dainty sound that drew his gaze. She managed to convey camaraderie and sympathy in a single look, and it suddenly mattered much less whether he was making a fool of himself or not. He didn't have to tell a lie to raise a glass to her. Their connection had begun on an odd premise, but he couldn't deny that she was the most appealing woman he'd met in years. If they'd become acquainted on some other footing, in different circumstances, when he still believed in love and possibilities, perhaps . . .

Clayborne cleared his throat, a drawn-out awkward sound, with none of the grace his daughter had managed.

"Yes, yes, a toast to Katherine. Finally a bride-to-be. We doubted the day would ever come. Many thanks for taking her off my hands, Wrexford. My suffering shall now be yours." He raised his wineglass halfheartedly and then gulped the contents in one swallow.

He was the only one who drank. The rest around the table still held their glasses aloft or had set them down again. None could miss his snide tone or the insult to his daughter.

Seb glanced at Kat again, but she'd turned her attention to studying the pattern on her dinner plate. She deserved more than her father's dismissal. Seb feared she'd experienced it far too often. Any man who'd truly won her hand in marriage wouldn't stand for it.

"We can do better than that, surely, my lord."

Her gaze locked on his and words welled up faster than he could raise his guard or make an effort to temper the emotion in his tone. "To the most intriguing woman I have ever met."

Seb wouldn't take back the words, even if he could. Intrigue was only the edge of what he felt for her, and he'd happily admit it if he could avoid examining the rest. His admission earned him a glance of surprise, and he relished the tremulous grin just tempting the corners of her mouth too much to regret a word of it.

"High praise for my daughter, Your Grace, though I suspect you're acquainted with few women for comparison. There can't have been many to catch your eye at Cambridge."

Clayborne's false joviality wasn't enough to cover the pointed dismissal of his daughter.

Pippa cut in the moment he'd finished speaking. "The number of women at Cambridge might surprise you, my lord." She turned her gaze to Kat before continuing. "My brother knows his mind, and he never offers praise lightly."

A moment of kinship passed between Kat and his sister, and the sight of it might have pleased Seb if Clayborne's cruelty hadn't already deadened his appetite. More than dishonesty and scheming, he loathed a bully. Ollie had been small for his age until a recent growth spurt, and Seb had spent their school years defending him. But fists and brute strength were nothing to the cleverer sort of bully who bludgeoned with words.

Sitting through the rest of the meal's courses was only tolerable because of the lively conversation between the ladies over their favorite art at the South Kensington Museum. Pippa preferred portraits of thinkers, scientists, both men and women, and Kat expressed a fondness for art that told a story, like the vivid landscapes of Mr. Turner and the bold realism of the Pre-Raphaelite Brotherhood. Harriet joined the conversation at the last moment to declare the portrait of Lord Byron her favorite, and though she didn't expound on her choice, all of the ladies got a far-off wistful look in their eyes and none raised a single objection.

Lord Clayborne was too far away to require Seb to

engage him in conversation, and the man seemed, as he had in his study, more content to observe than offer any more barbs to injure his daughter. Seb couldn't muster an ounce of disappointment when Lord and Lady Clayborne insisted on departing shortly after the meal rather than withdrawing for after-dinner conversation. Better yet, they allowed Harriet and Kat to remain, promising to send the carriage back to retrieve them.

"When are you going to show me *your* conservatory?" Kat asked as they sat together on the drawing room settee.

"I'm afraid we don't have one at Wrexford House."

"For an intelligent man, you do have a tendency to be quite literal. I meant the place where you escape. You found my haven. Now I want to see yours."

Seb didn't think she intended the request to be seductive, to sound like a siren's call, but his body responded as if she did, thrumming with barely suppressed energy. It was hunger too long unsated, desire too long denied. He flexed his fingers, wishing they were pressed against her skin.

It was precisely the wrong moment to lead her to a room where they'd be alone, where no one would see if he breached the line of propriety.

But she tilted her head as she waited for him to respond, and her emerald eyes glittered as she scanned his face, no doubt reading each illicit thought that crossed his mind. The woman was an irresistible provocation.

"Come with me."

## Chapter Fourteen

"COME WITH ME." He demanded more than asked, and it sent an odd tremor skittering across Kitty's skin.

No man commanded her. Only her father tried, and she'd been bucking his control most of her life. She should have loathed Sebastian's tone of command, but she didn't. She loved the strength of his much larger hand enclosing her own, the heat of his palm, and the tickle of his fingers as he tugged her along. He'd snatched her away from Lady Stamford's ballroom like this, guiding her out into the garden. She'd done the persuading that night, but caught against the warm wall of his chest, he could have convinced her too. Convinced her to accept more than a fleeting kiss if they hadn't been distracted by this silly ruse between them.

"This is where I retreat each time I enter Wrexford House."

When he turned up the gaslight and lit the study,

Kitty could easily picture him behind the massive cherrywood desk or bent over the table covered with books and papers and scientific gadgets she struggled to identify. The dark blue wallpaper suited him, and the shelves of books matched the image she had of a devoted scholar. Then she remembered how recently he'd inherited his title and begun living in the late duke's residences. Perhaps the books lining these shelves came with the house, and the late duke had favored literature over science. Perhaps they didn't reflect Sebastian's taste at all. How strange it must be to step into another's life. He achieved it with more grace than she suspected she'd manage.

"What's all that?" Pointing to the cluttered table in the center of the room, she suddenly wished she'd spent more of her education on scientific study and less time on deportment and acquiring bland ladylike skills.

"The makings of a paper for the Mathematical Society. Believe it or not, all of that boils down to a few pages that will take me an hour to present and be as quickly forgotten."

She might find the topic of his paper beyond the limits of the basic math she'd learned from her governess, but she understood devotion to a beloved task.

"I spend months tending a plant for a few glorious blooms. They're well worth the effort."

She cast a wary glance at his face. If her father could be trusted as a guide, a man's pride was easily offended, especially when it came to his life's work. Perhaps his study of mathematics and her efforts to bring the family conservatory to life wasn't the most apt comparison. But Sebastian didn't look offended.

He nodded, his eyes crinkling around the edges. "Yes, I imagine they are. Though I'm not sure anyone will say the same of my paper."

Kitty blinked, then again, before narrowing her eyes. He continually surprised her. As if he worked at overturning all of her expectations. Could any man be so affable, or look so at ease pretending to be, if that's what he was doing?

"Is that feigned humility, Your Grace, or are you truly so self-effacing?"

Crossing his arms, he tipped his chin and studied the ceiling as if her question required thorough consideration. It was a tactic she sometimes used with her father to avoid his chess game altogether. But she and Sebastian were locked in his study. He couldn't escape her questions or her curiosity about his true nature.

"Perhaps a bit of both?"

"So you are capable of prevarication after all."

"I prefer to think of it as moderation. No man should be all one thing or the other. You have to allow room for gray."

The duke couldn't have been more unlike her father. He turned Papa's philosophies on end.

"My father would say otherwise."

"I suspect your father and I will often disagree."

"That's something to look forward to."

She stepped over to inspect his scientific equipment and a flash drew her eye. He stood, arms still crossed,

leaning on the edge of his desk, a smile lifting his handsome face. Men smiled at her all the time, but not like
this. It wasn't a lascivious grin or even one meant to
charm. His look signaled contentment, pleasure, that he
enjoyed her company and whatever she'd just said. She
couldn't recall at the moment. His smile set her belly fluttering and brightened the room as effectively as it light-
ened her mood. Even the irritation over Papa's sarcasm at
dinner melted away.

"You should smile more often, Sebastian."

Kat bit her lip and he immediately stopped smiling,
shooting her a guilty look, as if he'd been caught enjoying himself when she'd banned merriment of any kind.
Is that what he thought of her? She'd spent years telling
herself she feigned pleasure well, that she look amused
when a lady should, but never too often. But honest and
unfettered laughter was a rare indulgence, and smiles like
his, pure and artless, never came easily for her. She stifled
them or tried to smile naturally and then found that too
much thinking drained the pleasure out of it all together.

Sebastian saw more, past the polite grins and inane
conversation she'd perfected. The notion of him seeing
beyond her façade frightened and thrilled her. He'd find
fault behind her walls, surely. Such a decent man would
disdain all the pettiness and the imperfection she kept
hidden from view, but at least he would see her. Truly see
her. She wanted him to. Stark honesty had never seemed
possible with any man, but Sebastian was a different sort
than she'd ever expected to meet.

She'd watched him too long. One of his eyebrows

lifted and he no doubt wondered why she stood gaping at him like a fool. She turned away, desperate for any sight as appealing as his eyes. His cluttered table begged for attention, the glass and metal of various gadgets glinted in the light and books lay open, causing her to wonder why that particular page caught his eye. She approached the table and reached out to touch the one object with which she was familiar.

"I had a telescope once." His was far grander than the child's version she'd treasured, but the excitement of potential discovery, what she might see through its far-reaching eye, was as potent as when she was a girl. The instrument sat in a stand on the table, too far from a window where she might gaze up into London's night sky.

"Shall we move it over to the window?"

He read her mind, and understood her eagerness. She saw it reflected in his face, sensed it in his movements as he rushed around her to arrange a wooden structure in front of the long study window and then lifted the telescope onto the scaffold. When it was secured, he glanced at her over his shoulder.

"Are you going to come and have a look?"

Not only did he offer her a look, but he refrained from taking a glimpse himself first. Another mark of chivalry and restraint she couldn't help but admire.

Leaning in front of him, she gazed through the eyepiece and saw beauty, a sapphire blanket encrusted with diamonds. A bittersweet pang racked her body, a hollowness gaped in her chest, and a silly tear welled at the corner of her eye. She'd missed this.

She sensed him behind her, but he kept silent, allowing her to look her fill. Only when she lifted her head, swallowing down the irritating tear, did he speak, his voice low and gentle.

"What happened to it?"

Talking about the incident would bring back the memory, and then she'd lose her battle with that tear. But she couldn't resist the tenderness in his gaze, the curiosity in his tone.

"My father took it away."

The look of disgust flashed so quickly, she might have missed if she hadn't been staring at him again.

"Why would he do such a thing?"

None of it had made sense to her then, though now she understood her father's motives. But knowing why he did it, even with years of distance, did not erase her memory of the pain. So many of his actions came down to his disappointment in her. She'd never been what he wished—too tall, too opinionated, too boyish, too silly. She never succeeded at impressing him, never succeeded at pleasing him, but she'd exceeded at disappointing him. Could she count that a victory?

"Would you believe I was a bit of a tomboy? At first I think he enjoyed having a child who wished to learn to fish and ride and shoot. But then he didn't. He insisted I give up my boyish pursuits."

The duke managed to look appealing, even with a frown twisting his features.

"Curiosity about the heavens and the celestial bodies is a boyish pursuit? Astronomy is set aside for men?"

His voice boomed off the walls of his study and echoed through her.

"In his mind, yes. He wished for me to behave like a lady."

"There is no doubt you're that."

"My father has doubts."

He lifted a hand and ran it through his hair before moving toward her. A zing of anticipation dipped into disappointment when he didn't reach for her. Apparently, he wanted to have a look too. He leaned down to press his eye to the telescope.

"I don't." Despite the low timbre of his voice, the two words rang in her ears.

After moving the telescope a fraction to the left, he lifted a hand to urge her over.

"Have a look."

The patterns emerged the longer she looked.

"Ursa Major." Names came back to her, and she recalled the sky map she'd treasured and traced with her finger over and over. "And Orion's Belt!"

"You remember the constellations." She didn't look up at him, but she could hear the smile in Sebastian's tone.

"It's all coming back to me. Oh, and there's Cassiopeia. I named my cat Cassiopeia."

"Did you?"

"Mmm. I struggled to spell the word, but I loved the sound of it."

He stepped closer, his boots just brushing the edge of her skirt. In the quiet, her gaze focused far into the night sky, all of her other senses sharpened. She could hear him breathing, faster as he took another step, and savored his clean masculine scent. Bergamot and juniper, and something deeper and woodsy. Sandalwood, perhaps.

"Kat?"

His leg pressed against hers, and his breath had gone ragged.

"I . . . need to kiss you."

Relief rushed her, as if someone had cut her from her corset or smashed a lock in the center of her chest.

She turned to take the kiss she'd wanted from that first moment when he'd chastised her during Mama's ball.

He didn't wait for her to turn. He pressed his body to hers from behind and dipped his head to kiss the slope where her shoulder met her neck. She'd never realized the spot was linked directly to her knees, but they buckled the minute he touched her skin with the heated tip of his tongue.

Reaching an arm around, he braced her body against his. A bulwark of tall firm male warmed her back and his long legs pressed into the folds of her skirt. She stopped resisting and let herself lean on him, into him, testing the feel of allowing a man to hold her up.

"You smell of lavender tonight. And vanilla."

His voice turned raw, shaky, and she turned in his arms to face him.

"I didn't eat dinner. Nothing seemed as appealing as what you might taste like. I sat through the whole meal craving lavender scones."

Suitors had compared her to Aphrodite or Helen of

Troy, called her a goddess or an angel and all manner of ridiculous names, but none had compared her to a baked good. Kitty was on the cusp of protesting when he stilled her with a touch. His hands trembled when he caressed her face, and he met her gaze for a long agonizing moment before pressing a kiss to the corner of her mouth.

She protested with a little cry of frustration.

An almost kiss wasn't enough. She needed more.

Reaching her hand up to clasp his, she guided his palm to her neckline and pressed it to her chest. She wanted him to feel the wild thump of her heart, to know that whatever affected him, she felt it too. Her hands weren't quivering like his, but the rest of her body was.

"Are you frightened?" He whispered the words, his breath warming her skin.

"No." She couldn't be afraid with him close. His nearness blotted out her fears, and it inspired something else—a yearning so strange and new it left her breathless. Anticipation welled up, as if she was just on the cusp, teetering on the edge, and she craved the next step.

"Are you?" It could be dangerous to ask a man about his fears. Would any man admit them?

"A bit." Apparently this one would.

She studied his eyes, burning with a kind of inner glow, and his mouth, tipping a bit at each edge as if he barely held back a smile. As she watched him, he moved his hand, slipping down, skimming the edge of her chemise, tugging until his fingertips dipped inside her corset.

She'd never allowed a man such liberties, and yet it wasn't enough with Sebastian. She wanted to give him more. Their hands tangled when she reached up to slip the ribbon on her chemise, and he mistook her, drawing back as if she'd scorched him.

"No, please." He snapped his head up when she begged, tilting it as if uncertain he'd heard her. In this moment, with her body drawn taut as a bow, she didn't mind repeating herself. "Please. I don't wish for you to stop."

The stiff line of his shoulders eased before he stepped forward again and reached for her, pressing her backside against the edge of his desk, and, finally, easing his mouth onto hers. Supple, warm, his lips teased at hers, coaxing her to feel—not think, not worry—just feel. He used his much larger frame to surround her, to shelter her. She'd never been so close to any man, and yet it wasn't close enough. Leaning into him, so near his heartbeat reverberated against her chest, she cursed all the layers of fabric between them.

He kissed her gently at first, tentatively, but when she grasped his arm, tugging him an inch closer, her breasts dragging against his waistcoat, he gave her more. Emitting a delicious moan, he caressed her lips with his, exploring her, teasing and tasting her languorously, as if they had hours for this kiss and the night would stretch out endlessly, but only for them. Only for this moment. When he lifted his head and they both struggled to catch their breath, the haze of pleasure cleared enough for Kitty to recall that they weren't truly alone in the house. Her sister and his were in the drawing room, no doubt wondering what had delayed them in his study.

"Do you think we should go back?"

"I'm trying *not* to think."

"What would happen if you did? Regret?"

"No, Kat." He drew back and lowered his chin, assessing her. "And you? What will you think of all of this in the light of day?"

Her fingers found the button of his evening shirt, the first one above his waistcoat, and she fondled it, memorizing its shape and anchoring her fingertips behind it as if a tug might bring his mouth down on hers again.

She'd never found it so difficult to meet a man's gaze as she did now, when he might see all the unladylike hunger brimming inside.

"I suspect I'll wish you'd kissed me more and I'd talked less." She meant the words as a hint as much as a confession, and hoped he'd kiss her once more before they settled their clothes and tamed their urges prior to rejoining the others.

He traced the edge of her bottom lip with his forefinger.

"You should talk as often as you like, and not hold back. And as for kissing . . ." He swept his fingers up across her cheek and she felt the stroke as if he'd touched her lower, down her neck, slipping down her middle, and settling with a tantalizing heat between her thighs. "I'm happy to oblige."

He pressed his mouth to hers and waited, tempting her but letting her take the lead. Easing up her toes, she balanced by leaning into him, and took her turn exploring, marveling at the intimacy that came so easily with a man she knew so little. She'd wanted him to touch her from the first, and being in his arms felt as if the space had been made for her.

When she touched her tongue to his, he moaned into her mouth, and clasped her tighter, nearly lifting her off her feet.

*Too much.* The thought cut in, like the chime of an enormous bell. Too much sensation. Too much pleasure.

She pushed at his chest to create distance between them. Her own chest hummed. Her whole body burned, oversensitive and pulsing, the feelings he stoked in her too much to contain.

And none of it was real. They were actors fooled by their own play.

She finally caught her breath enough to speak. "I don't want you to oblige me, Sebastian. Don't ever kiss me out of obligation."

"You know that's not what I meant."

"Do I? How do I know? We've known each a week." He may sometimes see past her artifice, but he wasn't familiar enough to know that she thought too much about every word she spoke, every expression that crossed her face. Or that nearly every choice she'd made in her life had more to do with spiting her father than finding her own happiness. "We don't truly know each other at all, Your Grace."

Soon they'd part ways, and she might hate herself for this fragile, fleeting moment when she wished for more.

Extracting herself from his embrace was easy. He lifted his hands the instant she pulled away. But walking out the door was harder, and the composure she'd perfected, the elegant walk Mama had taught her, the neutral expression that gave nothing away—all of it was gone. As if she'd been stripped of her armor during those precious minutes in Sebastian's study, and none of it would ever fit properly again.

## Chapter Fifteen

"I won't wear that." Kat continued shaking her head as he dropped the cloth on the seat beside him. He didn't think she'd willingly let him use it to cover her eyes, but he wanted to keep their destination a secret and thought it worth a try.

"Then you'll have to put your hand over your eyes for the next few minutes. We're almost there."

"We've been on this train for nearly an hour."

He knew it all too well. Seb's resolve not to repeat the madness in his study wavered the moment they stepped into the enclosed first-class train carriage and her fresh floral scent surrounded him. He'd asked the name of the fragrance and she'd gone on about *Convallaria,* also called lily of the valley, describing its tiny white bellflowers so lovingly that he grew as eager to see the flower itself as to draw near Kat and get a deeper whiff of its perfume from her skin.

He'd been sitting across from her for nearly an hour, the belled edge of her skirt brushing against his legs, and attempting to make conversation while his mind indulged in cataloging her slopes and curves and angles. Proximity to Kat was necessary until they could celebrate Ollie and Hattie's marriage, but he had to find a way to keep his hands, and the rest of his body, to himself.

He'd vowed to be levelheaded in her company, but as she pouted about covering her eyes, he thought only of tracing the shapely bow of her upper lip with his tongue.

"Can't I simply promise not to look out the window?" She answered her own question by lowering her hand from her eyes and glancing through the glass. Turning back to glare at him, she huffed out a frustrated sigh and lifted her arm to cover the upper half of her face again.

"You don't enjoy surprises, I take it."

"I hate them. Papa says only a fool allows himself to be taken by surprise. Clever men are always two steps ahead."

"And you agree with him?"

Silence told him she didn't. The man's beliefs were there, ready to spill from her tongue, no doubt imprinted in her mind, and yet Seb suspected she disagreed with most of what her father believed. He hoped she at least disagreed with the man's tendency to dismiss *her* worth.

"He's my father."

And a father's admonitions—right or wrong—stayed with you, shaping you and your behavior, like it or not. Didn't his own inner compass sound like his father as often as not? Reginald Fennick had been a titan in his fields, admired by those he met and taught, a man who enriched the lives of those around him. From what he'd seen of Kat's father, the man brought no comfort. He might be intelligent and a brilliant politician, but if he poisoned the air each time he spoke, what must it be like for Kat to have his voice ever in her head?

"Would you like a hint about where we're going?"

"I'd like to put my hand down." She heaved a frustrated sigh but didn't lower her arm. "But, yes, I shall settle for a hint." Her cheeks went a delicious shade of peach when she was irritated.

"Very well. I suspect you've been there before."

"Then it won't be much of a surprise." She even managed to look fetching while complaining.

"Perhaps, but I think you'll enjoy it nonetheless."

She slumped against the seat, dipping her shoulders, and her corset pressed in, forcing her breasts up, offering him an enticing view of creamy flesh threatening to spill over her neckline.

Damn his urges and his eyes and all the blood rushing to his groin. He'd denied himself female company for too long. Somewhere beyond the haze of lust and desire and all of the rest of what Kat sparked in him, he'd forgotten what the pleasure of her company was truly about. They were playing the besotted couple to aid Ollie and Harriet.

He clenched his fists, gripping the seat on each side of his thighs. He had to reclaim the cool head and chilled heart he'd been quite content with for years.

He couldn't take advantage of the situation between them. Society might turn its eye on a few liberties between a man and his betrothed, but that intimacy didn't truly exist between them. Attraction hadn't led them to this moment, cloistered together in a train car. Necessity and practically had. Now he simply had to find a way to tell his body that.

"I hope it's a very public place." That was the practical Lady Katherine speaking, and she was right to worry about whether this outing would serve its function to allow them to be seen about town as an engaged couple. He was grateful one of them could keep a clear head.

"It is. I do remember why we're doing all of this." He did, truly, if he concentrated hard enough. Ollie. Lady Harriet. Young love. A blissful future. All those prospects that were lost for him now.

"Good." She sighed again, and he tried to look anywhere but at her bosom. Her mouth. No. Not there either. Her hand encased in white dainty lace. No. The empty expanse of the railcar's plush bench seat beside her seemed a safe spot to cast his gaze, but the block of dark velvet upholstery was only interesting because of the way her hip curved against it.

"We really should be quick about this outing and then find a place where we might talk and plan. I've brought a list of all of the preparations I've begun and what's yet to be done."

She liked her lists, and he admired the orderly way her mind worked. He liked the way she conducted herself— self-possessed and graceful. And he understood the way she loved her sister, her need to ensure her sibling's happiness, even if he'd have preferred helping Ollie and

Harriet via some means that did not involve the falsely constructed engagement between them.

All this artifice because of one pompous, stubborn man. When it was done, and the young couple went off to begin their life together, Seb quite liked the notion of throttling the Marquess of Clayborne, or at least never laying eyes on the man again.

Gazing out the window, he noticed a sign indicating they'd soon arrive at their destination.

"We're here." And thank God for it. He needed to walk and get blood pumping in his limbs, to see fascinating plants and flowers, anything that might distract him and allow his mind to focus anywhere but on Kat.

"Can I look now?"

He could have said *yes* and kept his hands to himself. But resolve failed him completely. Reaching up, he clasped her wrist, and pulled her hand down to her lap.

Rather than turning to gaze out the window, she sat still and watched him, until he realized he wasn't simply holding her wrist but stroking the expanse of skin above her glove.

He released her, flexing his tingling fingers, and settled back in his seat as the train came to a stop.

"We're in Richmond. At the Kew Bridge train station." She fisted her hand against her mouth as her eyes went wide. Then she blinked and blinked again, her thick tip-tilted lashes fluttering against her cheek. "You're wrong, Sebastian. I haven't been here before." She gulped. "But I've always wanted to visit the Royal Botanical Gardens. What a perfect surprise."

A perfect surprise for the woman who purported to hate them. The hint of a smile curving her mouth and the astounding admission that he'd managed to please her despite her determination not to be pleased hit him in the center of his chest with a burst of warmth, spreading out to allow him to unfurl his fingers where he clenched the edge of his seat again.

She stepped from the train without waiting for him to assist her and bound forward so quickly he lost her in the sea of disembarking passengers. He found her at the entrance to the gardens, bouncing on her heels.

"Where shall we start?" He'd never been to Kew Gardens either and relished the notion that they'd be first-time explorers together.

"At the beginning, of course." A pucker appeared between her brows. "I understand the gardens are quite extensive. It could take much of the day."

Did she truly think he considered time spent with her a burden? He couldn't have endured more than ten minutes at each of the balls he'd attended without her presence to lure him into staying. And the anxious dread he'd felt since taking on a dukedom had suddenly turned to an eagerness for each day's encounter with her.

"Then lead on, my lady."

She shot him a look at his use of her honorific. He'd said the words before, but after last night, after holding and kissing her, the meaning had changed. *My lady.* His alone. For a fraction, just a sliver of a moment, he allowed himself to imagine it. That he could call this strong, clever, beautiful woman his partner, his lover, his future.

The notion had him trembling as much as touching her had.

*No.* He forced the images from his mind and focused on the ground under his feet and the blue firmament above. No matter what he wanted, no matter how these moments with her might haunt him when their scheme came to an end, no matter how she provoked him—body and mind—he had nothing to offer her. She deserved more than an embittered man still haunted by the past.

As they walked, every single item seemed to thrill Kat, though she turned back to check on him often. He'd fix his gaze on a random plant, so she wouldn't realize he'd been studying her reactions rather than the impressive flora around them. Many of the flowers weren't yet in bloom and a pair of sisters who'd come in just behind them insisted June was the best month to visit. But nothing, not the over-chatty sisters, nor the flowers still cocooned in bud, daunted Kat's enjoyment. He noticed that she bit her lip each time a smile curved her mouth, as if she wasn't allowed such excessive enthusiasm. He suspected her father had some saying stuck in her head, reminding her to never to enjoy anything too much.

Seb favored the rock garden, admiring the tenacity of the vines and creeping plants clinging to stony structures, embracing jagged boulders, and beautifying the plainest of stones. Kat crouched down, drawing disapproving moues from the visiting sisters, and pointed to a patch of green in the shade of a craggy gray stone. Bright pink flowers with hot yellow centers, as tiny as teardrops, dotted the clumps of green plant.

"Beautiful." And he didn't just mean the flowers. The strong breeze had loosened the pins in Kat's hair, a few strands lashing against her cheeks, and she'd dirtied the hem of her white and black striped gown to show him a bit of beauty in the darkness.

She tilted her face toward him and he offered a hand to help her up, barely resisting the urge to touch his fingers to the honey strands whipping around her face.

"Thank you." She grinned but turned her gaze from his.

Awkwardness loomed between them now, not unlike the elderly sisters who'd shadowed them from the moment they entered the gardens. Their presence was a matter of chance, but the awkwardness with Kat was his doing. He had given into impulse in his study, to his own needs too long ignored, and he'd touched her as he'd wanted to from the moment he'd seen her glittering at the edge of her mother's ballroom.

She'd been right to put an end to it last night, and his choice of an outing today was meant to be an offering of sorts, a means of making peace between them.

"You never know when you'll find color in a shady spot. Many flowers prefer a bit less sunny attention." She took in the flowers shooting up from a winding watercourse along the path but kept turning her gaze back to the tiny cup-shaped pink-gold flowers hugging the rock.

"Is it fair for them to spend their days hidden by a broken lump of stone where few will even notice them?"

She lifted a hand to shade her eyes from the sunlight and gazed up at him.

"I don't think they'd wish to be anywhere else. That rock needs a bit of cheering, and perhaps they only care to be seen by those who'd bother to take a closer look."

He pressed his lips together to resist smiling like a fool. Kat seemed to have a terrible habit of inspiring smiles. He'd smiled more in the past week than he had in years.

The sisters had gotten lost somewhere behind them, and he and Kat took a bend in the path into an exotic corner of water running over a block of stone and vines bearing purple flowers. Kat grasped his arm and a current of sensation rushed through him, all the way to his toes.

"Look! *Passiflora incarnata.*" She rushed over to stand before the extraordinary flowers and then turned back as if she intended to introduce him. "The passion-flower."

The flowers were strange and beautiful, a vibrant shade of purple with curling sprigs, like tendrils of corkscrew hair, of the same shade surrounding the bloom.

Kat's face had gone soft, awestruck, and he watched her eyes dance over every aspect of the plant as if she wanted to memorize its color and shape. The flower's sweet spicy scent tickled his nose, but Kat dipped her head and closed her eyes to breathe it in.

She reached down to work the glove off her right hand and lifted it tremulously, looking back at him, her fingers an inch from one of the blooms. "Just one touch?"

Not waiting for the permission she didn't truly need, she reached out to gently stroke the edge of the flower.

One touch seemed enough, and she clasped her hand tight as if she could capture the memory in her palm.

"So beautiful."

"Yes." He saw the moment of realization. The instant she recognized that he wasn't referring to the plant but to her. That he had to touch her. That he was going to kiss her.

She stepped toward him, toe to toe, and tipped her face into the sun to gaze at him. He lowered his head to offer her shade and draw near enough to study the shards of gold in her eyes, the sable spikes of her lashes, and the constellation of pale freckles across her nose and cheeks.

Then he kissed her, not a hurried press of his mouth against hers, but a slow savoring. Too long and lush a kiss for the public space they were in, and not nearly enough to sate his hunger for the taste of her.

He liked the dazed look in her eyes when he finally lifted his head, and he couldn't resist touching the soft curve of her cheek. But he pulled back after a single stroke. If he continued touching her, he'd continue kissing her, and all of his resolve after their last encounter had already been shattered.

Glancing over his shoulder, Seb half expected to find the two disapproving sisters wagging their fingers at him, but there were three individuals in view. Two women with a boy between them. All of them were turned in his and Kat's direction, as if they'd been watching their intimate display.

Wonderful. The idea of these outings was for them to be seen, not to create a scandal.

He braced a hand over his brow to block the sun and get a better look, and shivered. His stomach plummeted to his feet and he felt seasick.

The trio began walking toward them, and there could be no mistake. His aunt and Alecia stared at him as they approached.

"Kat, excuse me a moment."

Her hand gripped his wrist.

"If you intend to speak to them, I'm going with you."

His wish to keep her out of the ugliness with Alecia warred with his desire to have Kat by his side, but she didn't allow time for his inner battle. She slid her hand down and clasped his before beginning a determined march toward his aunt and former lover.

"Lady Stamford, how nice to see you, and you, Lady Naughton. Such a lovely day for a walk through the prettiest garden in London."

Both ladies agreed with Kat's assessment and then turned their gazes toward Seb. The boy positioned himself near Alecia but seemed more interested in the greenery than the adults' conversation. Naughton's son was a mirror image of his mother—black hair contrasting with pale-hued eyes. At least he'd been spared his father's weak chin and overlarge head.

Seb caught his aunt's eye as Alecia and Kat carried on a conversation of inane questions and practiced answers.

His aunt took two steps to her left and tipped her head to encourage him to join her. "Do look at this unusual vine, Sebastian."

Before he could ask any of the half-dozen questions burning his throat, she leaned toward him, balancing gloved palms on her upturned lace parasol.

"I see questions in your gaze, my dear. Pay me a visit tomorrow and you'll have your answers."

## Chapter Sixteen

THE MYSTERY OF why his aunt invited Alecia to her ball and spent the next day promenading with her in the Royal Botanical Gardens were the questions that had kept Seb up most of the night.

An acquaintance between the women was unexpected, but Alecia's husband held a minor position in the government. Perhaps Lord and Lady Naughton were popular among London social circles.

He still shivered at the memory of looking up from kissing Kat to find his aunt and Alecia on his heels. Between the letters he'd destroyed and Alecia's tendency to pop up where he least expected to find her, he felt hunted, pursued. Irony of ironies, by the woman he'd once pursued to the point of forfeiting every bit of his peace of mind.

He spun the paradox in his mind as he waited for his aunt to join him in her drawing room. Tapping his fingers on the arm of his chair, he studied a painting of a blond country girl walking through a meadow. The artist had achieved a fine composition, with a golden mean sort of proportionality. The female figure in the center looked back at the viewer over her shoulder, a surprisingly seductive pose for such a wholesome subject, and the line of her neck and shade of her hair reminded him of Kat.

A pang of longing—for the sight and scent of her, to hear her voice saying something impertinent and clever—struck him as his aunt swept into the drawing room with a maid bearing a tea tray following in her wake.

"Where should we begin?"

*At the beginning, of course.* Kat's words from yesterday's outing at the Botanical Gardens rang in his mind.

"How long have you been acquainted with Lady Naughton?"

His aunt took a sip of her tea before looking at him square. "You needn't be quite so polite, my dear. Ask me what you truly wish to know."

Seb frowned. So perhaps there was more than a polite acquaintance between the women. He suspected he didn't know enough of the truth to ask the right questions.

"I'm content to start with how long you've known her."

She sighed, clearly disappointed. "Not long. She approached me at a dinner party a few months ago."

"A few months ago? Or was it two months ago? After I inherited my cousin's dukedom."

His aunt dipped her head in a curt nod. "I hadn't missed that connection, my boy, but do hear me out. Ned knew her husband, and I vaguely remember Naughton saying years ago that he was considering marriage."

"Ten years ago."

"Yes, perhaps it was." She offered him a sad grin before setting aside her teacup. Leaning forward, she clasped her hands in her lap. "Alecia—"

"Alecia, is it? My, you two are close."

"Don't be peevish, Sebastian. I have much to tell you, and some of it will be quite difficult. But I know how you value honesty, as did your father and my Ned. You deserve honesty."

Seb lifted his teacup and took a long sip, savoring the flavor and nearly scalding heat of the liquid.

Honesty. His aunt wished to speak of honesty? And in the same breath in which she mentioned Alecia? Clearly she didn't know the woman well at all.

"Forgive me, Aunt Augusta. Please carry on."

"The circumstances of your . . . relationship with Alecia are not unknown to me. She has conveyed a bit of your shared history."

He took another sip of tea to hide a bitter grin. What had Alecia told her? What version of her twisted truth?

"That must have been an interesting story."

Alecia only told interesting stories.

His aunt stood as if she was too full of frustrated energy to remain sitting. Pacing the carpet in front of him, she cast him a look now and then, as if contemplating what to tell him or how to tell him what she seemed compelled to say. Finally she stopped in front of him and planted her hands on her hips.

"She told me you were lovers."

He cleared his throat but met her questioning gaze. He'd never expected to have such a conversation with his aunt, but she seemed determined to speak plainly, to get to the heart of the matter. Such straightforwardness matched everything he knew about his aunt.

"That part is true." Unfortunately. If he could return to his younger self, he would avoid Alecia Lloyd and the pain she'd wrought in his life. But what was done was done. Why deny the truth of their history now?

"May I?" Lady Stamford indicated the space next to him on the settee and he scooted tight against the edge to make room for her.

She stunned him by reaching for his hand.

"She told you she was with child?"

He barely resisted pulling his hand away and storming out of the room.

"She lied. It wasn't the first lie, and it certainly wasn't her last."

Augusta patted his hand like a headmistress comforting a homesick child.

"That's the rub, my dear. She didn't lie about the child, though she did mislead you, everyone, about the boy's sire."

He shook his head and found he could not stop shaking it. Years of misery and grief were behind him now. The past. And he wanted to live in the here and now.

"No. I won't hear this. Not again."

Extracting his hand, he rose and stalked toward the painting on the wall, standing inches from the flaxen-haired milkmaid's face. This close, she wasn't half as beautiful as Kat.

"She tells me the boy is your son, Sebastian."

The boy at the gardens, the one sticking close to Alecia's side. He was small, and Seb had guessed him several years younger than ten. He couldn't be his son.

"You refer to the child with you yesterday? He looked to be eight or nine, perhaps younger."

"Alecia says Archie is small for his age. And he does look a good deal like his mother, but he—"

"This is beginning to sound like one of Alecia's tales." He twisted around to gaze at his aunt. "Don't blame yourself. Everyone is taken in by her. She can be quite convincing."

"Do not underestimate me, my boy." His aunt's tone turned steely. He knew she wouldn't like his implication that she'd been as duped by Alecia as he'd once been. "Do you take me for a fool, Sebastian? Do you think I didn't suspect the woman of some scheme? You've taken on a title, an estate. None of us wish to see you damaged by this revelation or create any challenge for your future heirs."

The mention of heirs, of a future, brought Kat to mind, and then his family—Pippa and Ollie. He wouldn't let Alecia and her lies damage any of them.

"Thank you for the tea, but I must—"

"Meet the boy, Sebastian. For his sake and yours, we must resolve this." He still hadn't turned from the painting and his aunt came up behind him, resting a hand on his back. "I am sorry this is so difficult, and that your son, if he is your boy, has been kept from you and you from him."

His son. Everything in him rebelled at the notion. There'd been months between his break with Alecia and the last time he'd seen her in the village. There'd been no indication at all that she was with child. And back then, with his heart still torn and bleeding, he'd wished she was. Wished she might have been telling the truth when she'd first told him she was bearing his child.

But now, two months after his unexpected inheritance of a dukedom, a decade since he'd had any connection with Alecia at all. No. He couldn't bring himself to believe any of it.

Money motivated Alecia, and it seemed the only sensible reason for this sudden revelation that coincided with his newly acquired wealth.

Was the woman truly brazen enough to use his aunt for her own gain? A bitter laugh rumbled at the back of his throat. Of course, she was. Alecia had nearly caused a man's death, nearly cost him his own life. She'd have no compunction about using Lady Stamford.

"I suppose she wants money. To keep quiet? Not to spread this lie?" It had always been about money with Alecia. He'd taken on a title and inherited wealth, and suddenly her son was his son. Not bloody likely.

"Only enough to help provide for Archie as a duke's son should be." Alecia's voice sounded from behind him and he whirled to find her standing at the drawing room threshold. "Of course, I also want Archie to know you."

An ambush, just as she'd attempted at his aunt's ball.

"Stop this, Alecia. Why not tell my aunt what you told me a decade ago? You said you carried my child, and then that the babe was Charles Page's, before finally admitting you weren't with child at all. How many versions of the story have you told this time?"

"What if he *is* your son?" His aunt's emphatic tone made him wince. He knew how fervently one came to believe Alecia's lies. He remembered arguing her cause with more passion than she'd defended herself. Why did she need to, when she had such a talent for winning over zealous supporters?

"Archie is here. Shall I call him down so that you can meet him?"

She used her soft, almost childlike voice, a voice she'd often used to cajole and convince him.

"No." His voice cracked off the walls like a gunshot. Both women flinched.

The anger turning in his stomach had nothing to do with the boy. Alecia was the sole focus of his wrath, but his bitterness soured the entire room and the hostility was palpable. The boy didn't deserve any of it. He wouldn't bring a child into such a situation. The fact that Alecia would consider doing so made him even angrier.

He glanced at his aunt, who stood strong and solid at the edge of the room. Her gaze brimmed with worry and concern, not the pitiful, beseeching look Alecia wore.

"I must go. Now is not the time."

"Sebastian." Both women spoke his name and it echoed through the room in a discordant whine.

"No, not like this. Not today."

He stalked to the door, ready to be done with all of it. But his aunt didn't deserve rudeness.

"Good day, Lady Stamford." He tried to convey with his gaze and tone that he would consider all of it. That he simply needed time. Then he dipped his head toward Alecia, careful not to meet her gaze. "And to you, Lady Naughton."

---

"So you've caught a duke. Well done, Kitty." Cynthia Osgood's mouth twitched in rebellion when she attempted a smile, belying all the saccharine in her tone. "And so efficiently. One waltz and you had him on bended knee."

"You must tell us your secret, Kitty." Bess Berwick's eagerness couldn't be feigned. She edged forward in her chair and leaned toward Kitty, prepared to absorb any courtship wisdom she might offer.

Kitty reached up to slip a strand of loose hair behind her ear and found the shell warm against her fingertips. No doubt her ears were as flushed as her cheeks. Sniping with Cynth was a long-standing habit, but she found it harder to play coy in the face of Bess's sincerity.

She reached for a plate brimming with tea cakes and biscuits and held it out first to Bess and then to Cynthia. Playing hostess was an excellent distraction, but Cynthia wouldn't let her off that easily.

"Come, Kitty. Tell of us of your whirlwind engagement. Did he, in fact, bend the knee?"

"It was too cold for that, I'm afraid. We were in Lady Stamford's garden."

Cynth sputtered and a few amber droplets of tea arced through the air before disappearing into the intricate design of the drawing room's Aubusson carpet. Thank goodness her mother had chosen a design darker than the white walls and blush upholstery.

"He truly proposed to you moments after your waltz?"

"How romantic!" Bess bit her lip and Kitty heard a little hiccup, as if the young woman held her breath, waiting for the rest.

"Not immediately, no, but not long after."

Bess tipped so far in her chair, Kitty feared she might land on the Aubusson carpet too. "B-but what did you say or do to entice him? Did you know from the first moment you met him that he'd ask you?"

"I'm not sure, Bess."

What had she said to entice him? It was more what she'd done—leaning into him, resting her hand on his broad firm shoulder, waiting for a kiss that finally came. She'd been as breathless as he, caught in her own snare. But it had worked.

It would seem a good deal less romantic if she described her first encounter with Sebastian, when he'd chased her down the hall of Clayborne House to chastise her. Yes, she'd recognized something unique in him, and in her reaction to him, even then. But admitting it to herself didn't make their engagement real, and it did not mean he'd ever wish for anything but to end it when the time came.

Cynthia lifted a perfectly arched black brow at Kitty's admission. Kitty was always sure of herself in Cynth's presence, or at least she worked very hard to appear so. To admit that she was uncertain of anything was a bit like showing an enemy one's unprotected flank on the battlefield.

"Why such haste for the ceremony? *My* father would certainly never have approved of such a short engagement." Fluttering her eyes in what Kitty suspected was meant to be a semblance of innocent naiveté but looked a good deal more like she had a lash caught in her eye, Cynth added in a near whisper, "Is there something you're not telling us, Kitty?"

"Miss Osgood!" Bess's exclamation rattled the porcelain on the tea tray.

"I'm sorry to disappoint you, Cynth. There's nothing amiss. Wrexford and I merely saw no need to wait, and my father agreed. No one wants an engagement which drags on and on."

Cynthia felt the barb and stopped batting her lashes long enough to squint one eye.

"Some men are worth waiting for, surely," Cynthia squeaked, her voice an octave higher.

"You shall soon find out." Bess spoke so matter-of-factly that Kitty had to bite her lip to stop from smiling, especially when Bess offered a quick wink in her direction.

"Well, speaking of fine gentlemen, I must depart if I'm not to be late for a shopping excursion with my dear Molstrey." Cynthia stood and shot Bess a pointed look.

"Come, Bess. Don't dawdle. We mustn't keep Mollie waiting."

Bess and Kitty looked at each other as Cynthia pulled on her gloves, exchanging questioning glances, and mouthing *Mollie* in unison. Then Bess pressed her lips together and Kitty covered her mouth, both determined to keep their mirth suppressed.

What nickname might she choose for Sebastian? Kitty couldn't imagine adopting Violet's habit of assigning everything a girlish diminutive and calling him something like Sebbie or Wrexie. He was such a tall imposing man. Dainty and frivolous would never suit.

But as she watched Cynthia take care with slipping her left glove over the hand where she wore Lord Molstrey's emerald engagement ring, her mouth went slack, her body tight, and she clenched the ribbon at the edge of her gown.

Cynth assigned Molstrey a pet name because she would soon be his wife. That future did not await her with Sebastian. Why even waste a minute on the thought? Marriage may not be her fate. She'd accepted that long ago.

The Duke of Wrexford would be a brother-in-law of sorts, and nothing more.

Releasing the wrinkled ribbon, she lifted her hand and pressed it to her chest where she suddenly felt chilled.

Cynthia and Bess were saying their thank-yous as Kitty herded them toward the drawing room door, but it swung open as they approached and a housemaid popped her head in.

"The Duke of Wrexford to see you, my lady."

"Oh, goodness. Perhaps we should stay awhile." Cynthia's voice had gone even higher, and her eyes grew large and panicked at the notion she might miss out on some juicy bit of intelligence to be gathered by seeing the two of them in the same room together.

"No, Cynthia. We don't wish to be late for meeting Mollie." Bess managed to keep a straight face as she said the nickname, but she turned a beaming smile on Kitty as she shooed Cynthia out of the room.

There was a moment of awkwardness as the ladies stopped to greet and then offer parting words to Sebastian, but when they'd finally left and he stood facing Kitty in the entry hall, her legs began to quiver.

He looked dreadful, his skin ashen and hair askew, but more than the physical dishevelment, he looked . . . bereft. His broad mouth was fixed in a grimace and he clenched both of his hands at his sides. Her first instinct was to go to him, to embrace and comfort him. She'd never seen a man who looked more in need of it.

Instead, she lifted her hand and indicated the drawing room door, inviting him inside.

"May we go to your conservatory instead?"

"Yes, of course." She never invited anyone there. Other families entertained in their conservatories, taking tea or even luncheon in the well-lit space, but her parents disdained the scents and dirtiness of the room. It had become sacrosanct as her private retreat.

His footsteps fell heavy behind her, not at all his usual

firm, clipped gait as she led him to the back of the house. He followed so closely she could feel his breath displacing the fine hairs at her nape.

She didn't take him to her work area, but to a white-washed wrought iron bench near a small pool in the center of the room. She'd managed to grow a few thriving lily pads in the pond and hoped to add more.

"Shall I ring for tea?" she asked him.

"Have you not had your tea?"

"I meant for you."

He shook his head before leaning forward, bracing his elbows on his thighs and dipping his head down toward his hands.

"I don't want tea. I just . . . wished to see you."

An odd thing to say when his eyes were fixed on the black and white honeycomb tiles of the conservatory floor.

"Will you sit with me, Kitty?"

He'd never called her by that name, and it wasn't until she heard him say it that the realization came—she much preferred the nickname he'd chosen for her.

Gathering her skirt so as not to crowd him on the narrow bench, she sat and waited for him to lift his head.

With his back rounded, his muscular frame straining against the seams of his overcoat, he looked beaten, so bowed by troubles he didn't wish to raise his head and face to the world around him.

Kitty gripped the cool metal of the bench's frame, slipping her fingers into the swirling vines of the design to keep herself from reaching out to stroke his back and smooth his wildly ruffled hair. It looked as if he'd stuck his fingers through the locks, and then again, or tried to yank them out altogether.

Silence was common in this room. She often worked for hours without speaking a word to anyone, though she sometimes hummed a tune or rambled on to her plants. But sitting with Sebastian, misery rolling off of him in waves, made her want to fill the emptiness with words that might soothe him. What might they be? As she'd said to him that night in his study, they knew little of each other.

"Sebastian."

He lifted his head enough to glance at her lap.

"I am . . . willing to hear whatever it is you need to say."

Surely there was something weighing on his mind. Some reason he'd called unexpectedly and looked so forlorn.

He offered her nothing. No answer. Not even another glance in her direction.

But he moved, flexing his arm so that he could rest his right hand on the bench next to her left one. He spread his fingers so that the edge of his hand pressed against her own.

Lifting her smallest finger, she stroked against the edge of his, allowing herself that tiny means of reassuring him.

"Tell me what scent you're wearing today. It's deeper, but still sweet."

She felt the roughness in his voice as if he'd dragged it across her skin.

"Jasmine and a few notes of rose."

"You must have dozens of bottles of perfume."

Kitty bowed her head. How many times had her father chastised her for spending too much on scent?

"It's my weakness. Some ladies have too many shoes or can never buy enough hats. I buy too much perfume."

He finally straightened and turned his head to gaze at her.

"You like hats too. Don't forget your ill-fated feathered one."

"That was the first new hat I'd had in months. Will you forever remind me of that one?"

"I probably will. It was unforgettable." The skin around his mouth lost some of its tension, the hint of a grin chiseling at the edges. But his eyes. His beautiful gray blue eyes and the lines at their corners, the dip of his brow above, signaled so much anguish that Kitty felt it, a tight, sharp little knot of pain in the center of her chest.

"Is there anything I might do?"

He had come to her, and she'd happily ease his pain if she had the power to do so.

Finally, the grin she'd glimpsed the seed of bloomed into a devastatingly tender smile. And he heightened the punch of it by reaching for her, easing his hand over hers where it rested on the bench.

"You already have." He stroked a thumb over her hand. "And as to the rest, I haven't wrestled with it long enough to face the truth myself."

"My father says—"

In one swift movement he lifted his hand to stop her.

"Let's not invite your father into this moment."

Kitty drew her hand away from his and straightened her back. He was right, but the realization made her feel foolish and small. At three and twenty, was she truly still parroting her father's philosophies at every turn?

"I'm sorry, Kat. Tell me what your father says."

When she pressed her lips together, he reached for her hand again.

"Please. I want to hear it."

"He says . . ." Her voice sounded tiny and childish, and she cleared her throat to recapture a bit of self-possession. "The test of a great man isn't whether he tells the truth, but whether he can face the truth, no matter how difficult."

He edged away from her on the bench to turn his body toward hers, his long legs tangling in her skirts.

"For once, I think I might agree with your father." He grinned, but like the last, it didn't wash away the pain brimming in his gaze. "But what if a man can't tell? What if he's proven himself a fool and believed so many lies that he can no longer discern the truth at all?"

## Chapter Seventeen

AGREEING TO A dinner at Clayborne House was probably a mistake. Seb's patience was a thread beyond frayed and the likelihood of holding his tongue when Clayborne said something insulting to Kat seemed unlikely. Not to mention the fact that he'd kept the matter of his possible offspring from her when visiting her conservatory. Just sitting with her quietly had calmed his nerves. But he'd seen the question in her eyes. She was a clever woman and knew something was amiss. If she asked him tonight, he was liable to tell her all of it.

Kat deserved to know all of it. She would have to know all of it, because the longer their feigned engagement went on, the more he wanted her in his life, and not just until Ollie and Harriet wed. Perhaps Alecia's allegation had worn down his defenses. Perhaps they weren't as solid as he'd imagined them to be in the first place. Kat,

his feelings for her, had slipped beyond his guard and ignited him.

"Are you all right, Sebastian?"

"Yes, of course. Why do you ask?"

Pippa sat across from him in the Wrexford carriage
and shot him an incredulous look. "You returned late
this afternoon and locked yourself in your study. You
took no luncheon that I'm aware of, and you were surly
about having to dress for dinner. If you did not wish to
dine with the Adderlys, we shouldn't have accepted their
invitation."

Pippa was ever the practical one, but she didn't seem
to comprehend that social niceties sometimes required
one to be less than practical. It was natural for the Adderlys to invite them to reciprocate the meal they'd all
shared at Wrexford House. And as their eldest daughter's
fiancé, it would've been the height of rudeness for him to
refuse.

"It's not quite that simple, Pippa."

"I see. Then perhaps I'm missing something."

"I believe you are. She is my fiancée. Clayborne will be
my father-in-law."

He didn't even choke when he said it. In sifting his
feelings for Kat, he couldn't ignore her father. If she was
to be part of his life, the marquess would be too. Which
probably meant throttling the fellow wasn't an option.

*Good grief, man.* Now he was getting too far ahead
of himself. She might have enjoyed their kisses as much
as he did. And she'd proved herself willing to invite him

into her conservatory and give him a bit of comfort when he was sorely in need of it. They'd formed a companionship of sorts, but at times she retreated behind that cool self-possession he'd encountered the first night he'd met her. He had no real notion whether she might welcome a genuine courtship. Why would she accept his attentions when he was the fool who might have fathered a child and known nothing about it for years?

Seb looked across the carriage interior at his sister, noted the concern etched on her face, and tried to force the frown from his own.

"Thank you for being concerned about me."

"Until you're married, I believe that's still my job." Pippa seemed to lighten a moment, almost letting the worry slip from her expression and giving into a grin. "Since mother and father are gone, we must always look out for each other."

"And Ollie," Seb added solemnly.

Pippa looked down at her clasped hands and rubbed her thumbs together, a habit she'd had since childhood, one of her few outward signs of distress.

"Yes, and Ollie." Pippa lifted her head and looked out into the fiery dusk of the Mayfair skyline. Fragments of light pierced the empty slices between buildings. "No matter what choices he makes."

She still struggled with acceptance. And he couldn't blame her one whit. How long had he spun aimlessly in denial before finally embracing the end of his relationship with Alecia?

Turning his head toward his own carriage window, he

hid a wry twist of his mouth. And now the poisonous relationship wasn't over at all. An innocent boy was in the middle of it, and Seb mourned for Archie most of all. Whether the child was his son or not, he'd become his mother's pawn.

When the footman assisted Pippa from their carriage, Seb finally realized the vehicle had stopped moving and stepped down.

Clayborne House blazed as if Queen Victoria herself would be joining them, gaslight and candlelight glowing from every window, and liveried footman standing sentry on each side of the hallway as they entered. Far more fuss than Seb had encountered on any of his previous visits, and he wondered why Clayborne was suddenly so concerned with presenting a glamorous façade.

When they stepped into the drawing room, he saw Ollie's smiling face first and then scanned the room for Kat. His shoulders tightened when he didn't see her in the drawing room, but then he caught a whiff of fragrance, the same lavender-vanilla blend she'd worn to dinner at Wrexford House.

"I wasn't certain you'd come this evening." Kat's tone was soothingly light as she moved to stand beside him.

He offered her his arm. Together they walked to stand near the unlit fireplace rather than taking a seat among the guests.

"Perhaps I shouldn't have, particularly if you're expecting wit or charm. I'm not sure I have it in me tonight."

Finally, she turned toward him, and he watched her eyes move over each feature of his face and then sweep down to take in his evening clothes before meeting his eyes again.

"Do you always assess men so boldly?"

"No, and certainly not when they can see me doing so. But with you, I thought I might be allowed."

She seemed to sense he needed banter, or at least a conversation that did not delve into the reason for his unplanned visit earlier in the afternoon.

Reaching up to straighten his lapels and ease his shoulders back, he let himself be drawn into her mirth.

"So, what's your assessment, Lady Katherine?"

"Are you sure you want to hear it?"

Inhaling sharply, he nodded. "Do your worst."

"I was simply trying to find it."

"Find it? Find what?"

"Whatever it is about you that's so different from every other man of my acquaintance." She skimmed her gaze from his head to his toes and back up again. "You look every inch the titled gentleman, as well tailored and elegant as any. But you readily admit your faults and honestly answer each question I put to you. That alone marks you as extraordinary."

She'd been kind enough to avoid questioning him earlier in the afternoon, and those crucial answers would no doubt have soured the admiration in her gaze.

"And do you prefer honesty or polite and proper answers?"

Her sigh was loud enough to draw her mother's attention.

"If I am remarking on your honesty, then I must find

it to my liking. Otherwise, if I loathed it, I'd be polite and proper and not mention it at all."

"I don't recall that I spent my engagement to your father involved in nearly so much whispering in corners."

Seb pivoted to face the Marchioness of Clayborne. He'd yet to exchange more than niceties with Kat's mother, but on first impression the lady was far less fearsome than her husband. If not for the way her narrow blue eyes took in every detail around her, he would have considered the woman a charming antidote to her husband's sharp edges.

"But I suppose I can forgive you for monopolizing my daughter, Your Grace. We are so pleased. The prospect of two daughters married in one season. I may be the luckiest mother in London."

Talk of matches caused Seb to lift his gaze to Ollie and Harriet, who stood conversing with Pippa. Pippa seemed to sense his attention and turned to look at him, lifting her chin a notch.

She would come out of this challenge as she did each one life had dealt her, with courage and grace.

While Seb watched his sister, Clayborne drew up next to his wife. "Yes, my dear. Fortuitous, indeed, especially when one considers this was to be Katherine's fifth season. If not for you, Wrexford, the dusty old maid's shelf would have been her fate."

Kat didn't blush or drain of color as some young ladies might at such a declaration, but fire sparked in her gaze, more anger than hurt, as she looked in her father's direction.

The man refused to acknowledge her glare.

Ignoring propriety, Seb reached for Kat's hand to draw her attention.

"Thank goodness you had the sense to refuse all your other suitors."

For a moment all the rest receded—the chilly drawing room, their gathered family chatting and laughing over something Ollie said, and the pinprick gazes of Kat's parents. She wasn't wearing gloves and he slid his fingers over her warm skin, breathing in her scent, attempting to offer her the comfort she'd given him so freely earlier in the day.

"Lord Clayborne and I considered a party to celebrate both engagements." The marchioness's voice cut in.

"No." They called out the word emphatically and in unison.

Kat's mother reared back and clutched the diamond choker at her throat. "Well. Perhaps we can discuss a party another time."

Before the conversation with her parents could become any more awkward, the blessed dinner gong sounded and they begin filing in couple by couple to the dining room. Seb had been impressed with Wrexford House's staff and the effort they'd put into preparing the dining room for its first formal use since he'd assumed his title. But Lord Clayborne and his wife seemed determined to outdo him. Their table boasted twice as many silver serving dishes, thrice as many glasses, and more pieces of silverware than seemed necessary for the number of guests. Flowers dominated the space and Seb glanced over at Kat, wondering if her conservatory had been stripped bare to decorate the small dinner party.

Seb didn't have the advantage of sitting at the opposite end of the table from Clayborne this time. He had to endure the man's pointed questions to Ollie about his progress at the Inns of Court, his brags about his own accomplishments in Parliament, and his thinly veiled attacks on his eldest daughter.

Not all families were happy ones. He'd always known that his was one of the lucky few, but he'd never encountered a father who expressed such naked enmity toward his own daughter. His ire seemed especially reserved for Kat. Lady Harriet drew almost none of his attention, favorable or otherwise.

Much like Pippa, Kat seemed to bear pain with stoicism and grace, often ignoring her father altogether to speak to her sister or Pippa, but the more the marquess drank, and the more she ignored him, the more he seemed increasingly determined to pierce her poise with his words.

"You can't take that damned conservatory with you, you know."

"Pardon, Papa?" Seb knew she'd heard him, and he admired how calmly she responded to her father's provocation.

"When you marry the duke, you must leave your filthy hobby behind. You'll be a duchess, and duchesses don't dig in the dirt with their fingers like some farm laborer."

Seb slammed his palm on the table and shot up from his chair.

"Might I have a word with you, Clayborne?"

The man's eyes were glassy when he glared back at Seb. "I'm not sure you're aware, Wrexford, but we're in the middle of dinner service, and it's not yet time to leave the table."

"Make an exception."

The marquess didn't allow the smirk to slide off his face, but Seb could see in Clayborne's cloudy gray eyes that the man sensed his seriousness. As daintily as any fine lady, the marquess lifted his napkin and dabbed at the corners of his mouth before throwing the snow-white fabric on his plate.

"Very well, Wrexford, as you are our guest, I shall make this single exception. If you'll excuse us, ladies and Mr. Treadwell. It seems I must impart a few of the rules of decorum to the new duke. Shouldn't take long."

Seb expected Kat's father to lead him back into the drawing room, but he took a right into a cool dark room that smelled of pipe smoke and liquor. He only turned up the gaslight enough to lift the darkness, and Seb noted rows of book-lined shelves, well-worn leather furniture, and a massive desk that dwarfed his own.

"Have a seat, Wrexford. I'd like to get back for the main course."

"This won't require sitting. Your daughter, Katherine, is an extraordinary woman and yet after twenty-three years of knowing her, you seem unaware of that fact. Or perhaps you are, and the pain of losing her to any man has turned you bitter and angry. I don't know you, Clayborne, and I can't begin to understand you, but I can tell you this. As long as Kat is my fiancée, as long as she is my wife, you will never speak to her that way again."

The marquess dipped his head, but he didn't bend his shoulders or sag in defeat. In fact, he straightened to his rather diminutive height and reached up to smooth his beard before turning a Cheshire cat smile on Seb.

"Are we to speak plainly then? I have been so looking forward to the two of us speaking plainly to one another. Do you think I believe you're truly interested in my daughter? Do you think I believe you have any intention of marrying her? Do you think I'm such a fool that I accept the coincidence of your choice of my very challenging daughter at the very moment her sister needs approval to marry your, what shall we call him, not quite a brother?"

Seb doubted his ability to convince Clayborne from the beginning. But why had the man let them carry on with their ruse?

"You thought you'd done it so well. I've heard of your very public outings. Apparently you decided to go for a swim in the pond at Hyde Park and take liberties with my daughter at the Royal Botanical Gardens."

If Alecia's pursuit unnerved him, how must Kat feel to know her father watched her every move?

"Nothing goes on with my children or my family or any other cause in which I have an interest without my knowledge. Your Grace, you are a novice at this game. It takes decades to learn the rules."

"I'm not interested in the game, Clayborne. Nor the rules."

Seb stared past the man, over his shoulder, at a portrait of three women. Lady Clayborne anchored the center, with her swan long neck, rosebud mouth, and discerning eyes. Two blond girls shared the canvas, one leaning into her lap, an easy smile lighting her cherubic face, while the other stood with regal solemnity, one hand balanced on the back of her mother's chair as she stared at the viewer. Her green eyes glowed with hope, intelligence, and determination. Of the three she was the only one who looked as if she wished to break the confines of the canvas, leap out and make her mark on the world. She had all the determination of a prince, and her energy dominated the painting. Aside from her longish hair, there was nothing feminine about the child. Then he noted her hand and the flowers clutched in her fist. Long green spade-shaped leaves with dainty white bells nestled inside—lily of the valley. She told him it was her favorite flower, and he instantly recalled how intoxicating it smelled on Kat's skin.

He turned his gaze back to Clayborne.

"I wish to marry your daughter. I'm asking you now for her hand. No feigning or scheming. I want to marry Katherine."

"Is this more trickery, Wrexford?"

"I don't engage in trickery. I wouldn't be any good at it if I tried." He glanced up at the painting again, his gaze focused on those fierce little green eyes. "She's an intriguing woman."

When Clayborne glared, Seb offered the one thing that might persuade the man. "I can make her a duchess, and I know she will excel at running Roxbury."

"I wouldn't count on that. Katherine has never excelled at anything but defying every expectation I had for her. But how can I refuse you? She won't get a better offer after five seasons." Seb loathed the man's sneer almost as much as his dismissal of Kat, as if she somehow lost appeal each year of her life. He couldn't regret that she'd gone five seasons without accepting a proposal. He admired her for holding fast against the sort of pressure her father must have exerted.

Clayborne didn't offer his hand, and Seb was grateful for the omission. He turned to leave the man's study, but something in him, some petty defiant part couldn't let the man have the last word.

"You needn't worry about Kat missing her conservatory, Clayborne. I'll build her the most elaborate one in England when we return to Roxbury." Seb swiveled away from the marquess when all he truly wished to do was strike the man. Anger burned like bile in his throat. He turned back. "Kat *will* excel as Duchess of Wrexford. You may be blind to her merits, but I see them, and I'll remind her of them every time she hears your vitriol in her head."

Seb didn't wait for a reply before turning to stride from Clayborne's study.

"It made her strong." Clayborne's voice rang overload in Seb's ears.

He stiffened, turned on his heel, and charged across the carpet in two long strides. Clayborne flinched back, and Seb leaned over the man's desk, lifting a finger to point at the portrait behind him.

"Look at those eyes. I suspect Kat was born with

that strength you're so quick to take credit for. You can't nurture a child on cruelty. If you ask me, Kat deserves a bloody medal for putting up with you."

Clayborne began to splutter, but Seb walked out and breathed deep when he was finally free of the man's presence. Halfway down the hall, he stopped at the sound of conversation in the withdrawing room and walked toward the threshold rather than returning to the dining room. Ollie and Harriet stood together, hands joined in front of them, whispering nervously.

"Where's your sister, Lady Harriet?"

"She's gone out. When Kitty's upset, sometimes she likes to walk, but it's quite late. We were just discussing whether we should go after her."

"I'll go. Which direction?"

"Hyde Park."

She wasn't difficult to spot. Tonight she wore a shimmering gown that caught a bit of the waning light as she walked. With a few long strides, he drew up behind her on the otherwise empty pavement.

"I heard you got away."

Kitty stopped short so quickly at the sound of Sebastian's voice, she pitched forward before raising her arms out to regain her balance.

"I'd had enough." She turned. A tear pushed, hot and insistent, at the corner of her eye.

He jolted at the sight of it and reached for her, concern shadowing his features, as if he'd do anything necessary to take away her pain and stop her from shedding that tear.

She noticed the direction of his gaze and swiped the bit of moisture away.

"You needn't look so frightened. I'm not the blubbering sort."

"Thank goodness." When she didn't reach for his offered hand, he pushed it into his coat pocket.

She narrowed her eyes at his attempt at levity, and tried to ignore the tingling in her fingers where she wished he'd touched her.

"But I will cry if I wish to. I am capable of it when the occasion calls for it."

"I shall keep that in mind." He nodded solemnly, as if she'd imparted an essential fact.

She felt shaky and uncertain, and he was a tall enticing wall of strength just within arm's reach. Kitty sensed anticipation in his stance, a readiness to move toward her, as if the same magnet exerted a pull on both of them. If she stepped toward him, he'd embrace her. His scent, his warmth, his arms surrounding her, and she ached for him to hold her as he had in his study.

But tonight he'd almost ruined their entire plan. He'd displeased her father, and if Papa took against Sebastian, he might refuse Mr. Treadwell.

"What did you say to him? I hope you didn't make him angry."

He jerked back his head as if she'd struck him. As if he couldn't believe she was concerned about him angering a man who'd just insulted her, again, in front of everyone.

Her father's manner took some getting used to, not to mention a thick skin. Papa always reserved his harshest criticism for her.

"If we anger him, he may refuse Oliver, and all of this will have been for nothing." She lifted her hand and made a circular motion in the air, as if to encompass both of them.

All of this. Bantering in the dark. Kissing in his study. Saving an unsalvageable piece of headgear. Holding his hand as they'd explored the Botanical Gardens together. She didn't regret a moment of it.

No, a single regret had lodged itself in the center of her chest. She regretted that none of it had been real, that they were still playing the game, and that the only romance that seemed to matter to them was between Ollie and her sister.

He took a step toward her, so close she leaned back to look up at him. She needed to know what was true between them.

"I know you dislike this subterfuge, Sebastian."

He shook his head. "Doesn't it seem absurd that we must lie to your father so that he'll give consent for his daughter to be happy?"

They'd need more than a few minutes in the dark for her to explain her father to him.

"And the way he speaks to you. It's intolerable. No one should ever speak to you that way."

He touched her, pressing his palm to her cheek, and she leaned into his hand, turning her face to savor the slide of his skin against hers.

"I once asked him to be hard on me, to speak to me as he would if I was his son. Never to spare my feelings because I'm a girl."

Lifting his other hand, he cupped her face and took a step, closing the space that separated them, sealing their bodies together.

"Darling, Kat. You don't need your father's cruel words to make you strong."

She wanted his mouth on hers, needed his kiss to swallow the cry surging up at the back of her throat. His gaze, too tender and brimming with admiration, threatened to melt all her defenses, to shatter her self-possession. This might be one of those occasions that called for tears, and yet then he'd know she wasn't strong.

"We should go back."

Unlike every other time he'd held her, he didn't instantly release her when she pulled away. He slid his hands over her upper arm, staring into her eyes a long moment before releasing her. She sensed he held something back, as if he wished to speak but couldn't find the words.

Finally, he lifted his hands and took one step back.

Though it was a mild night, she shivered the moment he stopped touching her and fought the urge to reach for him again. Pivoting on her heel, she turned and began marching back toward home, trying to breathe past the gnawing ache in the center of her chest.

"Where are you going?"

She stopped to gaze at him over her shoulder.

"We both just walked out. We must go back and make amends with my father."

He narrowed his eyes a moment and then strode toward her.

Kitty waited for him to catch up and didn't hesitate when he reached to take her hand. His hand in hers had always fit like they'd been molded for the purpose of connecting with each other. No man's hand had ever felt so right against her palm.

He turned as if to speak, but remained silent. She wanted to speak, to tell him that, for her part, none of what had passed between them had been pretense, that she wanted more than their false engagement. But as the moonlight lit the pavement and the gas lamps twinkled in the fog, she gripped his hand tighter, forcing her busy thoughts to quiet. Closing her eyes, she breathed in the cool night air, allowing herself to indulge in one whimsically, ridiculously romantic notion that she could face anything—her father, the future—so long as she had Sebastian by her side.

## Chapter Eighteen

To ANYONE PEEKING through the windows of the fashionable jeweler's shop or passing on the busy Hatton Garden thoroughfare, Seb and Ollie must have looked like two eager grooms-to-be in search of the perfect rings for their brides.

Seb mimicked Ollie's behavior, bending to look closer into display cases, staring to assess this ring or that. He'd never felt like more of a fraud in his life. Before Ollie invited him on the outing, he hadn't considered buying Kat a ring. She didn't expect one. At least the task hadn't been among the activities outlined in her detailed list of steps they must take to pull off a believable engagement.

When Seb turned his attention to a collection of simple etched bands, Ollie shook his head and moved toward a corner cabinet.

"I think not, my friend. You'll need quite a large one

to impress Lady Katherine," he said, pointing toward an outrageously grand rock behind glass.

Seb's eyebrow shot skyward at the same moment the jeweler's clerk spluttered and covered his eavesdropping with a bout of coughing.

Ollie seemed to miss all of it. "Don't you think that's the sort of diamond she'll expect?"

"I don't." The faceted gem gave off a blinding glow, but the diamond was far too large. Seb imagined most women would find its weight and bulk uncomfortable, despite the impressive proof of wealth it was intended to be.

Kat's beauty had struck him with the diamond's blazing quality the first time he'd spotted her across the Clayborne ballroom, but now he'd seen more. A woman whose wit and cleverness and loyal heart were every bit as enticing as her outer appeal. The woman he'd come to know would likely be happier tending her plants than showing off such an ostentatious ring. Then again, she might say it would provide proof of the sincerity of their engagement. Such a stone would make an impression, and that goal *was* on her list.

But it didn't suit her.

Seb cast his gaze around the shop. One ring drew his notice. Nestled against black velvet, it sparked with the same vivid green as Kat's eyes. Seven leaf-shaped emeralds hugged one central round diamond, a jewellike version of the flower Kat wore in her hair the night he'd waltzed with her.

Ollie noticed his attention on the bauble and stepped

near to peer over his shoulder. "Are you sure it's enough for a marquess's daughter?"

"Which would you choose for Hattie? You're planning to marry a marquess's daughter too." The moment Seb uttered the words, his legs stiffened, his throat tightened, and the sensation spread, a squeezing constriction wrapping around his torso. Shock held him in place, and when he sensed his mouth agape, he snapped it shut.

The words had been easy, too easy. They'd slipped from his mouth effortlessly, not as a ploy, not to convince Ollie of anything. In that moment, he had believed he would marry Kat, just as surely as he expected Ollie to wed Harriet.

All those years of denial and protecting himself, and now he acknowledged marriage to Kat as easily as if it was simply the next thing on his list. And he didn't even keep a bloody list.

Marriage was not how their engagement would end. Jilting, perhaps a bit of manageable gossip, and then Ollie and Harriet's successful nuptials. Those were the items on Kat's list. Those were their objectives. Nothing more.

Some distress must have lingered in his expression.

Ollie watched Seb, his smile slipping down into a worried frown before tipping up again. "Strikes you all of a sudden at times, doesn't it, Bash? Bachelorhood will soon be behind us, and yet I suspect the reward will be worth the sacrifice."

"The reward?"

"Your wife. My wife." He quirked his mouth and

glanced up at the ceiling of the shop. "I quite like the sound of that. My wife."

Fanciful. That's how it sounded to Seb. And completely unlikely. He clenched his hand into a fist and released it, sensing some of the tightness in his body beginning to ease.

Without thinking, without reason or logic, he strode to the counter and indicated the flower ring to the jeweler. "That one."

Ollie chuckled behind him. "That's quite decisive. Does Lady Katherine like flowers?"

"Don't all ladies?" Seb didn't want to tell Ollie about Kat's conservatory. She seemed to share her interest with precious few, and he wished to keep that experience with her to himself.

Ollie went quiet, pensive. "I've never asked Hattie. Perhaps I should." He crossed his arms, and his brow creased with the effort of fretting. "Good grief, I'm going to marry the woman, and I don't even know if she likes flowers."

"You'll have plenty of time to ask her, Ollie." A lifetime, Seb hoped. And if Kat had her way, Harriet and Ollie's marital bliss would commence soon. Her ambitious plans called for the couple to exchange vows within a fortnight.

Ollie nodded, seemingly mollified, and turned to examine the main case again.

Seb settled up with the jeweler and clasped the small box. He could envision the ring on Kat's hand, and yet he couldn't imagine presenting it to her. What could he say? Would she call it frivolous, or laugh at him for his sentimental impulse?

Seb closed his fingers around the diminutive square, and then reached up to slide the box into his inner waistcoat pocket. When he settled his jacket and coat, the box's edges pressed into his chest, nudging the line of his scar.

How fitting. The reminder of his past mistakes side by side with a token of his present foolishness.

Ollie made his own selection of a similarly modest ring, and they made their way out onto Hatton Garden, moving toward Oxford Street.

"I am still surprised by . . . how it's all turned out." Ollie stumbled over the words in completely un-Ollie fashion.

When Seb glanced over, Ollie shot him a guilty look before continuing. "You did fix on her rather quickly."

Seb stopped walking. Ollie followed suit. Fashionably dressed ladies and gentleman flowed around them.

"You suggested this." Seb's jaw felt as tight as his body had moments before in the bauble shop. "Everyone thought a match with Lady Katherine a very fine notion."

All except Pippa, but she would come around.

Ollie nodded his head. "And I, of all people, am pleased by the turn of events. I simply . . ."

Seb held still while Ollie assessed him, searching for the truth. For a moment, Seb considered telling him the whole of it. Why not tell Ollie their plan? *Because the man can't keep a confidence to save his life.*

"Simply what, Ollie?" Seb worked to temper the irritation in his tone and failed miserably. None of his anger was meant for Ollie. Every ounce of it was directed inward.

"She truly has turned your head."

Seb nodded to acknowledge what was impossible to deny.

She'd turned his head, scrambled his wits, derailed his hard-won peace of mind, and made him yearn for her company each day. There was his list—all the ways Kat had wrought havoc in his life. And he'd only known the woman a week.

Yet she wasn't the only one to blame. He'd made his choices.

After all, he was the impulsive fool with a four-cornered bulk dragging down the corner of his pocket, riding the edge of a wound that should have taught him years before about the dangers of making sound choices when a tempting woman was involved.

"THE BOY SHOULD be down any moment. He's looking forward to meeting you."

Seb couldn't rally any of the giddiness he detected in his aunt's voice, but he believed the sincerity of her enthusiasm. He would be kind to the lad, of course, and civil to Alecia, if she was present for his meeting with the boy. Whatever she'd been to him, he preferred to leave it in the past, but she was the child's mother.

Queasiness shot through his belly as a thought struck.

"Who does he think I am? What has she told him?"

If this was all true, what rifts would it cause between

Alecia and her husband? And between the boy and the man who likely believed he was the child's father? Seb didn't know Naughton well, but he doubted the pompous lord would have married Alecia if he suspected she carried another man's child.

"I believe he's been told only that you're the Duke of Wrexford, a friend of his mother's, and that you wish to make his acquaintance."

Seb released his white-knuckle hold on the arms of his aunt's damask chair. He still doubted Alecia's son was his own, but he'd feared she might lie or toy with the child's emotions as she did with everyone else's. He released the breath he'd been holding and felt a moment of gratitude toward the woman who'd caused him such pain. At least she had the sense to protect the boy's feelings.

"I am so pleased you'll finally get to meet him. The rest can be managed. If the boy is your son, he should know his father."

Her lack of concern for Lord Naughton shocked him, but her willingness to believe Alecia's story did not.

"Aunt Augusta, there's a very good chance this boy isn't my son. You don't know Lady Naughton as I do."

She shot him a saucy look, clearly investing his words with a double meaning he hadn't intended.

"I've known Alecia for years, from my youth, and used to believe her every word. Bit by bit, I learned she rarely speaks the truth. She's told me lie after lie, about her own family, where she was born, even her age. You can't fault me for doubting her now."

His aunt tilted her head and her mouth puckered

in a sad moue. "Would a mother do this to her own child?"

Alecia was the one person in his life who never behaved as he expected. "I don't know. Does she need funds?"

"If the rumors about Lord Naughton are true, I suspect she might," his aunt acknowledged. "She claims her life with him hasn't been easy. He's not . . . an ideal husband. The earl drinks, gambles, and pursues his romantic inclinations elsewhere."

Seb shook his head. "Naughton was her choice, and he's her burden to bear. She had other options, believe me. I was only one of them." He knew of Charles Page, Naughton, and suspected there'd been others.

Aunt Augusta pinched her eyes in a thoughtful expression, and then stretched up tall, looking very much the poised genteel lady he'd first met when he was a boy.

"If the boy is yours, Sebastian, you must make peace with Alecia, for his sake. But if she's lying"—she lifted her chin and one dark brow winged up—"well, let's just say I will see that she regrets her lies. For attempting to wound you, and for entangling an innocent boy in her scheme."

The drawing room door swung open and her serious expression transformed into an indulgent grin. "Oh look, here is young Master Archie." There was no mistaking the genuine warmth in her tone. "Archie, may I present my nephew, the Duke of Wrexford?"

The boy strode into the room confidently, his head held high, but the tremor in his slim frame belied his direct gaze.

Seb studied the boy, seeking any signs that might remind him of himself. Then a figure loomed behind Archie, and Seb looked up to find Alecia's ice blue gaze locked on *his* face.

The child's demeanor changed when his mother walked in the room. He dropped his gaze to the floor as if uncertain, stifling all the curiosity of moments before.

Something in Seb rebelled. He didn't want to do this on Alecia's terms, or even his aunt's.

"Would you care to join me for a walk, Archie?"

Alecia's expression turned thunderous. "No, he doesn't want a walk. Why not sit and take tea with the ladies? Lady Stamford and I were just going to ring for some."

The boy struggled, his eyes darting from the window and then back at his mother's face. Archie seemed snared between his desire to be out in the sun and the impulse to obey his mother.

"It's a fine day for a walk," Seb added to encourage the boy. "Come, Archie. We must catch the sunshine while we can. What do you say?"

The child nodded his head before slanting another wary gaze at Alecia.

"Very well," she huffed, "I shall accompany you. Let me just get my wrap."

"Nonsense, Lady Naughton," Seb cut in. "I wouldn't dream of interrupting your tea with Lady Stamford. Does Archie have a nanny or governess who might accompany us?"

Archie piped up. "I have Miss Perkins. She teaches me

my lessons and looks after me when Mama cannot." Excitement fizzed up in the boy like the bubbles of a chemical reaction climbing the neck of a beaker. "And she likes to walk too, Your Grace. She walks every day or rides her bicycle."

"She sounds like my sister Pippa. Shall we see if Miss Perkins can join us?"

Alecia shot him a scowl that in days of old would have left a gaping wound of worry about how he'd offended or displeased her, but today it only sparked an almost pleasant tickle.

"I'm certain she's available to accompany you," his aunt reassured before arching a brow at Alecia.

After stalking out of the room, Alecia returned a moment later with an extremely tall red-haired woman in her wake. Beyond her bright hair and height, Miss Perkins seemed unremarkable in appearance, but she exuded a kind of constrained energy, as if her plain blue dress and the very walls around her were keeping her from action.

The governess's eyes popped wide when his aunt introduced her to Sebastian and she stuck out her hand before retracting it and executing a graceful curtsy.

"Then you'll join us, Miss Perkins?"

"I would be pleased to, Your Grace."

Seb breathed a chesty sigh of relief the minute they stepped out of his aunt's town house, and he was surprised to see Archie take a deep breath too.

"Spring is my favorite season. You can smell everything blooming." The child turned to him and smiled.

They started onto the pavement and turned the corner toward Hyde Park with Miss Perkins following a few steps behind.

"Are you fond of botany, Archie?"

Archie turned back to glance up at his governess. "Miss Perkins is teaching me about plants and trees and everything that grows. But I prefer animals, I think. Zoology."

"He's a curious boy, which makes my job more adventure than burden."

Seb turned back to gaze at Archie's governess. The woman bounced when she walked and took in the Mayfair streets with hungry glances in each direction, as if she didn't want to miss any details. Seb suspected she'd find a means of turning any burden into an adventure.

As they entered the park, they kept to the far side of the path, avoiding those on horseback. Seb directed the boy and his governess toward the waterside where he'd made a fool of himself—the memory of it and Kat in her elaborate hat made him smile.

A few steps later, he realized he was walking alone and looked back to find Archie and Miss Perkins chatting with a young man on horseback. Or, rather, they fawned over the young man's horse. The muscular bay with a white blaze under its forelock dipped its head so that Archie could scratch its snout. Apparently the boy liked horses. While it didn't preclude the possibility he was Seb's son, it certainly wasn't a trait they shared.

"Come meet Hellion, Your Grace." The boy stared at him expectantly.

*Sounds inviting.* Seb stepped gingerly toward the massive creature and nodded his head in greeting. A verbal introduction seemed a bit much.

"He's magnificent, don't you think?" The enthusiasm in Archie's tone left no doubt that he thought so.

Extraordinarily tall and probably capable of crushing the boy under his hooves.

Archie gazed at the animal like Kat looked at her plants.

"Impressive, indeed." Seb could allow that, at least.

"Do you remember the Latin name, Archibald?" the boy's governess prompted.

Seb's knowledge of zoological families only extended to *Equus.*

"*Equus ferus caballus,*" the boy rattled off as if the name had already been on the tip of his tongue.

"Do you have many horses, Your Grace?"

"A few." A fine stable full, actually, though they'd all been acquired by his predecessor.

"My father is one of the finest horsemen in England." The boy puffed out his diminutive chest with the declaration.

His father. Lord Naughton. It seemed the boy's opinion of his father was much higher than Lady Stamford's.

"Do you know my father well, or just my mama?"

"I knew him long ago." So far in the past that he couldn't recall the color of Naughton's eyes. Archie's pale green eyes didn't match his mother's, nor Seb's, but in all other aspects the boy's rounded childish face mirrored Alecia's—the high cheekbones, narrow nose, and a thin lower lip crested by a full upper Cupid's bow. Even the way he tilted his head and inclined his mouth into a half grin reminded Seb of Alecia. And nothing about the boy resonated within him. Wouldn't he sense if this was his child? Clever and polite, Archie would make any parent proud, but Seb knew, bone deep, that the boy wasn't his.

No relief came with the certainty. Instead, his heart rattled as if his chest had become a hollow space. Alecia would fight him. Of that he had no doubt. If she'd set her mind on convincing him and his aunt that he'd fathered the child, she would not cede defeat easily. And if she fought hard enough, if she argued Archie's paternity loudly enough, eventually the boy would hear the rumors and be snagged in the middle. He clearly idolized Naughton. Whatever kind of husband the man was to Alecia, he'd clearly made his son proud.

"Sebastian!"

Seb turned at the sound of a child calling his name and saw Violet Adderley bounding toward him. He stepped away from the massive stallion so that she wouldn't frighten the beast. She walked quickly but a bit stiffly, as if the exuberance of being nine challenged all the etiquette lessons she'd been taught. Stopping before him, she reached out a hand, as Pippa always did, offering a gentlemanly handshake. After taking his hand a moment and then nodding politely in greeting, she twisted back to stare at Kat as she approached.

The sight of her hit him like a physical force, pressing in on him, and he drew in a steadying breath. He'd dreaded this morning and the encounter with Alecia and her son, but now, seeing Kat, he could barely repress a grin. Sunlight washed over her, highlighting a few strands of hair that had slipped her coiffure, and painting a glow on the arch of her cheeks.

"Violet, you know better than to amble off like that." Kat didn't excel at chastisement. Her eyes were too full of tenderness whenever she looked at either of her sisters, but she managed to cool that emotion when she turned to look at him.

"Your Grace, what a delightful surprise." Her tepid tone belied her words and Seb watched her gaze swing from his to Miss Perkins, down to Archie, and up to the young man who'd begun tightening the reins to lead Hellion away.

"Lady Katherine, may I present Miss Perkins and her charge, Master Archie Naughton."

"Naughton?" The frown marring Kat's brow disappeared almost as soon as it appeared.

She suspected something was amiss. He saw wariness in her eyes, in the quick intake of breath and the tightening of her mouth. It must look odd to find him wandering Hyde Park with the child of a woman that she already suspected of being his former lover.

Eyes pinched, she shot him an inquiring gaze. He'd never truly appreciated the way she usually looked at him, with respect and admiration. But he recognized it now as he saw it fading, overshadowed by distrust and uncertainty.

A cramping pain shot down his back and shoulders,

and he stiffened as if his entire body had just been wrenched up and hung on tenterhooks. He should have explained the situation with Alecia to Kat when he'd had the chance.

"Do you know my mother as well? Or my father?"

Bending at the waist so that she could look at the boy eye to eye, Kat lifted her hand to him.

"I am acquainted with your parents, but it is a great pleasure to meet you, Master Archie." The boy looked momentarily abashed, tongue-tied, before gathering his wits again.

"And you, my lady." After sketching an elaborate bow, Archie tipped his head back toward his governess for approval.

Miss Perkins beamed with pride.

"The Duke of Wrexford knows my mother very well, and as Mama and I are visiting his aunt, he wished to make my acquaintance," he helpfully explained.

Seb couldn't stop looking at her face, hoping for the sharp line of her jaw to soften, but she only offered him her profile. He couldn't even read the emotion in her eyes.

"And do you find the duke to be a pleasant walking companion?"

The boy didn't answer immediately, but he raked Seb with an assessing stare, every inch the aristocratic young man his father would expect him to be.

"He seems to know his way around Hyde Park, although I don't think he much likes horses."

It seemed a sin among nobles not to revere horseflesh.

"Archibald!" Miss Perkins flexed the full prowess of her stern governess scowl, and the child ducked his head and bit his bottom lip, instantly contrite.

"It's quite all right, Miss Perkins." The last thing Seb wanted was to earn the boy a scolding.

"You'll find, Miss Perkins, that the Duke of Wrexford is very fond of plain speaking and honesty," Kat lilted.

He hated the disappointment in her gaze—not anger or even confusion—just a long piercing glare, as if she was looking at him again for the first time and found him far less impressive this go around.

"Come, Violet, we must get back in time for luncheon."

"Kat. Lady Katherine, may I call on you later?"

"No." The finality in her tone pricked like a thorn under his skin.

"Your sister and I are going shopping. Have you forgotten?"

He had forgotten. This business with Alecia, with her son, had consumed him. The worry of what he'd do, how he could make amends for missing out on years of the boy's life had gnawed at him from the moment he'd opened his eyes. And he still felt no certainty the boy was even his son.

"Then I shall see you when the two of you return with feathered hats?"

Not even his reference to their previous adventure in the park inspired a bit of levity in Kat.

"Perhaps, Your Grace. Good day, Master Archie, and to you, Miss Perkins."

He watched her walk away, and his body tensed, ratcheting tighter with every step. He held his breath, willing her to look back at him, to give him some sliver of hope. She never turned. He gulped in a breath of air, reminding himself he'd see her in a few hours, when she returned from shopping with Pippa.

But what would happen when their feigned engagement ended? He'd asked her father for her hand in marriage, but if Archie was truly his son, he couldn't offer for Kat.

He'd have to tell her the truth of it, and she'd walk away from him as she did now, without a second glance.

## Chapter Nineteen

"This one's my favorite. What do you think, Kitty?" Philippa Fennick held up a smart little hat, carnation pink with delphinium blue accents, and nearly dropped it when the Wrexford brougham hit a rough spot on the cobblestones and she lurched forward.

Rather than become irritated as Cynthia Osgood or some of Kitty's other friends might, Sebastian's sister simply chuckled and righted herself. The young woman had an unassailable cheerfulness about her, and guilt for how she'd treated Pippa during their first encounter niggled at the back of Kitty's mind.

"That one is lovely, but I like them all. You have excellent taste."

Pippa cast her a dubious glance. "I'm not sure that's true. I wouldn't have had any idea what to choose if you hadn't been with me. To be honest, I've never bothered much with fashion."

Kitty couldn't detect any embarrassment or regret in the statement. Much like her brother, Pippa simply stated the truth artlessly. Or at least it seemed Sebastian spoke the truth. She'd been fool enough to believe it also meant he revealed all of himself. But he'd never promised her that. In fact, he'd insisted in Lady Stamford's garden that they keep their secrets to themselves.

"I don't know a bit about fashion," Pippa continued. "When I buy a hat, it's to keep the sun off my skin. I never worry what they look like." Sebastian's sister grinned. "Thank you, Kitty. You've taught me a lesson today. I never imagined buying a pretty hat could be such a satisfying endeavor."

After gazing out the carriage window a moment, Pippa turned back, expression serious. "I must confess to being uncertain about you. Perhaps I'm too protective of Seb. Maybe I'm too quick to cast judgment." She grinned again, but it was lopsided and rueful. "It seems I have many lessons to learn."

For the first time in their half a day together, Kitty sensed insecurity in the young woman's tone.

"Do you think I'll know how to be a duke's sister? My desire to protect him is second only to my wish to never embarrass Sebastian."

Pippa had no mother, no one to guide or shepherd her through what Kitty knew could be a daunting gamut of social judgments and competitive games. But she still held to her initial impression. With a bit more polish and a bit less naiveté, Sebastian's sister could become one of society's jewels.

"You couldn't. Anyone can see your brother adores you, trusts you, and with good reason."

That made Pippa smile, her narrow cheeks plumping round. "I think it's clear he adores *you*."

Kitty instantly noticed the confines of the carriage, the doors trapping them inside, the impossibility of escape without flinging herself into a row of busy afternoon traffic. Had it been so hot in the carriage a moment before? A trickle of perspiration slid down her neck, and she reached to lower the window. The fixture wouldn't budge.

She wanted Pippa's words to be true. The sentiment was precisely what she most yearned to hear, and yet her immediate thought was to refute the notion. To escape the very contemplation that Sebastian felt about her as she did for him, as if some part of her nature repulsed any possibility of grasping her own happiness.

"We are very fond of each other." She tried not to squeak but all the air had drained out of the enclosed space.

"Fond of each other? Surely it's more than that. I see the way he looks at you and you at him."

Was there a special way he looked at her? As if he was here with them in the carriage, Kitty saw his gray blue gaze searching her own. She swallowed and her throat felt raw.

What nonsense. Men's gazes had been following her for years. Men and women looked at each other. She'd even caught Pippa exchanging glances with Hattie's Oliver now and then.

"I honestly never thought Seb would consider giving

his heart again," Pippa said quietly as she ran her fingers around the edges of one of the velvet flowers on her new hat. Then, pushing the hat aside, she shifted in her seat and folded her arms, pressing her lips together, as if determined not to let another word escape.

"Was Sebastian . . . married before?" The notion of Sebastian's wariness to risk his heart piqued Kitty's curiosity.

"No! Absolutely not." Pippa lifted a hand to bite her fingernail before seeming to realize the error of etiquette, and pressed her palm against her thigh. "But he was engaged once. It ended badly. I mean to say, they called it off."

Kat knew instantly who Seb had once intended to marry.

"Lady Naughton."

Pippa's eyes went round. "You already knew?"

"I suspected." Deep under her skin, in her heart, wherever intuition resided, she'd known. "When were they engaged?"

"Many, many years ago, when I was still a child. It must be ten years ago now, at least."

How had it been? Who'd broken whose heart? Why did they end the engagement? At Lady Stamford's ball, she'd assumed Sebastian had rejected Lady Naughton. She'd never forget the displeasure on the woman's face when she caught them together in the garden.

Had he loved her? He'd certainly been unwilling to discuss any romance with Lady Naughton. His secret, Kitty had called her, and Sebastian never denied it.

Why couldn't he speak as honestly of his connection with the woman as he did everything else? And why had he been walking in Hyde Park with the lady's son?

The boy looked younger than ten years old. Kitty guessed him a few years younger than Violet. Could Archie be Sebastian's son?

Kitty needed to move and stretch, to be free of her carriage-shaped cage. She slid her foot forward and encountered a hatbox, and then another. In her excitement, Pippa had taken out more of her purchases to study their details and try them on again.

"Perhaps we should put all of these away, Pippa. We're almost there."

"I wonder what Sebastian will say about my sudden taste for fashionable hats."

"Would you mind if I spoke to him alone for a bit when we arrive?" However much she dreaded the answers, Kitty had to know the details of his relationship with Lady Naughton and her son.

"Actually, my aunt invited me to join her at the opera this evening. I hoped I might convince you and Seb to join us." Pippa busied herself with resealing her hats in their boxes as she spoke, and then stilled. "Unless . . . please tell me what I've said hasn't made you doubt Sebastian. I couldn't bear to see him endure what he did before."

"Our situation doesn't compare, Pippa." Kitty's throat closed around the admission, and the pressure reached down to grip her heart. "Our engagement has less to do with romance than practicality."

Pippa ducked her head and pinched the edge of her skirt between her fingers. After taking a deep breath, she leaned forward to catch Kitty's gaze.

"It may have started as a ploy, but hasn't it grown into more? Do you truly intend to end the engagement?"

"I have no intention of ending our engagement." *At least for now.*

Plans had been made for Hattie's wedding. A joint wedding gown final fitting was scheduled for tomorrow. Whatever her feelings for Sebastian, she couldn't let their plan fall apart yet.

When the carriage stopped in front of Wrexford House, Kitty almost balked. After stepping onto the pavement and out into the cool evening air, the desire to turn and start the relatively short walk back home made her legs vibrate. Why question him about the matter of Lady Naughton at all? They weren't truly engaged. His past was his own. He'd keep his secrets, and she'd keep hers. They'd agreed on that from the start.

And yet . . . if the boy was Sebastian's son, and Lady Naughton was prepared to risk her own ruin by exposing the fact, that scandal would ripple out to affect everyone associated with him. His sister would suffer snubs from polite society. Oliver's career might even suffer the connection, and that would touch Hattie. Scandal had a way of seeping out and staining everyone nearby, even those innocent of any wrongdoing.

Father wouldn't allow any connection with Wrexford or his family if the child's paternity became public. Sebastian wouldn't be the first aristocrat to father a child out of wedlock, but he hadn't even been a nobleman for a year. Hypocrisy required much less effort than humility. Kitty feared the condemnation would be greater for Sebastian because he had just assumed the title, only to tarnish it in the eyes of those who claimed to hold themselves to a higher standard.

"Are you coming in, Kitty?"

Pippa stood on the threshold, urging her into the town house's brightly lit entryway. The space was illuminated so well, she could see Sebastian lurking at the end of the hall, gazing at her as anxiously as his sister. But whereas Pippa wore her usual open expression with a grin curving her mouth, Sebastian appeared as grim as when she'd left him standing in Hyde Park.

Alone but for one governess and a clever child who might be his illegitimate son.

Kitty willed her body forward and was shocked when her legs obeyed. With a promise of a future outing, she thanked Pippa for joining her hat shopping jaunt. Regardless of the fact she hadn't selected a single new hat for herself, she'd enjoyed their time together.

"I take it you two won't be joining Aunt Augusta and me at the theater." Pippa glanced between them before gathering a couple of her hatboxes and heading upstairs.

Despite how his solemn expression increased her desire to turn and avoid a confrontation altogether, Kitty approached Sebastian.

"May I join you in your study?"

He frowned, as if he'd expected her to say something else entirely. Without answering, he turned and began trudging back toward the room where he'd last kissed her.

Afternoon light transformed the room, brightening the wallpaper, lifting the ceiling and extending the walls. The space loomed larger and much less intimate, especially when Sebastian positioned himself in the corner, the farthest point in the room from where she stood.

Her breath caught as she watched him. She'd never seen his broad shoulders sag so decidedly, nor found his mouth so firmly set. Divots of displeasure drew down each corner. He'd crossed his legs at the ankles and clasped his arms across his chest as he leaned against the wall. It felt as if a door had been shut to her. She realized in that moment how open he'd been before, how much he'd let her in.

Her pulse picked up, fluttering at her throat and thrashing in her ears when she tipped her gaze up to meet his.

"Have you come to end it?" He stared down at his feet.

Her breath whooshed out and drawing in the next brought pain, a little stab of despair deep in the center of her chest. She pressed a palm to the spot.

Then it was true. No denial, no explanation. Simply the assumption she would turn her back on him.

Hurt and anger welled up, twisting the pain into a sour knot in the pit of her stomach. He assumed the worst of her, that she was judgmental and hypocritical like all the rest. That she would dismiss him as swiftly as her father.

He seemed uninterested in putting up a fight or defending himself.

"Is ending it what you're hoping I'll do?"

"Do my hopes matter to you now?"

Even as he waited for her answer, he refused to look at her. Turning his body toward the window, he gazed at the curtains as if he could see the same patch of London sky where they'd sought far-off constellations together. Where he'd stood behind her and touched her as if he could do nothing else, as if he found her irresistible. And then kissed as no man ever had.

After so many suitors, assumptions had been made. Most men believed she would allow a stolen kiss, but she hadn't. She guarded her kisses as fiercely as she guarded her choice of a husband. She never intended to give herself away easily. Before Sebastian, she doubted the possibility of giving herself to any man at all.

So, yes, what he wanted mattered. She was just beginning to reach out and grasp what *she* wanted, but she had to know Sebastian's wishes were the same.

"What you want matters most of all. I need to know."

He glanced back at her. "Ask me whatever you wish to know. I'll answer any question you put to me."

So he always had. Every question except the one about his past relationship with Lady Naughton. She wanted to know about the boy, but she also feared his answers. Not the facts, but the feelings. Did he still love Alecia Naughton?

"My first question, the most important one to me, is to know what you want, Sebastian."

She meant who he wanted, of course, but couldn't bring herself to speak so baldly. As she stood waiting, heat rushing up her neck and onto her cheeks, she prayed he'd sense her meaning.

If he loved her, all the rest could come after. She would face the rest with him. Scandal, rumor, condemnation. Come what may, she could face it if she could have him for her own and give herself to him.

Emerging from the dimly lit corner, Sebastian stalked toward her, a zinnia gold glow from the window burnishing the right half of his body and face.

He was only a footstep away, but Kat willed herself to wait, not to reach for him as everything in her wished to do. But her body betrayed her and she swayed forward, only her corset holding her upright.

Uncrossing his arms, Sebastian reached for her, offering her his hand and seeking hers.

She took his hand immediately, forming her fingers around his firm reassuring grasp.

"I want this," he whispered. "To touch you." He stepped forward and slid his free hand down, curving around her waist. "To hold you."

The pulse fluttering at her neck began to travel, into her throat, down into her chest, and then lower.

"And I want this." He bent his head but didn't take her lips. Just skimming his mouth across her cheek, he sought her ear, nuzzling her there before dipping lower to place a kiss on the sensitive flesh of her neck. Then he tasted her, flicking his tongue against her skin.

The pulsing sensation in her belly shot to the apex of her thighs, making her legs go jelly soft. If he hadn't been holding her, she feared she might have done something ridiculous, like faint or swoon. She'd never fainted and hated the notion of such an outward display of weakness, of losing control.

"Tell me." He spoke against the skin of her neck, his low voice resounding in breath and heat against her body.

He was asking her to confess what she suspected he already knew. She hadn't been able to deny it to herself, not with any success. Surely he'd read it in her eyes, in her responses to him, even before she'd admitted the feelings to herself.

"Tell me what you want, Kat."

She wanted to give her *yes* to the one man who'd never actually proposed.

"I want you."

The rest, words she'd never said to any man, welled up, but he kissed her and she forgot words. She forgot to think and worry over how she looked or how she behaved. Only Sebastian, the taste of him, the warmth of his body, the sound of his breath and little murmurs of pleasure rumbling in his chest—nothing more existed for a moment. And she wanted to feel more than think, love more than worry.

He groaned when she turned bold and pressed her breasts into his chest, lifting onto her toes and clasping his head in her hands to deepen their kiss, to dart her tongue out and dance with his, as he'd taught her. Then, bolder still, she reached up to tug at the top button of his shirt. She loved that he dressed casually at home and wasn't wearing a necktie, that a few slipped buttons brought her fingers in contact with his skin and the fine hairs at the top of his chest.

He lifted his head when she slid the third button free.

"Kat." The nickname he'd chosen for her never sounded as seductive as when he rasped it in hot gusting breath against her skin. If he meant to stop her or say something sensible, it was far too late. She'd been ladylike for twenty-three years, made choices to please others, to avoid her father's wrath and being snubbed by her watchful friends. This moment was hers, hers and Sebastian's, and she wished to live it to the full.

"Are you thinking too much?" she asked as she explored the warm muscled contours of his chest with her fingers.

Last time he'd kissed her, he'd insisted on trying not to think. An excellent philosophy she'd decided to embrace wholeheartedly. At least for tonight. At least for this moment. Thinking had never brought her this sort of pleasure, this sense of rightness, this feeling that she had found the part of herself she'd always been seeking.

"Probably. You?"

"As a wise man once said to me, I'm trying not to think."

She paused in unbuttoning him and put a hand on the rounded muscle of his upper arms, then trailed her palms down, pressing until he released her. Then she slid her palms down to catch each of his hands in hers. Never breaking his gaze, she brushed a kiss over the knuckles of one of his hands and then the other.

He swallowed before his beautifully carved mouth went slack, opening slightly, as he watched her.

When she raised her head, she guided his hands to the buttons at her neckline.

"Kat?"

"Please, Sebastian. I want you to see me."

Lifting a hand to her cheek, he cupped her face and drew her in for a lingering kiss.

She hadn't thought her heart could beat any faster, but as he stroked her face and tasted her again and again, it rattled wildly against her ribs.

He broke the kiss and tipped his head, assessing her. "I do see you, and you're exquisite."

His eyes skimmed her hair, eyes, and mouth, but those were the parts of her body she'd been praised for all her life. She could take no pride in having inherited her mother's blond hair or her grandmother's green eyes. If her face was pleasing, it had been a matter of good fortune and no effort of her own. Nor had she chosen the shapes and shades of the rest of her body, but she had a choice about who could see her, naked and unadorned.

She chose Sebastian. She suspected she'd been waiting her whole life to choose Sebastian.

"I want you to see all of me." Every inch of what his eye could see, and, yes, in time the rest of her too. The flaws beneath her skin, the imperfections of her heart, the too-busy whirl of her thoughts. With Sebastian, she might risk being exposed as her true self.

Her words ignited him and he reached up to slip the buttons at her neck, fumbling over the tiny rounded pearls, and then proceeding to the larger buttons hidden under a row of lace down her front. Each press of his fingers, kneading into her chest as he worked her free of the gown's bodice, pulled her tauter, every nerve in her body focused on the movement of his hands. Then he skimmed the tops of her breasts as he grasped her ribbon-edged corset, pressing each half together, forcing it momentarily tighter, stealing her breath, to slip one hook, then the next, and the next. The backs of his hands brushed her nipples and Kat couldn't hold back a moan as his touch reverberated down her body to the tips of her toes.

"So many layers to get to you."

"Am I not worth the effort?"

"You are, Kat. You're worth every effort."

Caressing her cheek, he leaned in for another kiss but stiffened at a soft scratching sound against his study door.

"Aunt Augusta's carriage has arrived and we're off to the theater." Pippa's voice rang through the closed door, and both of them stilled like guilty children caught making mischief.

"Enjoy yourselves," Sebastian returned as evenly as he was able while trying to catch his breath.

They remained quiet, holding onto each other and listening to Pippa's retreating footsteps until Kitty heard a thud she thought might signal her departure.

Sebastian clasped her hand and started toward the door.

"Where are we going? I'm . . . disheveled." She stopped him long enough to wave a hand in front of her chest to indicate her unclasped corset.

"Perfectly so, but if you remain like that in my study, I fear I'll never manage a rational thought in here again."

## Chapter Twenty

"Oh my." She'd expected his suite of rooms to be done in warm colors with dark woods, a masculine haven. But even the sitting room was decorated in light colors, mainly white, with intricate plasterwork arches and extraordinary accents of flower and vine designs etched into the walls.

"Is that stone?"

"Marble. The late duke and duchess spent time in India and took it as inspiration for these rooms."

He stood watching her, waiting, as if all the choices between them were hers to make.

When she reached for him, he pulled her into his arms, pressing his mouth to her forehead, as he had the first time he'd kissed her.

But that desire in Lady Stamford's garden was nothing to this need, this hunger to be closer to him. His scent, the hard strength of his body against hers, the desire to touch more of his skin, set off something pulsing and wild inside of her. Poise was gone. Self-possession had been jettisoned. There wasn't room for any of that now. Only this mattered. Only this moment, only the need to get closer to Sebastian.

She reached up to continue unbuttoning his shirt and skimmed the raised edge of a scar. Peeling aside his shirt, she traced the oblong mark gently with her fingertip.

"You were wounded." She wanted to know the when and the how, to know this and every part of his past, for them to reveal all of their secrets to each other.

"Many years ago. I was foolish."

The finality in his tone stopped her from asking more. Then his hands were on her, and she forgot about questions and old wounds. He grasped the edge of her corset, but he wouldn't get her out of it without removing her skirt and petticoats. She reached back for the hook at the top of her skirt. The movement pushed her chest toward his, and he hissed as if she'd burned him before cupping her left breast through the thin cotton chemise. When he slid his thumb over the tight mound of her nipple, she gasped and tried to remember how her fingers worked in order to unbutton each petticoat before nudging them and her skirt over the swell of her hips. Finally, she could shed her corset, and they both raced to untie the knot at the top of her chemise before tugging and pulling to get her free of it. She yanked so hard to free her arm that it jolted from the fabric, the flat of her hand slamming against the edge of his jaw.

She gingerly touched his face. "I'm so sorry."

Grinning, he whispered, "You're worth a little pain."

Turning his head, he placed a kiss in the center of her palm before gazing down between them.

"Let me see you."

For one pleasure-quelling moment thoughts rushed in, so loud they dulled the glorious rush of feeling and sensation. The room was too large, too bright, and she was far too bare. She became less aware of his heat and more aware of the sear of her own blush.

With one arm braced across her breasts, she reached down to—

"No, please. Don't hide from me now."

Then he was covering her, touching her, one hand cupping her shoulder before he dragged it down her arm, raising gooseflesh. His other hand began at her hip, sliding up to dip into the curve of her waist and then back down to grip the rounded flesh of her hip.

"I see you, every wonderful inch of you."

He lowered his head. She thought he'd kiss her, but he pressed his mouth first to the tender skin at the base of her throat, tasting her with his tongue, then kissing the cleave between her breasts before taking her right nipple into the warm wet cavern of his mouth.

When she arched back and moaned, he slid the hand on her hip lower, down to the flesh of her thigh, molding it with his hands before pressing his palm to her mound.

"Sebastian."

Releasing her breast, he tipped his head and gazed at

her, his smile arrowing straight into her chest, burrowing under her skin. Niggles of worry—that she'd been too loud, moaned too wantonly—melted away.

"That's how I've wanted to hear you say my name from the moment we met."

Before she could form a reply, he slid both hands to the base of her spine and lowered his head to kiss her stomach. Every spot his mouth and hands touched warmed, not just from the press of his mouth, but a deeper warmth, an inner heat, a secret thrill that he was the first man to touch her there, and there, and there.

Down on one knee, his other leg braced against hers, he stopped moving and looked up at her.

"I want to be the only man to touch you like this. Ever."

Locks of hair slid down over his brow, and Kitty reached out to run her fingers through the strands.

"Yes."

As she uttered the sibilant word, Sebastian pulled her closer and laved her belly button before trailing his mouth lower and kissing her tenderest flesh.

Kitty's moan broke into a keening cry as her knees began to buckle. Raking his hair with her fingers and then reaching out to grasp his shoulder, she felt feverish heat radiating off his skin through his shirt.

He turned his head, resting it against her stomach, and held her tight.

"I love you, Kat."

They were the words she'd longed for, imagined him saying. Needed to hear. And she hated the sting in her eyes, the tears beginning to force their way. Panic sprouting up to choke out all her bliss. Thoughts like weeds multiplying in her mind.

Hadn't a dozen men said those words with nothing of truth or sincerity behind them?

Ridiculous. Sebastian wasn't like any of those men.

So why couldn't she give the words back to him when they lay just there, heavy on her tongue? She'd never offered the three words to any man, never loved any man until Sebastian.

Sebastian stood, the strength of his body sheltering her, the comfort of his arms embracing her.

"What is it?"

She shook her head, unwilling to admit that even as she stood naked before him, having experienced such delicious pleasure, such precious intimacy, she was still afraid. Afraid of giving all of herself to a man only to disappoint him. Afraid that beyond her pleasing shape and outward appearance, he would find nothing in her worth loving.

He'd been a fool to say it. He who'd been guarding his heart for years. Who swore he wasn't capable of loving any woman again, let alone saying the words. He'd smashed their bliss with three overhasty words.

Worst of all, he wouldn't retract them. Too soon or at the wrong time, perhaps, but he couldn't deny the sentiment any more than he could deny the fever burning him from inside to touch her, taste her, pleasure her in every way he knew how.

When she finally lifted her head to look at him,

he expected regret. Instead, he saw yearning, uncertainty.

He reached for a coverlet to wrap her in, but she gripped his arm to stop him.

"Please, Sebastian. I want to see you too."

Her slim fingers worked at his last two shirt buttons and then gripped the fabric to wrench it up from his trousers. He bit back a groan when she went to work on his trouser buttons, her fingers grazing the firm ridge of him as she slipped each one. She kept her eyes turned down, but he needed to see her.

Sliding a hand along her jaw, he urged her chin up at the same moment she took him in her hand. Gasping as their gazes locked, he couldn't hold back the groan when she traced the length of him with her hand.

"Kat." He rasped her name on another groan as she pushed his trousers over his hips.

She smiled up at him. "I've wanted to hear you say my name like that since the night we met."

He reached to cup the delicious warmth of her breast, so soft, so full in his hand. "You wanted me to call you Kitty on the night we met."

"I prefer Kat now, but only when you say it."

He stepped out of his last bit of clothing and she slid against him, stretching up to mold her mouth to his as the smooth curve over belly caressed his aching erection. He gripped her hips to hold her still, though instinct urged him to lift her, lay her down, and love her.

"Kat?"

She bucked against the restraint, and he felt the curls

between her thighs tickling his abdomen. He licked his lips, remembering the taste of her.

"Please, Sebastian." She slid a hand down to curve over his hip just as he held her, then she tugged him closer. "Love me."

He lifted her, bending to scoop her up in his arms, and carried her to the edge of his bed. He lowered her slowly, gently. When she reached for him, he bent his head to kiss her tenderly and rested his hands on either side, easing her onto her back.

As he gazed down into her eyes, brimming with desire and eagerness to match his own, a latch inside him broke, some imprisoning bar of his own bitterness and regret. Colors brightened, Kat's rapid breaths rasped loud in his ears under the beat of his racing pulse, his skin tingled as the tension he'd hosted too long melted from his shoulders. Only Kat. Only this moment mattered, and the rest fell away.

She stroked the hair on his chest as he watched her, then reached around his neck to pull him down for a kiss.

He tasted her mouth, then trailed his lips down to her breasts, tasting one ripe taut nipple before laving the other. She lifted her hips each time he licked her, and he wanted to slip inside of her, draw her to the point of pleasure. But not yet.

Sliding down her body, he kissed the smooth expanse of her stomach, then lower, tasting her center again, slipping his tongue into her delicious heat. The taste of her tore away all pretense, all propriety and gentlemanly thoughts. She was his. Only his. No other man would touch her like this. Ever.

She lifted her hips off the bed as she cried out her release, fingers tangling in his hair, her other hand pulling at his shoulder. He kissed a trail up her body before settling between her thighs.

"Sebastian." The sound of his name on her tongue, spoken with such wonder and awe, warmed him, and he was already burning.

She opened her mouth and he thought she might say it, those three words he hadn't imagined hearing or wanting from another woman ever again.

Tracing his jaw with her fingers, reaching up to smooth the hair back from his brow, he saw it in her eyes.

"Love me, Sebastian." And he did. His heart ached for how deeply she'd burrowed inside.

The words were there, true and real and the most frightening words she'd ever say to a man. She wanted to say them to Sebastian, wanted everything with Sebastian.

She licked her lips to try again, but he flexed his hips and she gasped as he pressed inside. She savored the thick hard slide as he joined their bodies and she lifted her hips to urge him closer, deeper.

He moved again, emitting a low sound at the back of his throat, and slid against her, filling her. Too full, too much. She pressed her hands to his shoulders to still him, and he lowered his head to kiss her. Yes, she needed to taste him. She opened to let his tongue dance against hers, and then he moved inside her, against her. Slow, delicious thrusts that drew every nerve in her body tight as a harp string.

Lifting his head, he gazed at her with such tenderness, such love and desire. No pretense. No charm. Just Sebastian loving her.

"I love you." She spoke in ragged breath as much as sound, but he heard every word. He closed his eyes a moment and when he opened them to gaze at her, they were molten silver blue, glassier than before, and he drove against her faster, deeper, drawing her toward the edge. Her skin burned, breasts ached for his mouth, and she wanted him deeper, could not get him close enough. Then she burst apart, crying out, arching up against his body, as pleasure drowned her until she gasped for air. He broke, groaning her name, driving into her once more, repeating the name he'd chosen for her. The name she loved. The man she loved.

He turned and collapsed beside her, reaching out to gather her against him. Their legs tangled, and she adored the tickle of the fine hairs on his body against her skin.

They lay quietly, catching their breath, and he stroked long drugging ribbons of sensation across her back with his fingertips.

She turned her head to listen to the beat of his heart, marveling that any man's heart—this man's heart—could be hers. As her own heartbeat steadied, her mind took up the reins, speeding ahead.

Fear rushed in. Doubts. He knew her body now, how

she sounded when he brought her to the precipice of pleasure and caught her as she fell. He knew the taste of her body, the feel of her skin against his. But he still didn't know her heart. He looked at her and saw more good than anyone ever had, yet she hadn't shown him the rest. She had been cruel. She had been petty, manipulating others, just as she'd watched her father do so many times.

The heat of Sebastian's body warmed her skin, but inside she began to go cold, defenses rising, old habits settling into place.

"Would you help me dress?"

"Of course."

He sat up and then stood, quickly pulling on his trousers before assisting her. He touched her tenderly, refastening the clothes he'd helped her to shed, and watched her intently as she tried to avoid his gaze.

"Kat, is this a good-bye?"

Swallowing, she willed words to come, forcing herself to be the self-possessed woman who'd walked into his study less than hour before. But she wasn't that woman anymore. She would never truly be that woman again. Everything had changed. He loved her, and she loved him. But she feared reaching out and embracing love. Loving him would change her, and for the better, but losing him would break her.

Poise. Calm. She could put on the mask again. She'd spent her life pretending, mismatching actions and emotions.

Finally lifting her gaze to his, she dredged up a bit of the old Kitty, summoning the even emotionless tone she'd learned from her father.

"How could it be? Ollie and Harriet aren't married yet. We still have our roles to play."

## *Chapter Twenty-One*

SEB'S THOUGHT REGARDING the equation hid, dodging every attempt to grasp it. Finally he caught it by its tail and rushed to scribble down the one bit of coherence he'd managed all morning, but he pressed the nib of his pen too hard, splattering ink on the paper, the blotter, and his shirt cuff. Staring down at the ragged hole where his captured thought should have been, he ground his teeth and flung the damned writing implement at the pen rest, missing it entirely.

With the movement, a twinge came, deep in his chest. His rusty tattered heart protested like Victor Frankenstein's monster for being brought back to life.

He stared across his study at the unlit fireplace. The marble mantel and looking glass above faded, and she was there. Kat, gloriously nude, every inch of her luminous skin exposed. She wanted him to see her, she'd said, and he'd never seen anything more magnificent in his life. And not because she'd been some ephemeral nymph, some flawless goddess he could never deserve. She'd been solid and warm in his arms—smooth flesh, lush curves, tantalizing angles—and she'd tasted of vanilla and lavender.

What a brave woman, so determined to gift him with those moments of intimacy and pleasure. And Kat had given him more than a memory he'd never forget. She'd given him a revelation—about himself, about his bruised heart. He'd wanted her in that moment like he'd never wanted anyone or anything. And he knew, acknowledged to himself and to her, that he loved her. What he hadn't confessed, what he'd only realized as Kat stood before him, is that he'd never felt it before—desire that bowed and strengthened him in the same moment, certainty that she would be his and he would be hers and there'd never be another.

What he'd felt for Alecia hadn't been love. Obsession, madness, youthful preoccupation—whatever it had been, it didn't approach this. His feelings for Kat had crept upon him so softly he hadn't time to fear or deny them. They were as much a part of him now as his limbs or the blood pumping in his veins.

When a knock sounded at the door, he realized he'd clenched the scribbled paper in front of him into a crinkled ball.

"Come in."

A young housemaid pushed through the door and curtsied. "Your Grace, forgive the interruption. There's a lady to see you."

Kat. Thank God. He could reassure her, soothe whatever fears had precipitated her hasty departure the night before. He still couldn't reconcile the uncertainty he'd seen in her eyes as she walked out the door with the love she'd confessed moments before.

"Thank you. Please show her in."

"Oh, forgive me, Your Grace. I asked her to wait in the drawing room."

Perhaps the drawing room was best, especially if Kat had any regrets about what had passed between them in his study.

"Very well."

He licked his lips and clenched his fists as he followed the maid down the hall. Sniffing the air, he expected to detect one of Kat's floral brews, but he only smelled starch and the mild sweetness of a bouquet of hothouse roses artfully arranged in a crystal vase on the entryway table.

"Your Grace, forgive me for calling unexpectedly."

Not Kat. Not the woman he longed to see. Seb's shoulders sagged and a dull ache thumped at the back of his head.

Archie Naughton's governess stood in the center of his drawing room, pressing her hands together, a frown twisting her face and carving lines across her forehead. The matter of the boy and Alecia's claims hadn't slipped from his mind, but last night and this morning, Kat monopolized every thought.

"Please have a seat, Miss Perkins."

The middle-aged woman twisted her head one way and then the other, as if uncertain which chair to choose, before finally perching at the far edge of the settee. Her jerky uncoordinated movements didn't match the woman he'd met the previous day. They indicated nervousness, or fear.

"What brings you to Wrexford House?"

A long pause followed while the woman stared at her clasped hands, then glanced up at him before ducking her head again.

Seb still couldn't quite forgive her for not being Kat, nor for reminding him of the unresolved matter of Alecia's claim that he'd fathered her child.

"Miss Perkins?"

She finally met his gaze, her mouth trembling, eyes brimming with unshed tears.

"I will lose my place over this, so I beg you to understand if it's difficult for me."

She'd come to him and believed it would lose her the post as governess to Archie. Pinpricks rushed across his skin and he stifled a shiver. Only Alecia had ever inspired a dark sense of foreboding in him.

Miss Perkins struggled to swallow, as if she'd just downed a loaf of bread whole, and reached inside the pocket of her skirt. The document she pulled out looked old, with foxing on the paper and wear at the edges. She handled it with care as she flattened it on her lap and then lifted it out to him.

His hand shook as he reached for the paper. It looked to be a page from a family history or genealogical record of the Naughton family. Archie's name was listed near the bottom, with birth date and year recorded as tenth of June, 1883. The boy would turn nine in a few months, and he'd been conceived two years after Seb had last seen Alecia before the encounter at his aunt's ball.

"My father is in jail."

The non sequitur caught him off guard, tangling his tongue and scattering the words he'd been about to say.

"He's a screever, a forger of documents."

Seb shook his head slowly, aware that his mouth hung open and he must look a fool. He had no idea what the woman was on about.

"I thought it very kind of Lady Naughton to employ me and overlook my father's transgressions. She entrusted me with the care and education of such a fine young boy." Her voice broke at the mention of Archie and she inhaled sharply through her nose as if bracing herself.

"I will miss him more than I can say, but I can't be a part of Lady Naughton's scheme."

Like one of Mr. Turner's vivid paintings, the details of Miss Perkins's tale were hidden among the brushstrokes, and he began to glimpse the framework of one of Alecia's snares.

"She asked you to alter this document?"

The woman shook her head so fiercely, Seb feared she might sprain something. "Not me, Your Grace, never. But she believed, given my family history, I would know someone who would. And not to alter that one but to forge a new one."

He traced the writing where the boy's name and birth date were listed, pressing his finger to the last numeral in his birth year. A different number there might have changed his life, the boy's life, and destroyed the Naughton family.

"And the rest of her scheme? She forges a new document and then what? Ruins her marriage, destroys her reputation, injures her child. For what?"

"She said you would give her money. I'm loathe to say it, but funds are not plentiful in the household. Both master and mistress spend freely." The governess released a breath, perhaps relieved by the confession and yet she held her stomach, as if all the whole matter left her queasy. "Lady Naughton says she should have been your duchess."

Seb narrowed his eyes and Miss Perkins shrugged. Apparently, Alecia's rationales sounded as mad to her as they did to him.

Another of her schemes. Another betrayal. He let the truth of it settle in his mind and waited for the rage he'd felt in the past, the bitterness that had been his companion for years.

It didn't come. He clenched his hands over the arms of his chair, irritated that the morning had not gone in another direction, that he resisted calling on Kat as he'd convinced himself not to do. Beyond irritation there was an unexpected pang of sympathy—for Miss Perkins and the impossible situation Alecia had put her in, for Archie who'd unknowingly become a pawn to his mother's greed, and even for Naughton. Whatever the man's sins, he didn't deserve this.

"Lady Naughton intended to present you and your aunt with the forgery to convince you that Archie is your son."

"Yes, I see." Seb lifted the document to return it to the governess, but she shook her head in refusal.

"You should keep it, Your Grace."

Keeping a piece of Naughton's family history didn't sit well with Seb, but the document might be his only evidence to refute Alecia's claim.

"Thank you. I shall keep it for now. What will you tell Lady Naughton about the forgery?"

Miss Perkins caught the edge of her bottom lip with her teeth. "I considered telling her I was accosted and the original document lost on my way to find the man."

"Seems as good a tale as any. You truly fear she'll dismiss you?"

For the first time since her arrival, Miss Perkins sat up straight, gazing at him directly, regaining the poise he'd seen in her the day before.

"Despite my initial impression of Lady Naughton, I now find her to be quite unpredictable. And this plan to deceive you, with Archie in the middle, has soured me on the lady altogether. If she doesn't dismiss me, I suspect I'll have to leave."

He understood her reasons, but he hated the notion of her departure and the disappointment of the boy who admired her.

"I hope you don't, Miss Perkins, for the lad's sake."

For a long moment, Seb assessed Archie's governess and she took his measure in return.

"Seb?"

He turned at the sound of his sister's voice.

"Sorry to interrupt, and pardon me, miss, but I wanted to remind you of our trip to the gallery."

He'd ruminated the morning away pondering his future with Kat, and completely forgotten that they'd agreed to all gather on the portico of the South Kensington Museum at noon.

Miss Perkins shot to her feet. "I should be going, Your Grace."

"Thank you, Miss Perkins."

After showing the governess out, he headed back to his study but Pippa stopped him.

"Who was your lady visitor? And should a betrothed man have lady visitors?" she teased. He'd missed that light teasing note in her voice.

"She's the governess to Alecia Naughton's son."

He expected her frown of confusion, but if they were to meet Kat and her sister within the hour, he didn't have time to explain. And more than anything, he needed to see Kat.

When Pippa didn't question him further, he moved to pass her in the hall. "We should prepare for the gallery outing."

"Seb, wait. You look . . . altered." She examined him closely, squinting as she studied his eyes.

"Do I?" Seb felt a bit like an animal at market, and Pippa looked as if she might ask to inspect his teeth.

"What's happened to you?"

Lady Katherine Adderly was the simplest answer, but

saying as much would only lead to more questions. A flurry of them, he suspected.

Then, without him saying anything, Pippa's brown eyes rounded and she reached out to squeeze his arm so hard he winced.

"Oh my goodness! I can't believe it, and yet I can see it written all over your face." She held her breath a moment and then gushed, "You *have* fallen in love with her!"

Falling didn't seem the right word, though Pippa was usually the one to argue semantics. If anything, his feelings for Kat had buoyed him up, reviving him, giving him an eagerness for the future he hadn't felt in years.

"I do plan to ask her to marry me."

Pippa crossed her arms and glowered as if was a fool. "Haven't you already done that?"

"You know our engagement was contrived. We're past the point of falsehood now, and I'm finished with pretending."

He didn't need his sister's approval, but he wanted it. Though she was eight years his junior, he trusted Pippa's judgment. At least with everything but her taste in men.

Seb crossed his arms, mirroring her stance.

"Are you waiting for my blessing?" she asked.

He thought back to Pippa's displeasure when he'd told her of his plan to feign an engagement to Kat. Observing their truce at the dinner table had given him hope, but the two women had few other opportunities to speak and come to know each other.

Romance was never a topic he'd broached with Pippa.

He'd never even spoken openly about recognizing she'd developed feelings for Ollie. It seemed more of a sisterly topic of conversation, though he suspected Pippa didn't talk about matters of the heart with anyone.

"What is it you see in her?" There was no judgment in her tone. She was testing his precepts, forcing him to defend his reasoning.

Her judgment would have been easier than questions, and with her usual impatience, she gave him no time to answer before proceeding to her next ones.

"I may have changed my views about Kitty, but tell me why you wish to marry her. As much as I hate to admit it, her odious father did have a point. You encountered only a handful of women at Cambridge and the season's just begun. Why chose so quickly? Perhaps she's simply the only woman with whom you've had reason to exchange more than a few polite words."

"Why do you love Ollie?"

She took a step away from him and pressed her arms more firmly against her chest, turning her head down to study the carpet.

He hadn't meant to corner her or expose a truth that caused her pain, but her questions had come too fast and they'd implied too much doubt about his feelings for Kat not to spark frustration.

"I'm sorry, Pippa." He tipped back his head and sighed. "I'm happy to answer your questions, each and every one of them."

Stepping forward, he lowered his arms, eager to make peace with this sister.

"But there's more to choosing who we love than logic." Mercy, he almost sounded fanciful.

She finally turned her gaze on him in a pointed glare.

"Then perhaps we should look to logic more often and avoid the pain of terrible choices."

He wasn't sure if she referred to his misery with Alecia or her feelings for Ollie.

"Kat is intelligent and believes in the vote for women."

Pippa's raised eyebrow and the quiver of a grin at the edge of her mouth pleased him. He knew that bit of information about Kat would intrigue her.

"While she's aware of her beauty, she accepts it more as fact than conceit. She's fiercely loyal to her sisters, and even to her father, who I'm not sure deserves it." *And I adore the way she thinks and makes lists, the way she moves, the way she looks at me, and her ever-changing scents.* If he said all that, Pippa truly would count him a besotted fool.

"She'll be an outstanding duchess." The certainty struck him almost as an afterthought. If he'd set out to choose a woman who could take on the duties of the role with grace and equanimity, not even his aunt could have selected a lady as well suited as Kat.

Pippa nodded and released her crossed arms to place a hand on each hip. "So she's not bereft of charms and fine qualities. I'm glad to hear it. But aren't you forgetting something?"

In his current state of mind, he probably had.

"What does she think of you? None of us could approve of a woman who did not appreciate all of *your* fine qualities."

He lifted a brow at that. "That's a good deal of sentimentality from you, Pippa, for so early in the morning."

"Does she love you? Truly?"

That spot in his chest that had twinged on and off all morning began to ache with a pulsating pain—as if his heart hurt with every beat. Now who was being sentimental?

But Pippa's question drew him to a point he did not wish to ponder, that he'd avoided sifting all morning. He'd been too consumed with recalling the sight of Kat standing in the center of his study, her corset pulled loose, gilded in dim gaslight and a sunset glow.

In the elaborate bedroom he already thought of as theirs, he'd confessed his love, and she'd said it too. But her admission seemed to change everything between them. Soon after he'd sensed her waver, and uncertainty rushed in to replace all the passion he'd seen in her eyes moments before.

He couldn't have mistaken the feelings between them. They were powerful and real and, for the first time in his life, felt in equal measure. Kat might be practiced at artifice—polite smiles and inane drawing room conversation—but surely those moments between them hadn't been that. There'd been no one to see and assess, no one to pass judgments that might impact their social standing. Holding her, touching her, loving her—that had been true. It had to be, be-

cause in those moments with Kat he'd been more alive
than he'd felt in years.

"Seb? Don't you know whether she loves you or not?"

She had said it, but perhaps the depth of her feeling
did not match his own. Had he been so blinded by his
own desires that he'd misread hers? What had caused
the fear he'd glimpsed before she departed? He shouldn't
have let her leave in such distress. If she could find the
courage to give herself to him, he should have found the
courage to ask her, not only about the state of her heart,
her fears and doubts, but whether she'd be his wife.

More than anything else, he wanted Kat to be his wife.
Seb had to ask her.

"I suppose there's only one way to find out."

## Chapter Twenty-Two

As THE COOL satin slid against her skin, Kitty could think only of Sebastian's warm fingertips as he stroked her. On her legs, her arms, her face, even at her core, her body held a memory of his touch, spots he'd explored, staking them out as his own with this hands, his mouth, his tongue. He said he never wanted another man to touch her that way. Neither did she. Ever.

The dressmaker tugged at the fabric near her waist, adding a pin from those arrayed in the seam between her lips, snapping Kitty out of her erotic reverie.

She breathed deep and finally glanced at herself in her long sitting room mirror. A bride stared back at her, garbed in the loveliest wedding dress she'd ever seen. Buttery satin fabric embroidered with dozens of lily of the valley flowers, and sparkling beads sewn in clusters to mark the center of each flower bell.

"What will be the flower sewn on my dress?" Violet called out to Kitty from the sitting room sofa.

She hadn't even realized Vi had come into the room. Her youngest sister sat next to where Hattie's rose-embroidered dress had been carefully laid out after her morning fitting.

"Which flower would you like?"

When Violet didn't answer, Kitty approached.

"Careful, miss. It's only pins holding much of that gown together," the dressmaker's assistant warned.

"Just a moment, Vi, and I'll join you there on the sofa."

Kitty waited while she was carefully divested of the skirt and bodice of the gown. Before departing, the modiste promised the completed dresses in five days, and Kitty calculated that with all the other arrangements in place, Hattie and Mr. Treadwell could easily marry within a fortnight.

The question of her own wedding, if such a day might ever come, niggled at the back of her mind. She'd woken full of regrets, not for what she and Sebastian had shared, but for how she'd left him. He'd looked stunned as he saw her to the Wrexford House front door, and it was the last emotion she wished to leave him with after the intimacies they'd shared.

She'd been a coward. A fool. And she'd tell him so today if she could find a moment alone during their outing to the gallery.

After seeing the dressmaker and her assistant out, Kitty lowered herself onto the sofa next to her sister, resting an arm along the back, just touching the girl's slim shoulders.

Violet was at the age for pouting, it seemed. The girl spent whole parts of the day with her chin perched on her fisted hand as it was now, and a forlorn expression plumping her lower lip and drawing her tawny brows together.

"What is it, Vi? You look as if someone's eaten all your sticky toffee pudding."

"I'd want violets for my dress."

"Wonderful choice." For their rich scent and vibrant purple shade, they were a flower Kitty admired.

"It's a boring choice. My name's Violet. I like violets. You see? Terribly boring." She was already sagging against the sofa but she leaned forward so that she could flounce back with a dramatic sigh.

"Violets aren't boring. They're beautiful and have a lovely perfume."

"*You* never wear violet water. It's boring. And if I'm boring, I'll never find a gentleman who wants to marry me, let alone have a wedding dress with violet-embroidered satin." Somehow they'd gone from violets to perfume to Violet becoming an old maid. Kitty's mind tripped over the holes in her sister's logic, but pointing out the gaps would only lead to a row.

She pressed her forefinger to her lower lip, thinking how best to reassure the girl without filling her head with fanciful nonsense. She focused on the facts. She'd worn violet perfume plenty of times. Occasionally, at least.

And if she didn't wear it often, it was simply because it was a rather common scent. Not boring. Just a bit . . . commonplace.

And, anyway, a lady didn't snare a husband because of the scent she wore. Few men had remarked on her perfumes before Sebastian, and none had ever asked her to tell them about the flowers that made up the scents.

"You can't even think of anything comforting to say! You must agree."

"I don't. Not at all, but I do think you should worry less about what others think of you."

If there was an art to eye-rolling, Violet had perfected it. She reminded Kitty of the fact with an impressive eye-roll and sigh combination.

"Just be true, and to yourself most of all. One day you'll find a man who loves you for that, for the truth of who you are. He'll love that you adore books and sewing. That you're overly fond of sticky toffee pudding and sneak sips of Father's coffee when he's not looking. That you like to plan for the future and care dearly about details, such as which flower you'll have on your wedding gown. In fact, you have such a way with a needle, I suspect you could embroider your own gown."

Violet sniffed, but she lifted her chin and sat up a bit straighter, as if somewhat mollified by Kitty's words. "With violets?"

"With whatever you wish."

"Does the Duke of Wrexford love you like that?"

"I think he does." He did. Kitty knew it, felt it, no longer truly doubted it.

When Violet smiled, it lit up the room, and caught the tiny mole on her cheek—the one she hated and had once tried to scrub off with tooth powder—in the cleft of her only dimple.

"He seems very charming."

"Yes."

Was he? He could dress elegantly and had impeccable manners. He was distractingly handsome and a clever conversationalist. Presumably he could be charming, though Kitty didn't like the word. She associated it with men who fawned, men preoccupied with boasting about themselves while pretending to adore her. If Sebastian had attempted to charm her, she wouldn't have given him a second look. Well, perhaps she would have looked. She'd never found a man more appealing to the eye, but charm wouldn't have snared her interest the way his honesty had. Charm wouldn't have won her heart. And it still shocked her that he'd accomplished that feat.

Violet lifted her head and stared at the room's threshold.

"Hattie, we were just talking about the duke. It seems Kitty *is* madly in love with him."

"Thank you, Violet."

Her youngest sister shrugged innocently before Kitty turned her gaze back to where Hattie lingered in the doorway.

Hattie wore a serious expression and ignored Kitty's implicit invitation. "Papa would like to speak with you, Kitty. He's asked me to fetch you down to his study."

"Did he mention why?"

"He just asked me to call you down." Along with eye-rolling, Violet was quite adept at fibbing, but Harriet could never pull it off. If her cheeks didn't flush and give her away, she had a tendency to start blinking, her eyelashes fluttering like black butterfly wings against her face. She blinked now, rapidly.

Kitty turned and pressed a kiss to Violet's cheek.

Her baby sister reached up to pat her arm and whispered, "I'm glad he loves you as you are."

"Me too." Now if she could just assure the man she felt the same.

While Hattie tapped her foot impatiently, Kitty walked to meet her at the door, almost forgetting that she was wearing a simple outdated day dress and had yet to change in the one she'd selected for their outing.

"I should change before speaking to Papa."

"No, Kitty, there isn't time." She'd never heard such panic in her sister's voice.

"Hattie, what is it?"

Kitty asked the question gently, quietly, so as not to alarm Violet, but it only seemed to anger Hattie and she threw up her hands before bracing them on her hips. "Goodness, Kitty. Why not go and speak to him rather than cross-questioning me?"

The girl was distressed, and Kitty didn't doubt their father was the cause. Apparently he had all the answers.

She swept past Hattie without another word and heard her sister's footsteps echoing behind her own.

"I do remember where to find father's study. You should prepare for our trip to the museum." Without looking back at her sister, Kitty heard Hattie retreating up the hall.

She stopped and took a deep breath before knocking on the door of her father's study. Clashes with Papa required every bit of mental energy she could muster.

"You wished to see me, Papa? I haven't much time. Hattie and I are meeting Sebastian and his sister at the museum."

"Yes." He lifted a hand to indicate she should take the chair in front of his desk. The direction was unneeded. She always occupied the same chair in his office.

She sat and he followed suit, reclaiming the larger plusher chair behind his desk and settling with his hands crossed over his waistcoat.

"Harriet will not be joining you this afternoon."

Kitty frowned, curiosity and concern fizzing in her belly.

"Is Hattie unwell? She seems unsettled."

Her father grinned, the last reaction she expected. The man possessed an unnerving ability to take her by surprise.

"She is quite the opposite of unsettled, Katherine. In fact, just this morning your sister has settled her fate nearly as fortuitously as you've managed to settle yours."

He could only be referring to marriage, but he'd never been this pleased about Hattie's match with Mr. Treadwell. The buzzing in her stomach turning to stabbing jolts of dread.

Her father looked far too pleased with himself and Hattie had been decidedly troubled.

"Please explain."

"When a man finds no succor at one table, he dines at another."

Now they were talking about dining? Papa did love his aphorisms.

"You've lost me."

"That's what Ponsonby thought. 'I've lost her,' he said. And so he turned his attentions elsewhere. We can only be grateful his eye didn't stray to the daughters of some other family."

"Ponsonby?" Kitty knew a moment of guilt that the man who'd pursued her so tenaciously for years hadn't crossed her mind in days.

"He's asked for your sister's hand, and I have given them my blessing."

Ponsonby. Harriet. Ponsonby and Harriet. The two were like water droplets on an oily surface. They simply would not coalesce in her mind. By their very nature, they could not merge together. The man was as old as their father, perhaps older, and she'd always sensed him taking her measure, not as a potential life partner but for her ability to provide him with heirs. Kitty wanted children, and several of them, but she wanted a marriage based on more. Love, mutual respect, desire—qualities she'd previously doubted or belittled mattered now most of all. She'd found them, and so had Hattie.

"But s-she's engaged to be married to Mr. Treadwell."

"Is she? I can't see how that's possible, since I never gave the man consent to marry her."

More words that would not compute in her mind.

Even Sebastian's mathematical wizardry couldn't solve this equation.

"But she and Oliver seemed so happy after he'd spoken to you. I thought—"

"I gave the man reason to hope, but I told him that he and your sister needed more time to become acquainted. I asked him to give me a fortnight to consider the matter."

She realized she was shaking her head, and so quickly she felt dizzy. Hattie wanted to marry Oliver Treadwell. That was what all of this had been about—the scheming, the planning, the wedding dresses. Her feigned engagement.

"But you gave your blessing to Sebastian?"

"Yes, of course. The man's a duke. I could hardly refuse him."

Titles, wealth, power. She'd never doubted how much her father valued those qualities, but despite how hard he'd been on her, despite how stern he could be with all of them, deep down she'd believed in his decency. Her father was an honorable man. He might scheme for political and financial gain, and he collected information on others the way she collected perfumes, but she'd never doubted that, at his core, he was worth her admiration.

Until now.

"Does her happiness mean nothing to you?"

He shot up from his chair and winced as if she'd stabbed him, his cheeks mottling an awful puce shade.

"The future happiness of my children is my chief concern. Do you really believe my sweetest, gentlest daughter will be happy living in poverty with that young jacka-napes?"

Opening her mouth to answer his question, Kitty wondered where she and Violet fit in his ranking of daughters, but, as often happened during discussions with her father, he hadn't truly wished for an answer and cut her off before she'd gotten a syllable out.

"Do you know the fellow told me he may not perse-vere in the law but may try some other profession if it suits him better? As if a man can change professions as often as he replaces his shirt collars. He is aimless, pen-niless—"

"The Duke of Wrexford has ensured that Mr. Treadwell is not penniless."

When her father came out from behind his desk to argue, Kitty knew the topic had raised his ire and he was determined to win his point.

"And what if he falls out with the man? Mr. Treadwell has a fondness for betting on horse races. What if he's as unsuccessful with the ponies as he's been with every other profession he's attempted?"

She had no idea Oliver Treadwell involved himself in gambling or that he'd tried other employment before set-tling on the law. The news didn't please her, but not every man who gambled did so excessively, and not every man who pursued a profession found it to his liking. None of her father's revelations changed the fact that yesterday Harriet had been in love with the man. Now that she'd experienced the emotion herself, she knew Hattie's heart couldn't have altered overnight.

"Papa—"

He moved to stand in front of her, between his desk and her legs tucked against her chair, close enough to loom over her, his finger jutting out accusingly.

"And if you didn't wish Ponsonby to marry another woman, you should have married him yourself."

Ponsonby? How had the conversation become about him and not her sister?

"I haven't a care who the man marries. He's too old for me, and he's certainly too old for Harriet." Especially when she'd already given her heart to someone else.

"She's agreed to the match, Katherine. There is nothing left to debate."

If Hattie had a character flaw, it was that she was too malleable and eager to please. She never wished to disappoint anyone, least of all their father. Whatever he'd said to convince her, it wouldn't have taken much.

Kitty's chest burned and the stinging pain traveled up, pressing behind her eyes, but she ground her teeth. She'd determined long ago never to let her father see her cry.

"What of Mr. Treadwell? Has she spoken to him of this decision?" She didn't let the tears fall, but she hated the quaver in her voice.

"I've invited him to meet with me tomorrow. I'll break the news on her behalf."

So he'd take everything from Hattie. Her choices and her opportunity to part with Oliver on her own terms. To Kitty, that seemed the worst of it. Hattie deserved her own ending with Mr. Treadwell. She must have the opportunity to explain her choice or at least choose her last words to him. Why burden an eighteen year old with regrets that might last a lifetime?

Then again, perhaps if Hattie was forced to break off with Oliver face-to-face, she'd come to her senses and realize their father's wishes for her future did not match her own. At least she would have that choice.

"Then you should let Hattie come to the museum with me."

Her father instantly began shaking his head in refusal, almost before she'd finished her sentence.

"Her absence will be noted, and when all is said and done, some may think it cowardly that she did not face Mr. Treadwell one last time."

"Nonsense." He moved back around to settle himself in his desk chair, straightening his necktie before reaching for a cigar from his humidor. His relaxed air told Kitty that he considered the battle won.

"I'll be marrying a man who considers Treadwell his brother. Wrexford won't take kindly to seeing his friend snubbed."

A humming ring sounded in her ears and tension ran through her body as she gripped handfuls of her skirt below the edge of her father's high desk, where he could not see. She wanted a true engagement with Sebastian, but it would mean another battle with her father, especially if Lady Naughton could prove he was Archie's father.

But the matter of Hattie's happiness came first.

"Papa, please allow Hattie to accompany me today."

"Go then. And take your sister with you." He waved her away through the pungent smoke of his cigar. "Don't imagine you'll change her mind, Katherine. Unlike you, Harriet wants to do what's best for her future and this family."

*Stand up and go.* The temptation to stay and defend herself, to turn this conversation into an argument, as so many of theirs had been, battled with her impulse to get out while she could.

But more than winning an inch of ground with her father, she wanted to see Sebastian. She needed to tell him the truth of her feelings so they could end their feigned engagement and put away the pretense between them.

This time she wouldn't doubt. This time she would not run away.

And yet she'd never have contrived an engagement with Sebastian if not for the goal of securing Hattie's happiness with Mr. Treadwell. What if her father won? How could she grasp her own happy ending and leave Hattie to marry Ponsonby?

## Chapter Twenty-Three

"It seems silly for us not to speak to each other for the entire journey." Kitty leaned over to get a glimpse of the cluster of carriages blocking their way. It was as if all of London decided to take advantage of the unseasonably warm weather. "Judging by traffic, we'll be in this carriage awhile."

"We should have walked." Hattie wouldn't look at her as she said the words. She sat in the farthest edge of seat opposite her, arms firmly clasped across her chest.

"Shall we send the carriage back and get out? I do enjoy walking."

"It's too late now." Hattie's voice had the petulant tone of a young woman determined to be displeased with any suggestion.

Kitty had rarely argued with her middle sister. Violet could be a whirlwind of changing emotions, but Hattie had always been too agreeable. She'd never give an opponent a chance to argue before capitulating herself.

"Papa says you don't intend to marry Mr. Treadwell."

Hattie turned a momentary glare her way, and Kitty considered it a victory. If Hattie truly wished to marry Oliver, she would have to defy their father. Kitty would support her sister's choice every step of the way, but in the end, Hattie would have to be the one to stand up to their father, and she'd need that kind of inner fire to do it.

"I suspect he did not say it in that way at all."

No. He hadn't made it about Hattie's choice, more about her agreement with his.

"He said you've agreed to marry Lord Ponsonby."

Hattie winced. It was a fleeting tightening of the smooth skin around her eyes, but Kitty caught it. Seeing even that flash of pain in her sister's face hardened Kitty's resolve to prevent her sister's marriage to a man three times her age.

"Is that what you want, Hattie?"

At first it seemed she'd only be treated to more silence. Hattie tucked herself further into the corner and pressed her mouth tight and flat. Kitty closed her eyes and waited, imagining her love for her sister stretching out like a vine attempting to find a bit of sun.

"You ask me the question as if my wishes are all that matter. What I want. What I wish. What of our father's expectations?"

Kitty opened her eyes to find Hattie glowering at her, eyes glassy as if she might burst into tears at any moment.

"Hattie, love, Papa isn't the one who has to marry

Lord Ponsonby. I'm more concerned with your wishes than his."

"Lord Ponsonby is a fine man. He is kind, and he possesses wealth and status." Hattie's youthful voice echoed off the interior of the carriage, but Kitty imagined the words coming out of their father's mouth.

"And if you'd married him, I wouldn't have to." And there were father's exact words. He hadn't just persuaded her. It seemed he'd converted her completely.

Hattie's tears finally started trickling down her cheeks and Kitty gathered up the skirts of her gown and managed to maneuver from her side of the carriage onto the seat next to her sister. When she reached for her, Hattie stiffened but finally melted in her arms, sagging against her and weeping in earnest.

Each little moan of misery, each hiccupping sniffle tore at Kitty, but she let her sister cry her fill, rubbing soothing circles over her back and shoulders. The initial wave of sobbing subsided and she whispered against Hattie's hair, the same shade and texture as her own.

"Neither of us wants to marry Ponsonby. And neither of us must marry the man."

She'd expected the words to bring her sister comfort, to reassure Hattie that Kitty would join her in defying their father on this point, but Hattie pushed her away.

"You don't understand, Kitty. You never have."

"Understand what?" She wanted Hattie to have her say, to find her voice and make her own choices.

"Papa wants what's best for us. For all of us, and yet you've spent your whole life defying him. It's no wonder he's hardest on you. You've never obeyed him or sought to please him."

All the tenderness she'd felt for her sister while comforting her, the ache in her chest at the notion of Hattie promising herself to a man she did not love—it all receded with the bite of Hattie's accusations.

Years of disappointing her father, years of twisting herself in knots to be the heir he'd always wished for, and then a fine young lady who would make him proud. Hattie dismissed all of it in a single breath.

"I obeyed him. I idolized him."

Hattie choked out a dismissive laugh.

"You defied him for four seasons!" They'd never been adversaries, and Kitty hated the bitterness in Hattie's tone. "Don't you see that you ruined my season by still being out yourself? You should have been married years ago, but you insisted on having your way. Thank goodness Wrexford offered for you. I feared you might ruin Violet's first season too."

"Hattie, stop." The shouted words echoed in the confines of the small space and Hattie's mouth hung open. "This isn't you. You've never said a cruel word to me in your life." Or least she hadn't until this miserable carriage ride.

"I can't defy him." Her sister bowed her head, her voice weak and broken. "He's given me everything I own." She lifted an arm and tugged with the opposite hand at the cuff of her gown. "Every stitch of clothing, the food I eat. He provides all that I have."

Seeing Hattie struggle to find a dry patch on her

handkerchief, Kitty produced one from the pocket of her own skirt. She waited for her sister to dab at her eyes and then reached up to embrace her again.

"When you marry, your husband will be the one to provide your home and clothes. Perhaps you'll feel as beholden to him as you do to Papa. Do you really want that man to be William Ponsonby?"

"How LONG SHOULD we wait?" Pippa managed to withhold the question for longer than Seb expected, but the anxiety in her voice mirrored his own.

"I'm sure they'll appear soon." He'd been standing outside the museum with Ollie and Pippa for the better part of half an hour.

At first his sister didn't seem to mind the wait. Having hidden a little pocket-sized book in her skirt, she simply found an obliging bit of building to lean on and read. But then Ollie attempted to engage her in conversation, which seemed to work well until he said something that amused her enough to cause a burst of hearty laughter. She indulged her pleasure for only a moment before turning to glare at him and stepping away, as if she resented how much she enjoyed his company.

"Do you think they've forgotten us and found a couple of worthier gentlemen to marry?" No matter the circumstances, Ollie found it easy to jest.

Seb didn't offer an answer. He spotted the grand Clayborne Clarence carriage rattling along behind nimbler hansom cabs. Before either he or Ollie could make their way down the steps to assist the ladies, Kat and Harriet emerged, wearing nearly identical day dresses covered in ruffles and layers, and matching frowns.

He stepped forward to greet Kat, and she offered him a shaky smile but only met his gaze a moment before turning to glance at her sister and Ollie.

Following her gaze, he found the two greeting each other with their usual cordiality, if a bit less exuberance.

"Kat, let's find a place to talk while the others explore the gallery."

Eyes locked on her sister's face, Kat didn't turn to look at him when she answered. "I think our little group should stay together this afternoon." Finally she glanced up at him. "But, yes, we should find time to speak to one another privately."

She spoke without any particular warmth, as if they were mere acquaintances or friends and nothing more. But he wasn't content with nothing more. They were lovers and he could no longer imagine the days of his life unfolding without Kat as the brightest, best part of each one.

"Why don't we all take a late luncheon at Wrexford House after the gallery?" The housekeeper wouldn't be pleased and the cook might become apoplectic at the prospect of an impromptu meal with guests, but he needed to speak to Kat and settle matters between them.

As they proceeded into the first room of paintings, its rich hunter green walls soothed his eyes and set off each piece of art. He counseled himself to be patient, to tell her about Archie when they were in a less public setting.

Any questions about their evening together would need to wait.

She clasped his arm as they followed the others, and he managed to hold his tongue by focusing on the pleasure of her touch, the sweetness of her scent.

"Lily of the valley?"

"What? Oh, yes, I suppose it is." She'd never answered a query about her perfume with so little enthusiasm, and she didn't appear to take interest in a single painting. All of her energy seemed reserved for watching her sister's actions, and occasionally observing Pippa or Ollie.

Seb detected nothing amiss in their behavior. Ollie and Harriet walked arm in arm, remarking on various paintings they stopped to ponder, and Pippa followed a few steps behind. Pippa's occasional long glances at the couple were subtle enough. He didn't think anyone observing them would notice. Not even Kat.

He stopped in front of a painting of a family. The portrait was posed with the sitters staring out at the viewer, but the artist had captured the playful vibrant qualities of each. Seb could sense the children's eagerness to move and parental pride in the eyes of the husband and wife. The contentment of the scene kindled a wistful pang, a shallow ache in his chest.

Good grief, he was becoming a sentimental fool. For years he'd forced the notion of marriage and children from his mind. Focusing on his work, his studies—endeavors at which he knew he could succeed—had been easier than healing his heart.

And now, because of the woman at his side, he looked

at a painting of a merry family and could envision the same for himself. With Kat. Only with Kat could he imagine such a fate.

"The matter you asked me about yesterday," he began. "I have an answer now."

He had to clasp her arm tighter to get her attention.

"The matter? Oh, that matter. What *is* the answer?" For the first time today he caught her notice, a look of interest and concern shadowing her features.

"The allegation is untrue." The same lightness he'd felt after Miss Perkins's visit lifted in his chest now.

"How can you be sure?" He'd expected to see his relief reflected in Kat's eyes, but she seemed more dubious than pleased.

"I obtained a document that would be difficult to refute. Ironically, it's a matter of simple mathematics."

"He's too young." She'd turned her eyes to the happy family portrait before them and spoke in a near whisper. "I thought as much when I saw him in the park."

"By at least two years."

"That is good news, for everyone concerned."

Alecia wouldn't agree. But for Archie's sake and Naughton's, and for his future, it was the best outcome. But he'd expected more than Kat's tepid reaction. He frowned and turned so she might not see his frustration, but there was no need. Her eyes still trailed her sister's every move.

After tolerating a long silence between them, Seb stopped before the next painting, a rather bland landscape, but Kat tugged at their clasped arms as if she preferred to continue on. Harriet and Oliver were so far ahead, they'd almost turned a corner into the next room.

"Should I guess or can I convince you to tell me?" Seb tried to keep his frustration from his tone.

"Tell you what?"

"You've never been this hawkish about chaperoning your sister."

She finally turned and looked at him, almost as if seeing him for the first time. Her eyes and mouth softened, and she moved her hand to caress his arm where he held her. He thought she might grin and dipped his head to watch her mouth. He expected to see her lips curve up, but they began to tremble and turned down at the edges the moment he heard Harriet cry out, "No! I can't explain. Please don't ask me to."

Kat yanked her arm from his and rushed forward. By the time he reached her, she stood embracing a tearful Harriet while Ollie lingered nearby twisting his hands and looking miserable. Pippa waited off to the side, looking equally distressed.

Seb pushed in between Ollie and Kat and her sister.

"Are you unwell, Lady Harriet?"

Kat turned and whispered to him. "Might we have a moment, just Hattie and I?"

Seb nodded and reached out both arms to herd Ollie and his sister forward. Ollie continued to look back, as attentive to Harriet's movements as Kat had been, but he allowed himself to be led into the next gallery filled with sculptures.

None of them asked Ollie for an explanation of the

lady's behavior. By his bewildered expression, it was clear he knew as little as they did.

"She wouldn't let me hold her hand." Ollie looked up at Seb as if he might have answers. "She allowed me take her arm, but balked the moment I reached for her hand."

Kat's distraction. Hattie's chilly behavior. None of it made sense.

Finally he saw her usher Harriet over to stand near Pippa, and then approached.

She glanced at Ollie before turning her back on him.

"Shall we proceed to Wrexford House for that luncheon you offered?" she asked pleasantly, as if the distress of Harriet's outburst hadn't rippled out to charge the air between them.

When he hesitated, she clasped his hand and he felt her tremble. He wanted to hold her, comfort her, fix whatever had gone so wrong this afternoon.

"Please, Sebastian. She needs a chance to speak with Oliver."

And he needed to speak with Kat. But Ollie's interest in Harriet had led him to her in the first place. Whatever rift existed between the pair, he was as eager as she to see it mended.

### *Chapter Twenty-Four*

THE HOUSEKEEPER DIDN'T bat an eye when Seb requested an unexpected luncheon be laid out for six. Indeed, the staff introduced him to a part of the house he hadn't even known existed, taking advantage of the warm spring day to prepare a table under the arbor in the house's back garden.

As they gathered in the drawing room and waited for the food to be carried out, Seb offered Kat his study or the family sitting room for Ollie and Harriet to speak alone.

"Hattie says she's not ready." Kat tugged at the ribbon on the front of her skirt as she spoke quietly to him in the hall outside the drawing room, turning her head to watch her sister, who sat alone on the settee.

Seeing the young woman without Ollie seemed odd. From the moment Seb met her, the two had been all but inseparable. He'd been so thrilled at the notion of Ollie finally settling down that he could easily imagine the two married, the children they'd have, the contentment he hoped they'd find together.

Ollie stood at the room's only window, his back to all of them, with Pippa by his side. With his shoulders hunched, Ollie appeared smaller, vulnerable, the boy he'd spent his school days defending. And Pippa looked bereft. Seb had never seen the helpless look his sister wore now, but he understood it. The desire to comfort when the wound itself was still a mystery. He wanted to lift the misery that had descended over all of them.

"May we speak, Kat, alone?"

He feared she'd refuse, rejecting the notion of focusing on anything but her sister and whatever was amiss between Hattie and Ollie, but she dipped her head in agreement and started toward his study.

When he closed the door and turned to her, she stepped close and slid her hands under his suit jacket to wrap her arms around him, resting her head against his chest.

Pleasure rushed him as he embraced her, ebbing up into desire so intense he feared he held her too tight.

"Your heart's racing." The tenderness in Kat's voice tightened his chest.

"Yes, that's what you do to me."

She lifted her head to gaze at him and a tear glittered at the edge of her lower lash.

Comfort. She needed comfort. He stroked a circle across her back, the way his mother had soothed him as a child.

She pulled away and lifted his other hand to her chest,

above the ribbons and frills of her neckline, pressing his palm to her warm flesh. Her heartbeat thudded against his hand.

"Mine too."

He held her gaze, fighting the urge to kiss her, ignoring the desire reflected back at him and focusing on the tear that still hadn't fallen onto her cheek.

"Will you tell me?" His question lost him her gaze. She turned her head, staring at the wallpaper, and bit the edge of her lower lip with her teeth.

Perhaps she thought it a private matter between Harriet and Oliver, but they'd met over the hope of seeing the two wed. He wanted Ollie's happiness as much as she cared for her sister's.

"Has she decided not to marry him?" He prayed Ollie's changeable nature hadn't cost him the love of a young woman who seemed to adore him. "Has Ollie disappointed her?"

Kat snapped her to gaze at him and placed her hand on his chest. "No, not at all. And it isn't so much about what Harriet wants as what my father does."

Of course. How could have he missed the obvious? Yet Clayborne had already given his consent. Why withdraw it now?

"Do you recall Lord Ponsonby from your aunt's ball?"

"The one who eyed you as if he was starving and you were his next meal?"

She winced and nodded, the movement setting the tear free to trail down her cheek.

Realization hit with a sickening weight. "He wants Harriet to marry Ponsonby?"

Kat pulled away from him and took two steps to sink into one of the chairs arranged near the fireplace.

"I'm sorry, Sebastian. I asked you to lie to your family, your friends, and it was all for nothing."

Moving to kneel in front of her, he waited for Kat to meet his gaze.

"No apologies, and no more lies. I want to marry you. If you'll have me."

The moment stretched on endlessly and in the silence he could hear her father's voice, the amusement in his tone as he informed Seb that his was the seventh request for Kat's had in marriage. She'd turned down six other men, probably titled, perhaps wealthier, certainly more accomplished at social graces and polite conversation. One of them had certainly been Ponsonby.

She pressed her hand against his cheek. "Sebastian, I . . . "

Hurrying her made no sense. Why was he on bended knee when he could still see concern for her sister written all over her face?

"Kat, you don't have to say anything you don't—"

Lifting her hand, she brushed a finger over his mouth to quiet him.

"I love you."

The impact of the bullet from Alecia's lover's gun was nothing to the explosion that wreaked Seb's body at those three words again from Kat. Relief melted the tension he'd been holding since they'd parted, and he hauled her into his arms, finding heaven in the sweetness of her lips, the eagerness with which opened for him to taste her.

He lifted his head to gaze into her eyes. Beyond her poise and elegance, past the beauty that caught everyone's notice, in Kat's eyes he'd always read the truth of her feelings. Even when her expression didn't match her gaze, he believed the emotion he read in her eyes.

Now he saw love that matched her words, excitement echoing his own, and a shadow of worry he wanted to erase.

"Yes," she whispered in the inch of air between them.

"Yes?" For a moment, he'd gotten lost in the pleasure of holding her, her now familiar lily of the valley scent, and the certainty that she returned his feelings.

"You did ask me to marry you, I think."

He kissed her again, deeply but tenderly, as if this was the moment of their solemn vows and oaths. He was ready to bind himself to her tonight if given half the chance.

She lifted her head, the happiness in her eyes diminished by the frown on her face. "Harriet still wishes to marry Oliver. She simply fears defying my father."

If he were in Ollie's position, he'd start planning an elopement to Gretna Green, as the couple had once considered themselves.

Seb opened his hand and she fit hers inside before they both clasped their fingers tight.

"Let's go see what we can do."

WITH HIS HAND in hers, Kitty believed they might truly be able to find a solution. Her father wouldn't get his victory, but he didn't always have to win. Surely Hattie's contentment trumped his pride.

Pippa rushed up as they exited the study. "Thank goodness you two have decided to come out. The table's ready for us in the garden."

Returning to the drawing room, Sebastian's sister gathered Hattie and Ollie, and then led all of them to the back garden.

"Sit wherever you like," Pippa announced when they reached the prettily laid table with pitchers of lemonade, a variety of cold meats and sandwiches, fruits, and an impressive array of sweets. A bee buzzed above the spread, but Kitty knew the little worker was more interested in the lovely roses climbing the trellis against the edge of the arbor than any of the food below.

She glanced at her sister, hoping Hattie might take a place next to Ollie, but she immediately seated herself at the round table next to Pippa. Taking the chair on her sister's other side, Kitty left the remaining spaces for Sebastian and Ollie.

Sebastian sat next to her and reached out to give her hand a reassuring squeeze under the table. The joy of what they'd just shared, confessing her feelings and seeing every measure of it reflected in his eyes—all of it dimmed the minute she sensed the tension in Hattie's posture as she sat beside her.

Amid the clink and clatter of silverware on porcelain,

Kitty noted two conversations taking place, with Pippa in the middle. Hattie and Pippa seemed to be continuing an earlier chat about frightening books and haunted castles, but when the conversation waned, Pippa whispered now and then in Ollie's direction, sometimes raising a fleeting grin on the young man's face.

Kitty hadn't noticed such closeness between Pippa and Ollie before, but perhaps it made sense. If Seb viewed the man as a brother, Oliver and Pippa would have formed a sort of sibling amity.

And yet . . . there was something more. Pippa watched him a bit too long, especially when he was unaware of her examination, especially when Ollie ducked glances at Harriet, his expression seesawing between worry and hope. If a young woman looked at Sebastian like that, she'd be simmering with jealousy, if not boiling over.

"Pippa, I'm surprised no young gentleman at the university has caught your eye."

Seb released her hand the minute the words were out of her mouth, and all conversation at the table died.

Hattie turned to look at Pippa, as they all had.

"I am not . . ." Pippa swallowed, flicked her gaze to Oliver's face, and then reached for her lemonade. She tipped the crystal tumbler against her water goblet, nearly upending them both and Oliver reached out to assist her. When he inadvertently touched her hand, she pulled her arm back as if she'd been stung.

"I do not attend university to catch a husband." Pippa's shaky voice contrasted with her strident tone. "I go to study mathematics."

"And very successfully." Sebastian leaned an inch toward her as he praised Pippa, as if to emphasize his point.

Kitty couldn't look at him. She sensed tension in him now. Her sister sat stiff and miserable beside her, and he was no doubt displeased with her for challenging Pippa. Yet if she could get Harriet to see Pippa's admiration for Oliver, perhaps jealousy might spark her into action. Give her the strength to defy their father and make a future of her own choosing.

"I say no Cambridge man interests you because you've lost your heart closer to home." Kitty heard herself speaking in the same caustic tone she'd used during years of sparring with Cynthia Osgood. The same pettiness welled up too, the callous pleasure of landing a blow with a few carefully chosen words. She flushed, heat rushing up her face just as Pippa's face went crimson. "Have you told him of your feelings?" She shifted her gaze to glance momentarily at Ollie, and then looked back at Pippa. "Men can be so oblivious sometimes."

A piercing screech, the sound of Sebastian's chair as he pushed it behind him to stand, tore at the haze of ugliness Kitty had wrapped herself in. A chill swept over her skin. A clammy trickle of perspiration slid down her nape. She shivered and turned to Hattie, who'd clasped a hand to her mouth.

Sebastian moved around the table to stand behind Pippa, but she bolted from the table before he could touch or comfort her. Ollie rose next, his mouth pulled tight as he nodded once to Hattie and then turned to march determinedly along the path of Pippa's retreat into the house.

Hattie leaned toward her, whispering in her ear. "Kitty, we should take our leave." But her sister's small tremulous voice seemed far away.

Only Sebastian drew her back. He was a tall black-clad shape in the center of her vision, but she lifted her gaze slowly, knowing, fearing what she'd see in his eyes. She lingered on his strong square jaw, traced the shape of his beautiful mouth, and then finally met his gaze.

Worse, far worse than she'd feared. He didn't look at her with anger or even disgust, he stared at her with the same chilled look of disappointment she'd read in her father's eyes a thousand times.

The pain of displeasing her father had dulled long ago, but to see it now in Sebastian's blue gray gaze made it fresh, a hot searing burn in the center of her chest. The sting of it took her air until each breath brought a twinge of pain.

None of her intentions about spurring Hattie into action excused her. This scheme, like all her others, had come to nothing. Nothing but pain. Misery that multiplied the longer Sebastian stood watching her.

"Please, Kitty." Hattie tugged at her sleeve, her voice desperate and shrill. "I think we must take our leave now."

"Yes." She was surprised she managed the word. All her energy went with the effort, but she knew she still required a bit of strength to stand. She reached out to brace her hands on the table, nearly upsetting her plate, and ignored the stitch of pain in her middle to breathe as deeply as she could. As she pushed herself up, she saw Sebastian move, a blur of black in her peripheral vision. His large hand gripped her arm as he lifted her, helping her to stand.

"T-thank you."

He embraced her with one arm once she was upright, but she couldn't look into his eyes again, couldn't bear to see her failure reflected back at her.

Hattie took her arm. "Thank you, Your Grace. I can see to my sister."

But that wasn't the way of it. Hattie was the one who needed looking after. Hattie was the one whose heart was broken.

Kitty steadied her breath. Her father taught her to be strong. *Never display weakness. Never cry or lose oneself in sentiment. Never let them best you.*

"No, Hattie. Go inside. I shall be there directly."

Hattie obeyed reluctantly, glancing up at Sebastian and then at Kitty's face before finally releasing her arm and slowly trailing the others' steps back into Wrexford House.

The afternoon sun bore down on them but Kitty's skin pebbled with gooseflesh. That persistent bee buzzed past as she waited for Sebastian to speak, giving him the chance to rail at her, to chastise her as she deserved. Just as he had the first time she'd met him.

Somehow he'd seen past her bad behavior then and come to love her, want her, and ask for her hand in marriage. But he wouldn't overlook this blunder. This lapse hadn't wounded a stranger in a ballroom. She'd hurt his sister. His beautiful clever sister, who'd probably never disappointed her father or anyone else in her life.

"I'm sorry." She felt so much more regret than those two words could convey. "Please tell Pippa I'm sorry."

When he made no reply, Kitty moved out of his embrace, away from the heat of his arm against her body. That magnet pull between them tugged at her as she strode away, and the burning in her chest turned frigid, chilling her to the bone.

"Kat?"

She didn't look back when he called to her, didn't know what more to say. She'd ruined everything. She hadn't helped her sister, and now she'd injured his. If he'd done the same to Hattie, Kitty wasn't sure she could forgive him. She wasn't sure she could forgive herself.

## *Chapter Twenty-Five*

"I DON'T APPROVE of running away." Pippa sat on one of the plush sitting room chairs, her legs tucked underneath a knitted throw, and a steaming teacup cradled in her hands. "But I can't say I'll miss London."

He wouldn't miss London either. The memories of the past week—had it truly only been a week?—spun endlessly in his mind.

For two days the staff had been busying themselves preparing to close up Wrexford House and pack the family's essential belongs for their departure back to Roxbury. For the last forty-five minutes Seb sat staring at a blank sheet of paper, unable to settle the whirlwind of his thoughts long enough to convey anything sensible in written words. He'd sent one short note to Kat the morning after the incident in the garden asking to call on her, letting her know of their plan to return to Cambridgeshire, but he'd received no reply. Despite her silence, he'd called at Clayborne House the next day and been turned away at the door. Their train was due to depart in two hours, and this second letter in the afternoon post would be his last chance to say good-bye.

"You could simply try calling on her again. Push in. Insist she see you. Surely you can convince a housemaid to let you in," Pippa said, her tone matter-of-fact.

"I have considered it. And reconsidered it, and changed my mind again."

Pippa had recovered as Seb knew she would, though she'd spoken to him more openly than he'd expected of her feelings for Ollie. She seemed to find them as confusing as Seb did disconcerting. Speaking in lighter tone than her usual low rich timbre, she'd made light of what she dismissed as a foolish infatuation. "I'm far too clever for Ollie," she'd teased. Seb agreed entirely with her assessment.

For Ollie's part, the poor man seemed none the wiser about Pippa's admiration, even after Kat's pointed barbs. He knew Pippa had been embarrassed, but Ollie believed her feelings to be for a gentleman she'd met during their time in London. When Pippa begged him, Seb had been all too happy not to disabuse Ollie of the notion.

Pippa put aside her teacup and stretched her arms in the air. "You know when you think too much, it only leads to inertia."

He laid down his pen and stared at his sister. "You might be too clever for any of us, Pippa."

"Nonsense. That would make for a lonely life."

He didn't want that for her. He didn't want it for himself.

"Perhaps we should call on her together. I can reassure her that I'm well and forgive her, and you can . . ." She eyed him, twisting her mouth as if, with a bit of concentration, she could divine his thoughts. "You can tell her whatever it is you wish to say."

"I asked her to marry me." The words raked across his tongue, so painful he imagined he could taste blood on his tongue.

Pippa stared at her hands folded tightly in her lap a moment before raising her head. "I don't wish to be the reason you won't marry her."

"You're not."

Kat was the reason he was reconsidering their engagement, reconsidering the mad rush of hope and future happiness he'd let himself embrace.

She'd stood in his study days before and insisted on how little they knew each other, yet even then he'd believed he could perceive the heart of who she was. He could trust that the beauty he saw every time he looked at her wasn't just skin-deep. That her cleverness, her loyalty, her wit, her innate goodness were bone deep. That she was practiced at artifice but did not possess the heart of a liar. She might have been taught by her father to be cruel, but he could never imagine Kat capable of Alecia's craven malice.

He didn't believe even it now. Yet she'd hurt Pippa, purposely, ruthlessly. For what? If her motive was to help

Hattie, how had humiliating Pippa brought her sister and Ollie any closer?

Ollie had gone to Clayborne House after the incident and been turned away. As far as Seb knew, he and Harriet hadn't communicated since.

Kat's ugliness hadn't produced a bit of good, and it had pierced him far deeper than it had Pippa.

Her apology had seemed sincere, and he'd seen the horror in her own eyes at the realization of what she'd done. Yet he had not found forgiveness as easy as Pippa, who'd urged him that same night to make amends with Kat.

He'd always held grudges longer than she did. Forgiveness was an empty well inside of him. He still needed to find enough to forgive Alecia. And he knew forgiveness would free him. That had seemed possible with Kat in his life. But now nothing about his future was clear, except that the clock on the wall ticked on relentlessly, and their train departed for Roxbury in less than two hours.

KITTY CONSIDERED IGNORING her father's summons. They'd spoken more in the past few days than they had in months. And she didn't have the energy or desire to speak to anyone. Window watching seemed her main preoccupation, staring through the panes and battling the yearning to see the Wrexford brougham pull up to their patch of pavement or glimpse Sebastian himself, as his long confident stride carried him to her front door.

"Tell my father I shall be down directly." The poor maid had waited in the doorway long enough for her answer, and she'd hidden up in her room like a sullen child for as long as any grown woman should be allowed.

She stepped in front of the long mirror to take in her reflection. But for the crescents of shadowed skin under her eyes, she looked much as she always did—hair neatly arranged, fashionable clothes hugging her figure just so. A flawless woman without spot or stain. But underneath, below the skin, in her heart, the flaws had always been there. Pettiness and cruelty that she knew how to wield like a weapon. That she'd used to hurt the sister of the man she loved.

As she made her way down to her father's study, she marveled at the notion he was more likely to be proud of how she'd struck out at Pippa—he had taught her to use others' weaknesses to her advantage—than for anything she'd accomplished with benevolent intentions, like the charity work she'd helped organize with her Women's Union and the way she'd brought the conservatory to life.

"You know I have no tolerance for melodrama. I understand you would not take breakfast, and you did not come down for dinner last evening."

He'd never been concerned with whether or not she took her meals, but he disliked irregularity. He preferred discipline, order. He hadn't missed her at breakfast, but perhaps her absence had meant there were too many pieces of toast left on the sideboard or too many plates laid at table.

"Your sister says you've had a falling out with Wrexford."

So he'd called her down for an interrogation. She'd lost their family a duke and all the influence his wealth might bring.

Kitty offered her father one sharp nod. She wouldn't parse the details of the last time she'd seen Sebastian. The last time she might ever see him. She couldn't tell that story without tears, and she refused to give her father that. Ever.

"Perhaps it's for the best." Her father's tone was neutral, giving nothing away. Yet she couldn't imagine he approved of her break with Sebastian, unless he meant to foist her off on Ponsonby. At least it would free Harriet from that fate.

She'd turned her head down to study the carpet, anything to avoid meeting his cool gaze, but his declaration shocked her, as his words often did. "You're pleased to hear the news?"

"I am no longer surprised by your rejection of any suitor."

Snapping her gaze to his, Kitty sensed none of the anger she'd anticipated. Just resignation.

Her father rose from his desk chair. "Would you join me in the drawing room, Katherine?"

Body stiffening at the request, she shook her head. "Why can't we continue to speak here, Papa?"

"We have a guest in the drawing room. I would like you to join us."

There was only one person she wished to see and her body fizzed with anticipation. Could Sebastian be here? Just down the hall?

Her father had already approached the threshold of his study and held out his hand to urge her forward. "Come, Katherine. Let's not leave our guest waiting."

She stood to follow him. Sebastian would have asked to see her, and any of the maids would have brought him up, or at least let her know he was in the house. If her father had somehow kept them apart, why this elaborate dance of inviting her to his study and then into the drawing room? Did he simply want to watch the breaking of their engagement firsthand? She knew full well why she'd lost the chance at a future with Sebastian, but she couldn't fathom her father's reasons for no longer favoring their match in the first place.

"Lady Naughton."

Before she even stepped over the threshold, Kitty spied Alecia Naughton standing in front of the settee, her hands crossed daintily in front of her.

"Please, ladies," Father said, directing them. "Let us sit."

The lady perched as warily on the edge of the settee as Kitty balanced near the front of her chair. Seeing the woman took Kitty back to the night Alecia found her in Lady Stamford's garden with Sebastian. She was the first person Kitty told about their engagement, and now she understood the emotion on Lady Naughton's face that night.

She'd loved Sebastian once and lost him, and Kitty knew that agony now too.

"Lady Naughton has come to impart some rather sensitive and shocking information regarding her connection with the Duke of Wrexford."

Alecia ducked her head before blinking up at Kitty innocently.

"She says that her son is—"

"No." Kitty cut off her father's words and fire sparked in Lady Naughton's cool gaze.

"Katherine!"

She ignored her father's shout and Lady Naughton's glare and turned to face her father.

"The lady is lying, Papa. Prior to our break, Sebas—Wrexford informed me that he'd learned the allegation was false. Lady Naughton's son is too young to be his child."

Kitty had never been so grateful to her father as when he paused and considered her words, and then cast Lady Naughton a dubious stare.

"How old is your son, Lady Naughton? When was he born?"

Alecia cleared her throat and spoke with a soft breathy timbre. "Archie is ten years old, my lord, and takes after the duke in so many ways."

"I met the boy in Hyde Park, Papa. He's far too small to be ten years old, and he bears no resemblance to the duke whatsoever."

Her father tapped his foot against the Aubusson rug and then reached up to stroke his beard, all the while studying Lady Naughton's face, no doubt seeking the truth beyond her façade of feigned innocence.

"What do you say to that, Lady Naughton?"

"Might I speak to your daughter alone, my lord?"

As she asked the question, Lady Naughton ignored Kitty completely and oozed sweetness in her father's direction. Watching him out of the corner of her eye, Kitty couldn't gauge his reaction. Had the lady's lies convinced him too?

"No, I think not, Lady Naughton." Apparently not. "I find this all rather irregular."

Undaunted, Alecia turned directly to Kitty, reaching out a hand as if she might touch her, though she sat too far away to do so.

"Please, Lady Katherine. Might I just have a moment of your time?"

Her father didn't allow Kitty a chance to reply before rising to his feet, a clear sign of dismissal. "The answer remains the same, Lady Naughton. Good day to you." He didn't even offer the lady a nod before turning to Kitty. "Katherine, come with me."

She was as eager to be done with Alecia Naughton as he was. Yet his commanding tone set her teeth on edge. And something in the woman's beseeching gaze made her curious.

"It's all right, Papa. Might I speak to Lady Naughton? Just for a moment."

The tension of challenge and control zinged between

them, as it had so many times before. One momentarily scrunched eye was her sign he'd relent.

"A brief moment, I will allow." He cast one final vexed gaze at Lady Naughton before leaving the room.

Before the door had even slipped shut behind him, Alecia stood and approached to loom over Kitty.

"Has Miss Perkins been at you too, then? She has a fanciful tale to tell, I'll admit. But you should know this, Lady Katherine. Sebastian is a man of singular affections. He loves for life, and I am that love." Her whole countenance altered and she spoke with another voice, lower, full of anger, almost pained. "He is not a man to come to London and engage himself to a woman after three day's acquaintance. Whatever scheme you've concocted—"

"What happened between the two of you?"

She reared back as if Kitty's interruption was the last thing she expected.

"If he would have loved you for life, Lady Naughton, why are you married to another man?"

Alecia turned her back on Kitty a moment. "It was all a terrible misunderstanding."

"I see." Misunderstandings were plentiful. Ollie and Hattie had yet to speak since the incident at Wrexford House, and she suspected both of them misunderstood the other's reactions that day. She'd never explained her own actions to Sebastian and could only imagine what he thought of her now. Yes, misunderstandings were easily wrought, but she suspected whatever had passed between Sebastian and Alecia had been more than a mis-understanding, and she wouldn't get the truth from Lady Naughton. She'd come here to poison Kitty's relationship with Sebastian, not to explain her own.

"Would you mind seeing yourself out, Lady Naughton?"

The weight of it all poured down on her, as if she was still sitting in Sebastian's garden and looking at Pippa's shocked, flushed face. And then into his eyes, brimming with disappointment.

"I know your engagement is false. I don't know why or how you convinced him to involve himself in such a scheme, but I know Sebastian would never wish to marry a woman like you." As Kitty turned to the door, Alecia came up just behind her, hissing the accusation in her ear.

The drawing room door slid open and her father stepped inside. "I believe my daughter has asked you to leave, Lady Naughton. Good day to you."

Her father came to stand beside her, not touching her or reaching out to comfort her, but positioning himself close enough that Alecia could see the seriousness in his eyes.

She said nothing more but dipped into an obsequious curtsy before striding for the door.

"If you're lying, Lady Naughton, trust that I shall uncover it. And know that you are misguided on one point."

The diminutive woman paused, back straight, neck

taught, never turning her head to look back, but clearly interested enough in the rest to wait to hear what Kitty's father would say next.

"Wrexford did ask for my daughter's hand in marriage, and I gave my consent three days ago."

Alecia departed without another word, slamming the drawing room door behind her to mark her exit.

Kitty turned to her father. "He asked you three days ago?"

"In earnest, yes. I'd suspected his first request wasn't quite what it seemed."

Her scheme had not gone to plan. Indeed, none of it had worked out as she'd hoped. Hattie and Ollie weren't married, and she still didn't know her sister's true feelings about any of it. They'd barely exchanged two words since the incident at Wrexford House.

Yet she didn't regret a moment of her time with Sebastian. All but those last moments when she'd torn it all apart.

"He truly wished to marry me?" She knew it was true. He'd said as much himself, but hearing the words from her father's mouth seemed a reassurance she sorely needed.

"Yes, Katherine, though I am not certain of his intentions now." He raised a hand and she thought he might touch her, embrace her, and she stilled. Instead, he reached inside his waistcoat pocket and removed a letter. "He and his sisters are departing for Cambridgeshire this afternoon. The three o'clock train."

She snatched the folded paper from his hand, noting

her name addressed on outer flap. "How could you keep this from me?"

He lifted his head in the aristocratic haughty way she'd seen all her life. "I thought it best."

Kitty moved past him, rushing for the drawing room door.

"Where do you think you're going?"

She pulled the door open, not stopping as she called back her answer. "King's Cross Station."

## Chapter Twenty-Six

"WHICH TRAIN IS it?" Hattie trailed along behind her as Kitty moved through the throng toward the schedule board. Her sister had found her in her rooms, frantically changing into a traveling dress and out of the simple wrap gown she'd worn in the morning. Hattie had listened to her plan, tried to talk her out of it, and then insisted on accompanying her to the station.

"Platform three!" Kitty called back, though when she turned, panic welled up when she didn't immediately see Hattie in the crowd.

"Kitty, I think they're over here." She turned at the sound of her sister's voice and saw her gloved hand waving to draw her attention. Pushing to the point of rudeness, she made her way through a cluster of passengers waiting to board and drew up near Hattie.

"I think I just saw Lady Philippa get into that carriage." She pointed at one of the first-class carriages near the end of the train from where they stood.

Kitty grabbed her sister's hand and started along the platform, but halfway toward the first-class cars, the train released a cloud of steam and began its metallic grinding groan into motion. Running in her skirts was impossible, even if the platform had been clear of family members waving a final good-bye to loved ones.

The train moved toward them and Kitty stopped, realizing they were too late to board, but still might see Sebastian and his sister as their carriage window passed by. As the first-class cars approached, she uttered a little prayer under her breath. That she might see him, that he would look at her with something other than disappointment and disdain.

Light filtering through the station's high windows glinted off the glass of the closed carriage windows, but as the carriage drew near, she could see the unmistakable curve of an angular cheek, full lips, and dark waves against a blue dress.

"It's Pippa," Hattie shouted over the noise of the train as she tugged excitedly at the sleeve of Kitty's gown.

Before Kitty could open her mouth to call, she heard Hattie's usually quiet gentle voice cry out.

"Pippa!" They both began shouting as her carriage passed, and Kitty swallowed a painful lump when, across from Pippa, she glimpsed the wide printed span of a newspaper splayed open before the face of a gentleman with large wide hands.

Finally, when the carriage had just passed them, Pippa turned and spied them through the glass, her eyes huge, as she lifted a hand to wave. When the train car rolled past, all the air seemed drained from the world. Kitty sagged and reached up to grasp her chest, where that pain from the garden incident began to twinge.

Then she felt Hattie tugging at her sleeve again. "Kitty, look. Is that the duke?"

A man's face, *his* face, gazed back at her from the spot where Pippa had sat. He was too far away for her to read anything in Sebastian's eyes, but he'd looked for her. Pippa must have told him she'd seen them, and he'd cared enough to have one last glimpse of her.

"Come, Hattie." She turned and marched back toward the ticket booth. When she didn't turn toward the station's exit, Hattie called from behind her.

"What are we doing?"

"We're going to Cambridgeshire." She had to see him, speak to him, explain her behavior. Even if he wouldn't forgive her, she needed to see him just once more. And she also owed Pippa an apology.

"Kitty, we can't. We haven't any clothes. And we haven't been invited."

She swung back to face her sister, whose hat had gone askew, her neatly arranged hair disheveled. Kitty reached up to settle her sister's hat.

"If they turn us away, so be it. But I must try. I need to see him one last time." She cupped her sister's smooth cheek. "I can go on my own. Just tell Papa you lost me at the train station." She tried for a grin but her face felt stiff and wouldn't obey.

"I'm going with you. You started all of this because of me. I'm not letting you finish it alone."

FOR ALL THE hours on the train, and the carriage ride from the station, his mind whirled with questions. Why had she come to the station? Why hadn't she answered his morning letter? Why had she refused to see him when he'd called so late he'd almost missed the train himself?

"Ah, the duke has returned to Roxbury." Teague, the estate's butler, led a small army of staff out of Roxbury's grand front doors to welcome them. The footmen and maids turned their attention to trunks and luggage, while Sebastian escorted Pippa inside.

"I received your telegram and have prepared a small luncheon. I thought you might be peckish after your journey, Your Grace." Teague's enthusiasm actually made it feel like a homecoming, and Seb thanked him for his efforts.

A half an hour later, after he and Pippa had taken time to change and wash off the dust of travel in their rooms, they gathered again in the morning room. They filled their plates from a spread on the sideboard, though Seb found none of it appealing. His stomach turned at the very notion of eating. But he smelled the divine smoky aroma of coffee and spied a small silver pot at the edge of the table. The staff had remembered his preference for coffee over tea, and he silently blessed them for it.

Pippa seemed to have an appetite and Seb allowed her to tuck into her meal before speaking.

"How did she look when you first glimpsed her through the window?"

Pippa lifted her napkin and wiped her mouth. "Desperate."

Seb frowned, and Pippa sighed and lifted her gaze to the ceiling. Not quite an eye-roll, but almost.

"Oh, don't look so confused. Kitty looked desperate to see you. She'd come all the way to the train station to see, perhaps to stop you leaving, for all I know."

Hope flickered, that pitiful little ember of future happiness he still clung to.

"Why don't you telegram and ask Aunt Augusta to visit her? I'm not sure why Kitty ignored your notes, but perhaps she'd speak to Aunt Augusta. There *is* still the matter of your betrothal to settle."

The sourness in Seb's belly swelled, bile rising up in the back of his throat. Mention of his aunt brought up images of Alecia and her vile attempt to manipulate him. But then he turned his attention to the heart of the Pippa's question. His betrothed.

Kat was that still. He had not ended it. She hadn't sent word of her desire to do so. And she'd come to the train station. He still wasn't certain what it meant, what she'd intended to say to him, but he'd seen her face from a distance—the frown marring her brow while the bud of a smile bloomed at the edges of her mouth. Misery merged with hope. A fair picture of his own state of mind.

"And there is still the matter of her attempt to wound you, Pippa."

"I am *not* wounded. For goodness sakes, she merely pointed out a fact that I'd been silly enough to think I'd concealed."

She was right, and what had passed between Pippa and Kat wasn't truly what held him back. Pippa had forgiven her, and he'd known from the moment it happened that Kat regretted all of it. What held him back was simpler. Primal. Fundamental. What held him back was fear. With matters unresolved between them, he could still hope. Yet with matters unresolved between them, he couldn't have what he needed most of all. Kat in his arms and in his life.

Pippa had been watching him and threw down her napkin. "I've changed my mind. Don't involve Aunt Augusta. You should send a telegram directly to Kitty."

"Should I?"

"Yes, because if you don't, and you continue with that miserable look on your face, I'll write to her myself."

He stood and leaned over to kiss his sister's cheek. Pippa gasped and lifted a hand to the spot, then began rubbing furiously to wipe his kiss away as she had as a child.

"Thank you, Pippa."

Striding back to his study, he considered what to say in his telegram. Though an expedient form of communication, telegrams required a message to be concise. He couldn't say much, and yet brevity didn't match the jumble of what he wanted to convey to Kat. He needed her with him. Loved her. The further he stood from the debacle in the garden, the more he saw it as her misguided attempt to help her sister. The woman was deft at coming up with plans that never worked out as she hoped they would. The false engagement, the attempt to make Harriet jealous, if that's what it had been. From the start, Kat had been guided by a desire to help her sister, just as he'd wished to assist Ollie. He couldn't fault her for that loyalty.

Half an hour later, slumped in his study chair, he found himself trapped in the inertia Pippa warned him about. Too much thinking led to inaction. And inaction wouldn't get him face-to-face with Kat again.

He reached for his fountain pen and began scratching out the message he'd send to Kat via telegram.

So intent on finally taking action, a knock at the door made him jump.

"Your Grace, you're wanted in the entry hall."

Just a few more words and he'd have the message complete, ready to be taken to the station and transmitted on the telegraph. It could be delivered to her within hours if he hurried.

He replaced his pen and sighed. His half-finished message stared back at him. "Is there something amiss in the entry hall?"

"Unexpected guests, Your Grace."

Unexpected guests? Ollie said he might catch tomorrow's train and come for a visit, but he couldn't imagine who he might bring with him. Then the queasiness bubbled up in his stomach again. What if he and Harriet had decided to elope after all? Clayborne would have the constables at Roxbury's doors next.

He followed the maid down the hall and could see three feminine figures standing in front of the still open front doors. Pippa stood with her back to him as she spoke to their guests, and he glimpsed the dark silhouettes of two women in the light pouring into the hall through the open doors.

He picked up his pace, moving past the maid, and caught a scent on the air. Lily of the valley. Sweet, fresh, and mingled with the richer scent of Kat's skin.

Pippa turned to look at him and stepped back to allow him a direct view of Kat standing in front of her. His sister lifted her hand as if presenting him with a prize.

"And here she is. Your telegram must've traveled at triple speed."

"I hadn't sent it."

Pippa smiled at that. "Then it's destiny." She lifted her brow, as if shocked by her own fancifulness, and reached for Harriet's hand. "Would you like some tea, Hattie? We still have lunch laid out if you'd like something to eat after your journey."

Hattie nodded and grinned. She followed Pippa out of the entry hall, only turning back once to glance at him and then her sister.

Kat looked tired and disheveled, strands of hair falling down over her shoulder, her bodice askew, and a smudge of something on her cheek. She looked marvelous to his eyes.

He widened his stance to keep himself steady. The relief of seeing her again nearly buckled his knees. Her scent made his mouth water. He wanted to hold her, comfort her, love her, but he held back. If he touched her now, he wouldn't listen rationally to anything she said or be able to tell her what he needed to say. If he touched her, he'd never want to let her go.

She ducked her head. "I know it's rude to push in when we weren't invited."

He took a step closer. She hesitated a moment and then did the same.

"There's an unsent message on my desk asking you to come. I thought on it too long and didn't get it sent off in time."

He took another step and could feel the warmth of her body. He breathed deep, savoring her scent.

One more step and he closed the distance between them, reaching up to slide his hand against her cheek.

"W-were you considering not sending it?" She stumbled over the question and he missed the confident lilt he usually heard in her voice.

He stroked the smudge at the arch of her cheekbone and felt her shiver reverberate up the length of his arm.

"I was considering how to fit everything I wished to say to you into a telegram."

She tipped her face, nestling against his hand.

He lowered his head and felt her breath wisping against his face.

"Say it now."

Before he could speak, he had to kiss her. Brushing his mouth against hers electrified him, all the weight and worry of the past days slipping away, and he slid a hand around her waist, fitting her body against his.

Then he pulled back, lifting his head to gaze at her. "I love you, Kat."

"And I love you."

He knew he was smiling like a fool because he felt it, not just in the muscles of his face, but in the buoyant lightness that welled up inside him.

"Kat . . ." He reached into his waistcoat pocket and slid out the flower ring. He'd forgone the box and kept the band tucked in safe, close to his heart, since the day he'd purchased it for her. "I want to marry you."

She gasped at the sight of the glinting ring, and he took the pleasure breaking across her face as the answer he longed for her. But when he dipped his head for another kiss, she lifted a finger to his lips.

"But I act too often on impulse."

As he had when he'd just kissed her, embraced her. He lifted his mouth from her finger. "Impulsivity isn't always uncalled for."

She almost grinned at that and seemed to lift onto her toes for another kiss, but then held back.

"My plans, which seem masterful in the making, never come to good."

He slid his other hand up her back to pull her closer. "Scheme less. Kiss more. That's my new philosophy."

He bowed his head to nuzzle her neck, and she

moaned, sliding a hand under his jacket to press her palm over the spot where his heart thrashed in his chest.

Turning his mouth to her cheek, he grazed her lips to kiss her and the minx pushed at his chest and reared back.

"Worst of all, I'm prone to pettiness. I can wound with a few words."

Her words were beginning to feel like agony to him too, though he had been the one to tell her she should talk as much as she liked.

"Darling, Kat. All of us have regretted our words at times. We can't always bite our tongues when we should." At the moment, he had other notions about tongues and how they might use them.

"You can forgive me?"

He pressed his forehead to hers, breathing in her delicious scent, savoring the way her loose strands of hair tickled his skin.

"I have forgiven you, love. Pippa has forgiven you. As soon as we're able, I plan to make you my wife. Now, will you kiss me?"

She slid her fingers up to his shoulders, clasping her hands around his neck, pushing up to balance on her toes and leaning in to let him take her weight. She didn't answer him. No words were necessary as she lifted her mouth to his, carded her fingers in his hair, and pulled him down to deepen the kiss.

He let himself revel in the kiss, the wonder of having

her back in his arms. He let the past fall away as he held onto Kat and embraced the here and now. He'd never wanted to savor a moment more, and yet he'd never looked with more eagerness toward the future. Their future.

*Epilogue*

---

*Two months later*

"I DON'T SUPPOSE you'd ever forgive me if I throttled him." Sebastian stood near the vestry room door in the Roxbury parish church and tried not to look directly at Kat's father as he said the words. The man was already drawing too much attention to himself. They both suspected he'd imbibed before coming to the church. Either that, or he had thoroughly taken leave of his senses.

He'd insulted the vicar, started a row with two of the local barons, and accidentally sat on the village doctor's wife's hat. Seb knew how much women loved their hats.

Kat watched her father's antics a moment before answering, lifting her hand to slip it under and around Seb's arm. "Oh, I probably would, but if you choked him, it would make family gatherings rather awkward going forward."

Seb quirked a brow. That didn't sound half bad. "He might visit less." Flexing his fingers, he imagined them wrapped around Clayborne's throat, and then found placing them over his wife's hand and stroking her warm supple skin far preferable to violence. "It would satisfy me immensely."

"I thought that's what I did." With a few words, she had him hot and aching. She did satisfy him, and so much more. She thrilled him, challenged him, and helped him improve upon every single day.

"You do, love, and exceedingly well."

She cast a glance back toward the vestry door. They were waiting for Lady Clayborne to emerge, the sign that Hattie was ready to begin the bridal procession. Seb had already done his best man duty of attempting to allay Ollie's nerves, and Kat had been sequestered half the morning assisting with Hattie's last-minute preparations.

Seb took a step to move an inch closer to his wife. He relished the heat of her body pressed against his.

Kat responded by pressing in nearer, and he craned his neck to look ahead and scan the church entryway.

"What are you looking for?" she asked, turning to gaze in the same direction.

"The groom. The sooner this wedding is over, the sooner I can take you home and undress you."

Kitty laughed, a low throaty sound, and squeezed his arm. "Have you forgotten? We're hosting the wedding party at Roxbury. Most of these people will be coming with us when we leave, and half of them are staying in our home."

Seb dipped his head and leaned toward Kat, aching to kiss her and taste the lavender-vanilla scent of her skin. He whispered near her ear. "Can't we reconsider and send them all away to the local coaching inn for lodgings?"

He skimmed his mouth across her cheek before lifting his head.

"You're beginning to sound as unsociable as my father." Kat put up her other hand and fully embraced Seb's upper arm.

"Why *is* your father in such a state today? He gave his consent for this wedding. And your cousin is marrying Ponsonby next month, so he gains him as a family member as well." The notion of a familial connection to the earl didn't thrill Seb, but anything was better than seeing Harriet married to the man. Or Kat. He glanced at his wife again and a languid, warming contentment spread through him. It was a new sensation, but one he was learning to embrace.

A moment later, Oliver took his place at the altar. Hattie's groom vibrated with energy and his mouth continually twitched into grins he seemed unable to contain.

Mama finally emerged through the vestry door and swept past Seb and Kat, her tear-filled gaze seeking her husband. She captured Papa's attention and urged him toward the door she'd just exited. His turn had come for a few moments with Hattie before leading his middle daughter down the aisle. Kat watched as her mother reached up to offer him a soothing pat on the arm, and her father's shoulders sagged. He'd admit the truth to no one, but Kat suspected how difficult this day would be for him. Relegating oneself to the marital machinations of three daughters was far preferable to having no daughters to marry off at all.

"I think I know what's brought on Papa's behavior," she whispered.

"What is it? Has he failed to make someone cry today?" Sebastian was used to her father's garrulous behavior and no longer sought reasons or excuses.

Kitty tipped her mouth in a grin. "Violet."

She'd come to visit Roxbury ahead of their parents to help prepare for Ollie and Harriet's wedding and had quickly won over Seb and his sister. Violet was clever, witty, loved books, and was fiercely forward-thinking. More so now that she had begun to idolize Pippa.

"How could Violet have caused his outbursts?" Seb knew as well as Kat did that her father needed very little provocation.

"She announced to Papa this morning that she does not wish to marry. She told him she wants to be what he is." Kat watched her husband, eager for his reaction.

"A grumpy old man?"

"A soldier in the British Army, or a member of parliament."

Seb burst into a chuckle and then whistled quietly between his teeth. "My goodness, she will be a modern woman. Well done, Vi."

He looked toward the church entryway again. "Where is Violet anyway?"

"She decided she would be the flower girl after all, since Pippa is to be a bridesmaid. She's leading the bridal procession."

Kat had been in a state of euphoria for most of her own wedding, but today, for Hattie's sake, she'd worked to remain levelheaded, except for the temptation of her husband by her side. Still, a brew of feelings boiled just under the surface.

She glanced up at Seb and all of it washed over her as a tear welled up at the corner of her eye. Turning away from him, Kat swiped it away as daintily as she was able. Papa had taught her not to cry, and if Sebastian saw her tear, he'd rush to fix the trouble. But she wasn't suffering from weakness or distress. The tear was simply the bubbling over of too much joy.

Though her days of silly schemes were behind her, she'd never felt more gratitude than she did for how this one had turned out. Marriage, hers and Hattie's, and she didn't even loathe the word now. From the moment she'd met Sebastian, he'd been overturning her expectations about men and upending her beliefs about herself, and each day, in countless ways, he showed her that marriage needn't be about possession or control. He'd redefined it in her mind as a union of two hearts and minds, a partnership of love and respect and unimaginable pleasures.

They'd even managed to achieve a bit of peace with Alecia. With a helpful nudge from Aunt Augusta, Lady Naughton confessed that jealousy and a desperate need for funds had driven her to concoct the tale of Sebastian fathering her child. Ever practical, Papa had insisted on obtaining the woman's admission in writing. Most importantly, Aunt Augusta assured Seb and Kat that Archie had never been privy to his mother's scheme.

The organist began the bridal chorus, and Kat drew in a shaky breath as everyone in the church pews rose to their feet.

Violet walked up the aisle first, strewing rose petals ahead of her. She performed her role perfectly, and then winked at Kat.

Pippa came next. For a young woman who eschewed marriage as Kat once had, she seemed to have caught the blissful energy of the wedding day and smiled at her brother and Ollie before taking her place between Violet and Kat.

Finally, Hattie started up the aisle, her arm clasped tight around their father's.

"She looks beautiful," Kat enthused.

Her sister looked extraordinary, glowing with joy from the inside out. Pride and happiness welled up again, hot pinpricks at the corners of Kat's eyes. When she caught Hattie's gaze, she smiled, trying to convey all the love and well wishes in her heart.

The wedding guests seemed to hold their collective breaths as Hattie and Oliver exchanged their vows, and then broke into a chorus of giggles when Oliver fumbled the ring before getting it settled on Hattie's finger. With a sweet overlong kiss they sealed their vows, and Kat's sigh matched those of other ladies in the church.

As Hattie and Ollie proceeded back up the aisle, Seb drew near and slid his hand around Kat's waist.

"They will be happy," Kat whispered.

"As happy as we are, love?"

She leaned toward him and turned her head, her mouth inches from his. "I'm not sure anyone could be as happy as we are, but let's wish it for them just the same."

He kissed her then, one lingering taste, and she heard two older ladies from the village gasping as he lifted his head.

"You'd think a duke would know a bit more about propriety," one whispered to the other.

Seb looked out among the pews and offered the ladies a charming grin. "Forgive us, ladies. Despite my wife's admonitions, I fear I do lack social graces."

"Yes, and my husband loathes etiquette."

To prove how much, Seb kissed Kat once more.

# ONE SCANDALOUS KISS

THE ROOM WAS sweltering. Who knew a gallery event in Mayfair would attract such a crush? Lucius Crawford, Viscount Grimsby, darted his gaze from framed portraits to lush landscape pieces, fully expecting the paint to start melting off the canvases. No one could deny the colors were extraordinary and the compositions pleasing, but couldn't they have found someone with a better eye to hang the pieces? The arrangement of art was irritatingly haphazard, small and large side by side, some frames just inches apart and others an arm's length, or two, away from each other. Despite the impulse to find a ladder and impose order on the chaos, Lucius found focusing on the paintings preferable to meeting the eyes of those around him.

Glancing around a crowded room could be dangerous. Too often he'd find himself snared by a questioning look here, a disapproving frown there. They wondered about his father, of course, especially now that he had withdrawn from London society completely.

Lucius was prepared to admit his own lack of aristocratic tendencies—he was far more interested in discussing business than horse racing, technology than teacakes—but none of his faux pas or successes since becoming heir to his father's earldom eclipsed Maxim's infamy. The man had been so querulous and apt to initiate feuds with fellow noblemen that they'd dubbed him the Dark Earl of Dunthorpe.

Would the gossips be any kinder if they could see the frail, doddering man Maxim Crawford had become? Lucius doubted they would, and he had no intention of giving anyone the opportunity for either pity or pardon. Sheltering the earl from rumormongers was one of the duties that had fallen to him.

So he would learn to tolerate the speculative gazes and whispers. Eventually. But they still set his nerves on edge and made him wish for the haven of his study back at Hartwell. Never mind what else awaited him at Hartwell. Leaky roofs and crumbling masonry didn't daunt him. And regardless of the pain he'd experienced within its walls and the resentment that swelled and ebbed between him and his father as regular as the tides, the family estate in Berkshire was home now.

He'd accepted that it was no longer the home of his childhood, that idyllic Hartwell he'd longed for and missed with a searing, stubborn ache all the years he'd been away. The real Hartwell, a pile of wood and stones— some rooms as old as the Dunthorpes' Tudor ancestors, others as new as those Lucius had refurbished the previous year—was a bit of a mess. A mishmash of architectural styles, just as the estate itself had seen a mix of care and indifference over the years. Father's neglect had caused the most damage, and neither his ailments nor his obsessive love for Mother excused his poor stewardship. Lucius was determined to do better by the estate than his brother, Julian, or his father ever had.

Turning his head, he snagged the gaze of an elderly matron, her eyes as beady and hungry as those of any crow he'd ever seen. He acknowledged her with a minute nod, and she reared her head a fraction, as if utterly taken aback. And that, exactly that, her reaction and his failure to exude one tenth of the charm required to engage in any sort of social repartee, was why he came into town and mixed in society rarely. Even without an infamous father, he would have found the social rounds daunting.

So let them talk. Let them watch him tug at his neck-cloth like a man on the gallows might claw at the noose, and straighten and restraighten his waistcoat, running a finger down the four buttons at the bottom to make sure they formed a perfect line. This visit to London was necessary and would, if his aunt could be believed, allow him to settle his future—to meet Father's demands that he marry a woman with money and impeccable breeding and ensure the estate's future with an heir. Stability had always eluded him, and the notion of a settled future seemed as unlikely as a happy one, but if anyone could achieve such a coup, it was Aunt Augusta.

She'd been the one constant in his life, writing and visiting after Father shipped him off to Scotland, guiding him after Julian's death and the news he'd become heir to Hartwell, and comforting him when his own mother could not. She'd been as much a parent to him as either of his own.

"You look a bit seasick, my boy. But unless someone has failed to inform me, I don't believe Mayfair has set sail."

Aunt Augusta tucked herself into the space between him and the scowling crow woman. She lifted a glass and he took the crystal flute with a nod of gratitude.

"How long must we stay?"

"I believe the hostess is going to give a brief speech. It would behoove us to linger until then."

He sensed her eyes on him, assessing his discomfort, looking out for him as she always had.

"You will be attending many more social events once you marry. Get in as much practice as you can."

"Didn't you promise to find a candidate who'd be content to do the social rounds on her own?"

"Independence is one thing. Being forever without one's husband is another matter entirely."

Lucius closed his eyes a moment and imagined a life of house parties, elaborate dinners, and sitting room musicales. The prospect made him shudder. He opened his eyes, still avoiding Aunt Augusta's inspection, and took in the canvas before him—a man on horseback with a verdant English landscape stretched out behind him. It looked a bit like Hartwell's meadow, and though he'd been away only a week, longing for the place gnawed at him. In this hot, congested space of too many colors and a cacophony of voices, he missed Hartwell's spacious rooms, familiar scents and textures, and labyrinthine floor plan, so well-known to him he could navigate it blindfolded.

"She certainly enjoys London more than you do."

*She? She* was very specific. Far too specific. He'd come to London to discuss the possibility of marriage. No, more than that—the necessity of it. And to seek Augusta's help in securing the perfect candidate, a woman with an ample dowry to keep Hartwell afloat, enough connections to earn his father's approval, and such a rabid desire to be a countess that she might not notice how ill-suited he was to be an earl.

The notion that she'd found a match so quickly, and that the young woman might be here among the crush of attendees . . . that he did not expect. And in Lucius's experience, the unexpected never heralded a pleasant turn of events.

"Does she? I wasn't aware you'd settled on anyone. Is she here tonight?"

He looked around, scanning one perspiring feminine face after another. None of them stood out. None of them stopped him short and made him wish to continue to look, to learn what lay beyond a flushed cheek or bright, smiling eyes.

"Not tonight, no. She is traveling at the moment."

That finally earned his attention and he turned to question Augusta further just as an older woman approached and embraced her, gushing about how long it'd been since they'd last seen each other.

As Aunt Augusta allowed herself to be pulled away to

join a lively conversation, his sister, Julia, and brother-in-law, Marcus Darnley, approached. Marcus and Lucius exchanged nods. Julia merely sipped at the liquid in her glass as she watched him, much as his aunt had moments before. But Julia's was a different gaze. Her eyes narrowed, not out of concern, but in judgment.

"Do stop glaring at everyone, Lucius. People will think you as frightful as Papa."

His sister's tone held a note of irritation along with the command, and he allowed himself a slight twitch of his mouth that none but those who knew him best would ever mistake for a grin.

"He must continue glaring, love. I believe he enjoys nurturing his grim reputation." Marcus Darnley leaned in to whisper the words to his wife, though Lucius didn't care who heard him. His sister's husband tweaked him as often as she chastised him. And though he would never admit it, he found as much enjoyment in Marcus's teasing as he did in his sister's scolding. He and Julia had missed out on years of sibling squabbles as children, and he didn't mind catching up now.

But Lucius would never apologize for being discerning about how he spent his time and whom he took into his confidence. His reputation as one of society's most dour bachelors served him well. It kept giggling debutantes, scheming mothers, and nearly everyone else at bay. Marriage was necessary—he accepted it as his chief goal for the year. But not the game, the silly business of inane conversations, coy flirtation, and stolen kisses on balconies. Lucius was quite content to leave such carrying on to rogues like his friend Robert Wellesley and allow Augusta to find him a sensible, practical, and exceedingly wealthy bride.

Time was too precious a commodity to waste on games. Managing Hartwell, a task he loved but had never been groomed for, consumed his days and nights. But Julia played on his sense of obligation and had urged him to help make Delia Ornish's gallery gathering a success. Mrs. Ornish's friendship with their late mother had indebted them both to the wealthy social butterfly.

Marcus stood close to Lucius and leaned in to speak confidentially. "There are some lovely young women in attendance tonight. Don't you agree, Grimsby? Surely one of them must strike your fancy."

His sister and her husband were unaware of Augusta's matchmaking efforts.

"Yes and no." Lucius lifted the flute of champagne to his mouth and sipped.

Marcus quirked a brow at him, begging explanation.

"Yes, there are lovely women in attendance. No, none of them strikes my fancy."

The women in the crush of attendees were stunning in their finery. Every color and shape one could desire. But none of them stirred him.

Marcus wouldn't be deterred. "Are you never lonely, old chap?" His brother-in-law turned his eyes to Julia as he spoke.

Lucius caught the look, and an ember of loneliness kindled in his chest. He didn't desire any of the women before him, yet he did envy the easy companionship that his sister and brother-in-law shared. He could envy it but never imagine it for himself. Even if Aunt Augusta's scheme was successful, it wouldn't be a love match. He'd seen the results of what such an attachment had done to his father, a man whose adoration for his wife became a destructive obsession, sparking jealous rages that drove her—and Lucius—from their home.

He wouldn't lose himself in that kind of passion. Now, with the responsibility of Hartwell laid on his shoulders, he couldn't spare the time for it. Let his father indulge in maudlin sentimentality; Lucius had an estate to run.

"I haven't the time for loneliness." He lied easily and ignored the look Marcus shot him, fearing he'd read pity there.

A fracas near the gallery's entrance offered a welcome distraction. Turning away from Marcus, Lucius craned his neck to spot the cause of the ruckus. The room was so full of bodies it was difficult to see the front of the building, despite his height. But whatever the commotion, it caused a few shouts mingled with cries of outrage.

Then he saw the trouble. A woman. A bluestocking, more precisely, wearing a prim black skirt and plain white shirtwaist, spectacles perched high on her nose, pushed her way through the throng of ladies in colorful evening gowns and men in black tails. She looked like a magpie wreaking havoc among the canaries, though her hair was as striking a shade as any of the finery around her. The rich auburn hue shone in the gaslight, and though she'd pinned her hair back in a severe style, several rebellious curls had escaped and hung down around her shoulders.

As he watched the woman's progress, a gentleman grasped her arm roughly, and an uncommon surge of chivalry made Lucius consider interceding. But in the next moment the woman proved she needed no rescuer. Stomping on the man's foot, she moved easily out of his grasp and continued on her path—a path that led directly to Lucius.

Give in to your Impulses . . .
Continue reading for excerpts from
our newest Avon Impulse books.
Available now wherever e-books are sold.

## MONTANA HEARTS: HER WEEKEND WRANGLER

*By Darlene Panzera*

## I NEED A HERO

### A MEN IN UNIFORM NOVELLA

*By Codi Gary*

## BLUE BLOODED

### A BENEDICTION NOVEL

*By Shelly Bell*

## BEST WORST MISTAKE

### A BRIGHTWATER NOVEL

*By Lia Riley*

An Excerpt from

# MONTANA HEARTS: HER WEEKEND WRANGLER

*by Darlene Panzera*

Darlene Panzera returns with a sweet
new Western series perfect for fans of
Debbie Macomber's heartwarming romances.

Bree Collins has finally come home to Fox
Creek, Montana, to manage her family's guest
ranch. She knows she can handle any challenges
that come her way, but when the infuriating
Ryan Tanner reappears in her life, Bree suddenly
has doubts about her ability to stay professional—
and away from the handsome cowboy.

Bree stayed a few more minutes to watch them sway in time to the music, then spun around to search for the three CEOs and collided straight into a hard, chiseled chest. A soothing warmth spread over her entire body as she glanced up into Ryan's handsome face and gasped. "You're here."

"I wouldn't miss it."

She leaned to the side and glanced at the three men behind him. "And you brought your *brothers!*"

"Yeah, they're the reason I'm late. They didn't want to come but I knew how much it meant to you, and *why*," he said, giving her a mischievous grin. "So I had to negotiate a deal to get them here."

Bree smiled because of the way his mouth twitched when he grinned, because of the excitement in his eyes when he looked at her, and because of the way his dark navy blue dress shirt and jeans clung to his splendid physique. *Whoa, girl! Remember to keep it* casual. Recollecting her thoughts, she met his gaze and asked, "What kind of deal?"

Ryan placed a hand on either side of her waist, his touch firm and . . . pleasantly possessive. "I had to trade them my earnings from working your ranch so they can buy a set of new tires for their quad."

He did that for her?

"Which means," he continued, flashing her another pulse-kicking grin, "I'm a little short on money and I'd be willing to be your weekend wrangler for the rest of the summer, if you'll have me."

Stunned, Bree sucked in her breath and stared at him, unable to speak, unable to process exactly what this would mean for her family, unable to think of anything except that Ryan Tanner was absolutely, undeniably, the very, very best! With a little hop, she squealed, unable to hold back her delight, and with her heart taking the lead, she flung her arms around his neck and kissed him.

It was a quick kiss, over before she even realized what she had done, but when Bree pulled back she didn't know who was more surprised, she or Ryan.

His gaze locked with hers for several long, breathless moments, then he cupped her cheek with his hand and drew her back toward him . . . and this time he kissed *her*.

His mouth was warm, tender, and soft against her own and filled with such passion she blocked out every sound around them, every presence, everything except the fact that Ryan Tanner, the guy she'd wanted to dance with since high school, held her in his arms.

An Excerpt from

# I NEED A HERO
## A Men in Uniform Novella
### *by Codi Gary*

Sergeant Oliver Martinez joined the military to serve his country—not plan parties. But after a run-in with his commanding officer, Oliver is suddenly responsible for an upcoming canine charity event. Worse, he's got to work with the bossiest, sexiest woman he's ever met—who just happens to be the general's daughter. When tempers flare and a scorching kiss turns into so much more, Oliver and Eve will have to decide if this attraction is forever . . . or just for now.

The dog bounded to her, wiggling and licking wherever he could. She held her hand behind her, and Oliver gave her the leash. Once she had it hooked onto Beast's collar, she stood up with a mischievous smile. "I don't know why he gives you so much trouble."

"Oh, I'm sure Best put him up to it," Oliver grumbled.

"Ah, and he gets a kick out of messing with you, huh?"

"That's just because I've let it go until now, but the dude owes me a sofa and chair."

Eve laughed and held the leash out to him. "I wonder if maybe you two just got off on the wrong foot. Perhaps you should open your mind to the possibility that Beast has issues and this is his way of dealing with them."

Oliver took her advice with a healthy dose of skepticism. "What makes you think he has issues?"

"Well, for starters, he came from the animal shelter, so he's got to have some baggage. The question is, was he turned in because he has behavioral problems and his previous owners just couldn't deal? Or were the owners jackasses who just didn't want him anymore?" Her tone was sad as she added, "If he was loved, it's easy to assume that he is confused and misses it."

Oliver studied Eve. Her dreamy, sweet expression tugged at his heart and he wondered who she was thinking about. A loved one she missed? A past lover? A bitter rush of jealousy churned in his stomach. He didn't want to think about another man having even a sliver of Evelyn's affections. Not when he wanted them all to himself.

"How is it you seem to know so much about what he's feeling? Are you an event planner by day and dog psychic by night?" He had been trying to make a joke, but one look at her face told him he'd insulted her.

"I'm just making an observation," she said curtly.

"Hey." He reached out and touched her arm, turning her toward him. "I was just teasing you."

She remained silent, and he took her chin in his hand, tilting her gaze up to meet his. "Why does it always seem like I can never say the right thing to you?"

A small smile played across those bee-stung lips. "Maybe I make you nervous."

Oliver rubbed his thumb across her bottom lip and her sharp, warm breath spread over his skin. "Oh, you definitely make me nervous."

"I do?" Her breathless question stirred his cock to life.

"Yeah, you do. I can't relax around you, not with the way you make me feel," he said.

"How is that?" Her tone was soft, and Oliver dipped his head, his mouth hovering over hers.

"Like I'm standing in the sunshine every time I'm near you," he said.

"Oh."

Oliver didn't give her a chance to escape this time and

covered her mouth with his, groaning as the sweet taste of her overwhelmed him. His hands slid back to cradle the back of her head, sliding his fingers into her hair and loosening her ponytail. A tiny sigh escaped her and he took advantage, slipping his tongue between her parted lips, coming undone when her tongue tangled with his. He felt her hands grip his waist, pulling him tighter against her body and he wanted more. Never had he gotten so caught up in one kiss. And never had he ignored every warning bell for a woman, but with Evelyn, it was like common sense went out the window and was replaced by uncontrolled passion.

Oliver felt something pushing between them and opened his eyes to look down at Beast, who was trying to use his giant head to separate them. Ignoring him, Oliver maneuvered them toward the couch, tumbling Eve down onto the mangled leather.

The kiss broke long enough for Eve's eyes to pop open and she giggled. "Somehow, I never imagined making out on a cloud of couch stuffing."

Oliver grinned down at her. "What can I say? I'm an original."

"You're definitely different," she said.

"Is that a compliment?" His lips found the pulse point behind her ear and he felt her heart race against his mouth.

"I think so."

"You don't sound sure," he murmured against her jaw.

"Probably 'cause I can't think while you're kissing me," she whispered.

His mouth brushed hers. "Want me to stop?"

"God, no."

An Excerpt from

## BLUE BLOODED
**A Benediction Novel**
*by Shelly Bell*

In the next sexy and suspenseful novel from
Shelly Bell, an investigative reporter and an ex-
military Dom witness a murder outside of the sex
club, Benediction, and uncover a deadly political
conspiracy while trying to clear their names . . .

**An Avon Red Impulse Novel**

$P$uffing on his Cuban cigar, the Senator reclined in his chair, a tumbler of scotch on the rocks in front of him. He stared down the two men sitting on the other side of his desk, daring them to repeat the words that had just been uttered.

Sweating profusely, FBI Agent Seymour Fink tugged on his tie, his Adam's apple bobbing above the buttoned collar of his shirt.

For a moment, the Senator considered retrieving his gun from his desk drawer and shooting the agent in the head, but he couldn't risk getting blood or splatters of brain matter on his tuxedo. After all, he had an important dinner to attend in an hour and didn't want to disappoint his wife.

He downed the rest of his drink, then shook the ice in the glass the way he'd like to shake the mobster who was fucking with him. "Tell me what you're going to do to fix the problem," he said calmly, unwilling to allow this minor bump in the road to waylay his plans.

"Do, sir?" Using the sleeve of his suit jacket, Agent Fink wiped the sweat from his brow, cigar smoke circling around his head like a boa constrictor. "I'm not certain we should do—"

"You listen to me, you little prick. There is nothing that

will stand in my way." The Senator hurled his tumbler against the wall above the fireplace, shattering the glass into a million tiny pieces. "Do you understand me? I've got your balls in a vise underneath my blade, so let's try this again. What are you going to do to fix the problem?"

Seymour swallowed convulsively. "No one was supposed to get hurt."

"Don't pull that bullshit now. You knew when I approached you that lives would be lost for the greater good," the Senator said. He handed off his cigar and nodded to the other agent, a bruiser of a man who he'd chosen not only for his twenty years of service to this country, but for his lack of empathy. Agent Richard Evans understood the risks involved in his job, the three bullets he'd taken in the chest a testament to that fact.

Evans pinched the fat cigar between his fingers and in a flash, locked his partner's head under his arm, pinning Fink's hands to the table and singeing the top of one with the foot of the cigar. Fink screamed, his smaller body thrashing wildly as he fruitlessly tried to escape from his partner and the pain he was inflicting.

The acrid scent of burnt flesh overpowered the cigar's sweet one, a smell he would forever more attribute to power.

By the time Evans released him, Fink's skin had turned pasty white, his shirt completely drenched from his sweat. He breathed heavily, nodding. "Consider the problem solved, sir. By this time tomorrow night, Rinaldi will be dead."

The Senator leaned back in his chair and smiled.

God bless the USA.

Touring the dungeon located in the basement of a private mansion, Rachel Dawson ignored the decadent sights and sounds of sex going on all around her and kept her eye on the prize. After working her ass off to gain entrance into Benediction, the prestigious sex club owned by Cole DeMarco, she was finally here.

Although it was early in the evening and most of the upstairs fantasy rooms were still vacant, she'd gotten to play the role of voyeur as she'd observed two different scenes. The "teacher" bending the "schoolgirl" over his desk and smacking her with a ruler had titillated her, but Rachel had remained a removed observer, her body not engaged by the fantasy.

Then she remembered she wasn't at Benediction to fulfill her fantasies or to act as voyeur. She was there to do a story about BDSM and for that, she needed to go to the dungeon.

Unlike the fantasy rooms, the dungeon was packed. In here, the sights, smells, and sounds of passion and pain seduced her senses. The potent scents of leather, musk, and sweat teased her with the promise of sex. Everywhere Rachel looked, people indulged in their kinks without judgment or recrimination.

Her mouth grew dry at the sight of a naked woman suspended from the ceiling by rope and flowing white sheets, twirling as if she was an acrobat in a circus act.

Who had bound that woman? Was *he* here tonight?

An Excerpt from

# BEST WORST MISTAKE
## A Brightwater Novel
*by Lia Riley*

**Sometimes the worst mistakes
turn out to be the best . . .**

Smoke jumper Wilder Kane once reveled in the
rush from putting out dangerous wildfires. But
after a tragic accident, he's cut himself off from the
world, refusing to leave his isolated cabin. When a
headstrong beauty bursts in, Wilder finds himself
craving the fire she ignites in him, but letting
anyone near his darkness would be a mistake.

Quinn unzipped her jacket, pausing halfway. "You don't mind, do you? Seeing as I'm staying, at least for a while."

"No." *Yes.* Because the minute she slid out of that white, puffy coat, her breathtaking body was on full display. Those snug-fitting jeans weren't overtly sexy, but the way the denim contoured to the slight flare of her narrow thighs made him swallow. Hard.

It had been awhile since he'd been in the company of any woman who wasn't a medical professional or intimately involved with his brothers. Also, as much as he didn't want to admit it, he had a type and this forward, strong-looking woman fit it right down to that thick wavy brown hair pulled back at the nape of her long, sexy neck.

Necks were underrated female geography. He loved how they tasted when he kissed them there, how they smelled as he nuzzled.

Equally fascinating was her lush mouth, how the corner remained quirked on one side despite the natural pout, as if in perpetual secret amusement.

This woman was bright, spunky, and happy, despite her father's miserable situation. His heart sank. He had nothing to offer someone like her, not when his whole world had burned to cinder.

He shook himself inwardly, not moving a muscle. No point succumbing to the ugly truth, however true. Maybe he could pretend to be a normal guy for the night. Normal except for the scars, the missing leg, and the fact that he hadn't spoken to a living soul since Sawyer dropped off his groceries six days ago, and was tongue-tied around strangers at the best of times.

*Shit.*

What would Archer do? His younger brother was good with people, especially the ladies. He'd navigate this situation like a pro.

She gave him a tentative smile, probably because he was staring at her like a loon.

*Compliments. Women like compliments.*

"Your teeth are real white," Wilder blurted. God damn it, the words hung over them like a comic strip balloon. He wished for a string to grab on to, stuff the idiocy back into his mouth, swallow it down.

"Excuse me?" Her shoulders jerked as her lips clamped, clearly not anticipating the awkward flattery.

At least he hadn't said how much he liked her neck. Yet.